ECHOES OF DISTANT THUNDER

A Veteran's Story

Frank P. Slaughter

ARBUTUS PRESS • TRAVERSE CITY, MICHIGAN

Echoes of Distant Thunder © 2011 Frank P. Slaughter

ISBN 978-1-933926-36-0

Arbutus Press
Traverse City, Michigan
editor@arbutuspress.com
www.Arbutuspress.com

Library of Congress Cataloging-in-Publication Data

Printed and bound in the United States of America

Dedication

This is a story about a veteran of the Civil War, but it is an ageless story that has played out countless times in the aftermath of all of our country's wars, from the Revolution to the present day in Afghanistan. The uniforms change, the weapons change, but the men and women who go to war for us are always the same. They are our precious youth. We send them out to kill and sometimes to die on our behalf. Some of them come home maimed in body, some in mind; some come home only to die in our midst, because what we asked of them took them down a road of no return. To our veterans, from those of us who can never know the true cost of what you bought for us with your lives: please forgive our complacency. May our great nation always strive to be worthy of your sacrifice, and in so doing, sow the seeds of future generations of men and women who will go forward as you have done, to fight and die for the freedom that defines us.

"In the end, we take nothing with us. Who we were is what we leave behind with those who knew us. What we were is returned to the land, and the land binds us all together..."

Anonymous

Prologue

The big General Motors V8 pulled the Catalina effortlessly along the dips and rises of the two-lane blacktop of County Road 633. The early afternoon sun emerged from behind one of the low-ranging cumulus clouds that filled the summer sky and streamed through the windshield, prompting Paul Castor to pull down the visor and squint under the lower edge at the road ahead. On the seat beside him was a takeout bag from the Dairyville with the remnants of his lunch beginning to bleed through, slips of paper with hastily scrawled directions, and a plat map of Grand Traverse County. His poorly folded Michigan map lay on the passenger side floorboard with an empty Pepsi can that moved back and forth with the easy motion of the car. Up ahead, the road appeared to rise straight up between the distant trees lining the shoulders until it disappeared under their green tops.

"Well, there's the hill he was talking about, must be getting close," Paul said to himself, referring to the man back at the Shell who had given him directions. He felt a twinge of excitement, knowing that there was a very good chance the end of his long quest that lay just over the hill. It was a quest started nearly ten years ago with the death of his great-aunt Rose and the inheritance of an antique wooden box containing some old letters, a pocket watch, and a Civil War-era revolver.

The gift had come as a complete surprise. He had known about the revolver and the watch since he was a youngster, having seen them at his aunt's house on those occasions when they made the trip to Maysville for Sunday dinner. He was captivated from the first time he laid eyes on the contents of the box, and during every visit after, he begged her to get it out so he could hold the heavy gun and study the delicate face of the watch and the little gold winding key that hung from it on a yellow ribbon.

Aunt Rose, wisely, always made him wait until the dinner was over before giving in to his appeal. Sometimes as he sat before the box on the floor of the living room, he would pick up on snippets of conversation among the adults about their ancestors and one memorable thing or another that they had done. But by far the most interesting stories centered on the ancestor who had owned the watch and gun. Everyone agreed that the pistol was one that Paul's great great grandfather, William Castor, carried in the Civil War, but the watch was something of a mystery. On the back, worn almost smooth, was the inscription "Love Always, Mollie" in beautifully engraved script. Aunt Rose had once confided that as a young woman she had carefully examined the fragile letters for clues to Mollie's identity but found that they were all from a woman named Amanda.

The gun was an 1860 Colt Army revolver and had obviously seen hard service sometime in the last one-hundred-plus years. The walnut grips on the butt were nearly black with age and stood out in stark contrast to the yellow brass trigger guard and handle frame. All the other metal surfaces were splotchy dull silver and deeply pitted, completely devoid of the original blue finish. The gun's mechanism was frozen and had been as long as anyone could remember. The hammer would not cock and the cylinder would not turn. The most interesting thing about it was that the chamber directly behind the barrel was still loaded. Even though his father strictly forbade it, when no one was looking Paul would hold the gun up and look down the barrel. If he held it just right with the light behind him, he could see the white oxidized lead ball still waiting at the other end.

Since those early days, Paul hadn't stayed in touch with his aunt, aside from the yearly Christmas cards or the birth announcements of his children. When the wooden box had arrived in the mail on that blustery February day ten years ago, he had been deeply touched and not a little guilty. It had arrived at a time when he was suffering from a touch of "cabin fever" following a long winter, and he immediately threw himself into reading and making photocopies of the letters. From that day forward, genealogy was his hobby, or as his wife would say, his obsession.

There on the right shoulder of the road as he crested the hill was a green county sign that announced the village of Monroe Center. The road took a little dip, then rose again and disappeared into a dark cavern formed by the joined canopies of huge old maple trees that had been planted at regular intervals along each shoulder. On the left, just past where the trees began, was a large, boxy two-story building, the front of which was spanned by a high porch, giving it the look of an old general store. Someone appeared to be living in the upstairs. On down a bit further, on the same side of the road, was a beautiful little one-room Methodist church with white clapboard siding, three floor-to-ceiling arched stained glass windows on each side and a lovely picturesque steeple and belfry rising tall from the front peak of the roof. Out past the cool sanctuary of the trees, a lush green and gold patchwork of farm land covered with corn, oats, and barley rolled off to distant tree lines all around.

Paul touched the brakes to slow the car as he approached the highest point on the tree-covered portion of the road. Up ahead on the left was the little village cemetery that he was looking for. He pulled off on the right shoulder of the road in front of the entrance and switched off the ignition. The pastoral countenance of the land flowed around him, replacing the noise of the car's engine with the soft sounds of treetops stirring in the breeze, birds singing, and the faint *pop, pop, pop* of an old John Deere tractor creeping through a distant field. Whoever planted the trees along the road years ago also placed them on the other three property lines of the graveyard and scattered a few throughout for good measure. A somewhat rickety black wrought iron fence served to keep out livestock from the neighboring farms and was crowned by a high, matching arched sign that carried the moniker "Monroe Center Cemetery" in white letters. Old, but well cared for was the general impression.

Paul leaned forward and turned the key in the ignition, bringing the car back to life. He slowly pulled through the right entrance way and traveled about a hundred feet before stopping and switching the car off once again. There were grave markers of all descriptions and ages. Most were old, as he expected they would be, but there were some newer brass plates that lay flush on the ground scattered about, too. Some markers were dark polished granite, some were rough weather-worn white granite partially obscured with lichen, and a few were simple wooden crosses.

Paul stepped out of the car and gently closed the door. He stood for a moment, looking around and taking the measure of the task before him. The part of the cemetery closest to the road was obviously the oldest, so he headed in that direction as the likely place to start. About thirty minutes into his search he came across an elaborate white marble marker that had once stood six feet tall. Over the years, melting snow had found its way into hairline cracks around the base of the obelisk, and as it re-froze and expanded, the top portion of the monument had eventually snapped off. Someone, most likely a maintenance man, had thoughtfully stood the broken piece up and leaned it against the base. Much of the inscription on the face of the monument was worn and indistinct, but the name "Emma Castor" and the dates "1846–1914" directly under it were clearly discernible. With mounting excitement, Paul quickly turned to the much smaller Veterans Administration headstone to the left of Emma's grave and immediately recognized the recessed shield of a Civil War veteran's headstone. This marker was also white granite, but it had suffered the same indignities of nature as the larger one next to it, and the bas-relief letters inside the shield were even harder to make out. Paul silently congratulated himself for remembering to bring tracing paper and artist charcoal so he could make rubbings of each marker. He knelt down and studied the inscription. After several minutes, he ran his fingers slowly over the letters as if reading Braille and whispered, "William Castor 1844–1919 Pvt Bat D 1st Mich Art."

Paul went back to the car and retrieved a small satchel containing the materials he had purchased for making the rubbings. He knelt down in front of Emma's marker, and holding the stick of charcoal flat against the paper, he began to rub long, light strokes at first to judge the effect, then more determined as the letters began to appear. When he was satisfied that all the information from the stone had been captured, he stood up and backed away.

EMMA CASTOR
1846–1914
BELOVED WIFE OF WILLIAM
SLEEP WELL UNTIL WE MEET AGAIN

Paul moved over to William's stone and repeated the process, although with a little more difficulty owing to the recessed shield and raised letters. This time as he rubbed the charcoal over the paper, something completely unexpected began to emerge. Below the rank and unit designation on the government headstone was the single word "Peep." The lettering was worn, but it was without question a professional job, probably added by a local stone carver after it was delivered from the Veterans Administration. Paul said the word to himself several times as he considered its meaning. The story behind this simple word was probably lost forever.

WILLIAM CASTOR
1844–1919
PVT BAT D 1ST MICH ART
PEEP

Paul carefully removed the tape from the edges of the two sheets of tracing paper, rolled them up tightly, and secured each with a rubber band. Someday they would be copied and bound with the rest of his charts and documentation on the Castor family. The years of research, the countless inquiries to distant relatives, the poring over court records, and the hours spent fitting all the pieces together had finally led him to this place, this timeless shady grove surrounded by working farmland. He reached out and rested his hand on the top of the stone, looking off across the fields but not really seeing. The moment lapped at his feet, then washed gently over him, making the hair on the back of his neck tingle. In his mind's eye, he saw a young man in a dusty dark blue uniform, cap pulled low, leaning forward on the top rail of the far back fence. His gaze was steady but not unfriendly, and Paul held the vision as long as he could. Finally, it was gone.

He hung his head and looked at the grass between his knees, chiding himself for being so sentimental. Slowly he stood and looked around, having accomplished everything he had set out to do but not yet ready to leave. He backed away from the graves of William and Emma and eased down against an old tree with smooth bark and a comfortable lean. Paul closed his eyes and replayed the vision in his mind until he dozed.

Chapter 1

CHICKAMAUGA,
GEORGIA SEPTEMBER 20, 1863

The little fire hissed and popped in the still, half-light of morning, its flame like a beacon to the weary men who huddled around it, avoiding each other's eyes. Will sat on the ground, leaning back against the left wheel of the gun with his legs stretched out in front of him toward the fire, trying to dry his shoes, which were wet through from the heavy dew. Steam from the hot leather curled straight up in two tiny columns until it mingled with the thin wisps of low drifting ground fog just above his head. He imagined it was his soul seeping out through the bottoms of his feet and drifting away to join those of all the dead men who lay scattered everywhere around him. He was bone tired from another sleepless night. The unspeakable images and disembodied sounds of dying men and horses left on the battlefield after yesterday's fighting had become even more disquieting in the cold moonlight. The ghostly illumination had spurred his imagination and kept him looking hard at the dim shadows.

Will reached into the inside pocket of his blue wool jacket, as he had done a hundred times before, pulling out the small black hard-shelled Union Case that opened into two picture frames, like a book, joined in the center by delicate brass hinges. On one side, the side his eyes always fell on first, was Amanda's daguerreotype, and on the other, instead of an image, was a snippet of blonde hair pressed under the glass and surrounded by a gold oval mat. Even in this soft early light, diffused by a thick forest canopy, the reddish highlights were faintly visible.

When the battery left Michigan two years ago, she had been with him on the train station platform in the same dress that she was wearing in the picture, blue and white in his mind's eye, long hair parted in the middle and pulled back tight around her temples and ending in a bun at the nape of her neck. Her neck, with the wisps of fine golden hair that always seemed to escape the general upsweep as she bent forward reading, was his favorite place. She had stood close, facing him, fussing with his uniform and darting quick glances over his shoulder at the confused mass of soldiers and civilians. The air had been charged with a bravado made slightly hollow by the growing lists of dead and missing in the daily newspapers. Jimmy, his best friend, had drifted away from them, sensing the awkwardness of the moment.

He had known Amanda since childhood, having grown up on the same road, separated only by the Miller farm, but he had lost track of her until several years ago at the Andersons' corn shucking and barn dance. The transfiguration had been quite remarkable. A faint smile played across his mouth as he recalled that night sitting side by side on the benches that lined the walls of the main barn gallery, sipping cider and rather stiffly discussing their plans for the future. In truth, he hadn't really given the future much thought, and that oversight had suddenly become a glaring liability when he realized how important it was to Amanda. As it turned out, the future he threw together for himself on the spur of the moment wasn't a very good one. Being a relative newcomer to sparking with the ladies, he made the mistake of assuming forty acres of fallow land and a mule were lofty goals that would turn any woman's head. Be that as it may, after that night he began to think of her every day, imagining ways he might see her and the kinds of things they might say to each other. He started looking at every rig that passed by the farm, hoping to catch sight of her on her way into town.

His father's farm straddled the main north-south road leading out of Coldwater and was at the top of a low ridge line that ran east and west. The road split a grove of mature sugar maple trees just north of the house, and there were a few apple trees set back, just out of reach of the shade of the taller trees. There always seemed to be a wagon and team pulled up under the trees, resting during the hot summer days, and as a youngster, Will sold wild blueberries or blackberries to the drivers. It was the place he and Amanda would sit, side by side, when she read stories to him—it was the place he went in his mind now before he fell asleep.

Will snapped the little case shut and glanced sideways at Jimmy, who was sitting next to him, also leaning against the wheel. A twinge of guilt had become part of the ritual as he spent more and more time lost in thoughts about Amanda and less time sharing the realities of daily life in the army with his friend. He and Jimmy had grown up together on neighboring farms and shared a bond that even flesh and blood brothers seldom knew. They hunted and fished together, hired out together as farm hands during harvest to raise "walking-around money," and took long camping trips up to the big timber north of Saginaw. They called these trips "grand excursions." It was on one of these grand excursions that they hatched the idea of striking out for northern Michigan on their own and getting work in a lumber camp. There was real money to be made up there, they believed, and compared to the dirt farming they had grown up with, it all seemed rather exotic. It was said a man could work a few years and save enough money to buy some land and a few animals.

After the fighting yesterday, the possibility of a future had become greatly diminished in their minds. The whole idea of the body and the spirit being two separate things had seemed plausible enough when he sat in church with Amanda before the war, but back then it was just an interesting theory. The stark truth of the matter was now clear after seeing so many examples of one without the other. It was hard to resist looking at the faces, if there were faces, of the dead men for clues about what lay beyond.

"What?" said Will, with a touch of irritation in his voice as he tucked the small black case back into the pocket of his roundabout.

"I sure as hell hope she's worth all that hankering and that she's not snuggled up to some parlor officer back home while you're out here getting your ass shot off," said Jimmy.

Will chose to ignore the implication, and in an effort to change the subject said, "How's your ass treating you today, Jimmy? Seems like you're spending a lot of time hunkered down in the tall weeds," referring to the bad case of Tennessee Quick Step that Jimmy had been fighting for a week now.

"I'm telling you, Will, I ain't never had nothing like it before. This morning before we moved out I started to let one rip, and damn, I hitched up short just in the nick of time. Damn near shit my new government-issue britches. I'm so damned tired of being on a hair trigger, it just makes you wonder how a body can crap that much when I ain't had a decent meal in four days. If I get kilt today I'm for sure gonna shit myself, and I got to tell you, Will, that ain't how I had this war figured."

Will chuckled and said, "Well, Jimmy, the way I see it, you're gonna have the last word in the matter. There'll be one mighty disappointed Johnny when he sticks his legs down into what he thinks is a brand new pair of britches and finds what you left him. He for sure won't think no better of his northern brethren…"

"Damn it, Will, don't make me laugh," said Jimmy through a grimace as he looked to the right and scanned the ground in front of the gun. "And by the by, if you got any more of those Cincinnati newspapers, I'd be grateful for a few more pages. I find them quite superior to those Secesh papers we got up in Nashville. I don't know what they put in their paper, but it sure give me the red ass."

Will dug around in his haversack and pulled out his last two folded-up pages of the Times-Star, one with a corner saturated in grease, apparently from coming in contact with a piece of salt pork he was saving for dinner. "Here you go, Jimmy. I won't charge no extra for the grease. Who knows, you might find it soothing. I'd watch out for dogs if I was you."

Just then Al, the number two man on their gun who was sitting Indian-style across the fire from Will and Jimmy, poking at the coals trying to heat a cup of coffee in a battered tin cup, took up the conversation and said, "Now, Will, you may be giving the Johnnies just a little too much credit. From what I seen, they ain't none too particular about their appearance, or their general aroma, for that matter. Why, you'd be hard pressed to pick the one with a load of shit in his drawers out of half a dozen, even if you could stand to sniff 'em out. I remember back in '56;

was it '56 or '55, George?" he said, glancing over at his brother, "when I shit myself coming out of church? Well, no matter, it was a glorious sunny fall morning and I'd been pinching one back all through the sermon, just praying for the strength to hold out so's I wouldn't reflect badly on Betsy and Ma, and that dern preacher Kinick was fired up and letting her roll. Every time he made a point he would thump that pulpit with his fist, and I surely had to bear down to keep from lettin' fly. Well, I was doing fine until I missed that first step coming out of the church. Oh what a mess I was. Run down my leg into my boot. Whatever become of those boots, George? I surely did love those boots. Got them from Wilhelm's, I think. Of course that left one give me a little trouble when I was breaking 'em in…"

Will was always amazed how Al could talk non-stop, day in and day out, flowing seamlessly from one subject to another, never repeating a story or forgetting a detail. He quizzed his brother George from time to time, more to see if he was listening than to get help with his story. George was the younger of the two, maybe thirty-five or so, burly and as quiet as Al was wordy. Except for Sergeant Hazzard, they were the oldest men in the battery.

Since just before daylight the cold, heavy air had carried the deep rumble of artillery fire to them from somewhere over on the left, and it had steadily increased in volume and urgency as the morning wore on. When the first volley fire of massed infantry added its roar to the distant artillery, everyone knew the killing was about to begin in earnest. At first they could see smoke roil up out of the treetops in the distance, marking the location of the combatants, but the firing was spreading slowly down the line toward them, and now much of the area was blanketed in dirty gray clouds of smoke that hung in the trees and mingled with the few remaining pockets of ground fog around the cedar thickets. Will looked back toward the limber and watched Jonathon trying to calm the lead saddle horse Big Mike by rubbing his nose and talking into his ear. Big Mike was still wet from the last move and seemed to know as well as the men that something big was brewing. Nervous tremors rippled down his dark, glistening flanks as he shuffled his feet and fought the urge to bolt.

He was the only Michigan horse still with the battery and had become something of a celebrity. Back in Coldwater before the war, he had pulled the delivery wagon for Bidwell's Mercantile, and just about everyone in the battery knew him from there. Now he had become a symbol of home and good luck. Most of the men found a reason to pass by and scratch an ear or slap a hind quarter if they knew the enemy was nearby. As driver of the lead team on their gun, Jonathon took his charge very seriously and had developed a strong bond with the animal during the countless marches and gun drills. Will knew it would be a bad day for Jonathon when Big Mike finally went down, as one day he surely must. There was a lot of turnover in his line of work. The Rebs had a tendency to shoot the artillery horses first so the guns could not be moved.

Just as Will was about to look away, their gunner Corporal VanVleet, and Sergeant Hazzard, chief of the piece, came around from behind the limber box and headed toward them, heads bowed close together to be heard over the sounds of battle coming from Thomas's sector. As they came up to the wheel Will was leaning against, the sergeant quickly pulled off his gauntlets and slapped them down on the rim before burying his hand in a gap in his shell jacket and scratching vigorously. It was plain from the horizontal dark streak on the front of his jacket leading to the large opening created by a missing button, that this was not his first bout with body lice.

"These goddamn graybacks will be the death of me yet, Charley," he said as he switched sides and renewed the assault.

The gun corporal chuckled and said, "You're just getting 'em riled up that way, Dave. Pretty soon you're gonna be busier than a puppy with two peters."

Al, still working on his coffee, said, "George, who was it over by Lapeer that we hear tell of had a goat with two peters? Wasn't that just the damnedest thing…why, if I had two peters…well, there's just no telling the fun I could have."

The sergeant pulled his hand out of his jacket and pinched around on his crotch a few times and then stood up straight and said, "OK, let's

16

get on with this goddamn war. What I come over here to tell you is that the captain thinks the big push is going to be up on the left this morning. I know we already shifted position three times since sun up," said the sergeant, holding up both hands, palm-out, as if to block the hail of curses that he expected to erupt from the corporal. "But be ready to move out in a hurry. Artillery ain't been getting much advance notice lately. All that commotion down yonder is infantry pulling out of line and moving over to help Reynolds, and we may be next. If we get the call, limber up quick and move your gun down on the road before anybody mounts up. Your horses are going to have enough trouble with this underbrush as it is, without a lot of extra weight. Keep enough men with you to work the gun in case we get separated and make sure you got plenty of primers. That last batch we got had a lot of duds in it. You can put your numbers one, two, and three on the limber box and your number four man on the wheel horse. If you can pry Jonathon away from Big Mike, he can carry rounds for you."

Not able to resist the opportunity for a little sarcasm, Will said, "Excuse me, Sergeant, but I don't much like riding on the box. It's really very dangerous, you know, what with all that gunpowder and such. If you don't mind, maybe I'll get a head start and just mosey along right now and meet you over there."

Sergeant Hazzard chuckled and leaned over the wheel to see who was talking to him. "Let me tell you something, Willy, my boy, if some Secesh gunner gets lucky and puts a round through your limber box, it's gonna be raining brass buttons and assholes all over these damned woods. You just don't pay it no mind. Those Reb gunners couldn't hit a bull in the ass with a coal shovel."

The sergeant slapped Charley on the shoulder and started to walk back to the limber but stopped and turned. "Remind Will and Jimmy to step out far enough to clear the wheels after you go to the 'ready.' Double canister makes these parrotts buck like a scare't mule on this damned Secesh hard pan, and I don't need nobody getting run over."

With that, he continued on, pausing briefly to cuss out Jonathon for wasting his time on an animal whose days were numbered anyway. As the old sergeant walked away, Will marveled at the calming effect he had on the whole battery. As a young man he had served in a regular army battery during the Mexican War and was one of the few noncoms, or officers for that matter, who had actually seen combat prior to the current disturbance. Nothing seemed to surprise or rattle him, at least nothing that couldn't be rendered manageable by one of the many curse words or oaths in his impressive repertoire.

Jimmy kicked Will's boot and motioned with a nod of his head in the direction of the other gun in their section. Startled out of his thoughts, Will looked back over his shoulder in time to see Captain Church rein his big sorrel to a stop and shout something to Lieutenant Fuller. Even though they were too far away to hear what was said, it was easy enough to figure out from the wild arm gestures of the non-coms and the response of the crew.

"Time to go to work, Jimmy," said Will as he gathered his feet under him and stood up. He stuck his hand out and pulled Jimmy to his feet just as the sergeant came trotting back down the left side of the limber, yelling, "Limber up!" Gun Six, limber up now! Let's go, boys; praise the Lord if it ain't just a beautiful Sabbath day for doing God's work of killing Secesh! Chocks out! Move it, move it, move it!" He stopped and grabbed Big Mike's bridle, jerking it towards him and at the same time yelling at Jonathon to spur the horse forward. Big Mike lurched, shaking his head, but he was no match for the old sergeant and quickly settled into a steady pull to the left, bringing the back of the limber around to meet the gun. Jimmy and Will grabbed a handle on each side of the trail, briefly making eye contact to synchronize their efforts before putting their backs into the lift. As soon as the trail cleared the ground, the gun started rolling back toward the limber with corporal VanVleet and Horace pushing on the wheels, and Al and George leaning into the axle on each side of the barrel. Just as the lunette dropped over the hitch pin, the first cries of alarm began rippling up and down the line.

The voices of thousands of Confederate soldiers rose as one into a high-pitched twittering scream from what moments before had appeared to

18

be a deserted forest just on the other side of the corn stubble field in front of the battery. It grew in intensity as each successive rank came boiling out of the dark woods, row after dusty gray row, punctuated here and there by the glint of sun off the barrel or lock of a weapon. Choking dust rose up from their feet so fast that just the heads and shoulders of following ranks were visible.

At that moment, Lieutenant Corbin rode up frantically waving his hat and yelling, "Drop trail, action front, drop trail, action front! Sergeant, dump all your canister rounds out on the ground here, and send your limber down to the road. Fire low and quick on the captain's command. Give 'em hell, boys!" He shouted as he spun his horse around and rode off in the direction of the next gun in line, still waving his hat.

Having been first to receive the order to limber up, the two-gun section of Battery D farthest to the left had already pulled out, and both guns were nearly to the road that ran roughly parallel to and behind the Union defensive line. The order to take up their old positions and go into action transformed them into an astonishing scene of motion and disorder, turning in billows of dust as the men and horses fought the weight of the carriages to reverse direction. Just as all seemed lost in hopeless confusion, first one team, then the other burst from the dense clouds of their own making, drivers bent low, flailing frantically at horseflesh, the carriages bouncing wildly over the uneven ground and underbrush, all pulling together back to their original firing positions. The Ohio infantrymen close up on either side of the battery were torn between watching the Confederates dress their ranks for the attack or the choreographed efforts of the cannoneers struggling to bring their pieces back into line on their flanks.

Sergeant Hazzard still held Big Mike's bridle, impatiently looking back at Corporal VanVleet who was struggling to unhitch the gun. When the corporal's hand finally went up, he smacked the animal's flank and yelled to Jonathon, "Drive on! Wait down on the road but keep an eye out for the Rebs. If it looks like we been overrun, you git on across that cornfield as fast as you can." The corporal mounted the trail spike and used it as a handle to help Will and Jimmy lift the heavy trail and guide the gun forward into battery, with George and Al working the wheels. The order "action front" had come so quickly on the heels of the order to "limber up" that Gun Six was still very close to the original firing position.

As the wheels came up against the logs that they had previously used to mark the "in battery" position twenty feet behind the breastworks, Corporal VanVleet yelled, "Drop trail, load, canister," to set the firing sequence in motion. Jimmy spit on the leather thumbstall, covering his left thumb to make it pliable, stepped inside the right wheel, and placed it over the vent hole on top of the breech, nodding when he was satisfied that he had an air-tight seal. Al stepped up to the front of the gun, pushed a canister round into the end of the barrel, and nodded to his brother who stepped in to ram it home. As soon as George was clear, Corporal VanVleet yelled "Ready," which was the cue for Jimmy to reach over and push the long brass pick down the vent hole and punch a hole in the powder bag. Will then stepped up beside Jimmy, placed a friction primer in the vent, attached the lanyard, and side-stepped away, being careful not to stumble as the lanyard became taut. When Corporal VanVleet gave the order to fire, Will would give a sharp tug on the lanyard and the gun would go off, sending a deadly pattern of seventy small lead balls toward the enemy.

Captain Church was sitting astride his horse near the center of the battery, watching the Confederate line approach through field glasses and hoping he could delay long enough for the left section to unlimber and get their guns into action. He wanted to shock and confuse the enemy soldiers as much as possible by firing all six guns together, but when the range closed to 500 yards, he would have no choice but to open fire with whomever was ready. He let the glasses dangle against his chest on the neck strap, shifted the reins to his left hand, and drew his sword. Church looked to his left just in time to see the two James rifles on the end come to the "ready." He held the sword over his head, spun his horse around in a tangle of hooves to make sure he had everyone's attention, and yelled "Battery D, on my command." The captain hesitated for a moment as he watched his command repeated up and down the line, looked once more to the front to check the progress of the gray line, and then sharply dropped his sword and screamed "Commence firing!" at the top of his lungs.

Chapter 2

Almost as one, Battery D's six guns erupted, issuing a sheet of flame and a thunderous roar that shook the ground all along its eighty-yard front. The Confederate line in front of the battery disappeared in a maelstrom of fire, dust, and dense gray smoke. The low unnerving drone of hundreds of wounded men groaning in agony told of the horrors taking place on the other side of the veil.

By now the deafening roar of battle had become so overwhelming that spoken commands could no longer be heard, even from a few feet away. At such close range and using canister, there was no need to sight the gun, but the corporal grabbed the trail spike and nudged it to the right about a foot anyway, with the thought that their second shot might find an untouched section of the rebel line. Satisfied that all was in order, he took several quick steps back, scanned the crew to make sure everyone was in position, raised his arm, locked eyes with Will, and then yelled "Fire!" as he dropped his arm.

Will gave the lanyard a tug, and the gun went off with a loud crack. A plume of smoke followed by a twenty-foot stem of dark red flame shot out of the barrel, sending the whole gun lurching backwards ten feet. The blast of lead balls spread out as they traveled down range, sweeping away everything and everyone before it. The balls in the bottom of the pattern struck the hard dry ground about twenty yards out and ricocheted, kicking up a dense layer of dust and taking off the legs of men and horses. At 100 yards the expanse of human wreckage they created in the rebel line was forty yards wide.

As the gun came to rest, Corporal VanVleet yelled "In battery, load, canister double," and the four cannoneers grabbed the wheels and rolled the gun forward until the rims once again rested against the stop logs.

As the crew of Gun Six worked quickly but deliberately to reload their gun, the men of the 35th Ohio Infantry, whose works started just a few yards to their right, unleashed a crashing volley from their Springfield rifles that marked their battle line in a long flat sheet of fire and made even the hardened artillerists flinch. Gun Six got one more round off before the order to cease fire was passed to give the captain a chance to survey the effects of their work.

It took a few tense minutes for the smoke to rise away and the dust to settle, giving them at last a panorama unlike anything they had seen before. Where there had been rows of Confederate infantry advancing shoulder to shoulder across the open field with regimental flags waving bravely, there was nothing. What appeared to be rough broken ground to their front was actually the bodies, or pieces of the bodies of the attacking rebels, so completely covered with a fine layer of ocher-colored dust that they looked like fallen statues, what the citizens of Pompeii must have looked like after the great eruption. As disturbing as the sight was, it brought a feeling of relief to the men of Battery D and the Ohio regiments on their flanks. A few of the green recruits in the 17th Ohio started to cheer and shout taunts toward the enemy line but quickly fell silent under the disgusted glower of the old hands.

Will replaced the last primer he had readied back in his pouch and looked on with Jimmy as Al and George stomped out the grass fire set by the muzzle blast of their gun. Jimmy looked sideways at Will and said, "Old Al'll be shitting and gitting if that fire spreads over to the pile of powder behind him," referring to the spot where they had cut the powder bags off some of the canister rounds.

"George, get that spot just behind your left shoe," said Al. "We need Ma here to help with this, God rest her soul. I'll never forget that morning she almost burned the shithouse down, hiding out there smoking her pipe."

This memory struck a particular nerve in George, and he spoke for the first time. "She didn't take too kindly to our general merriment, neither, as I recall," he said. George rested the rammer on the toe of his boot and looked out over the corn stubble field littered with the dead and the near dead. "Good God almighty, Al. What a mess that canister makes."

Just as George was about to turn away, he noticed movement on the edge of the woods across the field. "Get ready, boys, looks like they ain't had enough yet."

Corporal VanVleet jumped up and spun around, looking for their lieutenant and the order to load. Again the tree line was transformed as the first two lines of gray infantry stepped into the sun and started forward. This time, however, their tactics were different. The first line halted about thirty paces from the cover of the trees and waited for the second line to come up close behind them. When the two lines were an arm's length of each other, the foremost raised their rifles and took aim at the dark woods that held the Yankee guns. The second line of soldiers also raised their rifles and took aim over the shoulders of the men directly in front of them and all waited for the order to fire.

As soon as Sergeant Hazzard saw the first line of rebels stop and raise their rifles, he came running up to the gun screaming, "Get down, boys, get down. As soon as they fire, get up quick, load and fire, double canister and be quick!"

Up and down the line, infantrymen and cannoneers alike were getting as flat on the ground as they possibly could to avoid the coming storm of lead. Jimmy and Will dropped down on their bellies side by side with the gun trail between them. Neither man tried to speak above the continuous roar of battle, but they searched each other's face for reassurance. The only comfort to be had this day was from seeing the fear, and the resolve to overcome it, reflected in each other's face.

Will had just rested his head on his crossed forearms when the volley from the enemy line exploded in a sheet of flame and a rolling crash that started way over and out of sight on the left and traveled swiftly down the line and out of sight on the right. Thousands of .58 caliber miniballs swept the woods and the hastily constructed Federal breastworks along a 600-yard front. Whenever the lead balls encountered a wood fence rail or a flat surface like a limber box, it sounded like hail on a barn roof. When they hit flesh they made a hollow thud. Even though the rebels did not have a clear view of the Federal line inside the woods, the volume of lead more than made up for any difficulties finding a target. Curses and screams of the wounded seemed to come from every direction, as did shouts from noncoms and officers trying to steady their men. Corporal VanVleet was already on his feet yelling "Load, canister, double," his face contorted with urgency and his eyes wide. The crew of Gun Six needed no more encouragement and jumped to load the gun.

The Confederate generals had learned a hard lesson well. This time they would not feed their troops in piecemeal and advance in ranks as they had with the first attack. Before the Union soldiers had recovered from the first devastating volley, the rebels rushed the blue line at the double quick, supporting troops pouring out of the woods behind them by the thousands. The infantry regiment to the right of the battery rallied first and fired a ragged volley, followed almost immediately by the 17th Ohio on the left, but the gray mass continued to advance over the bodies of their own men as they fell. The guns of the battery once again began to add their thunder to the overpowering noise of the battle, shaking the ground and hurling huge billowing dirty clouds of smoke streaked with fire into the face of the enemy. The hundreds of lead balls flying through the air from the double canister sounded to the rebels like gusts of wind, and they instinctively bent forward and pressed on.

The guns of Battery D were taking a terrible toll on the Confederates as they crossed the old cornfield, but they could not fire fast enough to stem the tide, and all six guns were running out of ammunition. The Ohio regiments on either side of the battery began to fall back, firing into the rebels as they backed away but leaving the artillerymen unsupported. Captain Church was suddenly out of options. Reluctantly, he ordered the section of Battery D on the left, the James rifles, to stay in place and hold out as long as they could, firing canister to cover the retreat of the remaining four guns. Not wanting to expose the limber horses to enemy fire, he sent a lieutenant back to the road to alert the drivers and then ordered the guns manhandled fifty yards to the rear where they could be limbered up and pulled to safety.

As soon as he received the order to pull back, Corporal VanVleet stepped up to the trail of Gun Six and yelled, "Cease fire, secure the implements," at the same time drawing his hand, palm down, across in front of his neck in case his verbal command was lost in the deafening noise. Al and George secured the water bucket and rammer underneath the gun carriage and stepped inside the wheels, ready to lean into the axle as soon as Will and Jimmy lifted the trail. Horace dropped to his knees and started stuffing the few remaining rounds of ammunition into the gunner's haversack. Corporal VanVleet leaped forward and grabbed Horace by the collar, jerking him to his feet. "You dumb son-of-a-bitch, leave it be and get on a wheel," he yelled as he pushed Horace roughly toward the gun. He then spun around, shoved Will away from the trail handle, shouting for him to get on the other wheel, and together with Jimmy, lifted the trail and started the gun rolling through the underbrush to the rear.

Chapter 3

As Corporal VanVleet and his detachment reached the road with their gun and prepared to limber up, the rebels passed through the firing position the battery had just vacated, closing fast. The limbers for the James rifles that were left behind to cover their withdrawal had already started out across the trampled cornfield amidst the swirling mass of fleeing Union infantry, and from a distance they looked like two giant insects borne aloft by a hoard of angry ants. Of the four remaining limbers standing side by side, the Napoleons were the next to pull out. The buzz and hiss of miniballs passing overhead was becoming more intense by the moment. With increasing frequency they struck a gun carriage or limber with a resounding crack like a hammer blow. The horses harnessed to the limbers were rearing and stomping their feet, their eyes wide with terror.

Sergeant Hazzard stood in front of the lead horses of Gun Six, holding Big Mike's bridle and yelling instructions up to Jonathon in the saddle: "You see the bald spot on the left end of that ridge over yonder?" He pointed across the open field to where other Union batteries were already firing. Jonathon nodded his acknowledgment as he reeled in the saddle. "As soon I turn Mike loose you git across there quick and look for the first lieutenant in the woods to the right of that clearing– he'll put you into line. You boys lean forward and stay low," he said, turning to the other two drivers behind Jonathon. "Don't stop for nothing…even if somebody falls off."

The sergeant was looking back impatiently at Corporal VanVleet and Jimmy struggling to line up the gun's lunette and drop it over the hitch pin on the limber carriage, when he saw a volley of infantry fire flash on the edge of the tree line behind them, followed instantly by the sound of splintering wood and the unnerving screams of wounded horses. In the blink of an eye Gun Five was doomed. Four horses and all three drivers went down as one, shaking the ground as they collapsed in a squirming tangle of harnesses, animals, and men. Two of the drivers were killed outright, but the corporal on the lead team was trapped under his horse and getting crushed as the horse rolled in agony, spilling its glistening entrails from a gaping gut wound. The stunned crew of Gun Six looked on as he calmly fished his revolver out of his belt and shot the animal twice in the head and then did likewise to the two remaining horses that were struggling to regain their feet. As the shock and pain of a crushed leg and pelvis gripped him, he lay back in the dirt and closed his eyes.

Corporal VanVleet had missed the drama unfolding next to them as he and Jimmy secured their gun to the limber, and now he waved his arm, signaling to the sergeant that they were ready to move out. The crew immediately began to scramble up on the limber box, desperate to get away from the approaching enemy. Will ran along the right side of the limber, stopping next to the right horse of the wheel team. He could see the sergeant yelling at the drivers and knew he had only seconds to get up on this horse or get left behind. Without further thought, he threw his arms over the back of the animal and jumped forward, pulling himself up until he lay across its back on his belly. He hung there for a moment, flailing his arms, trying to get a purchase on anything that would help him spin around and get his leg over the horse's croup, finally settling on a fistful of mane. The horse lurched forward, straining at the traces, just as Will was able to straddle its back and grab onto the harness.

Sergeant Hazzard glanced over quickly to make sure Will was set and then jumped out of the way, yelling "OK now, git!" Big Mike didn't wait for Jonathon to touch him with his spurs but shot forward as soon as the old sergeant released his grip on the bridle. The sudden move caught the other horse of the lead team by surprise, and the limber lurched and started to veer sharply to the right before both horses settled in and began pulling together.

Will glanced back at the wreckage of men and equipment that had been Gun Five and noticed a body lying apart from the others directly behind them. In fact, the right wheel of their gun had made a clearly defined track across the back of his blue jacket. It dawned on Will that the man was one of their own, and he quickly checked the men on the box to see who was missing. It was Horace. In the excitement he must have forgotten to find a handhold on the limber box and toppled off the back and under the wheel of the 1800-pound gun when they started out across the cornfield.

Union infantrymen of Wood's Brigade, which had been in the process of pulling back and moving north to support Reynolds, had been caught at the worst possible moment by the Confederate attack and were now scattered and fleeing for their lives across Dyer's once tranquil cornfield. Units that were still in line and holding their own began to comprehend the magnitude of the disaster, and their resolve weakened. They gave up ground in ever-increasing numbers until finally the rout was complete. The open ground surrounding the Dyer farmhouse and the ridge a half mile to the west was choked with masses of men in various stages of panic and retreat as the rebels overpowered everything in their path. Here and there a Federal general officer, surrounded by his staff, would attempt to stem the tide, but they inevitably were swept up and carried along in the retreat. Any man fortunate enough to be at a distance on high ground, with the leisure to observe, would have beheld the grand spectacle of sixteen thousand Confederate soldiers attacking across half a mile of open fields, dozens of regimental flags tilted forward and waving bravely, and shells from the Union artillery streaking over their heads and bursting in flashes of light up and down their ranks.

For the men of Gun Six, Battery D, in the midst of the maelstrom, the view was very different. Choking dust kicked up by the limber horses and the thousands of army boots crossing the field on the run, mixed with the slowly drifting cloud banks of gunpowder smoke and closed in tight around the men of Gun Six, limiting their field of view to only a few feet. Riding on the limber box, Al, George, and Jimmy linked arms to make sure that Jimmy, seated in the middle with no handhold, did not suffer the same fate as Horace. The collars of their roundabouts were pulled up over their faces in an attempt to filter out the dust that caked their eyes, noses, and mouths. Shadowy figures of men running in all directions darted in close and then just as quickly faded back into the dirty cloud. With unsettling frequency, lead balls nearing the end of their trajectory buzzed past like angry bees, sometimes even tugging at a coat or hat. Will was bent low over his horse, gripping the harness as tight as he could and looking down to protect his eyes when suddenly, for just an instant he was face to face with a terrified screaming soldier as he swept past under the horses and carriages. As they approached the base of the ridge where they were to unlimber and go into action, the twenty-three guns of the Union artillery reserve already in place were firing over their heads as fast as they could shoot and reload, the blasts from the guns overlapping to create a continuous unearthly roar that shook the ground and dominated the battlefield.

Jonathon, riding the lead horse, was bent over, straining to keep the barrel of the Napoleon in front of them in sight, hoping that its driver knew where he was going. There was a narrow line of woods and tangled underbrush at the bottom of the ridge and for the last few minutes they had been angling to the left, searching for a path through it that was wide enough for the carriages. Suddenly the gun in front of them slowed and turned sharply right onto a road. Big Mike reacted to the change a second before Jonathon saw the barrel of the Napoleon materialize out of the dust cloud and reared as he crabbed to the right, forcing the whole rig to slow and follow the turn. They had only gone about fifty yards when they reached the place where the long low ridge flattened out and ended at the road. The land had been under tillage at some time in the past and was clear of obstructions all the way to the line of trees at the crest. The three remaining guns and crews of Battery D turned right off the road in succession and followed the gradually rising spine of the ridge, the horses slowing as they strained against the weight of the guns and limbers. When they were nearing the tree line, a horseman appeared on the edge of the woods and broke into a gallop toward the guns laboring up the hill.

Lieutenant Henry Corbin reined in his horse and neatly reversed direction, pulling abreast of the lead horses on the first gun. He leaned in close to the driver and yelled "Just up ahead you'll see tracks leading into the woods. Follow them until you meet the captain and he'll put you into position." Without waiting for an acknowledgment, he spurred his horse and once again reversed direction, coming to a quick gallop by swatting the animal's hindquarter with his slouch hat. With the same smooth horsemanship that he had displayed at the first limber, he spun around and pulled in next to Jonathon and Big Mike, slowing to match their speed. The lieutenant rode beside them in silence for a few minutes, seemingly unaware of the bullets buzzing close by, right arm hanging straight down from his shoulder and hat still in hand. Fatigue and shock from leaving the crews of the James rifles, his men, to fend for themselves were etched on his gunpowder-blackened face. The line where his hat had rested on his forehead, clearly denoted by white skin, would have been amusing in a more benign situation. "How's Big Mike?" he finally said, looking over at Jonathon.

"Nary a scratch, Lieutenant," replied the driver. "But he don't much cotton to all this commotion."

Lieutenant Corbin nodded, looking the big lead horse over and said, "I reckon he's thinking he's a long ways from Bidwell's about now, Johnny." After an awkward moment of silence, the lieutenant looked up with a pained expression on his face as the images of the peaceful world he had known in Michigan unexpectedly collided in his mind with the horrible scenes of death and destruction that were his current existence. "Sergeant Hazzard and your corporal are just inside those trees up ahead, and they'll put you into line when you get up there," he said, and with that, he touched his horse with his spurs and galloped away toward the crest of the ridge and back to the darkness of the woods.

The first Napoleon, and then a few minutes later, the second, following ruts worn deep by a farmer's countless trips to his wood lot, disappeared into the shadows of the forest. Will leaned back and threw his leg over the withers of his horse, sliding on his backside to the ground as they approached the trees. Taking that as a cue, the three men riding the limber jumped off either side and took up positions behind the gun, ready to push if needed.

As they entered the trees, the thunder of the guns farther along on the ridge took on a deeper and sharper quality. Occasionally the rhythm of the overlapping explosions was broken by a brief pause that allowed the resounding crack of a single detonation, followed by distant shouts and cheers of cannoneers, to carry down the line. Brush fires from the muzzle blasts of the guns burned furiously all along the ridge and added their smoke to that of burnt gunpowder, infusing the space under the high canopy of the forest with a thick fog that cast everything into hues of gray. Here and there the haze was ripped by long angry streaks of red from the mouths of the guns that set huge swirling eddies adrift in the dense smoke. Screams of dying men and the trembling of the ground made the vision of Hell complete.

Sergeant Hazzard was just off to the right of the trail, impatiently waving them forward and yelling curses that were carried away in the uproar. As they approached, he pointed to the spot where he wanted Jonathon to start his turn to bring the gun around. When the lead team was within reach, he grabbed the bridle of the horse next to Big Mike and manhandled the team sharply right to clear the trunk of an old hickory tree before switching to the other side and pulling the team left around the tree in a "U" turn. Once the gun was trailing straight behind the limber and both were perpendicular to the trail, Jonathon reined in and stopped the horses so the gun could be dropped off and wheeled into firing position by the crew. Will and Jimmy quickly jumped in behind the limber, pulled the key out of the pintle and lifted the trail of the gun clear, both waving their free hands to Jonathon to move the limber forward and out of the way. With Sergeant Hazzard's help, Jonathon executed another "U" turn and brought the limber into position with the six-horse team and their drivers facing the gun. Al, George, Jimmy, and Will quickly took their implements and prepared the gun for firing. From their vantage point on the crest of the ridge, the men of Battery D could now clearly see the entire southern end of the Federal line dissolved into total chaos and being swept westward toward them by the triumphant gray juggernaut.

The crew of Gun Six did not have long to wait for the order to begin firing. After a short exchange with Sergeant Hazzard, Corporal VanVleet turned slightly toward the limber and shouted "Load, shell, 900 yards, load!" The target was the tree line half a mile away, where the rebels were still pouring out of the woods and forming up. Will stepped sideways to the end of the lanyard and looked back at VanVleet for the signal to fire. The Corporal's arm dropped and Will pulled, igniting the charge. The explosion slammed the heavy barrel down into its fully depressed position and sent the gun recoiling back ten feet. Before it had even stopped rolling, the crew jumped to the wheels and started it back the other way to begin the firing sequence all over again.

Something odd about the way the gun corporal had signaled the order to fire nagged at Will, and as he waited for George to sponge the barrel, he glanced back over his shoulder. VanVleet was lying on his back in the dead leaves, arms motionless at his side but legs alternately bending and extending at the knee as if trying to walk. His face held a grimace, but the eyes were fixed and vacant. Blood pooled around his head creating a dreadful backdrop for his pallid skin.

Back at the limber, Sergeant Hazzard, who had been poised to observe the first shot so he could make adjustments in range for successive rounds, saw the miniball strike VanVleet in the side of his head just as he was about to lower his arm to fire the gun. Will, who was expecting only a hand signal from the corporal, pulled the lanyard as soon as his arm started to drop, even though the gunner was most likely already dead. Will looked up and locked eyes with the sergeant, who simply nodded and pointed to the gun, indicating that Will should mind his duty and forget what was going on around him. By now the rest of the crew knew that their gunner was down, and when Will turned to prime the gun, they were all looking at him, fear and uncertainty showing on their dirty faces. Will hesitated a moment and then deliberately fished a friction primer out of his pouch and nodded to Jimmy to pick the charge. When he was ready to pull, he looked back at the limber, and Sergeant Hazzard mouthed the word "fire" and pointed at him. The gun recoiled with a thunderous roar, and once again the men jumped to service the piece.

Chapter 4

Below them on the cornfield, the routed Federal infantrymen streaming west away from the pursuing Confederates began diving into the underbrush and fleeing straight up the face of the ridge directly under the cannon fire of their own army. First to pass through Battery D's position were several wild-eyed, riderless horses, one of which nearly trampled Al before he could jump inside the wheels of the gun. Next came the equally panicked soldiers, in ones and twos at first but soon in large numbers, many without rifles, some shouting at the cannoneers to run for their lives, nearly all with eyes locked straight ahead. The appearance of friendly troops in front of Battery D forced a temporary cease fire but also gave them valuable time to prepare canister rounds for the rebels who were in hot pursuit.

George had just finished sponging the barrel after the last shot and was standing inside the left wheel facing forward, gripping the rammer in each hand diagonally across his body, when a hatless, disheveled infantry lieutenant suddenly appeared out of the haze in front of the gun. He stopped at the end of the barrel and started shouting something unintelligible while stabbing his sword at the sky to emphasize whatever it was he was trying to say. None of the battery men could hear a word he said over the sounds of battle around them. George stood watching the man as he ranted but gave no sign that he understood or even cared what the message might be. In frustration, the lieutenant reached out and put his free hand on the end of the gun barrel while turning slightly and pointing behind him with his sword.

George's reaction was immediate. His head snapped to the left as he eyed the lieutenant's hand touching the gun, and then with no more effort than swatting a fly, and just as quickly, the big man struck the lieutenant in the side of the head with the gunpowder-caked sponge end of the rammer, leaving a rather shocking solid black circle on one side of his face and knocking him ass-over-applecart down the slope and into the underbrush. As the officer disappeared back into the smoke, George shot a quick glance over his shoulder to gauge the reaction of Sergeant Hazzard, but the old man had already ducked behind the open lid of the limber, shaking his head.

The rapid success of Longstreet's attack had caught both armies by surprise, and the resulting confusion had prevented, at least until now, the Confederates from making effective use of their own artillery. The odd ringing sound made by exploding enemy shells and the crash and splintering of trees toppled by solid shot began to mingle with the thunder of the Federal guns, portending an ominous change in the fortunes of war for the Union artillerymen. The cacophony was so overwhelming that it physically pressed in on the men and blocked all means of communication except visual, and even that was greatly diminished by heavy smoke. The thick layer of dead leaves that covered the floor of the forest was tinder dry after the rainless summer and was ablaze all along the ridge in front of the guns. The fire spread rapidly uphill and through the tall grass along the margins of the old farm fields.

Will was standing inside the wheel of the gun, waiting for the mass of fleeing soldiers to pass, when Sergeant Hazzard came up behind him and placed his hand on his back, causing him to jump in surprise. The sergeant leaned in close to Will's ear and shouted, "As soon as this sorry lot starts to thin out, load double canister, come to the ready, and hold until I give you the order to fire. We got to make damned sure we got Johnnies in front of us before we let fly." Will nodded his understanding and returned to watching the skedaddlers flow around his gun like a slow river around a rock.

The flow continued unabated for another ten minutes and then abruptly stopped, catching the battery men by surprise. The brief time their gun had been silent had allowed some of the heavy smoke to dissipate from their front, giving them occasional glimpses of the open field that stretched away from the bottom of the ridge; it was so densely packed with rebels advancing toward them at the double quick that it appeared as though the ground itself was moving. No man facing them on the ridge now believed they could be stopped.

The quick movement of Jimmy stepping up next to the breech and covering the vent with his thumb caused Will to refocus his attention, and he began digging in his pouch for a friction primer. The sergeant stepped around in front of Big Mike and took the gunner's position, next to the now motionless body of Corporal VanVleet, as Will and Jimmy primed the gun. Will pulled the lanyard taut, turned, and immediately received the order to fire. As they continued to load and fire, Sergeant Hazzard moved the trail of the gun a little to the left each time so their canister would slow down the Confederates attempting to flank the gun line on the ridge.

Small arms fire from the approaching rebel infantry was beginning to sweep the forest around the battery in ever-increasing intensity, striking down men and horses. The gun crews knew it was time to pull out if they were to avoid being overrun and anxiously glanced back toward their officers as they continued to fire into the gray ranks. Sergeant Hazzard kept an eye on the two guns to the left for any signs of limbering up, because he knew the order to pull back would originate somewhere down the line in that direction and would travel toward them from crew to crew like wildfire. An enemy battery to their front had found the range and was beginning to place shells on them with disquieting accuracy in support of the attack.

At last the signal came from Captain Church, now hatless and on foot, standing on the wagon path behind the limbers. He was yelling at the top of his lungs and waving his right hand in a circle above his head. The words were lost, but the motion of his arm was all they needed to start the withdrawal.

Sergeant Hazzard slapped Will and Jimmy on their backs as they were priming the gun for the next firing and yelled, "Limber up, boys. Let's get the hell out of here!" With that, he spun around and headed back toward the limber, shouting for Jonathon to mount up and start the horses forward to pick up the gun. As he drew near the lead team, he realized that Jonathon was not there. He quickly looked from the men crowded around the limber box to the ground close around the team but saw nothing of the boy. The sergeant cursed under his breath, stepped up to Big Mike, and climbed aboard the animal in one fluid motion. "OK, Big Mike, let's git," he said, half to himself, and dug in his spurs. At almost the same moment came the deafening crash of a rifle volley fired close on their right flank by a mass of Confederate infantry. As one, Big Mike and all the horses of the Gun Six team dropped straight down in their traces, all mortally struck. Seconds later, an enemy shell came twittering through the trees and exploded with a resounding crack directly above the gun, the concussion knocking all four battery men off their feet.

Will opened his eyes and stared up through the trees, wondering if he was dead or alive. He could feel the ground vibrate through his spine and the back of his head, but now it was from thousands of running men. He rolled onto his stomach and tried to reorient himself. His ears rang, and the sounds of the battle around him were muffled as if he were hearing them from under water. He turned his head and looked along the ground to his left where Jimmy should have been, but there was no sign of him. He turned back and looked toward the limber, expecting to see the frenzied activity of his battery mates preparing to pull out, but there was no one. Finally his gaze fell on Sergeant Hazzard, still astride Big Mike, but obviously badly wounded.

Will rose up on his hands and knees and paused, checking himself over for injury before standing up and hurrying back to the sergeant's side. The sergeant sat slightly hunched in the saddle with his left forearm held tightly across his middle below his belt in an attempt to stanch the flow of blood from a gut wound. Blood soaked the front of his uniform jacket and pants, ran down the side of Big Mike, and pooled around his boot in the dead leaves and pine needles. In his right hand he held his army revolver against his thigh. Will reached out to touch his sergeant's shoulder but pulled back quickly when the old man turned and looked at him. He had been shot through the side of the mouth and his lower jaw hung down on his chest, still attached by a strip of skin from his left cheek. His tongue was completely exposed and wagged as he tried to talk.

Will forced himself to focus on the sergeant's eyes and was surprised to see the intense look of command in spite of his terrible injuries. He followed the sergeant's gaze as he looked down at the blood seeping out from under his arm. The old man pulled the arm away from his body just enough so Will could see the glistening silver intestine protruding from the long horizontal tear in his jacket. He turned once more and looked at Will. When he was sure he had the boy's attention, he raised the pistol and shot Big Mike in the back of the head. The horse was already dead and made no sound or movement in response to the shot. The sergeant, still holding Will's eyes, handed him the gun and turned away. The message was unmistakable. There was no decision to make as Will looked down at the gun in his hand and hesitated. He knew he was about to do something that he would never be able to forget or be able to share with another human being. He raised the gun and shot the sergeant behind the ear. The force of the ball striking his head knocked the old man out of the saddle and down into the space between the two dead lead horses. When Will leaned over Big Mike to make sure the old man was dead, he noticed another pair of boots with spurs sticking out from under the sergeant's body that could only belong to Jonathon.

Will stuck the pistol in his belt and took one last look back toward the gun to make sure no one had been left behind. When he did so, he noticed the lanyard, still attached to the primer hanging down from the breech and trailing along the ground to where he had fallen after the shell burst. He knew if he left the gun loaded and ready to fire, the Johnnies would quickly turn it around and use it on them. Without further thought, he dashed forward, grabbed the wooden handle of the lanyard and gave it a hard pull. The foremost of the Confederates that were just clearing the underbrush and preparing to rush the gun literally vanished in a blinding flash and almost solid wall of lead shot. In his haste to fire the gun and be gone, Will had violated one of the cardinal rules and was directly in the path of the recoiling left wheel. He tried to step out of the way at the last moment, but it was too late. Just as the gun was nearing the end of its rearward travel, the wheel caught Will's leg halfway between his knee and ankle, snapping the bone and sending him sprawling in agony. He lay still for several minutes trying to collect himself and then rolled onto his back, provoking a stab of pain that brought tears to his eyes. His right foot reluctantly followed the movement and came to rest unnaturally on its side, pointing out. Will looked to the ground in front of the gun to see if the rebels had renewed their attack after that last round of canister, realizing at the same time that he must find some cover. Fighting off a wave of nausea, he rose up on his elbows and pushed himself backward with his left leg, aiming for a nearby tree that had been broken off by a cannon ball about three feet up. The top part of the tree lay on the ground beside the stump, offering a little protection and concealment from the approaching enemy. When he finally reached the tree, he gave one more push and walked his back up the trunk until he was in a sitting position. Will surveyed the scene before him and for the first time noticed a body in a blue uniform jacket, face down next to the sponge bucket and about to be consumed by the fast-moving brush fire. He closed his eyes tight and prayed that Al was dead, but seconds later came the screams that spoke otherwise, primal screams that bore into his brain, screams he would hear for the rest of his life.

Like the deep rumbles of a passing summer thunderstorm, the sounds of battle moved slowly off to the north, leaving in their wake a huge swath of death and destruction. Will had been drifting in and out of consciousness as shock threatened to overtake him, and when he opened his eyes this time, the gun and limber were gone. He had no memory of the Johnnies being there at all, and that scared him. He fumbled under his coat for his watch and was startled when his hand brushed against the butt of Sergeant Hazzard's pistol stuck in the top of his britches. The sudden memory of how it came to be there was enough to clear Will's head and start him working on a plan to find his army.

He was leaning over as far as he could to look behind the tree he was propped up against, searching the ground for something to use as a splint for his broken leg, when he was startled by the snort of a horse close by. He quickly turned back and plunged his hand under his coat, feeling for the butt of the pistol. In the small clearing a few feet away where the gun and limber had been, was a Confederate officer astride a tall, beautifully proportioned gray dappled horse, the kind of horse you didn't see much of up in Michigan. The rider was lean, with a long, drooping mustache and white wide-brimmed hat pulled low over his eyes. Despite the thin layer of dust that covered them, the man and his horse were the picture of quiet elegance. From the supple, brown, knee-length cavalry boots and matching saddle bags, to the swirls of gold braid that adorned the arms of his gray frock and twinkled through the grime of battle in the slanting rays of afternoon sun, he was the vision of a cavalier. The officer sat easily on the big gray and studied the six dead artillery horses, still in line, and the body of the Union sergeant wedged in between the lead team. Will's quick movement caught the Confederate officer's attention, and he turned to regard the young man leaning against a shattered tree.

"You the one who put down this gut shot sergeant?" he said after a fashion.

Will was too taken aback to speak at first, so he simply nodded, casting his eyes downward.

"Well, son, it's a helluva thing, and I'm sure you'll be thinking on it for some time to come. When you look back on this day, just remember it was something that needed doing."

Will nodded again and said "Yes, sir, I will do that."

"Now tell me, boy, whose battery was this?" said the Confederate officer.

"Captain Church's Michigan Battery, sir," Will replied with a little defiance in his voice.

"If you live to see Captain Church again, son, you tell him General Preston sends his compliments, and tell him he had the damnedest battery I ever fought. I've lost over four hundred men in taking it, but thank God I have it now, and I intend to keep it."

"I'll see that he gets your message, General," Will said, betraying a little pride now.

"You do that, son, and tend to that leg. Make sure you tie it up good now."

With that, the General nodded, touched his horse with his spurs, and disappeared over the crest of the ridge.

Will closed his eyes again and leaned his head back against the tree, easing his grip on the pistol. The next thing he knew, he was being shaken and someone was calling his name over and over again. It was almost dark now, and for a moment he thought he might still be dreaming. He wearily opened his eyes and looked into the anxious face of his friend Jimmy. A great sense of relief washed over him, and for the first time since morning he thought maybe things would be all right. Jimmy looked him over in the fading light and asked how badly he was hit.

While Will was explaining that he wasn't shot but that his leg was broken, George came out of the dusk and knelt down beside them. "Brother's dead, Jimmy. Killed and half burned up, he is." They all looked at each other for a moment, trying to think of what to say, but nothing seemed right.

Finally George broke the silence and said, "How bad is Will?"

"His leg is broken pretty bad, but I think we can tie it up with a couple of small limbs off this tree and get him out of here before it gets too dark."

"I'll make the splints while you find something to tie 'em up with," said George.

In a few minutes they had Will's leg secure enough to stand him up and support him between them with his arms around their necks. In this fashion they moved off the way they had come, towards the road leading west to McFarland's Gap and the retreating Union army. As they picked their way through the dark woods, they could hear muffled voices and see the dim flickering lights of lanterns drifting through the trees as the enemy soldiers searched for their dead and wounded.

Chapter 5

They had traveled about two miles when Jimmy called a halt. Aided by the light of a full moon, they moved off the road to the edge of a small pine forest and sat shoulder to shoulder, leaning back against a tree, exhausted. The nights were cold now in this part of the country, and none of them had more than the clothes on their backs to protect them against the chill. The three men rested in silence for a while, each trying to deal with what he had seen that day. George spoke first, stating flatly that he was going back to bury his brother. Both Will and Jimmy started talking at once, trying to dissuade him from such a foolish notion.

"Those woods are crawling with Rebs looking for their own people, George. Why, they'd nab you before you got halfway there and you'd end up in some Secesh prison for the rest of the war," said Jimmy.

"I know, I know. But Al's all I got… had, in this world, and I just couldn't live with myself not knowing how he was fixed for the Hereafter. If I can just get him covered with a little dirt and mark the spot, maybe I can come back here after all this is over and take him home to Lapeer. I'll be back before sunup, but if you get a chance at a wagon, don't wait for me." George started to get to his feet but then stopped and settled back against the tree. He spoke softly now. "Did you see him go down, Will?"

Will hesitated, staring off into the darkness while he wrestled with the image of Al's final moments, and with the question George was really asking. Finally he said, "I didn't see him get hit, but he was for sure gone before the fire got to him."

There was another long silence before George spoke again. "Thanks, Will. I reckon I'll be going." With that, he stood and slipped away without a sound in the thick carpet of pine needles, his retreating figure darting between the moon shadows of the tall trees. Will and Jimmy sat side by side, drifting in and out of sleep, as an endless procession of shadowy figures trudged slowly past along the road toward McFarland's Gap.

Sometime after midnight, Jimmy became restless and awoke feeling feverish and lightheaded. He opened the bottom buttons of his jacket and dug out his shirt to expose the skin where he thought he had just been nicked by a piece of shrapnel when the shell had exploded over the gun the previous day. He couldn't see much in the moonlight, just a short dark puckered line about four inches long on the pale skin of his left side. No blood, so it couldn't be too bad, he thought, but as he twisted his upper body around to get a better look, he felt a sudden sharp pain that took his breath away.

"Will…Will, wake up," said Jimmy, as he shook his friend by the shoulder. Will came awake with a start, reaching inside his jacket for the sergeant's pistol as he quickly scanned the darkness for a threat.

"You got any lucifers?"

"Damn it, Jimmy, you scared the shit out of me! What the hell you want with a lucifer?"

"I got nicked in the side when that shell burst next to us yesterday and it hurts something fierce. I don't feel too good neither. If you got any lucifers, light one and have a look at it for me, will ya?"

Will dug in his pocket and pulled out several matches and the crushed box that had once held them. He scooted down until his face was even with the bare skin Jimmy had exposed for inspection and struck one on the side of the box. In the sudden illumination, he saw the wound, which looked a little strange, but not too serious. What concerned him more was the large area of discolored skin surrounding a small thin entrance wound that spread out covering most of his lower back.

"Well?" said Jimmy.

"It don't look too bad, but you got a big black and blue patch all around it that seems kind of strange. How bad does it hurt?"

"It's damned uncomfortable, I can tell you that much. I could sure use a drink, too."

"You got a lot of needs, Jimmy," Will said, as he carefully pushed himself back up the tree with his good leg.

"Try to get some rest and I'll look at it again when it gets light. Maybe we can find some water, too. George ought to be back by then if he's coming." Will reached into his jacket and pulled out the revolver, tucking it under a fold of his wool pants next to his leg.

"Thanks for coming back for me, Jimmy," he said after a while, feeling a little guilty about being short with his friend. Jimmy didn't respond, so he figured he had already fallen asleep.

For the next several hours, Will drifted in a narrow layer of consciousness between being fully awake and fully asleep. He began to hear unintelligible voices, far off at first, but moving closer in the darkness. Eventually the environment around them became so charged with danger that it pulled Will up out of his troubled dream state. A strange light played on the outside of his closed eyelids, and an unfamiliar voice, very close, said, "Hot damn, over here, Bobby, we got us a couple dead bluebellies and they both got good shoes."

Will's eyes snapped open and looked into the dirty, gaunt face of a man kneeling next to him with a lantern. The dim flickering light revealed the startled look on the man's face as he realized this Yankee was not dead. Will was still disoriented and almost as a reflex extended his right arm, placed the long barrel of the revolver against the man's forehead and squeezed the trigger. The man's face was lost in the muzzle flash of the gun, and he was knocked backward into the darkness. Suddenly there was another voice close by, this one younger and more desperate,

"Pa, Pa, where are you, Pa? It's me, Bobby …where are you?" Finally the boy came near enough to the lantern light to see what had happened to his father. He looked too young to be in the army and was dressed in filthy rough homespun like the older man.

"You dirty Yankee, you murdered my pa, you murdered him over a pair of dead man's shoes," he screamed as he lunged toward Will. Will raised the pistol again, and without a word shot the boy in the face, killing him instantly. He lay his head back against the tree and closed his eyes, trying to catch his breath and calm his pounding heart. Suddenly it dawned on him what the boy had said about dead man's shoes and the fact that Jimmy hadn't stirred or said a word during the whole confrontation. Will reached down by his left foot, picked up the old man's lantern, and brought it up to Jimmy's face. What he feared was confirmed by the vacant, unblinking stare of his friend's eyes. Jimmy had died quietly, leaning against him. Died without a word. Without knowing he was going to die. He had just slipped away.

Will lay against the tree in the early morning darkness, wide awake now and fighting off despair. He stared into the gloom and took what comfort he could from the sounds of the forest waking up around him. One bird broke the silence first with a slow methodical chirp, and then others joined in with their own particular styles and songs. None of them were on the move or feeding yet, just sitting tight and waiting for the sun.

Gradually things began to take on form and substance, the most disturbing of which were the three bodies arrayed around him. About halfway between where he sat on the edge of the pines and the Rossville Road, a swaybacked dark mule hitched to a two-wheel cart stood motionless in the dim light under a huge, spreading maple tree. The yellow and orange leaves at the very top of the tree were luminous in the first soft rays of autumn sunlight that spilled over the ridge behind him. Ground fog pooled around the animal's legs and hung on clumps of underbrush. It drifted silently between the shadows. Will closed his eyes, thinking to himself that the rig must have belonged to the man and his son who lay dead at his feet. The buzz of a bold black-capped chickadee flitting between the low branches near his head reminded him of warm autumn days back in Michigan, hunting fox squirrels with Jimmy and dozing at the base of an old-growth hickory tree. Will felt a downward tug on the bill of his kepi and opened his eyes. As he was about to push the cap back up on his head, the chickadee swung down, still gripping the bill with his feet, and scrutinized Will with a comical but still defiant upside-down look. The audacity of the little bird made Will smile in spite of the desperate situation he was in. "Must be his tree I'm leaning against," he thought to himself. His curiosity satisfied, the chickadee flicked his tiny wings and was gone about his business. It wasn't much, but the visit from the little bird had broken Will's downward spiral into despair, and he started hatching a plan to move north before the Confederate army swept him up.

Before Will could go anywhere, he had to figure out what to do about Jimmy. He forced his feelings aside and started going through his friend's pockets.

"Easy there, Yank, don't shoot. I ain't part of nobody's army no more and I ain't gonna do you no harm." The soft voice came from directly behind him. Will pulled back from Jimmy, and his hand closed over the butt of the pistol, but he held his tongue, waiting.

"By the looks of things, y'all might be just a little trigger-happy, if you don't mind my saying so. If it's all the same to you, I'd just as soon chat a bit and then say our goodbyes if we don't see eye to eye," said the stranger in the same soft Southern drawl.

"Come on around where I can see you, then, and we'll talk. I won't shoot," Will said warily.

A Confederate soldier cautiously stepped from behind Will's tree, moving slowly and keeping his hands in front of him as a sign of his peaceful intentions. He lowered himself to the ground and sat Indian-style between the bodies of the old man and his son, never losing eye contact with Will as they sized each other up. The Confederate was somewhat older than Will, but both were exhausted and equally covered in grime from the battlefield. The Southern man's uniform was in tatters. Crude field patches made from all different types of material were liberally scattered over both his coat and his pants, the legs of which were paper-thin and worn off halfway between his knees and his bare feet, giving him more the air of a scarecrow than a soldier. A new-looking but dusty bummer sat atop his long scraggly black hair, and except for a Federal issue canteen, he was otherwise not accoutered.

"What can I do for you, Johnnie?" said Will.

"Name's John Dean. Most folks call me Jack. 17th Tennessee, or at least I was till yesterday," said the rebel.

Will studied the man for a moment and then said, "Will Castor, Battery D, 1st Michigan."

The other man nodded and said, "The way I see it, we may be able to help each other. I expect you're hoping to get up north and find your army, and just so happens I'm going that way myself. I been walking all over this dern country and sleeping on the ground without even a decent meal for three years, and I figure I've done my share. After yesterday, everyone in my regiment is dead or scattered to the winds and I just ain't going to do it no more. My folks live a little northeast of here around Thompson Creek, and that's where I'm headed."

Will pondered what Jack was saying for a moment, and for the first time began to see a solution to his immediate problem of getting away from this spot and the bodies of the local farmers that would seal his fate, should he be taken prisoner by the Confederates.

"That rig down yonder by the road belonged to these two fellas and I don't think they got much use for it now. I can't walk on this leg, but that cart would work just fine. What do you need from me? You could just walk home or take that cart for yourself and just leave me be," said Will.

"True enough," said Jack, looking to his left where the road disappeared into a distant growth of scrub, "but there's nothing but Yankees north of here, no offense, and I got no mind to die in some Federal prison." He looked over at Jimmy's body and said, "I need that uniform and those shoes, and I need you to do the talking if we get stopped."

Will looked at Jimmy's body and then back at Jack and said, "It's a deal if we can take him with us and give him a decent burial when we get the chance."

Jack leaned forward and stuck out his hand. Will released his grip on the pistol and shook.

Chapter 6

The road leading west from McFarland's Gap was poor and undulated over hillocks and small ridges around the base of the mountain. It was lined on both sides with the debris of a defeated army in full retreat. There were dead and dying men every few yards, lying where they had fallen, exhausted and too weak to go on. A few begged for water, some lay quietly beside a companion, perhaps a brother or buddy, but most were still. Of the latter, some had been attended to and left behind rolled in a blanket. The rest had simply died alone during the cold night, in a strange land, with only their own thoughts and fears to see them on. One older soldier they passed was leaning against a rock a few feet from the side of the road with his chin resting on his chest as if in sleep. His left hand rested in his lap holding a brass picture frame that shone bright in the morning sun. His right hand lay at his side, clutching a bundle of letters. Some of the pages had slipped from his grasp and were fanning out downwind in the old farm field behind him.

Will turned away from the disturbing sight and looked at Jimmy's body lying next to him under a blanket in the wagon. He had seen how his own army buried the Confederate dead after Murfreesboro, and he was sure that these dead men would receive a like amount of respect when the rebels got around to interment. Evidence that they ever existed would be found only in family bibles or daguerreotypes on far-away mantles, the memories of who they were only in the minds of their friends and kin. Will was determined that Jimmy's remains would not be lost.

The farm cart they were riding in looked as if it might fall apart without a moment's notice, but what it lacked in beauty was more than made up for in utility. Its previous owner had added a driver's seat that was nothing more than a plank laid flat across the cart's width and supported on either end by the sideboards. Jack's body swayed with the motion of the unsprung cart as it lurched in the dried-up mud holes in the road's surface. Occasionally he cursed the mule for this or that, but luckily, the animal seemed to know the way and was content to get on with his job.

"You Yanks are mighty fine dressers, Will. I ain't had a suit of clothes this good since I joined the army. My only complaint is that this wool is a little hard on my tender hide, and of course the color don't have much to recommend it, if you follow my drift."

Will looked up at Jack's back and for the first time noticed a dirty white cloth tied around his neck with a large dried blood stain on the side closest to him. "You're awful damned picky, Jack. I can tell you straight out, you weren't turning many heads in that dirty bundle of Secesh rags you were sporting when you snuck up on me a while ago. And by the by, I don't recall you having a wound…"

Jack reached up and fingered the makeshift bandage around his neck, "Smoke and mirrors Will, smoke and mirrors. When we catch up with that army of yours, I'll have a good reason not to do any talkin', as trying as that might be for me."

Will nodded his head in understanding and didn't ask about the blood.

"What's your plan now that you're done soldiering, Jack? You going back to whatever it was you did before the war?"

"I reckon so," said Jack. "I got a wife and a couple young'uns back in Missouri waiting for me. My brother Sam and his boys is working the farm while I'm away. I'll do what I can for the folks—make sure they're fixed for winter, then I'll be on my way home to Ailcy. How about you?"

"I hope to be married when I get back. Reckon it all depends on whether or not this leg is bad enough to get me out of the army. All I've ever known is dirt farming, so I guess I'll use the money I got saved up to get me a little spread and a few animals, start a family."

The autumn afternoon sun was low in the sky this time of year, but it still had enough left in it to warm Jack and Will, and they fell into an easy silence as they moved slowly along the road west, away from

McFarland's Gap. They were beginning to pass abandoned campfires now, still smoldering from the previous night. At one there was a body covered with a gum blanket and topped with a sheet of white paper held in place by a rock. The paper, most likely containing the soldier's identity, fluttered sporadically in the breeze. Beside the dead man sat a forlorn little brown and white dog. As they passed, he gave out one half-hearted bark then turned his head and looked back down the road as if expecting someone else. Will looked down and adjusted the lie of his broken leg in an attempt to find some relief. The pain was growing worse with every bump in the road. He knew he would have to get it tended to soon.

Jack looked back and broke the silence first. "I figure we'll keep heading west until we hit the rails going in to Wauhatchie and try to hitch a ride. Can't be more than five miles, give or take." Jack turned back around and continued, "That broken leg won't keep forever. I expect there's a passel of your wounded people headed up to hospitals in Nashville on the rail. Might be an easy thing to tag along, with all the confusion and such."

Will looked up at Jack and said, "I ain't exactly all fired up to talk to any army doctors, nor end up in one of those army hospitals. I never knew anyone who came out of one better than when he went in."

Will had never been part of a defeated army in headlong retreat before, so he had nothing in the way of experience to draw on. Jack, on the other hand, seemed to have things figured out pretty well, even though he wasn't ready to show all his cards yet.

"I thought you said you weren't going that far. Thompson Creek or some such you said," Will observed.

"So I did, so I did," said Jack, pausing in thought for a moment. "I'm counting on the train stopping for water at Tullahoma like they did before the war. I got kin there and my folks' place is just up the road a short piece."

"You know of any doctors there that might be willing to fix a Yankee leg?" said Will.

Jack turned and looked at Will, considering his question for a moment before turning back. "Let me chew on that a bit, Yank," he finally said. Will pulled the bill of his kepi down and closed his eyes against the sun that had begun to bore in since the last turn in the road.

He sat straight and still on the hard wood of the church pew, his head bowed forward at the neck and a drop of sweat growing on the end of his nose as the Reverend Purpura droned on in prayer, asking forgiveness for all manner of transgressions. Will's devout posture let him blend right in with the members of the congregation sitting close by, the only difference being that they were trying for eternal salvation, and he was studying Amanda's slender hand and wrist fringed in lace as it rested gracefully on her hymnal. He was nudged out of his thoughts by the shuffling of feet as the congregation stood to deliver a hymn. His momentary hesitation in standing up had not gone unnoticed by Amanda, and she cast him a stern sideways look. Unruffled, Will leaned in closer under the pretense of looking over her shoulder at the shared hymnal, and marveled at her perfect left ear, delicately adorned by the finest of tiny blonde hairs and supporting a simple gold wire earring with a small cut crystal ball that danced with each movement of her head. The morning sun streamed in through the tall arched side windows of the church and burst into an array of colors against her pale skin as it passed through the facets of the earring.

Suddenly the singing stopped, followed almost immediately by a discordant sound from the pump organ as it trailed off to silence. Horrified parishioners filed out of the pews and took up positions on the outside walls of the sanctuary. From there they fixed Will with looks of either disbelief or outright condemnation. Will turned to Amanda for reassurance but discovered that she, too, was backing slowly away from him, shaking her head slowly from side to side with a cold look in her eyes that he had never seen before. Will turned toward the front of the room and found Reverend Purpura smiling a wicked smile and holding up his right hand, pointing to the alter and the crucifix that was now missing the ceramic body of Jesus Christ. He looked down and saw that a single person had remained seated in the pew in front of him. The man turned slowly, and Will gasped when he saw the mangled face of Sergeant Hazzard, his tongue wagging as if possessed in the red mess that had been his mouth. Will raised his right hand to obey the unspoken command in the eyes of the old sergeant, but when he did, his hand was empty. There was no gun. He tried to run, but he could not move. He screamed, but there was no sound.

Someone was shaking him by the front of his jacket and slapping his face as he rose out of his nightmare toward the cool air of the evening darkness. The mysterious rhythmic chuffing hardened into the sounds of a steam engine passing close by and slowing to a stop. A long hiss of escaping steam was followed close on by the metallic clank of box car linkage, starting softly on the far right, moving closer and growing louder, then passing away to the left and diminishing as it traversed the length of the train.

"Easy there, Will. Come on, wake up now. We got to get on this here train before it gets filled up." Jack was speaking softly into Will's ear. Will sat up and slid forward on the bed of the cart until he could ease his legs over the edge and put his feet on the ground. He was still fighting off the effects of his dream, and only at the last minute before attempting to stand did he realize that Jimmy's body was gone. Jack watched as Will looked over his shoulder at the empty bed of the cart and spoke first to head him off.

"I left your friend with all the other dead by the field hospital we passed a ways back. I cut a button hole in that little cloth with his name and outfit on it and attached it to his drawers. We got no way to bury him and we got to git out of here while the gittin's good. I figure we did the best we could by him."

Will looked down at his feet and paused, trying to collect his thoughts. Finally he looked up at Jack and said, "Thank you. Let's get on the train."

In the days before the war, the train ride from where Jack and Will were picked up, to Tullahoma, would have lasted just a few hours. On this night, the journey seemed to go on forever. The interior of the boxcar was in pitch darkness and reeked of human excrement and the unwashed bodies of men in various stages of dying. In fact, some were already dead, and their numbers were growing with every passing mile. The wounded soldiers lay packed tightly together on a thin layer of filthy straw, each struggling with the horror of his situation as best he could. The less severely wounded men sat shoulder to shoulder on the creaking, sagging roofs of the cars, trying to ignore the groans of agony that rose out of the big open side doors below them with each lurch or sway of the train on the uneven rails. At dawn the train was stopped in Stevenson, Alabama, exchanging those men who had died during the night for those still clinging to life. The old engineer stood silently in the cab, looking back at his charge and watching in dismay as his human cargo of young men expired and was tossed beside the tracks in ever-increasing numbers. When the grim work was done at each stop, he pushed the old locomotive as hard as he dared for the hospitals in Nashville, anticipating every grade, and easing off only slightly in the bends.

Jack had found them a good place on the floor of the boxcar. Will lay on his back along the wall just behind the open door, with his broken right leg tucked out of the way against the sideboards and his head far enough forward to catch what fresh air there was to be had as the train labored up the tracks through the green mountains. His fever was rapidly getting worse, and he was only partly conscious much of the time, alternating between sweats and chills. Jack had no means to relieve either condition, so he just lay close and stared out the big door at the passing countryside, rendered nearly unrecognizable, even to his familiar eye, after being scoured clean repeatedly by both armies since the war began. At last there was a blast from the steam whistle and the engine began to slow, sending a shiver down the long line of cars as the train pulled into the little Tullahoma depot.

Jack's older sister had married a man who owned a small saddlery in Tullahoma before the war, and their living quarters were above the shop, located on Atlantic Street facing the railroad. A few years back, when war talk was running high and everyone was choosing up sides, Katherine and her husband Crawford had come down on the side of the Federals, defying almost everyone on both sides of the family. Harsh words were exchanged, the least offensive among them being "home-made Yankees," and they were cut off from all family matters from that point on. Jack had no expectations that the hard feelings his sister had for him had mellowed over the intervening years, but he hoped they might at least be able to set them aside long enough to get Will's leg doctored and find a way to get him out to the farm. That's where he was headed now, after getting Will off the train and laid out under a tree.

Chapter 7

As Jack approached the gray, weathered two-story frame building, he slowed his pace and studied the structure for signs of habitation. One of the upstairs windows had been boarded up in a crude attempt to block the hole left by broken glass, and the other was opaque with grime and neglect. Jack stepped up on the front porch of the gloomy little building, and out of the corner of his eye he caught sight of a slight stirring of the coarse gray blanket that hung down covering the store window from the inside. He knocked and waited, staring down at his hand-me-down brogans. After a few minutes of silence, he heard the shuffling of feet on hard wood, and once again the blanket was pulled back briefly and then dropped back into place. The heavy wooden door swung open, casting Jack's shadow along the floor in the pool of afternoon sunlight. At first he thought no one was there, but as his eyes adjusted to the room's dim interior, the figure of a thin woman, sitting in a straight-back chair emerged, facing him across the charged space. An antique double-barrel fowling piece rested across her legs, and lazy dust eddies from the swinging door crept along the floor, passing through the beams of the setting sun and disappearing into the void behind her.

Katherine's face was gaunt and prematurely old with fragile looking parchment skin stretched tight over her angular cheek bones. Despite the squalor of her surroundings, her hair was neatly pulled back tight, her eyes piercing and defiant, blazing from somewhere deep within.

"Well Lordy be, if it ain't the high-falutin' Jack Dean of Bedford County. Home from the war and turned out in a Yankee suit, no less," she said, breaking the uneasy silence.

"Hello, Kate," said Jack, stepping forward into the room and removing his hat. "It's been a while…"

"Do tell, little brother…do tell," she said, softening a bit. "Jeffery, you born in a barn, boy? Shut that door before I catch my death."

Jack turned his head to the left following Katherine's sharp look and for the first time realized that there was someone else in the room, standing against the wall and partially hidden behind the open door. It was Kate's boy Jeffery, grown into a young man since Jack had last seen him. He was lanky and thin. His growing out hadn't caught up to his growing up yet. His dirty clothes hadn't kept up either, and he would have been laughable if it were not for the look of cold hatred twisting his smooth, unwashed face. This was a hatred that Jack had never seen on a face so young.

"What do you hear from Craw?" Jack said, looking back at his sister.

"Last I heard he was up north around Nashville fixing tack for the Federals—5th Tennessee Mounted. Letters stopped about two months ago, so I don't know what to think now," she said. Jack looked down, nodding his head.

"You seem to have made out better than the rest of the Dean boys, Jack," Katherine said. "But then you always did, flashing that big smile of yours and slinging the bull like you do."

"What have you heard about our brothers, Kate?" said Jack.

"Tom and Casper was killed in that big fight over at Murfreesboro – killed on the same day. Chris is fightin' somewhere in Virgina," she said quietly. "My information ain't too reliable, though. I get everything second hand, you know." The enormity of what she had just recounted in such an off-hand manner shocked both of them into silence, a silence that stretched out as they struggled with their memories and weighed their loss.

"You coming from that ruckus south of Chattanooga?" Katherine asked.

Jack nodded and said, "The Thompson Creek Grays are gone, Kate. All the boys I joined up with back in '61 are dead or captured." Jack paused, bowing his head and running the fingers of his right hand through his matted hair. "I've just had enough – I can't do it no more. I'm going to take the oath and go home."

They both fell silent, neither having the right words for the moment. Finally Jack decided to get on with his business and looked up at Katherine.

"I need your help, Kate," he said. "I got a Yank with a broken leg lying in the weeds over by the tracks and he needs doctoring real bad. I want to bring him here and get Doc Crenshaw to set the bone. We'll be on our way as soon as the deed is done. I plan to get him out to Pa's tonight."

"Pa ain't going to take kindly to you showing up with a Yankee, never mind his favorite son dressed in blue," said Katherine. She started to speak again, but just then Jeffery jumped into the center of the room facing his mother and said, "Ma! You can't bring no scum-sucking Yankee in here! Why, it's bad enough we got traitors fer kin without bringing no bluebelly around." Jack stepped forward with the intention of putting some respect, or at least fear, into the boy, but a sharp look from Katherine pulled him up short.

"That's enough, boy!" she yelled. "You had your say, but you ain't the one making the decisions around here. Now go fetch Doc Crenshaw and tell him to bring fixings for a broken leg." Jeffery stared her down for a few moments but then jumped when she shouted at him to "git."

When he was gone, Katherine said, "He's all I got in this world and he's got the itch to go fight. They're taking young'uns his age now, you know. I don't know how much longer I can hold him." She bowed her head and dabbed at the corner of her eyes with the hem of her once-white apron. Jack stepped up close to her side, wanting to put his arm around her, but she read his movement and raised her hand to stop him.

"There's a wood tote out back if you need it to fetch your Yank. Go on now, and be quick. I 'spect the doc will need hot water," she said as she stood and walked over to the small parlor stove they had been cooking on.

Jack hesitated for a moment and watched his sister as she bent to stoke the fire. The flickering yellow light from the embers spilled out of the little stove door and onto her troubled face, twinkling in the moisture of her eyes. She added a couple small pieces of split wood, shut the door, and straightened up. When she turned, Jack was gone.

The old doctor studied the Union soldier lying at his feet, taking the measure of his task. He had retired from his one-horse practice six years ago, but when the war broke out, all the younger men with any notion of medicine had been taken by the army, leaving him alone to look after the small community. During the last two years, when he should have been spending lazy afternoons catching his dinner and napping on the banks of Rock Creek, he had seen more suffering than in all the previous years of his practice put together.

The boy in front of him now was delirious with fever, and his right leg was crudely splinted and tied up with strips of cloth that appeared to have been the sleeves of a shirt. He knelt down and rummaged through his worn doctor's bag, finally pulling out a pair of scissors and a roll of white sheeting.

"You get down here, young man, and make sure this leg doesn't move when I cut the bindings away," he said.

Jack got down on the floor on the other side of Will and held the leg while the doctor cut off the leg of Will's britches above the knee and removed the splint. The inside of his shin was caked with dried blood where the bone had punctured the skin, and when he squeezed gently on the wound, grayish green pus drained freely.

"Reckon we're going to need that hot water now, Katherine," he said without looking up. Kate fetched the bottom half of the cast iron Dutch oven off the wood stove that she had used to heat the water and set it carefully down beside the doctor. He rolled up one of the shirt sleeves that he had cut off the splint, dipped it in the water and dabbed the wound clean, expressing it as he went. When he was satisfied, he dropped the wadded-up sleeve in the water and rolled the leg carefully from side to side, watching how the foot followed the movement.

"All right. Let's get this bandaged up and we'll use the same sticks for a splint. His leg seems to have set itself, albeit a bit turned out. There's too much infection to go messing about trying to straighten it. When you get him out to your Pap's place, you make sure to keep that leg looked after. Press your thumb around the wound like you just seen me do every time you change the bandage. As long as this greenish pus comes out, that's good, that means it's healing," he said, looking up at Jack.

Both men worked in silence for a few minutes, Jack holding the splints in place while Doc Crenshaw wrapped the leg with bandage material. Suddenly the doctor stopped and exclaimed, "Whew, good Lord in Heaven! Either you or this Yank smells like the south end of a north-bound mule! I highly recommend you avail yourself of a convenient creek as soon as possible, sir."

Jack chuckled and said, "I ain't had much opportunity to make a proper toilet these last few months, with our army chasing tail all over these parts and such. I'll think on your recommendation, though."

Jack and the old man stood up and surveyed their handiwork for a moment.

"How do you plan on getting him out to your folks' place?" said the Doc.

"Well, I was hoping you might see your way clear to lend me your buggy for a few hours."

The doctor was expecting the request and answered without hesitation. "Yes, you can use it, but make sure you have Mort back in the shed behind my office before sunup. He ain't much, but he's all I got to get me around. Now you listen to me, young man, and you listen good. There's some very bad people of both persuasions ranging up and down this countryside causing mischief and looking for any reason to have a hanging. You just stay clear of everyone you see."

Jack nodded and followed Doc Crenshaw out the door and down the street to fetch Mort and the buggy.

An hour later, he was back standing in the desolate little saddle shop saying goodbye to his sister. Jeffery sat on a stool next to the parlor stove, glaring at his mother and uncle as they talked. His face was stiff with loathing, and the light of a single oil lamp falling sideways across his features gave it an evil cast.

"Thank you, Kate," said Jack. He put his arm around her shoulder, and this time she did not resist, but he felt a shiver run through her as he pulled her close.

"You mind what Doc told you and lie low when you get out to the farm. Don't come back here until this war is over, Jack Dean. You hear me? You stay away." Jack squeezed her against his side one more time before walking through the door and into the cold night air.

The windows of the farmhouse were dark, but Jack could feel his father's eyes on him as he turned the buggy off the road and into the turn-around that curved up to the front porch. The two ribbons of bare, hard-packed earth stood out in sharp contrast to the dark vegetation in the moonlight, making it easy for Mort to find his way. Jack glanced to his left as they straightened out on the tracks and noticed that the big flower pot that normally sat atop the old oak stump by the road was sitting on the ground, a sure sign that his father had heard them coming. The last time Jack was home, his father had asked him to hollow out the top of the stump so he could hide his pistol inside and cover it with the flower pot. He didn't want to lose the weapon if they were searched by the Federals. When they were even with the porch, Jack gave a little tug on the reins, bringing them to a halt. He bent forward, resting his elbows on his thighs and bowing his head, letting his fatigue wash over him. He breathed in deep, filling himself up with the rich familiar smell of the land where he was raised. He looked over at Will, who was hunched forward and tied to the frame of the seat to keep him from bouncing out on the rough country road. He was still breathing at least, and perhaps now with a little bed rest, he would start to mend.

"Who the hell are you and what the hell do y'all want at this ungodly hour?" said a gruff voice from the darkness under the roof of the porch.

"It's me, Pap—your son Jack."

"Jack, that you?" his father said as he stepped down from the porch.

Before Jack could answer, two smaller figures in white bedclothes, luminous in the moonlight, emerged from the shadows behind the old man.

"Jack, Jack!" cried his youngest sibling Mollie, as she bounced up and down on her bare feet, clapping her hands in excitement. Jack climbed down out of the buggy and threw his arms around his sister and mother, holding them tightly against him, tears of relief flowing freely on every cheek. As soon as he could bring himself to break the embrace, he reached out and shook his father's hand.

"Who you got with you in that buggy, Jack?"

Jack had been working on a response to this question during the ride out from Tullahoma and was glad now to be able to answer with at least an air of confidence. "I got me a Yankee with a bad broke leg. He saved my life back in Georgia a few days ago, and I couldn't just leave him to die. It's my wish that you will let him stay here until he can walk well enough to go home."

There was a long silence as everyone waited for Pap to speak. "Let's get him inside, then. We can't stand out here all night," Pap said. "We'll chew on this some more in the morning."

Chapter 8

Will was gradually becoming aware of his surroundings, and sooner or later he would have to open his eyes, but not just yet. His body was sunk deep in the embrace of a feather bed, big puffs pressing in around him and the smell of fresh linen mixed with just a hint of dried lilac floated in the air. The soft rhythmic lament of a nearby mourning dove, answered each time by a distant companion, passed only slightly subdued through the single panes of the window by his bed and marked the passage of the early morning.

In his dream he'd been stretched out on a blanket and propped on one elbow, watching Amanda sitting on a large rock and dangling her feet in the creek that ran through the back of her father's wood lot. Narrow shafts of sunlight streamed through holes in the dense treetops and splashed the forest floor with patches of brilliance. As he looked on, she bent forward to examine her toes under the clear cold water and one such sunbeam fell on the side of her form farthest away from him, backlighting her golden hair and giving her a supernatural glow. Will was drinking in the beauty of the scene before him when he heard a shuffling in the dead leaves that lay thick on the ground. At first he thought it was a squirrel searching for acorns, but as the sound grew closer, it took on the rhythm of human footsteps. Amanda heard it, too, and a smile of familiarity spread across her face when she looked up. Confused, Will froze, like a hunter waiting for his prey to step into a clearing.

The dream faded away as muffled voices from the next room penetrated his sleep. The talk seemed spirited, but he could not distinguish any of the words or the gist of what was being said. When he finally opened his eyes, just enough to see out while still appearing to be asleep, he was amazed to see a young woman sitting in a straight-backed chair at his bedside near his feet. She was bent over, concentrating on her mending, with a large sewing basket on the floor next to her. The chair faced the side of the bed so the woman was in profile to Will and not aware of his watching. Her brown print work dress was neatly pressed, although threadbare in places, and a spotless white apron was pinned to her bodice and tied around her slender waist with a neat bow. Her hair was something of a mystery. It was dark, and at first glance it seemed to be rather short, but with closer scrutiny, Will could see that it was tucked and intertwined in clever feminine ways that only length would allow. The effect was very pleasing indeed. He had not been this close to a woman in many months, and he savored the stolen moment. As women tend to do, she had a sense about her that set off alarms when it detected the gaze of a man, and she suddenly cocked her head and looked hard at Will's face. The sudden turn of events startled him, and his eyes opened wide even as his cheeks blushed crimson with the embarrassment of being caught out.

"Good morning, ma'am," said Will, finally regaining his composure.

"You must be my nurse. Please forgive my manners. I'm just a little befuddled at the moment. In fact, I'm not real certain if I'm alive or dead."

The young lady didn't respond immediately but stood as she collected her thoughts. When she was ready, she turned and faced him again with a decidedly cold but amused look and said, "I can assure you, sir, that for the moment at least you are with the living. Before I take my leave, Mr. Castor, is there anything at all I can do to make you more comfortable?" she said with a hint of sarcasm as she bent over to scoop up her sewing.

Will's throat was dry from sleeping with his mouth open, and he thought this would be a good opportunity to request some water. "Perhaps a glass of water, if you will, nurse…and please have the doctor stop in as time permits."

The young lady looked at him for a long moment, like a cat watching a mouse, but it was completely lost on Will. When she returned with the glass of water, she set it on the table next to the bed—somewhat indelicately, Will thought, and she said, "Should you need something more, you may address me as Miss Dean. I shall be in the next room." With that, she turned in a swirl of skirts and was gone.

Will spent the rest of the morning sizing up his situation and working on the puzzles he had been presented with since regaining consciousness. Foremost among them was a simple question: Where was he? The air carried the smell of cooking and wood smoke—not exactly what he would expect of a hospital. It made him think of home more than anything. It had that warmth about it. His hands were remarkably clean, perhaps more so than at any time since he had joined the army, and he was wearing a soft cotton dressing gown. Will looked down his nose at the other end of the bed. His broken leg lay outside of his blanket and was elevated atop two large feather pillows. He briefly considered how he might have come to be clean and dressed for bed but quickly rejected that train of thinking in favor of speculation on the whereabouts of his uniform and possessions.

"Good day to you, Will," said Jack, appearing in the door. "It looks like you might live after all."

Will did not recognize him at first, although he seemed vaguely familiar. His hair was neatly groomed and straight back on his head, dark and shiny. He was clean shaven, his skin still holding a blush of pink from its unaccustomed encounter with the blade, and his blue eyes held a sadness that was at odds with his easy smile.

"I owe you a debt for that, Jack," said Will.

Jack came into the room and pulled the chair up to the head of the bed so they could talk confidentially. "We need to have a word about that," he said when he had settled in. "By my reckoning I call us even. In fact, in this house, it's commonly known that you saved my life. It was the only way I could figure to get my folks to take in a Yankee."

Will nodded his understanding as the final pieces fell into place. "I'll need to send a letter to my captain telling him where I am and asking for a medical leave. I'll just say I'm staying here with kin until I can walk again."

Jack stood up and said, "I'll have my sister bring you in some paper and a quill. I'm going up to Shelbyville tomorrow to take my oath, and I'll post it for you."

Will nodded again and stopped Jack just as he was about to leave. "One more thing, Jack—about my clothes and getting washed up…"

Jack paused in the doorway and flashed his famous smile. "All us rebels can peel a Yankee lickity split, even Ma and Mollie," he said. After savoring Will's discomfort for a moment, he turned and disappeared into the adjoining room.

Will sank back into the feather bed and stared at the ceiling, assessing the magnitude of his gaffe with Jack's sister and pondering what he might do to recoup the situation. For lack of a better plan, he decided to match her surliness and let come what may. The afternoon sun was beginning to come through the window and warm the dark blanket that covered most of him, except for his broken right leg, and that cheered him a bit. The toes of the exposed foot were cold, but he would damn well suffer with it before he would ask for help. Just as he was starting to doze off, the rustling of the bedclothes brought him back with a start. Miss Dean was at the other end of the bed pulling a puffy wool sock over his needy foot. For a moment Will thought perhaps he had judged her a little harshly, but when she spoke, animosity flowed freely between them.

"My dear brother Jack requested that I bring you writing materials so you might compose a letter to your army informing them of your whereabouts," she said, rather high-mindedly. In fact, her contrived formality was so ill-suited to her that Will was forced to stifle a smile. This, of course, had the predictable effect of infuriating her. She slammed the little bottle of ink down on the side table along with two quill pens and a penknife, then turned slightly and slapped a smooth board that he was to use as a writing desk, on his stomach, causing him to sit up abruptly. From the chair behind her she produced several sheets of stationery and tossed them on his chest.

"Judging from the amount of correspondence you carry with you, I must presume you can write, Mr. Castor," she said as she headed for the door.

"Are you always this cantankerous towards your house guests, Miss Dean, or have I offended you in some way?" said Will. "And by the by, just where are my possessions?"

Mollie turned and retraced her footsteps until she stood beside the bed, hands on hips, looking down at him. Without breaking eye contact, she leaned sideways enough to jerk the little drawer of the bedside table open all the way to its stops. "Mr. Castor, you are not a guest in this house. You are a Yankee, and as such, my mortal enemy. You and your ilk are not welcome in Tennessee, or in this household. Why Pap and Jack have allowed you to mend here is beyond my powers to reason."

Will glanced over and took a quick peek at the contents of the drawer and saw the little bundle of letters, his wallet, the Union Case containing Amanda's picture and the sergeant's revolver. This time Will held his silence as Mollie hurried through the door. He leaned over to retrieve the picture from the drawer but stopped and instead just pushed the drawer closed. He shut his eyes in exasperation and gave in to the fatigue that was becoming a way of life.

It was dark and in the early hours when Will was jolted awake out of a terrible nightmare. In the dream he stood in front of the dull green brass barrel of a Napoleon, watching as a Confederate gunner pulled the slack out of the lanyard and gazed at him with cold, empty eyes that held only death. Will screamed as he watched the flare of the primer illuminate the far end of the dark barrel and the fireball start towards him in slow motion.

He hoped his screams were only in the dream, but when he saw Jack next to his bed holding a chamberstick with the flickering stub of a candle, he knew they weren't. The flame cast just enough light to reveal the presence of someone else in the room, hanging back on the edge of the darkness. Without a word, Jack set the candle on the little table beside the bed, turned, and faded back into the dark house, leaving Mollie alone in the far corner, looking at Will's desperate sweat-streaked face framed by the small circle of yellow light.

The next morning Will lay awake with his eyes closed, listening to a cold heavy autumn rain drum against his window in sheets. It was driven by a fitful northeast wind that made the dense branches of a nearby crepe myrtle bush scour the side of the house in a steady cadence. The sounds made him feel safe in his warm bed. He could smell her in the room, and against all reason, that knowledge added to his comfort.

Will opened his eyes and found her sitting in the chair beside the bed looking at him. He braced for the anticipated rebuke, but it was never delivered. Instead, in a soft voice she said, "Good morning, Mr. Castor. I will need to change this dressing as soon as you are ready. Jack is still determined to make the journey to Shelbyville today in spite of this horrid weather, and he asks that you have your correspondence in order within the hour."

"Good morning to you, Miss Dean. Thank you for tending to my leg, and I am ready at your convenience," said Will. "My compliments to your brother, but I think my letter will have to wait until I can sit up."

"Perhaps if you will speak your business to me, I can write it for you."

"That would be very kind of you indeed," said Will, not quite believing the complete about-face in the demeanor of the young woman. Mollie pulled her chair up closer to the head of the bed, retrieved the writing board from the floor, and prepared to write. Will closed his eyes and began to compose the letter to Captain Church in his mind, stopping to speak the words to Mollie as he completed a sentence. Mollie would suggest a word from time to time when Will stumbled, or she would arch an eyebrow at a sentence. Sometimes Will would pause and press his eyelids tight together as the horrible scenes replayed in his mind. She felt a lump rise in her throat as she watched him struggle.

Mollie turned the writing board and laid it across Will's stomach, loaded the quill, and passed it to him so he could sign the letter. When he handed the paper back to her, she set it aside on the bed to let the ink dry and looked down, studying her hands as they lay folded in her lap. When she looked up, Will had closed his eyes and turned his head slightly away from her to hide the shiny tear trace down the left side of his face. Mollie stood and straightened the bedclothes for a moment, but before she turned to leave, she reached down and gave Will's hand a gentle squeeze.

Chapter 9

The October days were growing noticeably shorter and colder—colder than normal for this part of the country. Jack and Pap filled the daylight hours putting up wood for the winter, while Ma and Mollie dug taters and canned corn and green beans from their hidden patch out behind a distant stand of scrub oak. Pap had put in two gardens back in the spring. One was near the house where you would expect to find a garden, and one was tucked back on the rear property line of the farm, out of sight from the road. As expected, the passing soldiers of both armies helped themselves to the decoy, and once satisfied that they had gotten all there was to be had, did not pursue the matter any further. It was a simple enough ploy, but it made the difference between starving and just being hungry.

Mollie spent most of her evenings making a suit of clothes for Jack to travel back to Missouri in. Often she would sit with Will and talk as she worked, late some nights, or until her mother scolded her for wasting a candle. How she could see to make such fine stitchery in the dim light was a mystery to Will. Ma and Pap never entered his room or even spoke. Ma would occasionally look his way as she passed the door, but Pap would have nothing to do with him. Jack said the old man couldn't get past the thought that his two sons may have died by Will's own hand at Murfreesboro.

"I reckon I'll head off home in a week or so, Will," said Jack as he tilted back and struck a balance on the rear legs of the chair next to Will's bed. "Ever since that damn Bob Blackwell and his band of thugs executed those Federals who were guarding the depot in Shelbyville things have taken a real nasty turn around here. I reckon if they don't pick me up for deserting, sooner or later the Yankees will get around to it, even though I took the oath. Bushwhackers don't care much for paper work. How's the leg coming?"

Will looked down and rubbed his shin as he spoke. "It doesn't pain me as much as it did, and the wound seems to be healed over. I would be much obliged if you could fashion me a crutch of sorts before you set out. If 'Nurse Mollie' will give me her blessing, I plan to test my leg a bit," he said.

Jack gave him an amused look and said, "It seems my little sister has softened her stance on Yankees in recent days. She's always been one to take in strays—birds with broken wings, the odd cat or dog. When we were young'uns, she found a baby raccoon and somehow sweet-talked Pap into letting her keep it as a pet. We called him Raycoon. When he got older he would hide under the skirt of Ma's chair and reach out and grab your ankle when you passed by. Used to scare the bejesus out of me."

Will nodded, taking Jack's subtle meaning, but he didn't say anything.

"What about the lady you're sparking back in Michigan? You 'spose she's still waiting for you?"

"I guess I don't know," said Will, rearranging his blanket to hide his discomfort. "I worry how she will take this gimpy leg more than anything."

"Well, I guess you'll find out soon enough. I don't think even my army would take you back with that bad leg."

"I hope you're right, Jack. I just want to put this damn war behind me and get on with living."

"I reckon it's going to take a powerful lot of forgettin' to set things right for men like you and me," said Jack.

Will nodded his agreement and they sat in silence for a while, each in his own memories.

Finally Jack eased the two front legs of his chair down until they rested on the floor and stood up to leave. "Looks like another day of splitting wood tomorrow, so I guess I better call it a night," he said. "Mollie's good with the spring wagon and can give you a ride up to Shelbyville when you're ready to make your move. I'll poke around in the barn tomorrow and see what I can come up with in the way of crutches."

Jack was as good as his word, and a couple of days later Mollie brought him a pair of rough but sturdy crutches made from yellow poplar saplings that grew in abundance along Thompson Creek. She propped the crutches in the corner of the room when Will was done looking them over and fished a letter out of her apron and handed it to him. The envelope was a little shopworn and covered with numerous cancelling stamps, the most recent from the military post office in Nashville. It was a reply from Captain Church. Inside was a quickly scribbled note expressing sorrow over the loss of the Gun Six crew and thankfulness for Will's survival. Enclosed with the note was an official document granting Will sick leave for the duration of his recovery. He was instructed to report to a military hospital in Nashville when he was well enough to travel, and a determination as to his fitness for future duty would be made at that time.

Mollie positioned the room's only chair at a slight angle from the bed and stared out the window while Will finished reading his letter. As usual, Will was a tick or two late reading her mood and merrily launched into his plans for trying out the new crutches. When she turned and looked at him he saw at once that they were on very different paths.

"What is it, Mollie?" said Will.

She turned back to the window and brought a delicate embroidered linen hankie up under her nose and held it there. Will saw her hand quiver ever so slightly, but she did not cry or speak.

"Mollie, please—what's the matter? Talk to me." Suddenly she jumped up and spun on him.

"Damn you, Will Castor. How dare you come into my life, a Yankee, and then turn out to be a decent human being! Every day here is a struggle just to get by, and hating Yankees somehow made it easier to cope. You were at the root of all our tragedy. But now—now I have nowhere to lay all this blame, thanks to you. Two of my brothers are dead for sure, and we've had no word from Christopher in months. Katherine might as well be dead. Jack is leaving next week and Ma can barely do her chores for the grief. Just three years ago we were happy and prosperous – starting families, raising young'uns, sitting down to Sunday dinners with all the fixin's, bickering about who borrowed a hammer from whom. It's all gone, gone forever, gone for the 'Cause'," she spat. Will watched in stunned silence as her face contorted and a floodgate somewhere inside her burst, releasing a torrent of tears and raw emotions. When her frustration finally overwhelmed her ability to speak, she leaned over Will and began to pummel his chest with hysterical blows of her clenched fist. The attack had a much more serious look to it than actual bite, and but for the wrenching circumstance, Will might have been able to draw her up from her despair with a few careful words. By now, though, his own wounds lay open and all he could manage was to be still, looking past her toward the ceiling and taking solace in receiving what he considered to be his due, letting her fist land, again, and again, and again. He brought his hands slowly up around her back and pulled her down, holding her tight against him with his arms.

"Damn you, Will…Damn the 'Cause,' damn, damn," she whimpered between sobs, her voice muffled against his chest. Will slid his hand up and gently tucked the back of her head under his chin. As he stroked her hair, he could feel the tension begin to slip away from her. They lay together that way for several minutes, until finally Mollie lifted her head and looked into Will's eyes from only inches away. Both were caught off-guard by the unexpected intimacy of the moment but were held in fascination by the rich current of emotions flowing unabated between them. There was sadness, of course, and there was the uncertainty of youth, but there was something else, something that neither one expected or even thought was still possible – hope, the spark of human hope that rose up in each one, inexorably seeking its counterpart in the other to complete the circuit and become whole. Neither was willing to break the connection, but they both instinctively knew they were at a junction with no high road. They were marked, however, indelibly so, and they would never forget.

"I'm so sorry," Mollie whispered as she slowly pulled away, still holding Will's eyes.

"I'm sorry, too," he said as he relaxed his arms and let her go. She sat on the edge of the bed for a moment, collecting herself and dabbing at her eyes with the hankie. She looked over at Will, then reached out and wiped the tears from his cheeks with the tips of her fingers.

"You hurt so badly, dear Will…" she said.

Will caught her wrist before she could pull back and gently kissed the soft palm of her hand. "Thank you, Mollie Dean," he said. "Thank you."

Chapter 10

The day before Jack was to leave for Missouri was clear and cold. Hoarfrost lingered on the short grass up close to the house where it was still hidden from the sun, and it crunched under Will's shoes as he practiced with his crutches. His leg had begun to improve quickly, once he was able to get around a bit and build up his strength. Just being able to breathe the brisk late autumn air and smell the turned earth did wonders for his soul. If he could only reach in his pocket and pull out a nice fresh apple, he'd have a pretty good morning going, he thought to himself. He sorely missed the smell of his mother's apple pies baking on chilly morning, spreading warmth and that heavenly aroma throughout the house. There were a couple of trees out next to the road, but the fruit had long since been stripped. He paused next to the fieldstone well and used it to steady himself as he adjusted the placement of his crutches. Across the way, Jack and his father were digging the last of the turnips and tossing them in the back of the spring wagon, every breath they exhaled hanging briefly on the air in front of their faces like little puffs of steam.

Jack looked up and saw Will leaning on his crutches up by the house. He waved, planted his pitchfork, and then walked over to exchange a few words. "Morning, Will. A bit chilly this morning for these parts. I suppose a Michigan man can take a little cold weather now and again."

"Yep, we do get some powerful winters up in my neck of the woods."

"Looks like you're getting around pretty good on those finely crafted crutches, if I do say so myself," said Jack.

"Couple more days and I'll be out here digging root food with you and Pap," he said with a chuckle.

"You better hold off on that until I'm on my way. You'd look like a one-legged man in a butt-kicking contest, and I ain't sure my heart could stand the sight."

They shared a laugh. "I'm headed up to Raus this afternoon to see if I can collect an old debt, and then I'm leaving for home before first light tomorrow. I reckon I better say my goodbyes now in case I don't see you again," said Jack.

"I don't see how I can ever repay your kindness, Jack."

"Like I said, I figure it's a wash."

"I had some money saved up that I was going to send home before the big fight in Georgia, and I plan to give most of it to your folks for putting me up all this time," said Will.

"They won't take your money, but I reckon you could leave it in that little table by your bed so they would find it after you're gone."

Will nodded his understanding and held out his hand. Jack took it and they locked eyes.

"You take care of yourself, Yank. Put this war behind you."

"A safe journey to you, Johnny Reb."

Jack nodded and flashed his big smile, tempered a bit with sadness as he released Will's hand. He turned and walked back out into the field to take up his work.

Mollie had seemed a little distant these last few days, but Will supposed she was worried about finishing Jack's new clothes as the time for his departure drew near. The fact that it might have something to do with their recent encounter never occurred to him. He spent the rest of the day alternating between lying in bed with his leg elevated on a pillow reading a copy of Les Misérables that Mollie had lent him and hobbling around the yard behind the house on his crutches, working to regain his strength. He had decided to start for Nashville the day after next.

He heard a floorboard creak in the doorway to his room and looked up to see Mollie standing there with a tray containing his supper. The aroma from whatever was steaming in the single bowl arrived a second later reminding him how hungry he was.

"Good evening, Will," she said. "I have a little nourishment for you. It's not much, but it's hot and it will stick with you on a chilly night like this." Even after Will had started getting around on his own, he had continued to take his supper alone in his room so as not to disrupt the family meals. Mollie would usually sit with him and sip tea from a delicate hand-painted china cup and saucer while he ate. This night was no different, and she sat quietly, very straight and proper with the cup and saucer resting on her lap. Between slurps of tater and turnip soup, Will marveled at her simple beauty.

"Jack's setting out for home tomorrow morning," she said. "But then I guess you knew that already. I know he misses Ailcy and the babies terribly, but I hate to give him up. It's so quiet with all my siblings gone."

"Jack and I said our goodbyes this morning," replied Will, finally meeting up with the bread he had smelled cooking earlier in the day. "It's too dangerous for him to stay around here much longer, what with all these Home Guards combing the countryside and such. All a bunch of murdering cowards just trying to stay out of the regular army, if you ask me."

"I suppose you're right. I worry so about him making the journey. We all expected him back in time for supper tonight on his last night with us, but he said not to wait for him, since he might be late. I suppose if he ran into one of the Prince boys he might have shared a drop or two of corn-juice. Can't say it would be the first time."

"I reckon he might feel in the celebratin' mood, knowing he's bound for home tomorrow," said Will. Mollie looked on absentmindedly as he swept the bottom of the bowl with his last morsel of bread and popped it in his mouth with a sigh. "My compliments to your mother. She certainly knows her way around a tater. And thank you very kindly for attending me."

Mollie stood up, placed her empty cup and saucer on the tray, paused to give Will a chance to return his napkin, and then picked the tray up and headed for the door. Just as she reached the threshold, she stopped and turned back to look at Will. She wasn't at all surprised to find him watching her. Words would have only diminished the moment, so they simply held each other's gaze until Mollie finally turned away and continued through the door.

Will woke with a start, lying on top of the bed in the dark, his book open and upside down on his chest where it had fallen when he dozed off. He could hear excited feminine voices and the sounds of a winded horse coming through the open front door of the house. Sensing trouble, he eased his right leg to the floor with a wince, then swung around and sat on the edge of the bed, clearing the cobwebs from his brain. He lit the candle in the chamberstick and then gingerly hopped over to the chair and began pulling his shoes on. The voices of Mollie and her father had risen above the others, and it was clear they were in serious disagreement. Will pulled on his roundabout and then reached behind him and grabbed the crutches from where they were leaning against the wall. He stood, letting his good leg take his weight, then leaned over and pulled the revolver out of the drawer of the little bedside table. Holding it next to the candle, he pulled the hammer to half cock and spun the cylinder to see how many rounds were left. Two shots were left and the percussion caps were still in place. Will eased the hammer back and stuck the gun down the inside pocket of his coat.

The spring wagon was hitched to Abby, the Deans' only remaining horse, and stood on the path leading from the barnyard to the road. Pap was working his way around the rig, checking buckles here, pulling on a link there, making sure nothing had been overlooked in haste. Mollie sat up on the bench seat, holding the reins and talking to a young woman on horseback that Will had never seen before.

As Will approached, Mollie broke off her conversation and turned to face him. Even by the light of the half moon, he could see the look of shock on her face.

"What's all the commotion about?" said Will.

"Oh, Will, Sarah just brought us some terrible news. Jack was set upon by some Yankee bushwhackers tonight up near Raus and they shot him. I don't know if he yet lives, but I'm going up there to fetch him home one way or the other. Pap thinks it's too dangerous, but I'm going anyway."

Will shifted his weight to his left leg and threw his crutches behind the seat of the wagon. With one hand on the sideboard, the other on the footrest, and his good leg on the step-up, he swung into the seat beside Mollie before she could protest. She opened her mouth to speak, but Will cut her off. "I'm going with you," he said with a look that invited no objections. By this time, Pap had completed his inspection and stood silently under the overhang of the porch with his arm around the small figure of Mollie's mother.

Will turned as the wagon started forward and said, "I'll look after her, Mr. Dean." The old man looked back at him but made no acknowledgment, and Will finally turned away.

The road leading north toward Raus was mostly light-colored clay mixed with a little gravel, and the small amount of moonlight there was made it stand out in sharp contrast to the dark vegetation along each side. Mollie and her friend Sarah both knew the way well, having used this road all their lives for school and church, but the soft luminance was still welcome. After about thirty minutes, Sarah leaned in towards Mollie and pointed to the farmhouse just ahead on the right side of the road. Will motioned for Mollie to stop the wagon, and she tugged on the reins and spoke to Abby until the rig was halted in the road. He leaned across Mollie and spoke to Sarah.

"Where is he?" said Will.

"On the front porch of the house just over yonder," she said, nodding in the direction of the next house up the road.

"Who lives there?"

"Old man Hutchens, his sister, and a nephew who's touched," said Sarah.

"We're going to pull up as close as we can get to the house, but you stay back on the road until Mollie comes to fetch you. If there's any trouble, you ride for help," said Will. She nodded her understanding. Will reached under the seat and fished around for the oil lantern that Mollie had wisely thought to fetch from the barn for the trip and motioned for Mollie to drive on.

The two sides and back of the house were set into a stand of giant tall oak trees that afforded its inhabitants a measure of relief from the hot days of summer, but on this night it also cloaked everything in almost impenetrable darkness. With the aid of the few slivers of silver moonlight that found their way through the high treetops, Mollie was able to steer the wagon off the road, but only a short distance along the drive leading up to the house. They sat in silence for a moment as Will looked the house and grounds over for anything amiss.

"Wait here, Mollie. I'm going to walk up to the house and see if Jack is there. If he is, I'll come back and guide you in with the light. Anything don't look right, you turn around and high-tail it on up the road."

Will swung out of the seat and hopped on his good leg until he could retrieve his crutches from the back of the wagon. He was about to reach for the lantern when Mollie screamed. Will spun around so fast he became tangled up with his crutches and started to lose his balance. As he fell backwards he saw the dim outline of a bulky figure in a broad-brimmed slouch hat swinging a pistol at his head. The barrel and front blade sight of the gun caught him a glancing blow across the face, leaving a long diagonal cut from his left cheek across the bridge of his nose and up across his forehead above his right eye. Will staggered back into the side of the wagon and then slumped to the ground and rolled on his back, struggling to make sense out of what was happening.

The man pointed his pistol at Mollie and motioned for her to get down out of the wagon. "You climb down and get over here – and bring that lantern with you. I'm going to need to see what I'm about this night, sure enough."

Mollie stopped in front of the man, set the lantern on the bed of the wagon, and drew herself up to her most defiant self. In spite of her best efforts to remain calm, a shiver ran through her and that seemed to fuel the man's excitement.

"Well, my sakes if it ain't the sweet young Miss Dean, come to fetch her fresh dead Secesh spy of a brother. I just had a hunch I might meet up with the likes of you tonight."

"You murdering scum!" Mollie shouted. "Who the hell are you and how do you know my name?"

"Gracious sakes, Miss Dean, you have some horrid manners," the man said with a sneer. "I hope to cure you of those unladylike ways directly." He reached out and grabbed a fistful of hair from the top of her head, spun her around to face the back of the wagon, and bent her over at the waist, slamming her head into the rough wood of the bed. He set his gun down next to her to free up his hand and then reached down and pulled her dress and petticoats up as one and threw them over her back.

"My sakes, Miss Dean, I hope you won't be offended, but I do so fancy a poke about now," he said. He reached for her again and ripped her pantaloons down with one rough jerk, exposing her naked backside to the cold night air.

"Oh my, my, my, what a sight to behold," said the bushwhacker as he dug in his britches for his manhood. "I declare, prettier hindquarters I never see the likes of."

The man's euphoria was brought to an abrupt halt by the click, click of an 1860 Colt Army hammer being pulled back and the cylinder locking into place. His head jerked up and he looked down the barrel of the service revolver and into the hard eyes of the young man he thought he had properly dispatched just moments earlier.

The look of pure and certain death that Will fixed him with sent a bolt of icy fear through the grizzled old bushwhacker. "This ain't none of your damned business, boy, so y'all just back away and leave me to finish up here," the man snarled. "I'm settling an old debt between me and her Pa and having a touch of pleasure in the bargain, so you just butt the hell out. Besides, looks to me like we're wearing the same uniform." There was a long silence, and the bushwhacker was beginning to think things would be all right after all.

"Don't seem like you're gonna make much of a first impression when you meet St. Peter, with your dick hanging out and all," said Will. Without waiting for a response, he calmly pulled the trigger, shooting the man in the bridge of his nose and blowing the back of his head off.

As soon as the gun went off, Mollie straightened up and turned around quickly, dropping her dress and underclothes back in place. The yellow light angling up from the lantern reflected off the prominent features of Will's bloody face but left dark pools in the recesses around his eyes and under his lower lip, presenting a terrifying visage to her as she struggled to regain her composure. Will slowly turned to look at her as he tucked the gun back into his coat. He mistook her look of shock for one of revulsion at how matter-of-factly he had just ended a man's life.

"A lot of folks have died by my hand in this war, Mollie, but he's the only one I'm sure of that needed killing," said Will. "Now take the lantern and fetch his horse over here."

When she returned in a few minutes with the dead man's horse in tow, Will leaned over the side of the wagon and retrieved a length of tie-down rope from under the seat, knelt down, and lashed the man's feet together with one end of the rope, and then secured the other end to the saddle on his horse. He stood up, grabbed the man's gun out of the wagon and said. "All right, Mollie, let's get this sorry carcass out to the road." After a few starts and stops, they were finally able to get the horse, dragging the dead bushwhacker by his feet out on the road heading north.

"Throw the reins over the saddle horn and come back here," he said to Mollie. As soon as she was out of the way, Will slapped the animal on the rump and fired the man's pistol over its back. The horse squealed and reared up on its hind legs and then took off down the road at a run. The dead man with his arms stretched back over his head and his britches around his knees went careening wildly from one side of the road to the other as they faded into the darkness.

Will tossed the man's gun into the weeds across the road and then turned to Mollie and said, "Let's tend to our business. The sooner we're back home, the better."

They walked back to the wagon, guided by the lantern that Mollie held out in front of them. Even though Will struggled a bit to keep up with her, limping along using only one crutch to take the weight off his bad leg, he felt better having one hand free in case he needed the pistol again. The nasty cut across his face pained him, but at least it had stopped bleeding into his eye. When they reached Abby, Mollie shifted the light to her left hand, took hold of the bridle, and led her forward toward the front of the dark house. Jack's body lay stretched out on the floor of the porch, hands folded over his midsection and a smile frozen on his face, as if he had simply decided to take his evening's repose in the fresh autumn air and overslept.

As they drew near and the yellow area of illumination cast out ahead of them by the lantern crept over Jack's body, Mollie's heart sank. The dreadful violence of his execution at the hands of the Yankee bushwhackers was all too clear. Jack's last earthly purpose was to be an example, albeit an imperfect one, to his weary neighbors of what fate awaited them if they acted upon any Confederate leanings they might have. Mollie knelt down next to the body and began to weep as she straightened his collar and tugged at his coat here and there.

Will eased carefully down beside her and said, "Come on, Mollie, we need to go. Knock on the door and see if someone will help us get Jack in the wagon." She sat back on the counters of her shoes and rested her hands in her lap as she gazed at her brother's remains.

Will respected her moment of grief and then struggled to his feet and offered his hand. As she straightened up, she fished a little hankie from the sleeve of her dress and dabbed at the tears in the corners of her eyes.

"I'll get help," she said after taking a deep breath. Mollie stepped up on the porch and moved quickly to the front door. She was getting ready to knock a second time when the door opened suddenly and a stooped old man stuck his head out and swiveled his face up sideways to regard her.

"I'm Mollie Dean, your neighbor down by Thompson Creek," she started to say, but he waved a hand at her cutting her off.

"I know who you are and why you come. Damn shame about your brother. Tell your folks I said so, and give my condolences. Did you meet up with that Yankee straggler up yonder by the road?"

His question caught Mollie a little off-guard and she stammered as she answered, "Why, yes, yes we did, as a matter of fact. He seemed to be in a hurry to be on his way, so we didn't speak much."

"Yes, he certainly was in a hurry. Weren't much of a rider, though, was he?" the old man said with a little smirk and a glint in his eye.

Mollie realized he had seen the whole thing and decided just to state her business. "Would you be so kind as to help us get my dear brother in the back of my wagon so I can take him home?"

"I'd be pleased to help you, Miss Dean." The old man disappeared back into the house and yelled for his boy to come out.

Hutchens bent down and pushed his hands under Jack's shoulders while his odd-looking nephew grabbed the ankles. The old man nodded to his boy, they lifted together, staggered up to the back of the wagon with Jack's body, and slid him along the bed until just his feet were sticking out. As Mollie turned the wagon onto the road toward home, Will dabbed and wiped at his facial wounds with a piece of white cloth he had picked up by the back of the wagon after shooting the bushwhacker. He had no idea what the cloth was or how it came to be lying on the ground, but it suited his purpose just fine and he gave it no more thought. Mollie was glad that the dark night hid the blush on her face when she looked over and saw that Will was using her ripped pantaloons to stem the flow of blood from the long cut on his face.

Pap had been waiting on the front porch for a sign of their return and met them halfway up the drive that ran between the road and the front of the house. Sarah was there, too, having ridden hard back to the Deans' farm at the first sign of trouble to warn them that Mollie was in danger.

Mollie reined Abby to a stop next to the porch and quickly dismounted, thinking to grab the bloody underclothes from the floorboard where Will had let them fall. She nearly bowled Pap over as he came around the back of the wagon. She wept hysterically and threw her arms around his neck as if he could ward off all the evils of humankind that she had witnessed that night. Ma and Sarah came up and gently pulled her away from Pap and led her into the dimly lit house.

Will hopped down from the last step onto his good leg and steadied himself with the sideboard of the wagon. When he let his right leg take some of his weight, he grimaced and felt the odd sensation of dried blood crinkling on his face.

Before he could retrieve a crutch from the back of the wagon, Pap came up and stood close behind him. "What happened back there, son?" he said.

Will jumped, not expecting the old man to be so close and certainly not expecting to be addressed by him. He briefly considered sugar-coating what had happened back at the Hutchens farm, but in the end he was just too tired and discouraged to care. "One of the bushwhackers that killed Jack hung back and was laying for us; said he was settling an old debt with you. He pistol-whipped me in the face and I was stunned for a moment; when I come to, he was fixing to rape Mollie… so I killed him."

Will held Pap's eyes, trying to gauge his reaction in the darkness. The old man was unnerved by Will's directness and the air of death that clung to the young man as the smell of freshly turned earth clings to a farmer's boots. He looked down at the ground and said, "The girls can help me fetch Jack. You better get on in the house and tend to that wound."

Chapter 11

Mollie and her parents worked by candlelight long into the night, preparing the parlor for Jack's visitation. Pap built a platform by taking the pantry door off its hinges and setting it across two sawhorses. Mollie's mother placed her best bedspread over the door, letting it drape to the floor to hide the makeshift structure underneath. They laid Jack's body out on top of that, covered with a rough blanket until they could properly dress and prepare him for burial. Mollie would take the spring wagon into Shelbyville the next morning after sunup and buy a proper casket for Jack after she dropped Will off at the depot.

Before retiring for the night, Mollie went to Will's room with a dish of hot water to cleanse the wound on his face. Even though they had been guarded about their feelings for one another in recent days, Will still felt the strong undercurrent of emotion flow through the tips of her slender fingers to his face. She had lingered over each dab of the warm cloth, her face reflecting the struggle to hold back the words she so wanted to speak. Will held his tongue, too, not wanting to end the moment, but afraid for it to go any further. As the silence between them stretched out, they both knew their paths were drawing apart. Mollie sat on the edge of the bed in profile to Will, regarding her own reflection in the small side window. She sighed deeply and turned to find Will watching her. With her right hand she brushed a wayward lock of hair from Will's brow and then dropped the hand gently, palm-down on his chest. Will took it up and held it between his own two hands, feeling her life force resonate in the delicate long bones of the back of her hand.

The house was quiet now and the mantel clock in the Deans' parlor began to chime its top-of-the-hour preamble, calling attention to the telling hour strokes that would follow. He was hoping the clock would prove that he had slept at least a few hours, but it struck at 4:00, as it had at 3:00 and at 2:00 before that. He lay on top of the bedclothes, fully dressed except for his boots and hat, staring into the dark space above him. His worldly possessions lay beside him in a little canvas haversack that Jack had scrounged from the barn.

At 6:00 Will sat up, pausing briefly to clear the cobwebs from his head before donning his boots and hat. He opened the drawer of the little side table and dropped in forty dollars folded inside a sheet of stationery with a note attached. The day before he had penned the note to Mollie's parents, thanking them for allowing him to recuperate at their house and hoping that they would accept the money as payment for food he had consumed during his stay. Before closing the drawer he retrieved Sergeant Hazzard's service revolver, turned it slowly in his hands, confirming its readiness to fire, and then dropped it into the inside pocket of his roundabout. Will stood up, tucked one of the crutches under his arm, then turned and took one last look around the room, trying to fix it in his memory.

Will and Mollie rode in silence for the first hour. Wherever the road bordered the west edge of a farm field, they could look off far enough to see a streak of red morning light low in the eastern sky. It was cold and they sat close to one another with a single heavy blanket draped over their shoulders to conserve body heat. Nearly every house they drove past had a light or two showing as working folks cobbled together what they could for breakfast before heading out to do their chores. A dog, sometimes two or three, heralded their arrival at nearly every farm along the way.

"I reckon you better let me off on the edge of town and I'll walk the rest of the way in. Better if folks don't see you riding with a Yankee," said Will. Mollie looked sideways at him and nodded and then huddled in closer to his warmth.

An hour later they crested a little hill and the town of Shelbyville came into view, spread out before them in a shallow river valley. There was no wind this morning and the chimney smoke from every house rose through the heavy air in tight gray columns straight up for perhaps five hundred feet, where they stopped and spread out horizontally, merging to create a thin but distinct gray layer that touched all sides of the valley. Will climbed down slowly from the wagon, stiff from the long ride and the cold. He grabbed his haversack and crutch out of the back and then hobbled around to Mollie's side, where he handed her down to the road. They stood close, facing each other, holding hands. They both knew that they would in all likelihood never see each other again, but it was so much easier to leave the door open just a crack.

"Will you write and tell me how you fared?" said Mollie.

"I will, whether I'm sent back to the army or sent home. I will write —I will never forget you, Mollie Dean."

Mollie looked up into Will's face and lightly traced the ugly cut with the tips of her fingers. "I fear you will remember me every morning when you look in the mirror, dear Will," she said sadly. Will gently guided the soft palm of her hand to his lips and kissed her there.

Mollie pulled back, fighting off tears, fished something wrapped in white cloth out of her pocket, and pressed it into Will's hand. "I gave this watch to Jack when he was home on leave last Christmas. I know he would want you to have it. The handkerchief has my name embroidered in the corner for you to remember me by."

Will unfolded the hankie and exposed a beautiful gold pocket watch. A small winding key hung from a yellow ribbon that was tied to the bow. While she was digging in her other pocket, he held the hankie to his nose and breathed in, gratified that it carried her sent.

Finally Mollie held up her hand and displayed a little pair of scissors. "And if you will permit me, I would like to take a lock of your hair as a keepsake."

The lump in Will's throat would only allow him to nod in the affirmative. Mollie reached up and clipped the lock of his hair that always seemed to be out of place and carefully placed it in a small envelope that she had brought just for this purpose. Will started to help her back up in the wagon, but she suddenly stopped and threw her arms around his neck. He

88

wrapped his arms around her waist and they hugged each other as tightly as they could. Then just as suddenly, she pushed him away and climbed up onto the seat of the wagon. She grabbed Abby's reins and turned one last time.

"Godspeed, Will Castor."

Will couldn't speak, but he smiled a sad smile and tipped his hat as she drove away.

November 26th, 1863
Thompson Creek, TN

Beloved Sister Ailcy,

I this golden evening lift my pen in response to your sad but thrice welcome letter come duly to house. Your missive found us yet living but still in great distress. Mother and myself are up but not well. Pap has been very ill for several days. The medical attendant thinks that with strict care he will recover, though he has never seen one well hour since our great trouble, and I fear he never will. I sincerely hope that when you receive this you are recovered from your first thunderbolt of utter despair. Though you may live to number the gray hairs of three score and ten, you can never outlive the miserable year 63. Never, no never. Such is the fate of men. Sister, as you requested I will as plainly as possible give you the detail in full. As to the way your beloved was drest it was very neat yet decently plain. I have made him clothes to return to you in. His vest was gray mist, his pants were shoot-about gray and bright brown and made in the nicest order, well-lined and stitched. When I made them he told me to lay them by and he would wear them to meet Ailcy in. And he would keep them as long he lived to remember me. "When I get to see Ailcy she will have plenty for me to wear so I need not take everything, only what I have on." His shirt was as fine as ever you could wish to look at.

His coat was black cloth, black kid gloves, white hose which sister Lizier had given him which he was saving to wear home. A white swiss winding sheet and talton veil completed his burial attire. His coffin was black walnut raised lid lined with white and a case of poplar. Sister, it was the best we could do under the circumstances. You also requested to know how many times he was shot and where. He was shot through the right arm, the left wrist, the middle finger on his right hand, in his bowels by the right hip. Four shots in his breast, one in the hollow of his neck, four in the head three above the left eye, and one in the crown, two in the back supposed to have passed through his body. As to his talking after he was shot, I am satisfied that he never spoke. One of the detail told a cousin of ours that he pled innocence to the last and when they told him to dismount they were going to shoot him, he did so telling them that they had the power but that they would be killing an innocent man. Then he raised his hat and stroked his hair and dropped his hands to his side and fell a lifeless corpse. Thousands and tens of thousands have died on both sides since this bloody war began. Sister, I censure not the men who did the deed, but those who reported and I have no idea on earth who did it, for I don't think he had an enemy in this state that would have sought his ruin so harshly. He told me the night before his death that he was going to wind up his affairs and start home in two or three weeks. He was always talking about you and the children. Catherine's conduct seemed to distress him more that anything in all his trials; he knew not the cause of her removal. When he heard of Dan starting on such a long journey he said let him go. I don't blame him for traveling, for that was one of my great passions. He left no evidence behind of his future welfare more than the smile on his face when we was dressing him. He smiled as fair a smile as you ever saw in your life and it remained on his features until he was laid under the sod. I am perfectly satisfied in my mind that his angelic form is flying around the throne of him who doeth all things well. I am sending a lock of his hair and whiskers also. Will send his daguerreotype as soon as I have one copied from it. I will keep yours if you have no objections and send you mine. Tell your sweet babes to be good children and try to live a pious life and make useful men and women. Sister call your babe Allen instead of Alice, as that was the name I and he selected, Mary Allen. Give our best regards to Samuel and family, tell them we have written to them. Polly's folks are well and looking for a letter from them. Pap and Mother send their compliments to you all and say they would give everything in the world to see you and the children. What must I do with what is coming to you here? Write soon and fail not.

Your Affectionate Sister,
Mollie Dean

Part Two

Chapter 12

The cold glass of the train car window felt good against Will's scalp and the skin of his temple as he sagged against the armrest of the seat and dozed to the hypnotic rhythm of steel wheels riding over the rail joints. The air in the car was heavy and foul with the smell of unwashed working men in damp wool clothing, and it was heated almost to the point of being unbearable by a little coal stove that sat in the middle of the floor. Curled, brown leaves and scraps of newspaper collected in corners of the coach, trapped by eddies of cold wind whenever the door at either end was opened. The last time he had traveled by rail, he had been freshly discharged from the army in Nashville and was on his way home to Coldwater. That was back in '64. He had spent the years since the war trying to put some order and purpose back into his life, but nothing seemed to take. He tried living at home for a while, in his old room and helping out on the farm, but his heart wasn't in it, and he bumped into Jimmy's ghost at almost every turn. His folks had tried so hard to understand what he had been through, but it was no use. Only those who had been there themselves could understand, and like Will, they mostly just wanted to forget. He was still going through the motions of living, but he was adrift in a world he no longer understood; he felt hollowed out.

The one bright spot in all of this had been his discovery of the numbing effects of whisky. He and Jimmy had pinched a bottle from his father once and experimented in the seclusion of the hayloft, but the results were somewhat mixed, since neither could remember what had happened after a certain point, and of course there was the hangover to consider. After they had joined the army, the opportunities to partake were much more frequent, and they rarely passed up a chance to take a manly swig when a bottle was passed, but it was never more than that. Medicinal would be a better way to describe the purpose of whisky for him now. If he was careful he could fortify himself just enough to smile and carry on a friendly conversation or to laugh at a funny story without appearing to be intoxicated. It was a fine line to be sure, but as the months passed and his tolerance increased, he became very good at hiding the truth. And there were kindred spirits aplenty in almost every saloon, in every town: the loner sitting at the bar looking into the mirror with a "thousand-yard stare," or sitting alone at a table in the back, hat pulled low, watching his fingers endlessly turning a brimming shot glass. They were his people; they were the ones who understood.

Today he would not take a drink, at least not yet. He was on his way to find a job and make a new start. There was one long blast from the steam whistle on the engine, and the train began to slow as they approached the outskirts of East Saginaw. He had been to this town once before when he and Jimmy passed through on their way north to camp and explore the vast wilderness in the center of the state, and even though that was only eight years ago, the entire Saginaw River valley had been completely transformed. What lay before him as the train rolled to a stop in front of the depot was a good-sized city bustling with activity and purpose. Will stood up, threw one of the straps of his knapsack over his shoulder, and waited his turn to exit the car. The cold air that greeted him as he stepped down onto the platform was a welcome relief, and he savored the first few breaths as he took his bearings. He already felt better than he had at any time since coming home from the war. Perhaps on some level he could sense the closeness of a new life, a new existence where the past would finally stay put.

He started up Water Street, moving slowly and taking in the sights of the riverfront. On the river side of the street, there was one sawmill after another belching smoke and steam, filling the air with the smell of fresh-cut pine and hot machinery. The cacophony of gang saws and circular saws ripping through the huge logs overpowered all other sounds of daily life. Extending out into the river behind each mill were long curving booms made from sixteen-foot logs connected end to end with chain that formed a mill pond of sorts for the hundreds of logs that were feeding the saws. Men wearing spiked boots and armed with peaveys moved about from one log to another, herding their charges into the jack ladder that would lift them out of the water and into the mill.

The other side of the street was a mixture of shops, restaurants, and lumber company offices with a disproportionate number of saloons and bordellos mixed in. Even though it was still late morning, sounds of drunken revelry and fighting emanated from many of the establishments in varying degrees of intensity and in several different languages. The shanty boys, or lumberjacks as they would later be called, were coming into town to sign on to the crews that would soon be heading out into the wilderness to spend the winter in isolation felling the great pine trees.

Will stopped in front of a well-kept, two-story brick structure that was slightly separated from the other buildings and that occupied the south corner at the foot of Cedar Street. It had the look of a storefront, and at one time it had been, but according to the sign stenciled in bold letters across the windows on each side of the vestibule, it was now the Bert Heimbaugh & Sons Lumber Company. Will pushed open the heavy door and was startled momentarily by a bell hanging from the transom that announced his arrival. The front half of the large high-ceilinged room was nearly empty except for long backless benches that lined both sides of the dark wainscoted walls. The upper walls were hung with heavy framed photographs of sawmills and memorable events having to do with the lumber business. One such photo was of two draft horses hitched to a sled piled impossibly high with huge logs. Hardy looking men stood around and on the logs posing for the picture. Their jaunty attitudes reminded him of artillery men during the war. Someone had written "Camp No. 2 1866" across the bottom in white letters.

Will's inspection of the photographs was interrupted by a short, slightly overweight balding man wearing spectacles. His sleeves were rolled back to just below his elbows and his brown vest had a big patch of chalk dust near his right hip, as if someone had smacked him with an eraser.

"Can I help you with something?" he said.

Will turned away from the wall and walked up to the counter that separated the long room. "My name is William Castor, and I'd like to speak to someone about a job."

"All hiring is done at the main mill office. Turn left when you go out the door and down two blocks to the public dock. A boat to the mill runs about every hour and a half. Don't get your hopes up, though. We only hire experienced men." The little man turned on his heel, dismissing Will, and returned to his desk. Will picked up his pack and started for the door.

Ben Heimbaugh, who managed the lumber company for his father, had been sitting at his desk in an office off of the main room, poring over plat maps of the upper Tittabawassee River area and had overheard the exchange between his clerk and the stranger looking for work. He stuck his head out of his office in time to see Will limping toward the door.

"Clarence, catch that man before he leaves and show him back to my office," he said. Clarence made no attempt to hide his annoyance but jumped up and carried out his boss's order. Will introduced himself and apologized for barging in. They shook hands and the older man motioned to a straight-back chair in front of his desk. Will took a seat and waited for Mr. Heimbaugh to speak.

"You get that leg in the war?"

"Yes sir, Chickamauga," said Will.

"What outfit?"

"Battery D First Michigan."

Heimbaugh turned that over in his mind before continuing. "I was a lieutenant in the 11th Michigan. We had hot work that day. Lost almost half our men in Longstreet's attack. I'm pleased to meet you, Will. I always heard good things about Battery D."

"Thank you, sir. Your boys done themselves proud that day, too."

"So what kind of work are you looking for, Will?"

"Well sir, I'd like to try my hand at land looking. I've done a lot of hiking and camping in the woods north of here and can find my way around pretty good with a map and a compass. I'm savvy in arithmetic and can read tables, too."

Mr. Heimbaugh covered his mouth with his hand and stifled a chuckle at Will's naiveté. If it had been anyone else sitting in front of his desk, this is the point in the conversation where he would have sent him packing. This young man was different, however; he had mettle, and he was a veteran like himself. He would do whatever he could to help him find his way.

"There's quite a bit more to being a successful land looker than you might think, Will. For instance, you'd need to learn how logging camps operate so you could choose the best locations for setting up. There are a lot of beautiful stands of cork pine out there that can't be harvested simply because there's no river close by to float them out on. You would have to learn basic surveying and how to estimate board feet of lumber from a particular stand of timber, and of course it is a solitary endeavor. Not everyone is cut out for it…"

"Yes sir, I see what you mean," said Will, sensing a letdown coming.

After a moment of uneasy silence, Mr. Heimbaugh opened the top drawer of his desk, pulled out paper and pen, and began to write. "Here's what we'll do. I'll put you to work this winter with Camp Four. You'll be responsible for the livestock and driving the tote wagon. Make sure they're fed and healthy and hitched up when they're needed. The foreman will go over your responsibilities. Keep your eyes open and learn everything you can about cutting trees and getting them to the mill. Keep a journal and write everything down. Next spring you ride the cook raft during the log drive and follow the river hogs back down here. You come and see me then and we'll talk about land looking. Pay is forty dollars a month plus room and board."

Mr. Heimbaugh folded the paper he had been writing on in thirds and handed it to Will. "Now catch that boat out to the mill and give this to Lee Strom in the front office. He'll get you settled in," he said, extending his hand.

Will's mind was racing, trying to keep ahead of events as he jumped up and shook Mr. Heimbaugh's hand. "Thank you, sir, for giving me a chance. You won't be sorry," said Will.

"Remember, keep your eyes open. See you next spring."

Chapter 13

Will sat on the edge of the bed in the tiny third-floor boarding house room that would be his home until his crew was assembled and ready to leave for Camp Number Four. He struck a match and lit the wick of an oil lamp that sat on the little table next to a copy of the New Testament. With the help of its dim light, he picked loose the knots in his bootlaces and slid them off before flopping back on the bed and staring up at the ceiling. As if following some perpetual script, his thoughts turned to Amanda. It had been almost two years since he had seen her, but he still thought of her almost every day, and after a few sips of whisky he would begin reliving the pain of losing her. When he was discharged from the army in Nashville back in '64, he had decided to forego sending a telegram to his folks informing them of his return so he could slip back into town unannounced and put to rest once and for all any doubts about Amanda's fidelity.

When he had stepped off the train in Coldwater that snowy evening, it was dark already and the platform and depot were deserted, except for a boy hoping to earn a little tip money handling bags and the man behind the counter selling tickets. They had seen so many soldiers in blue coming and going since the war began that they hadn't even looked up as he passed through the waiting room and out to the sidewalk.

All of the shops had been closed at that late hour, but there were two saloons open, one on each side of the street. He remembered them from before the war but had never actually been in either one, so he chose the closest, "Billie's Tap Room," and crossed the street. Billie's was dimly lit and pleasantly warm from the large open fireplace on the wall across from the bar. The bar itself ran the length of the room, and its ornate carved oak sideboard and mirror covered the entire wall. All the woodwork was dark, nearly black from years of pipe smoke. A metal trough built into the floor ran along the base of the bar for chewers.

Will dropped his knapsack in a corner by the door and took a stool at the end of the bar. He fished a dollar out of his pocket and set it on the bar.

"Well I'll be stitched, if it ain't Will Castor," said the barman as he walked up to take Will's order. "It seems like an age since we was peppering old lard ass Thomas with spitwads," he said, referring to their school days.

Will looked up and forced a smile. "That seemed like pretty risky business back then," he said. "How the hell are you, Bruce?"

"I'm doing fine, doing fine, I got no complaints. I was sorry to hear about Jimmy, though. Saw his name on the list in the newspaper a while back. They did a nice spread on Battery D and Chickamauga, too. Yep, that was a bad one, all right."

Will almost asked him how he would know a bad one from a good one but decided against it at the last moment and just nodded.

"What are you drinking tonight, my friend?"

"Whisky straight up and a glass of water," said Will.

Bruce was back in a moment and sat the bottle, shot glass and water on the bar. "On the house, Will. So what brings you out on a blustery night like this?"

"Just got off the train. Got a medical discharge from the army, and I'm going home to see my folks, and then I'm going to look up Amanda Felter."

A look of surprise flashed briefly across the barman's face, but he was good at his job and the mask quickly fell back into place. The shadow passed between them unnoticed as Will continued making small talk.

"Amanda sure turned out to be a beautiful lady," said Bruce.

"That she did… that she did," said Will, a genuine smile lighting his face this time. "We've been exchanging letters since I joined the army back in '61."

"What do you hear from her lately, Will?"

"Well, I been moving hither and yon all this last year and I reckon her letters were never able to catch up with me, so all and all – not much."

"Seems like I heard she moved into town and was living at her aunt's house over on Chicago Street. That might have had some play in it," said Bruce.

Will nodded and mulled this new information over. "That the big red brick place at Chicago and Jefferson?"

"That's the one. Her kin are pretty high rollers."

Just then one of the two other patrons in the saloon that night signaled for a refill, and Bruce headed down to the other end of the bar. Will thought about his options for a moment, but the opportunity to see Amanda right away was just too good to pass up. He downed the shot and then poured another and downed it, too, before chasing the burning liquid with water. He left the dollar on the bar, waved to Bruce, and was out the door.

As he headed up Division Street toward the center of town, the snow was still coming down, heavier than before, but there was no wind now, and the big flakes floated down, driven only by their own weight and design. Some of the houses he passed had candles burning in the windows for the holiday, and it made him think of Mollie. She had been afraid her mother would catch her staying up late, wasting a candle to read by. The smell of wood smoke made him feel a little lonely.

At last he stood in front of the big three-story brick house owned by Amanda's aunt and uncle. He paused in the middle of the dark street and savored the moment he had dreamed about so many times since leaving home. Large glass balls hung suspended from pieces of garland in each of the three parlor windows to the right of the front door. The warm yellow light of the room twinkled randomly off their shiny surfaces as they rotated slowly in the disturbed air.

As Will stood taking in the scene of domestic tranquility, the front door of the house opened, spilling light onto the small cement porch and down the snow- covered walk. A man and a woman emerged and stood facing each other on the porch. Their forms were dark, silhouetted by the light of the vestibule behind them, but Will recognized Amanda immediately. The man put his arms around her waist and pulled her close as she tilted her head back to accept his kiss. After a moment, she turned her head and rested it against his chest as they held each other in one final embrace. Will felt her eyes on him as the bullet of this new reality tore through him, striking the one remaining part of the old Will that he had been clinging to like a drowning man. His demise was now nearly complete. The only difference between him and his friends who had perished in the war was that he was still breathing.

The couple finally pulled away from each other, and the man hurried away down the sidewalk without even glancing in Will's direction. Amanda reached down, picked up her skirts, and stepped back into the house. She started to shut the door behind her but paused and took one more look out toward the street where she thought she had seen the dark form of a man watching them. If there had been someone there, he was gone now, so she shut and bolted the door.

Will got up and dug around in his knapsack for one of several fifths of Walker's Club Whisky he had packed from home. He determined after much trial and error that two healthy belts before retiring for the night minimized the frequency and intensity of his reoccurring war nightmares. He held the bottle up to the lamplight and squinted through the amber liquid for a moment before putting it to his lips and taking two big gulps. It burned all the way down and set off a little quiver through his body. He stuck the cork back in the bottle, giving it a little tap, and making a mental note to secure a few more, that might, with careful rationing, hold him through the winter in the woods.

Chapter 14

Will's first day as an employee of Heimbaugh and Sons was a humbling experience, to put it mildly. He showed up at the front office of the mill before dawn and was met by the Camp Four foreman, one of the biggest men he had ever seen. In spite of his size, he spoke in a soft, heavily accented voice that was hard to understand the first time around. His first name was Ole, and his last name was something that sounded a lot like "Horsepickle." Will guessed he was a Swede. His penetrating eyes and impatient manner left little doubt that a man would do well to learn the vagaries of his speech quickly.

Since Will knew nothing of the lumber business, everything he was told to do required a degree of detailed instruction that seemed to annoy almost everyone. By the end of his third day, he felt like a complete idiot. The note from Ben Heimbaugh that Will had presented at the mill that first day was probably the only thing that prevented Ole from tossing, as he put it, his sorry carcass into the cold Saginaw River. What he lacked in experience, he tried to make up for with persistence and hard work. He made a point to be the first one there in the morning and the last one to leave at night, and if he was in the middle of an important task when dinnertime came, he often would work right through it. The road monkeys, who would be going up the Tittabawassee on this first trip to open up the camp and extend the access roads into the new work area, just looked on with amusement. Word had spread that the boss man had a special interest in this greenhorn, and no one wanted to risk getting too carried away with breaking him in—and besides, the nasty scar across his face and his odd gait from the injured leg promised a grit that none of them cared to challenge.

By the end of the week, Will was beginning to think things might be OK after all, and the long, hard days were taking his mind off the past. When he showed up for work Saturday morning, there was a large scow tied up to the pilings next to the mill. Its wide flat bottom made it ideal for transporting animals, equipment, and supplies up the shallow rivers to pineries north of Saginaw. Will spent his days leading up to their departure fetching fodder for the animals they would take with them and making repairs on the heavy harnesses and pulling gear that would be used to skid the big logs to collecting points on the cross-haul roads. Once the animals were settled in at the camp, he would begin re-shoeing them with calked or spiked shoes that would allow them to pull heavy loads without slipping on the ice-packed roads.

The trip upriver to Camp Number Four was uneventful, but it was four days of hard work poling the scow against the lazy current. Fortunately, there were enough men on board to rotate the work and give everyone a chance to rest. Twice they encountered wide shallow places in the river where they had to unload the horses and oxen to lighten the vessel enough to slide over the sand into deep water. Will was stunned by sights of total destruction as they started up the Tittabawassee. For many miles on both sides of the river the great forests had been completely cut away. In many places even the dense slash left by topping and branching the logs had been burned off, leaving an ugly black landscape for as far as the eye could see. Will and Jimmy had hiked and camped in these forests before the war, so unlike the other men on the scow, he could weigh the loss.

For the last day and a half of their slow journey upstream, the forests on both sides of the river appeared to be untouched by the lumber companies. Camp Number Four was located roughly two miles south of the confluence of the Pine River and the Tittabwassce, about equidistant from each. The land around the camp was covered by a mixed forest of white and red pine. The white or cork pine, as they were called because the logs floated high in the water, were the most sought after of the two. They grew to over one hundred and fifty feet tall, and many were five or six feet in diameter. In most cases the cork pine were found sharing the landscape with other species, namely red pine, hemlock, or oak, but whoever their neighbors were, they always towered over them. In areas where the white pine was the only species present, they grew amazingly close to one another and sometimes rose over eighty feet from the forest floor before they sent out branches. Standing in an old growth forest of white pine was almost a religious experience. It was quiet with huge branchless trunks growing impossibly close together, their dark columns fading off into the murk all around. High above there was the faint sound of the wind whispering through the distant tops of the trees. A man's voice or the sharp crack of a double-bladed axe biting into wood echoed as if in a great hall.

Will was dozing on a stack of fifty-pound sacks of cornmeal near the blunt bow of their vessel when he became aware of a subtle change in the voices of the men handling the poles. He sat up and rubbed his eyes, blinking as his pupils adjusted to the afternoon sun reflecting off the water. The scow was very close to the left shoreline and was crabbing sideways toward a clearing in the forest. A stark white-washed sign proclaiming this to be the Camp Number Four landing in crude black lettering was nailed to a tree near the water's edge. Will climbed down from his comfortable perch and moved back to the center of the vessel to check on the welfare of the animals. The oxen seemed quite content with whatever was in store for them, but the draft horses either sensed a change or had been here before and were beginning to move their feet in anticipation. Ole saw Will moving about and came over to give him instructions.

"Soon as ve get snugged up, ve take da horses off first. Get your team hitched up and take dem to da camp, about a mile down da road. Ve left two wagons dere last spring. You bring da biggest one back here so ve can get her loaded. Take Merle and cookie back vit you so dey can tell da men vhere to put things by in da cook shack. Ve got no time to move things more dan once, so you get it right da first time. Get me?"

Will nodded his understanding but kept silent, sensing there was more to come.

"You vill have little time vile da men unload da wagon, so you open up da stable and see vhat you got—make your plans. I keep da oxen here until you ready for dem. Get me?"

Once again Will nodded. Ole bobbed his head and moved off to supervise the men engaged in securing the scow. Will would learn over the months ahead that Ole ended all orders with the question "Get me?" and that when he gave that odd little bob of his giant noggin, he was done with you. Will went over Ole's instructions in his head a couple of times to make sure he had everything right, then started picking through the jumble of tack he would need to set up his team.

The three main log structures of Camp Number Four had been built the year before, so setting up operations this year would be relatively easy. Sweeping the floors, evicting the critters that had taken up residence over the summer, and restocking the shelves were the first order of business. Will did as Ole said and walked over to the stable to see what needed to be done while the wagon was being unloaded. When he opened up the wide doors on one end of the long building, he heard a rustling inside and stepped back around the corner of the building to wait for whatever it was to come out. After a brief moment of suspense, two portly skunks waddled out and stopped to look around and sniff the air. Will was careful not to move a muscle, and eventually they overlooked him and moved off into the underbrush. A long walkway ran the length of the stable with stalls on either side, each one wide enough to accommodate a team of horses or oxen. There was space for ten teams on each side.

The end of the stable to the right of where Will stood appeared to have been used to store a few long-handle tools, pitchfork, flat-edged coal shovel, grain scoop and the like, and walls were hung with whiffletrees and harnesses, some of which had been damaged by squirrels. There was a small pile of hay on the floor from the previous winter, but when he pulled a clump of it apart, the smell confirmed what he had suspected. Rain water had come through the roof in a few places and set the stage for mold. It wouldn't do for the animals, but perhaps he might pile it outside against the walls to help block the cold winter winds that would eventually come. To his left in the corner behind the door stood a small rusty cast iron box stove perched on a wooden frame filled with sand, and next to it a three-foot section of a large-diameter log stood on end to make a crude table. A single straight-back chair lay on its side under the only window.

Will swung the doors closed and started walking back toward the cook shack with his head down, thinking through some of the tasks that lay just ahead. It was clear that his predecessor had shared quarters with the animals in the stable and that would suit him as well. The nightmares, though less frequent in recent days, would not endear him to the tired lumberjacks in the bunkhouse, and besides, he would be able to take a nip now and then if he needed a little help sleeping. With a bit of preparation he thought he could stay warm, in even the worst weather. He would need to get up before everyone else to get the teams in harness and ready to move out with the men when they were done with breakfast.

Will stopped and turned around to look at the stable, thinking that something he had missed earlier might now show itself. For the first time he noticed that there was a small structure attached to the opposite end of the stable from where he planned to sleep. He walked back and peeked inside through a gap in the door frame. It was a surprisingly complete blacksmith shop. Tools hung from pegs, filling the entire back wall above a sturdy work bench. Underneath the bench and piled on the floor along the back wall were rusty pieces of iron in every imaginable shape. There was a wooden box containing farrier tools, and several larger boxes overflowing with caulked shoes for both draft horses and oxen. A forge stood against the right wall with a hood made from what appeared to be scrap wood, and a dented section of stove pipe poked up through the roof. A large anvil sat on the butt of an oak log in the middle of the floor, and to the left of that a double door on the inside wall opened into the stable.

Will spent the next few days bringing supplies up from the landing and getting himself and the animals settled in. The oxen would eat just about anything, so that was no problem, but he was a little concerned about running out of timothy and oats for the horses before the next scow arrived with supplies. The old bull cook who had been working in the Michigan woods for years said he could "feel" the first winter storm of the season approaching, and everyone took his word. Snow and the lumberjacks were the only missing elements, and the latter were due to arrive with the fodder on the scow's next trip. Ole seemed to be everywhere, solving one problem or another or breaking up one of the many fist fights that seemed to erupt out of thin air. Ole's way was to let the combatants settle matters for themselves, and he only stepped in if someone was about to be injured severely enough to interfere with the job. Untimely death was also frowned upon, mostly, as Ole explained it, because he hated doing the paperwork. Rumor had it that he had actually docked a man's pay once because the individual was stupid enough to get himself killed and leave them short-handed. The one thing that everyone agreed on, even the cocky lumberjacks, was that Ole's word was law, and justice for lawbreakers was swift—generally in the form of a crashing blow from a giant fist, or for the more severe cases, immediate expulsion from the camp, miles from civilization in the dead of a Michigan winter.

Chapter 15

As foretold by the old bull cook, winter descended on the camp with a vengeance. One day it was partly cloudy and warm enough to work in shirtsleeves, and the next the temperature plummeted and the wind-driven snow began piling up against the shanties high enough to touch the eaves. Ole held four of the swampers back from extending the skid roads into the new area that would be logged and sent them to the stable to help Will pull the wheels off all the wagons and drays and replace them with runners. He was grateful for the help and amazed that after four years in the army there were still cuss words he had never heard before. They were finishing up the last dray, when as if on cue, they began to hear distant voices and laughter coming from the direction of the river landing. The sounds were hollow and echoed in the stand of giant trees. Will and his helpers stopped working and looked down the tote road as far as they could to see who was coming.

"Must be the jacks walking up from the river," said one of the swampers. "Reckon Heimbaugh lit a fire under 'em when he see the weather changing."

"I hope you boys have enjoyed the peace and quiet around here, because we'll be having no more of that," replied one of the other men.

When the lumberjacks finally emerged from the distant bend in the road, their gaudy Mackinaw coats made an impossible splash of color on the solemn grays of the winter woods. Most carried a duffle bag or knapsack containing their personal belongings and a double-bitted axe, sometimes two, across their shoulders. An axe had to fit a man properly, and the lumberjacks were very particular. As they came up to Will and his helpers, the group began to disperse. Some kept walking to the bunkhouse and some stopped to question the swampers about the new areas of the forest they would be working in. Some were glad to meet up with old friends again. They were a rough-and-tumble group, all right—cocksure and ready to fight as the fancy moved them. Will was glad the long ride up the river from Saginaw had given them a chance to sober up.

Bringing up the rear of the group was a big man in a deep red plaid wool coat pulling a wooden box that was mounted on runners. His cheeks were red, stung by the frigid air, and Will couldn't help but think that if his hair and beard were white, he would look like St. Nicholas. To Will's surprise, he walked right up and extended his gloved hand.

"Name's Jerald Steiner. You must be Will Castor. The bossman told me to look you up. I'm the smithy. Reckon we'll be working together quite a bit this winter, shoeing and re-shoeing the animals like and such," he said.

Will liked him immediately. "Pleased to meet you," he said. "You're welcome to bunk with me on the other end of the stable and share my stove if you like."

"That's right neighborly of you, Will. I believe I'll do just that." He tipped his wide-brimmed black slouch hat to Will and resumed his trek toward the blacksmith shed.

Later that afternoon, Will walked down the center aisle of the stable and poked his head through the door to the blacksmith shop and asked Jerald if he needed help getting settled in. Jerald was just finishing up unloading his tools from the box he had been pulling behind him up the tote road.

"Hello again there, Will," he said. "I figure I'm about fixed in here. I'll get a fire going in the forge after supper and let it burn down all night so I got a nice bed of coals to work with in the morning. Tomorrow's the Sabbath, so I reckon the jacks will spend the day sorting themselves out and sharpening their tools. We'll get some of the youngsters to help us, and we'll shoe up the skid teams with calked shoes straightaway so they can go out with the men first thing Monday morn. Maybe we'll have time to get a sled team done, too. I don't know…gets dark real early nowadays." Jerald turned away from the work bench and regarded Will.

"That about how you had it figured?"

Will couldn't help himself and smiled a little sheepishly. "Reckon so, Jerald. That's exactly what I had planned." Both men laughed easily at the not-so-subtle joke about Will's inexperience.

Jerald and Will spent the rest of the afternoon arranging their sleeping quarters. They placed the empty tool sled between them for a makeshift nightstand and spread a bed of straw on each side to sleep on that would insulate them from the cold floor. Will moved his kerosene lamp from the log table to the sled table and buried a couple of bottles Canadian whisky in his straw bed for safekeeping. Before they could get to building a fire in the box stove, the cookie blew three deep blasts on the long Gabriel to alert the men to prepare for supper. The six-foot dinner horn was certainly overkill today, when all of the men were in camp already, but later when they were out in the woods felling trees they would be able to hear it calling them in from several miles away. Thirty minutes later the short horn was blown and the men came pouring out of the bunkhouse headed for the cook shanty. Will and Jerald walked over and stood in line as the men filed through the door.

Once inside, Will started toward the long table next to the far wall where there seemed to be plenty of room for the two of them to sit. Jerald reached out and caught his arm, holding him back. Surprised, Will spun around and shot a questioning look at his new friend.

"Let the jacks sit where they want first. They all have a certain place where they sit for each meal, and they don't take kindly to anyone who trespasses."

With this new information in mind, Will turned back to the room and watched the lumberjacks sort themselves out. Sure enough, in just a few moments there were several quick but intense flare-ups between men who thought they had rights to one place or another. As rowdy and unmoved by authority as these men generally were, they all, to a man, respected the universal cook shanty rule of no talking during the meal. The only exception was "pass this" or "pass that." When everyone appeared to be settled in, Will and Jerald found space at a table already occupied by mostly teamsters, and like the lumberjacks, they ate their meal in silence.

That night, both men sat easily with one another on their beds of straw, smoking their pipes and basking in the radiated warmth of the little stove. The small circle of light from the kerosene lamp seemed to hold the heat. The sweet aroma of burning tobacco mingled with the wood smoke, the smell of fresh cut hay, and the scent of the animals who shared their world out beyond the light. They would recreate this little retreat on most nights throughout the long harsh Michigan winter, sharing Will's whisky, and some that Jerald had, and serving up their life stories to each other a little at a time.

"What tobacco you using?" said Jerald. "Kind of reminds me of Peerless."

"Climax," said Will. "Bought it for the name the first time I seen it, but it's not too bad. Been using it for a couple of years now. You're welcome any time you want to try it."

"Looks like you done some soldiering," said Jerald after pulling on his pipe a few times in rapid succession to get it going.

"I was in the artillery—four years. Got this leg at Chickamauga. That was enough for me," replied Will. "The war still gives me fits at night sometimes. Don't be surprised."

Jerald nodded his understanding. "I didn't go in. Always carried some guilt for it," he said.

"You don't need to feel poorly about it. Next time you see some poor son-of-a-bitch with no legs sitting on a sidewalk selling apples, ask him if he would trade places with you."

A long silence stretched out between them as they let the trail of the conversation go cold. Finally Will said, "I try real hard not to think on it, but there's always something. I've been told it would do me good to get it out, but I just can't seem to let go. I feel like I'd crack."

"You ever need to talk, I'm your man," said Jerald. "Might cost you a touch of that Canadian Whisky you're sleeping on over there."

Will smiled and nodded as he looked over at Jerald. He was touched to see his friend's eyes looking back.

Sunday was spent, as planned, re-shoeing the oxen and horses with spiked shoes that would enable them to get a purchase on the frozen surface of the logging roads and pull sleds piled high with heavy logs. To ease the burden of these heavy loads, the youngest members of the camp, called Chickadees, would work all night spreading water on the roads so the big sleds would have a bed of ice to run on the next day. Before Will and Jerald began working on the animals, they helped the youngsters rig up the special watering sled and got them started down to a nearby creek to fill up. The sled had a wooden box as wide as the road mounted on it and sealed so that it would hold upwards of five hundred gallons of water. The Chickadees would fill it from the creek with a two-handle water pump. Two holes in the back of the wooden tank lined up with the runner tracks in the road, and they could be opened or closed using tapered wooden plugs and a mallet.

The lumberjacks had set up two grindstones and a couple of clamping racks for the crosscut saws next to the bunkhouse. One would crank the round stone while the other would dress up the cutting edges of his axe. The sawyers took turns with their saws in the racks, working the teeth with a file.

After dinner, the jacks spent the rest of the afternoon in the bunkhouse smoking their pipes and either playing cards or their favorite contact sport called "Hotass." The rules for Hotass were fairly simple, and there was always room for improvising. One man would get down on all fours in the middle of the room. Someone, usually the cook, would place a burlap sack over the man's head. The rest of the men would stand along the walls and pass a plank, or in the case of Camp Number Four, an Indian canoe paddle with a cut-down handle, from one to the other until someone would step up and whack the kneeling man in the ass as hard as he could, holding the paddle in one hand. The paddle would then be placed on the floor next to the man and the sack removed. If the victim could correctly identify his assailant, then that man would take his place. If not, then the process would be repeated until he guessed correctly. As Will and Jerald continued working outside getting the teams ready for the next day, they could hear spasms of cheering erupt at regular intervals until it was nearly dark.

The next morning as Will lay awake staring up into the darkness above his face, he heard the small side door to the stable open and turned to watch the cook, Fred Longwell, step through carrying a lantern. Fred walked over and dangled the light next to Will and was startled and momentarily tongue-tied to find Will watching him. He expected someone half asleep and maybe a string of mumbled curses, but not this.

"Morning, Fred," said Will, ending the awkward moment.

"A good morning to you, too, Will. It's 4:00 and time for you boys to get after it," he said. "Come on over for breakfast directly."

"Be right there," said Will. The teamsters were always turned out quietly before anyone else so they could eat first and then get their teams hitched up while the lumberjacks ate. Will lit the oil lamp and walked over to the stove to retrieve his boots and a pair of warm socks that had been drying all night. While he was there he pulled down a pair of Jerald's socks, stuck them in his boots and dropped the lot on top of his friend's blanket about where he figured his belly should be. There was a grunt and then, "And a good morning to you too, Will. You're just lucky that I'm such a benevolent soul, my friend."

After breakfast Will and Jerald each poured a cup of steaming coffee from the huge enameled coffeepot by the door and headed back over to the stable. Will lit four lanterns for the teamsters to use while hitching up their teams and set them in the snow just outside the big stable doors. From across the way they heard the bull cook giving the wakeup call to the lumberjacks.

"Hurrah, you beauties! Daylight in the swamp!" was followed by the low-pitched growl of sixty-five men groaning and cursing in unison. Pretty soon they started coming out of the bunkhouse in their shirtsleeves and either heading for the cook shanty or the sinks. The teamsters for the big log sleds and skid teams were sorting out their gear and hitching their animals together for the walk out to the cutting. Everyone worked together, holding a lantern or steadying an animal while the other made adjustments to the rig. By the time the lumberjacks were finished with their meal, the teams and teamsters were ready to move out.

Will had hitched his team to the tote wagon early on and was able to stand back out of the way and observe the morning routine of the lumber camp unfold. As he surveyed the activity before him, his attention was drawn to one man over and over. At first, it was his booming voice that seemed to crush all other conversation around him, but later it was his enormous nose. No matter how hard Will tried to ignore it, he found himself staring like a kid at a freak show. After about ten minutes it was clear that the huge proboscis that dominated the man's face was dwarfed only by his immense ego. Will looked on incredulously as the man walked over to a grinding wheel, grabbed the lumberjack who was sharpening his axe by the collar, and tossed him aside. He then casually stepped up, laid the head of his own axe on the spinning wheel, and shouted in the face of the hapless man who was turning the crank, "Faster, numb nuts." What was even more amazing was the fact that the two jacks who had been minding their own business offered no resistance, not even a curse.

Ole stepped out of the cook shanty where he had his office and looked up as if to sniff the air. Satisfied with whatever he had learned from the action, he plucked a gold pocket watch from inside his coat and studied its face in the gathering light.

"Ve go now," he yelled as he snapped the cover shut and returned the watch to its pocket. The men shouldered their tools and funneled onto the logging road ahead of the ox and horse teams.

As soon as they were gone, Will stuck his head into the blacksmith shop and said to Jerald's back, "I'm off for the landing, if anyone is looking for me." Will's friend was working the bellows on his forge and didn't turn around but waved his hand in acknowledgment. Will climbed up on the wagon, settled himself on the spring seat, and gave the reins a little snap and said "step up" to start the horses moving down the tote road. The trip to the landing took about thirty minutes and it was just about his favorite part of the job. There was only one road and it ended at the river, so Will just sat back and let his mind wander while the horses worked. When he was beyond earshot of the camp it was easy to imagine he was the only human being left in the world. Sometimes he could feel the eyes of Jimmy or Al on him. Sometimes he could hear the voice of Sergeant Hazzard in his head, mostly when he was weighing some choices. Sometimes he would think of Mollie. Although she was part of the dreaded abyss that his war experience had become, her memory beckoned to him like a beam of hope from a dark shore. As he swayed absentmindedly in the driver seat of the tote wagon, he vowed to himself that he would write a letter to her on Sunday.

Will was back in camp late morning, unloading the hay that he had picked up at the landing, when the cook called him over to the cook shanty.

"We're ready for the swingdingle as soon as you can get it over here, Will," he said.

"OK, Fred," said Will, with a little uncertainty showing on his face.

The old cook smiled and said, "Don't know what the hell I'm talking about, do you, son?"

Will smiled a little sheepishly at being caught out. "Reckon not, Fred."

"It's that strange contraption on runners behind the blacksmith shop," said Fred.

"OK, I'll need about fifteen minutes to switch my team over," said Will.

"Just bring it right up here close, right in front of the door," said the cook over his shoulder as he disappeared back into the kitchen.

Will walked over and looked behind the blacksmith shop to see how the swingdingle was sitting so he would know how to get at it with his team. He unhitched the horses from the tote wagon and walked them forward slowly down the length of the stable, talking softly to them and tugging gently on one rein or the other to reinforce his commands. He turned the team to the left as he cleared the blacksmith shop and then back to the right so they ended up in line with the swingdingle but separated by about twenty feet. "Back…back…back. Come on, Gerty, it's OK, I'm not going to let you hit anything," he said. The big draft horses eased back slowly, snorting and swinging their heads, clearly not comfortable with the maneuver. Will stopped them about ten feet short of the sled's tongue to give them a chance to calm down and to make sure that they would stop and hold on his command. Finally he backed them the last few feet and hitched them to the swingdingle. It was indeed a strange looking piece of equipment. Its base element was a long narrow flat bed surrounded by foot-tall sideboards. A raised platform ran down the center and was topped with two-by-three-by-one-foot-tall wooden boxes with lids. More such boxes filled the space between the platform and the sideboards all around. Some of the boxes held tin plates and cups, and one held flatware. There was a box for each item on the menu and a couple for dirty dishes. Once the sled was loaded and moved out to the work site, it was a simple matter for the bull cook or the cookie to remove the lids from all the boxes and let the lumberjacks serve themselves buffet style.

Will stuck his head in the door to the cook shanty and said, "Your swingdingle is ready to go, Fred."

"Thank you, Will. We'll need about four horse blankets to cover everything and keep it warm, if you would be so kind as to fetch them for me."

Will nodded and went to the stable to retrieve the blankets. On the way back he looked in on Jerald. "I'm fixing to take dinner out to the jacks. You want to ride along?" said Will.

"Hell yes, my friend! I'm so hungry I could eat the asshole out of a grizzly bear," said Jerald. "Give me ten minutes." Will chuckled and turned back toward the cook shanty shaking his head.

The run out to the work area took about twenty minutes. They stopped just short of where the logging road intersected the cross-haul roads. Two big sleds loaded fifteen feet high with huge white pine logs blocked the road ahead, waiting for transport to the banking ground on the Tittabawassee River. The cross-haul roads were used by the oxen teamsters to skid the logs from where they were felled and bucked into sixteen-foot lengths out to the logging road where they were stacked onto sleds by men with pikes, peaveys, and chains. As the sleds were loaded, a man called a scaler would record in his journal how many board feet were on each sled and then brand each end of every log by hitting it with a special hammer that left the company's trademark embossed in the wood. This insured that the proper owner of the log could be identified once it got to Saginaw, even if it got mixed in with those of other companies in the river. As soon as they were in place, the bull cook jumped down and slid the long Gabriel out from under the horse blankets and blew three long blasts to call the jacks in for dinner.

Will pulled the blankets off the wooden boxes containing the hot food and spread them over the backs of the horses. He whispered in Gerty's ear, "You girls should love me for this luxury. Nobody out here gets heated blankets." Will and Jerald shared a nearby stump as they sat back and watched the lumberjacks file past, filling their tin plates to overflowing. Once everyone had been through the line, Jerald, Will and the bull cook would eat. After that any food left would be offered up for seconds.

There were still about fifteen jacks waiting in line when Bellman showed up. He eye-balled the situation for a moment and then walked up to the front of the line and shouldered a jack out of the way just as he was about to pull a plate out of the box. There was no protest from the other men in line, but a pall of uneasiness descended on the group.

That night Will and Jerald were smoking their pipes and enjoying their customary nightcap, basking in the warmth of the little stove.

"Do you know anything about the jack with the gigantic nose?" said Will.

Jerald laughed out loud and said, "Boy-oh-boy, can you believe the beak on that one?" He's got a head only a mother could love, and I ain't real sure about that."

"He's got a head like a bastard rat, if you ask me. Got a personality to go with it, too," said Will.

"Yeah, I reckon so. You stay clear of him, Will. I've heard talk that he's gunning for you."

"What in the world could he have against me? I don't even know his name."

"His name is Tom Bellman. You just steer clear of him, that's all," said Jerald. "He heard the rumor that the Heimbaughs are going to build a sawmill in Manistee next spring and start logging way up north of here. He figures he's a shoe-in for the job of foreman at the next new camp. If I had to guess, I'd say that he also heard that Ben Heimbaugh has taken a shine to you and it ain't sitting very well with him."

Will drew on his pipe and thought about what his friend had said. "Well, I don't want no trouble, but I ain't one to turn the other cheek either," he said. "Truth be told, even dying don't scare me much anymore. I can't help feeling like I skinned out on my friends back in the war. It just don't seem right that one morning we was all sitting around jawing and the next morning they was all dead, and I wasn't." Will uncorked the bottle of whisky they had been working on and took a long pull before handing it to Jerald.

"You better go easy on this stuff. It's pretty hard to come by out here in the middle of nowhere," said Jerald. Will just grunted and lay back on his bed of straw. With his hands supporting his head, and the whisky numbing the pain in his heart, he once again took up the vigil in the darkness for the faces that he knew would come.

Dear Mollie,

I hope this letter finds you and your family healthy and in good spirits. I know you must be very surprised to hear from me after so much time has passed and I am heartily sorry for such a long silence on my part. After leaving Shelbyville I reported to army headquarters at Nashville and was promptly sent to the hospital there to be examined and a determination made as to my fitness for duty. I was deemed unfit for further service in the artillery but was sent to the military post office and spent the better part of a year sorting mail. As you may recall it was my wish to be granted a medical discharge and sent home. Finally just before Christmas of '64 I was let go and returned to my home in Coldwater. The woman I had hoped to wed had become engaged to a prominent lawyer in my long absence, so I found myself somewhat at loose ends. I lived at home for a time and helped Pa around the farm but I was not happy and I felt I was a burden to my folks. Last fall I took a job with a lumber company in Saginaw and I am currently a teamster at a logging camp somewhere around the center of the state. I am promised a job as a land looker next year, which is something like a surveyor who hikes the forests looking for the best stands of trees. A good land looker with a little luck can make his fortune in a few years, I'm told.

Mollie, I have thought of you often since we said good bye that morning on the road to Shelbyville and wondered many times how you fared during the last years of the war. I have always regretted not being present when your dear brother, and my friend, Jack, was laid to his final rest, but I still hold that it was best given the difficult times. I cherish his watch that you gave to me and I think of you both every day when I look for the time. My dear Mollie, I was never very good at small talk, especially in your presence. It is my fondest desire that you might entertain the idea of seeing me again at some time in the near future when I might travel to Tennessee. I feel like we shared a strong bond once, not that long ago, and if you were so disposed, I believe we could again. I will be working in the wilderness of Michigan until spring, but if you reply favorably I will come straightaway. Use the address on the envelope and I will get any word from you eventually. I anxiously await.

Yours Affectionately,

Will

Chapter 16

The Michigan winter tightened its grip on the forest and the lumbermen a little more each day. There were a few storms that howled in the tops of the great white pines and piled up the snow in graceful sweeping ridges at the corners of the buildings, but mostly it came in small amounts, and it came every day. It clung to the tops of the tree stumps in huge white mushroom caps, collected on the branches and trunks of every tree in the forest and pressed down hard on the crude roofs of the log shanties. The snow collected on the backs of the horses, on the hats and shoulders of the lumberjacks as they toiled, and it froze in their beards around their mouths and under their noses. It sparkled in the weak winter sun, and it muffled the sharp cracks of cold steel biting into live wood.

Will's routine varied but little from one day to the next. The supply scows were coming about every other day now, trying to deliver as much fodder for animals and men as they could before the river froze. Once that happened, resupply would be very hard, perhaps even impossible. Will made a couple of trips to the landing in the morning, delivered dinner to the jacks wherever they were working around noon, then made two or three runs to the landing in the afternoon. He had struck up a friendship with one of the scow men, and for a small handling fee he was able to get cheap barrel whisky in quart canning jars, cleverly labeled "Honey." Will figured he had about enough hidden around the stable to last him and Jerald until they got back to Saginaw in the spring. His biggest worry was that the lumberjacks would get wind of their stash and tear the stable apart looking for it. That would be the end of their happy arrangement and probably their jobs too.

Will was on his first run of the day to the landing, and he sat hunched over with his forearms resting on his knees, staring down at the ground through a wide gap in the floorboards. The runners of his wagon followed the deep furrows that had been cut in the frozen surface of the road by dozens of previous supply runs, and the horses knew where they were going, so there was little for him to do. The reins lay on the floorboard under his boot. He was a little thick-headed from drinking the night before, but he was starting to rebound, thanks in part to the strong black coffee the cookie let him have from the bottom of the pot before throwing it out.

The landing for Camp Number Four had been cleared of trees the year before in the shape of a large half circle, the flat side formed by the river. The tote road intersected the clearing at the top of the arc. The clearing was just big enough to allow a team of horses pulling a wagon to turn around and head back out. Out of boredom, Will had been letting the horses have their head to see what they would do when they came to the end of the road at the river's edge. This morning they stopped, as they had every other morning, in the clearing, but well back from the water. Still, there was a little edge to it, thinking they might one day keep on going into the river. He had gotten in the habit of pausing for a few minutes when he arrived at the landing to watch the river roll by and to savor being alone. Sometimes he picked at the wound that Amanda had left him with, sometimes he dusted off the promise of Mollie, sometimes it was just the war and his friends buried in the red Georgia dirt of some farmer's field.

Today for some reason, Gerty was uncharacteristically nervous. It took a moment for her foot stomping and snorting to break through the fog enveloping Will's mind, but when it did, he sat up straight and felt the hairs on the back of his neck tingle. He had heard stories about packs of wolves attacking horses when other food was scarce. He reached down and touched the stock of the Winchester he kept under the seat in case he had the chance to snag a deer for the camp. He turned slowly in the wagon seat and looked over his left shoulder. To his utter amazement, sitting on a log by the edge of the clearing were three Indians and a dog, all perfectly still, watching him. There was a thin old man flanked by two women, one about the same age as the man, and the other perhaps a daughter. The women each wore knee-length dark blue coats made from trade blankets, over golden brown deer hide dresses that were really just two rectangular panels, front and back, stitched together at the shoulders and belted at the waist. All three wore high-top puckered toe moccasins lined with rabbit fur and deerskin leggings heavily adorned with beadwork and worsted braid. The old man had a red three-point trade blanket coat and a gray knitted scarf that he wore draped over his head and tied under his chin to keep his ears warm. Over that he sported a black wide-brimmed slouch hat with a turkey feather stuck in the side at a rakish angle. Before them, lying on top of the snow, were their snowshoes, arrayed next to each other front to back, creating a platform on which rested six beautiful handmade baskets. Will had set his mind to think that he and the other men of the camp were beyond the boundaries of civilization and were the only humans for miles around. To see these three souls seem to materialize out of thin air jogged his reality.

Will climbed down from the wagon and walked over to say hello. The old man stood up and met him a few steps away from where the women sat. "Name's Will Castor," said Will as he stuck out his hand. The Indian regarded the offering for a moment and then quickly reached out and grabbed Will's hand as if suddenly remembering what to do. He said something in his native tongue that was unintelligible to Will, but had a "bob" sound at the end. Will leaned forward a little and said "Bob?" into the man's face. The old Indian laughed and smiled from ear to ear and repeated "Bob!" He reached out again and took a pinch of Will's coat sleeve as he pointed to the baskets. Will stepped over and picked up the only basket that had a lid and carefully examined the strange but very pleasing design and mixture of colors. He marveled that these people could find the elements in their environment to produce such shades of blue and violet. He looked up at the younger of the two women and met her eyes. They were dark and set far apart, expressionless, like the eyes of a deer. The skin of her face, like the faces of the other two, was deep bronze and its texture leathery from constant exposure to the elements. Will had the sudden realization that these were not just people who lived in the forest; they were part of the forest. They were part of the wild and beautifully complex fabric of their environment. Will envied them and vowed then and there to become more like them.

Will reached in his coat and pulled out his pocketbook to pay for the basket. He thought this would make a dandy Christmas present for his mother. He handed the man a dollar, which he thought was a fair price. The Indian held it up and stretched it out, squinting at both sides then handed it back to Will with a shrug. He then put his fist up to his mouth and sucked in his cheeks, pretending to smoke a pipe. The first thing that occurred to Will was that the man wanted to smoke a peace pipe, but he quickly rejected that theory as ridiculous. He reached in his coat once again and pulled out a pouch of tobacco this time. The old man started bobbing his head and speaking excitedly as he opened the pouch and inhaled the wonderful aroma. Apparently the deal was struck, as the old Indian walked back and took his place on the log. The Indians passed the bag back and forth taking turns smelling the contents.

Will made two more runs for hay before dinner, and as near as he could tell, the Indians, and the dog for that matter, had not moved. He waved to them each time and they returned the courtesy, if a little deadpan. By the time he returned in the afternoon, they were gone. They had melted back into the forest and the gently falling snow had erased any evidence that they had ever been there.

Chapter 17

One unusually mild Saturday evening after supper, some of the jacks were standing around outside by one of the bean holes, smoking their pipes, trying to out-fart one another and discussing the merits of various kinds of beans. Occasionally someone would poke at the fire or toss a log on to help the cookie build up a bed of coals for the next day's beans. Will and Jerald sidled up to the fire as far away from the smoke as possible and lit their pipes.

A few minutes later Jerald started waving his hand in front of his face. "Son-of-a-bitch, that damned smoke always finds me, no matter which way the wind is blowing," he said. Will nodded, holding his breath and moving to the side.

"Well, you can say whatever you please, but I'll take the old Yellow Eye over any damn bean you can name," said one of the lumberjacks. There was a little murmur of agreement in the group.

Finally another man spoke up. "Back in '63 when I was wearing the bottoms of my feet out in the army we had a fellow in our mess that could do things with a Marafax that would scare ya—it was like magic, I tell you. Those beans were so tender you had to pour 'em onto your plate to keep from breaking 'em – and nary a fart, my friend, nary a fart."

As if on cue, someone in the group let a massive gurgling fart. There was a moment of stunned silence followed by some jostling and groaning as men tried to distance themselves from the odor that was so heavy it resisted the efforts of the wind to carry it away. "Damn it, Dave, you know you're disqualified if you shit yourself," someone said.

In the confusion, no one had noticed Bellman joining the group. He made his presence known by grabbing Dave by his collar and jerking him backwards. "Go check your drawers, you idiot," he said and pushed his way to the front closest to the fire. "Well, well, look who's here – it's Heimbaugh's gimp. Listen up, men, I'm going on record. I'm extending a special invitation to our gimp driver here to join us tomorrow in the bunkhouse for a game of Hotass. It would be real unneighborly of you not to show up now," said Bellman.

Everyone in the camp liked Will, and the men standing around the fire knew he was being called out and would likely suffer from the pending encounter. A pall fell over the group as they began to disperse. Will held his ground, and his tongue as he calmly eyeballed Bellman. This was not the reaction the big man was accustomed to. He spit into the fire and stomped off into the darkness.

"I was afraid of something like this, damn it," said Jerald.

Will squatted down and poked at the fire with a stick. "It don't matter much, Jerald. My days of getting whooped and crying 'uncle' are long past. If he don't kill me first, I'll damn sure kill him. Don't make me much difference one way or the other," said Will, staring into the fire.

Jerald just looked at his friend in silence. Finally he said, "Let's go have a nip or two and call it good."

Sunday was a free day for the lumbermen, their only day off. Most of the men, with perhaps the exception of a few of the boys, still got up early and walked over to the cook shanty for breakfast. For some, like Will, Jerald, and the cooks, there were duties to perform no matter what day it was. Will spent the morning cleaning out the stalls, feeding the animals, and generally keeping to himself. He could hear Jerald sorting through a pile of iron stock down at the other end of the stable in his shop, in preparation for replacing a runner on one of the big log sleds. At dinner time they walked over to the cook shanty and got in line for the mid-day meal. As usual, there was no conversation allowed during the meal, but Will could feel the tension in the room. Every time he looked up, two or three men would quickly look away. Jerald had noticed too and whispered to Will, "They're sizing you up to see who they'll put their money on." Will nodded and tried to calm the butterflies in his stomach.

At the appointed time, Will and Jerald walked over to the bunkhouse and entered through its only door. There was one small window next to the door and the two men stood just inside waiting for their eyes to adjust to what seemed to be total darkness after coming in from the world of white snow. Except for Sunday when the lumberjacks were not working, their days started before dawn and ended after dusk, so there was really no reason to have windows. With the exception of a small area around the door, the room was lined floor to rafters with double bunks. Every jack had a bedmate. In the center of the room was a big iron box stove with round distressed-looking stovepipe rising straight up through the roof from a collar that glowed red. Every so often the stove would give off a mighty twang as the sides oil-canned from the intense heat. It did its job too well. The air in the bunkhouse was stifling. On every rafter, on the rails of every bunk, and on the web of clothesline that was strung in every conceivable manner were hung wet garments, mostly socks. Combined with sixty or so unwashed lumbermen, all smoking pipes, the scene that emerged out of the gloom as their eyes adapted to the dim interior was like nothing Will had ever experienced before. The pipe smoke was so thick that he could see only the half of the room that he was standing in, but he was grateful for its masking effect on the deadly confluence of odors that assaulted his senses.

There were two other men besides Will and Jerald who had not taken a turn at being "it," and they drew straws to see who would start the game. A young immigrant from Germany who was working in the camp as a Chickadee won the dubious honor. Spectators took their seats on the edges of the lower bunks, some still sorting out last minute wagers. Five potential paddlers were selected by the cook and made to stand shoulder to shoulder in the middle of the room.

The pomp and ceremony marking the beginning of each round of Hotass had gotten more elaborate and certainly more ridiculous every week. The cook was somewhat of a ham anyway, so he was well suited for the role of referee. He began by bringing the victim to the center of the room and having him shake hands with each of the five paddlers. He then held up the feed sack that would be placed over the victim's head and paraded it around the room so all could see that there were no holes that would allow the unfortunate one to catch sight of his assailant. Returning to the center of the room, he motioned for silence, then asked the young man to get down on all fours facing away from the five paddlers. He placed the feed sack over the victim's head, picked up the paddle, and presented it with a flourish to the lumberjack in the center. The cook stepped back, raised his arm, and dropped a handkerchief to start the game. The rules for Hotass were few, but they were iron-clad. To limit debilitating injury, the paddle was to be gripped in only one hand and the hand must rest between the two notches on the handle. The paddler was allowed one whack and he must land it on the ass, and only the ass, of the man on the floor. If the victim could correctly identify the paddler, then that man would take his place. If not, the paddler got to sit down and someone else would take his place. The process was then repeated.

The young Chickadee received his first whack and let out a visceral howling sound, something like a dog having a nightmare. The paddler sat the paddle on the floor next to the boy and took his place back in the lineup, trying to look as innocent as possible. The cook stepped forward, pulled the boy to his feet and removed the feed sack so he could face his attacker. The crowd of spectators erupted with a slow ten count, at the end of which the victim would have to make his decision known. When the moment arrived, the boy pointed to the lumberjack on the far right of the line, and on cue the spectators yelled "NO!" at the top of their lungs. The man in the center of the line took a seat on one of the bunks and the cook pointed to Jerald to take his place. The sack was once again placed over the boy's head and he got down on his hands and knees to await the next whack. This time he did not cry out, but when the sack was removed he looked like he was close to tears. Again, he guessed the wrong man and the lumberjacks roared "NO."

The cook pointed at Will to take the place of the jack who delivered the whack and helped the boy get in position for another round. Will knew the boy had had about had all he could take. So when the cook handed him the paddle, he made up his mind to go easy. He twisted as far around as he could, holding the paddle straight up behind him and waving it in little circles to build up tension in the crowd. With exaggerated arm and leg movements he swung the paddle around quickly but held back just before the paddle contacted the seat of the boy's pants to soften the blow while still appearing to have given it all he had. Will sat the paddle on the floor next to the young man and stepped back in line next to Jerald. When the feed sack was removed the spectators once again began to count in unison. Will saw a fleeting look of confusion pass over the boy's face as his eyes darted to someone behind them. He turned to see what had caught the boy's attention and immediately knew what was happening. Bellman was sitting on the bunk directly behind Will and had given him up to the boy by nodding in his direction.

The Chickadee looked down at his feet and pointed to Will. The lumberjacks broke into wild cheering and shouts of "YES, YES." The boy had no desire to sit down or to watch the rest of the game, so as soon as Will stepped up to take his place, he wasted no time finding the door. Bellman wasted no time either, stepping up to take Will's place as a paddler without waiting to be selected by the cook. Will glanced over and saw the concern on Jerald's face, then locked eyes with Bellman. To make sure none of the uneasiness he felt inside was reflected on his face, Will grinned and nodded to the big lumberjack before turning away and getting on his hands and knees. The cook, his festive spirit now forgotten, placed the feed sack over Will's head and picked up the paddle. When he attempted to hand it to the jack standing next to Jerald, Bellman reached out quickly, intercepted the handle and jerked it out of the cook's hand. Jerald looked down and shook his head. The stage was set, and no one would stop the show.

After several minutes of posturing and taking great sweeping practice swings at Will's backside, Bellman finally took his stance. The lumberjacks lining the bunks around the room began chanting "HOTASS, HOTASS, HOTASS." Bellman swung the paddle back, coiling his body up like a spring and holding it there to let the excitement build. Just as he was starting to swing the paddle the other way, he reached up with his left arm and gripped the handle with both hands. Everyone saw the infraction, but it happened so fast no one had time to call out a warning. Bellman put everything he had into the blow, even turning the paddle slightly so that the leading edge hit first. One thing he hadn't planned on was that the edge of the paddle landed right on the end of Will's tail bone. Stars exploded in Will's head, and the force of the blow knocked him forward on his face. A collective groan went up from the lumberjacks at this ugly turn of events. Jerald wanted to rush to the aid of his friend, but he hesitated in order to see what Will would do.

Will pushed himself up off the dirt floor and paused on his hands and knees, trying to get control of his breathing and the pain of a broken tailbone. Bellman stepped over to him, dropped the paddle by his side and said, "Maybe you better stay down on the floor where you belong." He then put his boot on Will's butt and shoved him back down. That was all Jerald could take and he yelled "You dirty son-of-a-bitch" as he lunged at Bellman. Two nearby jacks quickly grabbed him by the arms and held him back. Whatever control Will had up to that point was now gone. All the lumberjacks were on their feet, some because of the foul play they had just witnessed, but most were arguing with one another over who should collect on the bets they had made in light of the broken rules. Will laid his right hand on the handle of the paddle as he slowly pushed himself back up. This time he did not pause but pulled his legs under him into a squat while watching Bellman out of the corner of his eye.

Everything bad that had happened to him since 1863 now had a face, and that face was not three feet from him. He sprang up, gripping the paddle like a bat in both hands, channeling every ounce of strength he had into his arms. Bellman had been distracted for a moment by the pandemonium that had broken out among the lumberjacks and saw what was coming too late to react. Will struck him a crushing blow with the flat blade of the paddle directly on his left ear. The lumberjacks closest to the two men stood there in stunned silence, not quite believing what had happened. The force of the blow ruptured Bellman's ear drum and upset the delicate balance mechanism of his inner ear. The cartilage of his outer ear was torn in several places and blood was streaming down the side of his face into his beard. He turned slowly, opening and closing his mouth and rolling his eyes. He tried to take a step and then just crumpled to the floor on his hands and knees.

Will's demons had been uncorked, and they were not yet satisfied. With the intent to finish off his enemy, he lined up on Bellman's neck, raised the paddle up over his head, edge-first as if he were going to decapitate the man, and started a downward swing. Suddenly, as the paddle passed over Will's head on its way down, it stopped dead and big arms engulfed him in a bear hug from behind. "No, no, no, no, stop now. Ve don't kill in this camp," said Ole into Will's ear. The big Swede had slipped quietly into the bunkhouse to make sure the game didn't get out of control, and it was lucky for Bellman that he had. Will continued to struggle as Ole spun him around face to face. His eyes were wild and bent on murder, but he was no match for the camp boss. "You stop now or I vill knock you in da head, get me?" said Ole. Bellman was still confused and trying to stand up. When it looked as though he might succeed, Jerald put his boot on the man's hip and tipped him over like a big snapping turtle. Ole took the paddle away from Will and handed it to the cook. "No more Hotass today," he said to the room as he pushed through the door with his arm still gripping Will.

Chapter 18

In the days following the confrontation with Bellman, Will nursed his broken tailbone, which mostly meant not sitting on it any more than was absolutely necessary and killing the pain with liberal amounts of cheap whisky in the evening before going to sleep. He arranged horse blankets on the spring seat of the tote wagon in a way that would elevate his body enough to keep the broken bone from touching the hard wooden seat. The lumberjacks had a newfound respect for Will; whether it was because he had guts enough to stand up to Bellman, or because they thought he was a little crazy was unclear. For Will, there was no victory. The incident only confirmed what he feared more than anything else – that the war had permanently changed him into someone who could take the life of another human being without much purpose. He knew deep inside that he would have put Bellman to death if Ole had not intervened. Meanwhile, Bellman had lost his grip on Camp Number Four. No one much cared what the loudmouth jack said or did. He kept to himself and did his job, as Ole assured him he would do, unless he wanted to walk back to Saginaw through the woods. Whenever he and Will found themselves in the same vicinity, there was a lot of spitting and glaring, but nothing more serious than that.

Christmas came and went, with little to mark its passing but a few carols sung to a mournful harmonica and slightly off-key fiddle. No one knew more than the first verses of even the old favorites. The men who had families took the holiday the hardest, but even the single men were pretty quiet. The cook and his gang spent all day making pies, and at supper every man got to take a whole one for himself. There was dried apple, vinegar pie, and shoepac pie to choose from. Most of the men were relieved when the uneasy one-day observance was over and the work of turning the great trees into sixteen-foot logs for the sawmills in Saginaw resumed. Every day at least four big sleds piled high with logs would be pulled along the iced road by teams of draft horses and dumped at the banking ground to await the spring drive. By now there were hundreds of thousands of board feet of virgin white pine ready for the journey down the river.

About halfway through January, the Tittabawassee finally froze over, putting an end to regular re-supply until the spring thaw. It also meant that there would be no letter from Mollie, at least until he could get to the company office in Saginaw. Will and Jerald had developed a deep friendship over the many cold nights sitting in front of their ugly little stove, sharing whisky and their life stories. Jerald was careful not to bring up the war, afraid that it might spark one of his friend's terrible nightmares. One night, though, after they had polished off a jar of "honey," Jerald asked Will how he had come by that scar across his face. Will was quiet for a bit, the flickering yellow flames from the cracked door of the stove reflecting off his face as he stared into the fire and replayed the memory. Finally he gathered himself and told Jerald the story. When he was finished, Jerald looked over at Will and said, "Tell me more about Mollie." Will glanced over at his friend and smiled. "She's just a little slip of a thing, but damn if she ain't a firecracker. Damn, she sure is pretty too. She can cook and sew a man a suit of clothes better'n store bought – and drive a spring wagon as pretty as you please. I'm going down to Tennessee to look her up once we get paid off," said Will. Jerald gave a couple of understanding nods but was wondering what Ben Heimbaugh might think about his prodigy taking off on a wild goose chase after a woman.

That night Will lay awake remembering the moment when Mollie's face was mere inches in front of his own, the beauty of her face, borne not only by skin and bone, but by the force of who she was. Her hazel eyes darted quick glances down at his lips, wondering if he was about to kiss her; but he did not kiss her. That was the moment.

By the end of the month, the lumberjacks were in a race with Mother Nature. Even though the days were getting longer, February would go quickly and in March they would begin looking for a thaw. Fed by the run-off from melting snow, the river would rise, throw off her cover of ice and snatch the stored logs from the banking ground, putting an end to the cutting and marking the beginning of the spring drive. There had been a few warm sunny days when the jacks worked in their shirt sleeves, but it was just a taste, and soon the winter came back in spades. Most days, Will and Jerald lingered for a bit to watch the work after taking their dinner with the lumberjacks out at the cutting. On the forties they had worked so far there were liberal amounts of mature oak and beech still standing to soften the visual effect of the logging. They were working an area now that was made up entirely of white pine growing close together—a lumberman's dream, but a shocking sight when the trees were gone and there was nothing but slash, which, come summer, would be ripe for fire. The useless tops and branches of the mighty trees were so thick you had to pick your way through, and nothing was left standing taller than a man.

The first signs of spring came up on a stiff warm wind from the southwest and put the lumberjacks on notice. The slowly rising river pushed on the ice from below and the howling wind pushed down from above, breaking it into huge chunks with a rumble that sounded like distant artillery. Fights among the lumberjacks became fewer and farther between, even though fighting was just about their favorite pastime. Everyone knew that the most dangerous part of their job, herding the logs down the river, was still ahead. At least as river hogs they would be getting more pay and be headed in the right direction – toward the saloons and bawdy houses of Saginaw and Bay City. Even before the last chunks of ice had cleared the Tittabawassee and been picked up by the Saginaw River on their way out to the bay, the wanigan scow made its appearance at the landing and kicked preparations for the coming log drive into high gear. The wanigan was a floating kitchen and headquarters for the drive. Tote road trips to the landing were once again part of Will's daily routine, only this time supplies were moving the other way. When the level of the river was almost to the logs at the banking ground, the wanigan would be poled upstream so it could then follow the logs down to the mills, furnishing meals for the men along the way.

The lumberjacks, most of whom considered it unhealthy to bathe more than once a year, were beginning to give some thought to personal hygiene. The bane of all the men was the louse, body louse or crab louse; they all were hosts to both varieties. In the dead of winter one of the most popular non-contact sports for the men involved pitting a body louse against a crab louse in tournaments where the contestants would fight to the death. Now that breaking camp and returning to civilization was imminent, it was time to get rid of these colonies of freeloaders. Moving dandruff, some called them. The preferred method was to drop one's drawers into a big cast iron cauldron of boiling water and poke them down with a stick. Occasionally someone would take a long piece of curled bark and skim the gray scum of scalded lice off the surface of the water.

A day before the logs at the banking ground were to be rolled into the river, Will and Jerald had packed up their personal belongings and moved aboard the wanigan. Jerald brought along his rolling tool box, complete with the remaining jars of "honey" wrapped in extra pairs of heavy wool socks for safekeeping. Once the drive started, they would have little to do but observe and perhaps lend a hand poling the scow around bends in the river, and a little nip now and then would be in order. The warm, dry southern wind that had reduced the snow cover so dramatically over the last few days had finally begun to swing around to the northwest and take on the smell of rain. Where the winding tote road ran north and south, brief interludes of sunshine had burned through to the dark matted leaves of the forest floor, leaving ribbons of silver ice in the ruts made by the runners of Will's supply wagon.

Sometime during the night a steady drizzle had set in, and it showed no sign of letting up at dawn when they poled the wanigan upstream past the banking ground and secured it to a big cedar that was hanging out over the water. Will and Jerald sat on the tool box and leaned back against the front wall of the floating cook shack to watch the lumberjacks-turned-river hogs roll the big logs into the swollen river.

Ole had divided the men into three groups according to their experience and ability. The first group was made up of the most experienced men. They would ride the logs at the head of the drive and be responsible for dealing with any logjams that might occur. The second group would space themselves out along the river and make sure the logs kept moving freely downstream. The last group was made up of the younger men, and their job was to retrieve logs that may have strayed into backwaters or swamps. That usually meant wading in waist-deep, frigid water and once wet, they would stay that way until they got to Saginaw. The river hogs were fed four times a day, if they could get back to the wanigan. If not, they would eat what they had with them in their haversacks. At night the men slept on the bank of the river wherever they were when it got too dark to work. It was hard and dangerous work, but it paid four dollars a day.

The Tittabawassee was an easy river to drive compared to some. It was deep and wide, even when it was not over its banks with spring runoff. When all the logs had been floated away from the banking ground, they filled the river solid from bank to bank for three miles. It was like a great sluggish snake rumbling slowly along, men armed with peaveys and spiked boots leaping here and there, or running along the riverbanks, always poking and prodding. Will was fascinated watching these quick-witted, agile men herd the big logs down the river, and he was not alone. As they drew closer to Saginaw, they began to see people drawn to the riverbank by the distant thunder of the logs; old and young alike were captivated by the drama passing before them.

It took three days for the first logs from camp Number Four to reach the sorting boom where the Tittabawassee emptied into the Saginaw River. The boom company employed nearly a hundred men whose job it was to check the end of every log for a trademark, sort the logs by company, raft them together, and deliver them to their respective sawmills on the Saginaw. To accomplish this they cordoned off the river with two long booms made by chaining sixteen-foot logs together end-to-end and securing them to each riverbank. The other end was anchored to one of two log cribs filled with stones in the center of the river. There was just enough space between the cribs to allow a scow to pass, and of course several pine logs at a time. Just beyond the boom there were areas like corrals to keep the logs separate once they had been sorted. When the logs started piling up at the boom, the river hogs handed over their charges to the boom company and became free men. It would take a day for the front office to settle accounts, and then they could draw the pay that had been accumulating all winter. Usually a bath, shave, and change of clothes were next on the list, and then they would join the jacks from the other camps in the Saginaw valley and proceed to dismantle the town. The citizens of Saginaw would usually just lie low until the jacks ran out of money. The local economy depended on the bawdy houses and saloons being able to separate the lumberjacks from their newfound wealth, and it usually took only a few weeks.

As soon as the wanigan nosed into the riverbank at the end of the packed logs, Jerald and Will shouldered their duffle bags and jumped ashore. There were a couple of water taxis tied up just past the boom, and they hustled over there hoping to get a seat before the jacks took them all. Jerald thought they should go straight to Jerry's Barbershop on Lapeer Street and get a jump on a haircut and bath so they would be ready to go out on the town. On their way down river they passed several sawmills that already had their millponds full of logs. River traffic was heavy, with raft after raft of cork pine moving down to the mills and steam tugs pulling schooners up from the bay to be loaded with the freshly sawn planks destined for the New York or Ohio markets. The water taxi coasted up to a rickety looking dock and dropped them at the foot of Potter Street without tying up. Jerald pointed across the street at Koch's and said, "Let's go there first. I need a new shirt." Will nodded, thinking he could use one too, and they struck out with their duffle bags on their shoulders.

After spending the early afternoon at Jerry's getting a shave, haircut, and bath, they took another water taxi down to Heimbaugh and Sons and checked in at the boardinghouse. They paid their respects to the landlady and got a room on the second floor with two small beds and a dresser. They stayed there just long enough to drop their gear before heading back to town.

On Jerald's recommendation they entered a saloon called the Slanty Shanty about half way down the three-hundred block of Water Street, across from Coleman and Harvey's Livery. The origin of the name was immediately apparent as they stepped through the vestibule past a very big man who was guarding the door. The main room was long, front to back maybe fifty feet, and narrow. On the left side was a rather plain looking bar, its wood dark from a perpetual fog of tobacco smoke. The upper half of the long mirror that hung on the wall behind it was cloudy and streaked, clean only as high as the tallest barman could reach. From the front of the bar to the opposite wall, the pitch of the floor dropped a good twelve inches, making it almost impossible for a man to walk normally, drunk or sober. The sure-footed river hogs wearing spiked boots had a definite advantage here. In fact, the wooden floors of all of the businesses along Water Street bore the pockmarks of corked boots, as they were called. Toward the back of the room there was a battered billiard table. On one end the legs were adjusted as low as possible, and on the other end the legs needed the addition of stone blocks to make the table level. As the night wore on and the jacks began feeling the effects of their over-indulgence, the slanted floor would become more and more problematic. Passed-out lumberjacks tended to collect at the base of the wall on the low side. This particular establishment was one of the few with a dance floor on the second story. During brief lulls in the noise, they could hear faint piano music, shrill feminine laughter, and the creaking of floor joists coming from above.

It was a little past seven in the evening, and the place was packed with lumberjacks that had been drinking hard since shortly before noon, when the doors opened. Will and Jerald inched their way forward into the room and stood against the wall opposite the bar while their eyes adjusted to the dark interior. The place smelled of lemon, whisky, and tobacco smoke, with perhaps just a hint of vomit mixed in, and their shoes stuck to the floor from something spilled. Will noticed a small chalkboard hanging from the front door frame, announcing "BIMBO AND BEER, 10 cents till 9:00." He backhanded his friend's arm and pointed to the sign. "Explains the sticky floor and the lemon," he said. Jerald nodded and scanned the room. The jacks were two deep at the bar, and there were no empty tables in sight. There was, however, one table supporting the heads of two passed-out jacks that looked promising. Jerald motioned for Will to follow, and he eased through the crowd toward the underutilized table. Without batting an eye, he pulled the chair away from the table and tipped it sideways, pouring its occupant out onto the floor. Will shook his head and laughed and then did the same to the other man.

They had been sitting down for only a few minutes when a woman in a traditional German barmaid's outfit with enormous breasts spilling out over the top of her low-cut blouse swayed up to their table a little unsteadily and plopped herself down in Jerald's lap. "Good Lord, Jerald, honey, I have missed you in the worst way!" she said. "Why, as soon as I heard that Heimbaugh's logs were starting to hit the boom I said to myself, that big sweet fat butt boy Jerald will be coming for me soon. I'm so aflutter I ain't had a bite of food in two days."

"It don't look like you missed too many meals to me, Sugar Plum," said Jerald, slapping her generous rear. "Will, I'd like to introduce you to Patty from Cincinatti. Patty, this is my good friend Will, a dangerous man with a paddle."

"Oh, Honey!" said Patty. "I like the sound of that!"

"Be careful there, woman. When Will paddles you, you stay paddled," said Jerald. Will returned her smile but was having trouble tearing his eyes away from her ample cleavage. Jerald threw his head back and laughed, "Will, I thought you had better manners than that. I think he likes your titties, Patty. Be sociable, Sugar Plum, and take those big girls out so my friend here can have a proper look." Will could not believe what Jerald had said, and he was even more stunned when the woman complied, as if it were the most common thing in the world. After pulling down the front of her well-worn white blouse to expose her breasts, she squared up facing Will and began rhythmically arching and relaxing her back so that soon she had her amazing breasts rotating in opposite directions. Jerald laughed again at the look on Will's face. "As you can see, a very talented lady," he said. Will just nodded and continued to study the woman. What at first he had thought was some kind of feminine hair decoration on the back of her head was actually pieces of straw. Since it wasn't too likely that she had seen the inside of a barn recently, he surmised it must be from a worn straw-filled tick on her working bed. Further inspection of her breasts revealed puzzling pale flesh-colored patches around each aureole. After a moment, he grimaced as he realized that the odd discolorations represented the only clean places on her breasts, made by the hit-or-miss suckling of her intoxicated clientele.

As the evening progressed, the noise level in the saloon and Jerald and Patty's preoccupation with one another conspired to isolate Will. He wasn't complaining, though. The shots of bimbo and mugs of beer had done their work. Jerald, sensing Will's mood, spoke into Patty's ear.

"My friend needs some distraction, Sugar Plum."

"He seems awful quiet, Jerald honey," said Patty with a note of concern in her tone.

"He had a bad time of it in the war." said Jerald. Patty was thoughtful for a few minutes and then said, "I know just the right one for him." With that, she wiggled out of Jerald's lap, stood up, and extended her hand across the table to Will. "Come on, Will," she said, "I got someone I want you to meet." Will stood and let himself be led through the packed crowd of lumberjacks to the dim hallway beyond the billiard table. She went to the third door on the left and pushed it open without knocking. Will surveyed the small room over Patty's shoulder. There was an iron bed frame supporting a bare canvas tick, just as Will had guessed earlier. No point in using sheets when most of the clientele didn't even bother to take their boots off. A single kerosene lamp, along with a wash basin and pitcher, sat on a dresser by the wall on the left. A straight-back chair shared the wall on the right with the headboard of the bed. A young woman, Will guessed maybe nineteen or twenty, stood in front of the dresser, methodically sponging her forearms and hands with a wadded-up wash rag. She looked up suddenly when she heard the door open, and Will caught the shadow of alarm as it passed quickly across her face before it was replaced by a shallow smile. "Someone here I want you to meet, Sal," said Patty. "His name is Will and he's a real special guest tonight. You take good care of him." Sal nodded and with a pat on Will's back, Patty retreated down the darkened hallway to rejoin Jerald.

Will stepped through the door and closed it behind him. "Hello, Will," said Sal with a somewhat stiff familiarity. She smiled at Will, but there was only hopelessness in her eyes. She was dressed only in her underclothes, a white cotton chemise trimmed with blue ribbon and black cotton stockings with little bows at the top that seemed to stay up on their own.

"'Evening, Sal," replied Will, trying to muster his confidence. He looked down at the floor and kept passing the brim of his hat through his hands to calm his nerves. "How much?" he said, a little too quickly. Sal finished drying her hands and shot him a questioning look. "For a poke, I mean."

"Oh," said Sal, "I thought everyone knew this was a two-dollar house." Will just nodded and started digging in the inside pocket of his coat for his wallet. "You can pay me after," she said matter-of-factly.

Sal picked up the wash basin and carried it over to the chair. The worn caning in the seat of the chair cradled the bowl nicely. Smiling a little more sincerely this time, she motioned for him to come to her where she sat on the bed wringing out her only washcloth. Will took off his jacket and turned away to set it on the floor next to the dresser. When he looked up he caught the girl's reflection in the mirror hanging on the wall over the dresser. In the unguarded moment she was leaning forward with her elbows on her knees, dangling the rag from two fingers and staring at the blank wall across from her. The look on her face was so washed out that Will could not go through with it. He picked up his jacket, walked over, and sat on the bed beside her. When she turned to face him, he thought for a moment she was going to cry. "What's the matter? Am I not pretty enough?" she said. Will pulled four dollars out of his pocketbook and handed it to her. "You're pretty, all right," he said. "I just had too much to drink, is all." He stood up and walked out the door, closing it behind him.

That was Will's one and only experience with sporting women. In the remaining few days that he was in Saginaw, his drinking excursions with Jerald took on a familiar pattern. The two men would begin the evening playing cards and drinking at one of the saloons on Water Street, and then they would have some supper and more drinks, usually at Herman's. The next stop would be at a saloon with singing and women or maybe Bordwell's show house, and of course more drinking. Jerald would eventually find a suitable woman and disappear for a while, and Will would find a dark corner and drink until he was unconscious. When Jerald got tired or ran out of money, he would look for his friend and either find him sprawled across a table or on the sidewalk in front of the establishment, depending on how understanding the barman was. Jerald would pick him up, throw him over his shoulder, and stagger back to the boardinghouse to sleep it off.

On their first morning back in Saginaw, Jerald and Will ate a light breakfast in the dining room of the boarding house, in deference to the hangovers they were nursing and then walked down to the mill office to collect their pay. When Will got up to the window, the clerk asked for his name, then turned and searched a large array of pigeonholes that took up nearly one entire wall of the office. When he found what he was looking for, the clerk retrieved a little bundle of envelopes and slid them under the glass window, dismissing Will by looking over his shoulder for the next man in line. Will nodded his thanks absentmindedly and stepped aside thumbing through his mail. There were two letters from home, an envelope containing a company order that represented his pay, and a note from Ben Heimbaugh requesting his presence at the company office on Water Street. A little crestfallen, he stuffed the lot into the inside pocket of his coat and retreated through the front door of the office to wait for Jerald.

"Didn't make as much as you figured, or didn't get a letter from your southern belle?" said Jerald as he joined up with his friend. Will's face was a pretty easy read. Will just shot him a dirty look as they started walking toward the taxi landing.

Chapter 19

Will stepped through the door of Heimbaugh and Sons Lumber Company front office to the tinkle of the little bell hanging from the transom over the door. He had gained enough experience over the winter to realize how foolish he must have appeared the first time he was in this office looking for work. Clarence seemed to remember him and motioned for him to take a seat on the bench against the wall. Will sat his hat beside him and nervously flipped through the pages of his journal, trying to steel himself for whatever was to come. Fortunately he didn't have long to wait. Will heard a muffled conversation grow louder and take on a confrontational tone as the door to Mr. Heimbaugh's office opened. A short fat man with long greasy hair and pockmarked complexion came quickly down the aisle and pushed his way roughly through the section of hinged counter that gave access to the back offices. He was wearing an ill-fitting black topcoat that looked to be new, and he made a big show of patting down his expensive beaver top hat. Mr. Heimbaugh was a few feet behind him, and as the front door swung shut behind the man, he muttered "asshole" to no one in particular. He looked over at Will and waved him in as he spun on his heel and retreated back to his office.

Heimbaugh gestured Will towards a chair and settled in behind his desk, visibly struggling to rein in his temper. "Goddamn land speculator. Sold me some minutes last fall that weren't worth a doodly shit, and he's got the brass to come in here and try it again." Will shook his head as if he too were outraged, even though he wasn't exactly sure what "minutes" were or how badly Heimbaugh had been corkscrewed.

"Well, my friend, I hear good things about you," said Mr. Heimbaugh, finally getting control of himself. "Ole tells me that between you and Jerald, the animals were kept in tiptop shape. He says you're a quick study and reliable in all matters. Not bad with a paddle either, I hear." Heimbaugh threw the last thing out there to see how Will would react. Will pursed his lips and nodded, almost imperceptibly, but the sadness in his eyes told his boss what he wanted to know. "Tom Bellman is an arrogant son-of-a-bitch that had that whoopin' you gave him coming. The fact that the one who gave it to him is smaller than him and has a bad leg won't sit well forever. You watch yourself. He'll have another go at you someday." Will nodded and squirmed in his chair.

"OK, let's get on with our business," said Heimbaugh. "First of all, do you still want to be a land looker for me?" Will straightened up in the chair and said, "Yes sir, that is my wish."

"Good. First things first." He reached over his desk and offered his hand to Will. Will took it and said, "Thank you Mr. Heimbaugh. I surely do appreciate your kindness. Especially for not throwing my sorry ass out of your office last fall."

"I'll admit the thought crossed my mind," said Heimbaugh with a grin. "And don't thank me yet. There's a lot you still need to learn about this business. First off, you can start by calling me Ben. As a land looker, your expenses will be paid for, but you will be more like a partner and get a percentage of the take from the timber you find. A good looker can make some real money these days. I'm going to send you out for a few weeks with Henry Bolton, a man who used to work for my father. He's an old hand and will teach you everything you need to know about finding good trees, figuring board feet, and marking their location on a map so we know exactly what we're getting when we go to the land office. Write everything down. When you finally go out alone, there won't be anyone to answer a question for you. You with me so far?" Will nodded as he dug in his pocket for a pencil. "Day after tomorrow I'll send Henry over to meet you at the company store. He'll help you get outfitted. Just sign for what you need. Make your plans and go look at some timber. If everything goes well, I'll send you out on a short trip by yourself and then you will be on your own. Any questions?"

Will thought for a moment then said, "No, I guess not, Ben. I'll be waiting for Henry day after next, bright and early." Will stood up to leave. "Oh, I almost forgot. This came for you a couple of weeks ago," said Ben as he pulled a letter from the top drawer of his desk and handed it to Will. "Thought I might as well hold it here for you, since I knew you'd be in." Will glanced down at it and immediately recognized Mollie's handwriting. Ben came around his desk, put his hand on Will's shoulder, and walked him to the door. "As one old soldier to another, Will, leave the war and the whisky behind. Where you're going it'll get you killed." There was an awkward silence and then he said, "Good luck, my friend," and offered his hand. Will was taken aback by Ben's directness, and the fact that he had taken note of his drinking habits, but managed to disguise his surprise and thanked him for the advice as he shook his hand.

The late spring day still held the bite of winter, thanks to the cold air over the icy water of Saginaw Bay that followed the river inland, and fanned out over the broad valley. Will walked for a while, with the unopened letter from Mollie in his coat pocket, looking for a quiet, sunny place out of the wind where he could be alone. He finally came to an alley between a mercantile and a Lutheran church on Water Street just past German. One side was in shadow and the other in bright sun. He leaned against the building on the sunny side and slid down until his back rested against the warm foundation stones.

My Dear Will,

What a wonderful surprise to receive yours of last January. I am so happy to know that you survived the terrible events that gripped the country when we first met. I have often thought of you since those trying days and hoped you would find the peace you so deserve. Mother was never well again after dear brother Jack met his fate and she passed away year before last still watching out the window for Casper to come home from the war. Pap could not be consoled, though we all tried so desperately, and he would only sit hour after hour and stare out the back window at the overgrown fields he worked for so many years and raised a family on. He followed Mother last spring and by the grace of Him who rules over all things he is once again with my heavenly family, brothers Jack, Thomas, Casper, David, sister Sarah and Mother. Yes my dear Will, the war dealt my family a heavy blow. In the spring of '65 an old schoolmate who was raised on a neighboring farm came home from the army and asked for my hand in holy matrimony. We exchanged our vows in the fall and reside just up the road from the old farm at his ancestral home. Micajer is a good man and we are making a new life together. Brother Thomas's two boys were left orphaned by the sudden death of his widow Jane and we have taken them in as our own. They are so young and spirited! They have a good measure of "Dean" in their blood. I cannot keep up some days. Dear Will, I will always remember you and hold a special place for you in my heart. Your selfless deed that terrible night long ago saved me from certain ruin and I shall always be in your debt. May our Gracious Heavenly Father keep you safe in all matters. Please, oh please Will, drop me a line from time to time so I may know you are well.

Your devoted friend for ever,
Mollie Troxler

Will folded the letter up and carefully tucked it back into its envelope. He bowed his head, closed his eyes and breathed out long and deep, feeling one more dream run out of him and drift downwind like the little cloud of his warm breath on the cold air. At least his path was clear now. He sat there for a few more minutes and then opened his eyes and let Mollie go.

Chapter 20

The Heimbaugh and Sons company store was just west of the mill yard facing the river. In the beginning, it had carried only things the lumberjacks and mill workers needed: boots, overalls, gloves, coats, hats, tobacco. As the mill grew, the variety did too. It was now a well-stocked general store serving not only workers but also their families. If you worked for the company, you could buy anything from basic foodstuffs to clothes for your children with just a signature. Will stood with his hands in his pockets looking out the big storefront window and down the road leading up from the river. Henry Bolton would come up this road and he wanted to look him over before they met face to face. Instead, unexpectedly, he came face to face with himself reflected in the glass. The person looking back at him was dressed like everyone else, pac boots, flannel shirt, Mackinaw coat, but it still made him feel uncomfortable, and he was starting to turn away when he spotted a lone figure coming up the far end of the road.

The man who walked through the front door of the company store was not at all what Will expected. In fact he was almost certain that this man was not Henry Bolton, the land looker. The man came to a halt just inside the door, shrugged out of his knapsack and swung it around to the floor in front of him, pulled off his expensive looking deerskin gloves, the kind with a trap door built into the palms, and scanned the store. When his gaze landed on Will he took a second to look him up and down before speaking. "You Will Castor?" Will was still a little off his game by the man's appearance but managed to get out a "Yes, sir." Henry was turned out impeccably from head to toe. In fact, he looked like he had just stepped out of an English manor house to go fox hunting. His boots were not new but were shiny with mink oil and overlaid with spotless tan canvas gators that ended just below the knee. He wore fine dark brown wool pants and a brown and beige hound's-tooth waistcoat over a white duck shirt buttoned at the neck. Over it all he had a tan mid-length heavy canvas field coat with huge side pockets and a leather inset at the right shoulder to take the recoil of a rifle or shotgun. His hat was some alpine style with a big black feather sprouting from the left side.

"Henry Bolton," he said, extending his hand. Will gave him a firm handshake and said "Pleased to meet you, sir."

"What's the matter, son, you never seen a gentleman before?"

Will quickly pulled himself together and said "Oh, sorry, Mr. Bolton, just not what I was expecting is all."

"Well, be that as it may, let's start right out by clearing the air. I'm not doing this for the money. I don't need the money. I'm doing a favor for my friend, Ben Heimbaugh. Don't let these fancy duds fool you. I've forgot more about living off the land than you will probably ever know. I can teach you a lot and save you making a lot of stupid mistakes – but you got to listen. You watch everything I do and learn during the day and then write it down and ask questions before we turn in at night. Oh, and my name is Henry, not 'sir' or 'Mr. Bolton.' Fair enough?"

"Fair enough, Henry," said Will with a grin. He liked this man already. Henry frowned at Will's response and mumbled "Fucking young'uns" under his breath as he turned away.

Will followed Henry to the back of the store, where a big man in a canvas apron was filling an empty space on the shelf from an open crate on the floor. "Morning, Henry," he said. "What brings you around this fine day?"

"Morning, Tom. I'm fixing to make a land looker out of this greenhorn and he needs the whole caboodle. You got any of those engineer's compasses left?"

"Sure do, Henry. Hang on a second and I'll dig one out."

"OK. We're in no hurry. We're going to be out about fourteen days, so we'll each need fifteen pounds of corn meal and the same of salt pork. You a coffee drinker, Will?"

"I need a cup in the morning to get me going," said Will. "A pound each of coffee, then, ground," said Henry. Tom yelled at someone in the back room to start grinding a couple pounds of coffee. Henry tossed his list on the counter and said, "Here, Tom, you can read this as well as I can. That leg set you back any, as far as walking or carrying a pack goes? Them boots comfortable enough to walk in all day?"

"I've had 'em for almost a year and they serve pretty well. The leg is a little awkward, but I manage," said Will, a bit defensively.

"No call to get your nose out of joint, son. I'm asking for your own good. You'll be one sad sack after a day's hike if those boots start rubbing wrong."

"Sorry, Henry, I get a little put off when someone points out my bad leg." Henry looked hard at Will, in the eye, as if he were trying to decide something, but then turned away and strolled down the counter looking over the merchandise.

It was early afternoon when Will and Henry finished up at the company store, and before parting ways they agreed to meet the next morning at the land office in town. That would give Will a chance to finish packing and go over his plans with Jerald. After supper at the boardinghouse, they played a few rounds of five-card draw with a couple of jacks in the front room of the house. Jerald pretended to be too tired to go out for a drink, thinking it would not answer for Will to be hung over on his first morning with Henry. When they finally retired for the evening, they sat on their beds and talked as they shared a nightcap. "That Henry Bolton is a crusty old fart," said Jerald, "but you won't find a better man. If I was you, I'd surely leave the whisky behind. I've seen him rip snorting a few times, but he won't abide it out in the woods."

Will nodded and said "I've been given that some thought and I think you're right."

"I've decided to get into the livery business, Will. Harvey of Coleman and Harvey's is selling out and moving on. They're looking for a smithy anyway, so I figure I'm in the right place at the right time. I got enough saved to make a go of it."

"Damn, Jerald, that's big news. Congratulations!" said Will.

"I been thinking of giving up those winters out in the woods for a couple of years. Just couldn't make it work until now. I'll have quarters up over the office, and of course you'll stay with me when you're in town. I'll move your gear down there too when I leave here, so when you get back make sure you check there first before coming all the way out here."

Will stood up and turned his blanket down. "I'm happy for you, my friend."

The next morning Henry was standing in front of the land office when Will walked up. "Morning, Henry" said Will.

"Morning, Will. You planning on going hunting or land looking?" said Henry, referring to the lever action Winchester Will was carrying.

"I'm a pretty fair shot and I figure I might pick us up some local fare for supper along the way."

"Well, you may regret every pound that thing weighs once we start out. Just promise me you won't take a shot at a bear with that peashooter. I ain't as quick on my feet as I used to be. OK, here's lesson number one. When we go in there," he said, tilting his head toward the door of the land office, "we're going to be very cagey about where we're going and what we're about. We're only interested in two sections up around Coleman, but we'll buy plat maps and survey notes for four, just in case someone has the clerk in their back pocket. Understand? You can't trust anyone, and it's a hell of a lot of trouble to go through, just to come back and find some speculator has gotten tipped off and bought up the very sections you just looked at. Just keep your mouth shut and watch how I handle this." With that, Henry pushed open the door and stepped inside with Will right behind him.

After exchanging pleasantries and introducing Will around the office, they got down to business. Henry motioned for Will to follow, and he stepped over to a big map of the lower peninsula of Michigan that showed all the townships as set down in the original government linear land survey of the 1840s. In just a few minutes Will was able to pick up the logic of how the townships were numbered: The tier number, north or south of an east-west base line and the range number, east or west of a north-south baseline. The way the townships were further divided was a little harder to grasp, but once Henry explained it as divided into numbered square-mile sections arranged as the ox plows, Will saw the pattern right away. Henry pointed to the sections they were interested in and had Will write down the information to give to the clerk. They also purchased field notes for all the areas they were going to look at, as well as a smaller version of the big wall map showing all the townships. Will would keep that one with him on all his trips and make notations of roads, landmarks, Indian villages, and trails.

It was just a short walk from the land office to the depot at the foot of Potter Street, and when they arrived the train was already sitting next to the platform with steam up. This train was, as most were during this time period, a combination of passenger and freight cars. Will and Henry each bought a ticket to Coleman from the agent inside the depot and then walked out on the platform and swung their heavy packs down on a bench to wait out the departure time. "I usually have a word with the engineer before I board, let him know where I'd like to get off, if he's willing to stop the train for a few minutes," said Henry. "There he is now—let's go catch him."

Will and Henry stepped off the platform and headed toward the front of the train. "Morning, Lloyd," said Henry.

Lloyd looked up from squirting oil on one of the main crank pins and said "Well, Lord God Almighty if it ain't Henry Bolton! I thought you died, Henry. Ain't seen you in a coon's age." The men shook hands warmly and Henry introduced Will to the old engineer.

"Damn, Lloyd, I'm surprised that they still trust you to drive one of these big ass contraptions," said Henry. Lloyd pointed the oil can at Henry and threatened to give him a squirt but then relented when Henry put up his hands in mock surrender.

"So where is it to this time, my friend?" said Lloyd. Henry pulled out a small railroad map of Michigan, twirled Will around so he was facing the other way and pressed the map against his back while he and Lloyd studied it.

"We're looking at a few sections about five miles this side of Coleman. We'd be real obliged if you could let us off right in this area," he said, pointing at the map. "It would save us a few steps. We're going to be out about two weeks and we'll either flag you down or catch you in Coleman for the trip back."

"All right, gentlemen, I'll slow down to a crawl and watch for you to jump off. Be ready 'cause I can't wait."

Will and Henry started back toward the platform. "Thanks, Lloyd," said Henry over his shoulder. Suddenly he stopped and yelled back at the engineer, "I'll buy you dinner when we get back. You bring your wife and I'll get some other old whore and we'll make a fine time of it."

Lloyd waved and turned back to the engine. Suddenly his head snapped up as he realized what Henry had said. He shouted an oath and started running after them, blazing away with his oil can.

"Give Margaret my best, Lloyd," said Henry as they shouldered their packs and quickly hopped aboard an empty boxcar.

True to his word, Lloyd started slowing the train at the prearranged place, prompting Will and Henry to check their packs and prepare to disembark. The two men sat on the floor in the big open door of the boxcar with their legs dangling over the edge, waiting for the right moment. An impatient toot from the steam engine's whistle spurred them over the side without mishap, and Lloyd answered their waves with one long blast as he opened the throttle.

"Have a seat, Will, and let's figure out where we're going," said Henry. They both sat down on the ballast stones and leaned back against their packs. The receding noise of the train wheels on the rails had diminished to intermittent faint clicks as they studied Henry's plat map.

"Back in the '40s when the official government survey of Michigan was done, they placed a post at the corner of each section. I presume you know that a section is a square mile." Will nodded and Henry continued. "At each corner they also blazed two trees, one north or south, one east or west, pointing to the corner. That way if something happened to the post you could still figure out where it was supposed to be. The blaze carried the township name and section number. If you can find a section corner you can look at your map and know exactly where you are. Then, it's just a matter of following a line with your compass to get where you want to be. You know what a blaze is?"

"It's where a patch of bark has been skinned off a tree and numbers carved into the wood," said Will. "I've seen them before when I used to camp up around here before the war."

"Good. Well, they're hard to see at first, but as you get more experience they'll start jumping out at you. Well, I guess that's enough jawing for now. Let's go find a section line and see what we got. I always walk forty-five minutes and rest fifteen. That gives me about a mile and a half of ground covered in an hour." Will stood up, shouldered his pack, and fell in behind Henry, all the time working back over in his mind what he had just learned.

Soon after leaving the railroad tracks they picked up their first section line and turned due east, intending to follow it to a corner post. When Henry had first mentioned his routine of walking for forty-five minutes and resting for fifteen, Will had passed it off as being the easy pace of an old man, but as their fifteen-minute break drew near, he desperately wanted to sit down and shed his pack. The short Winchester carbine he carried seemed to get heavier with every step.

"OK, Will, I figure that's close enough. Let's take a break." With that, Henry swung his pack to the ground and eased down next to it.

"How you doing with that leg? You need me to slow down a bit?"

Will shot him a dirty look as he sank to the ground.

"I reckon not," he said.

"Well, that first corner ought to be just up ahead. We'll get us a good fix and then beeline a compass heading to the first land we're going to have a look at. Two and a half, maybe three more hours, before we make camp."

154

Will dug in his pack and pulled out a pair of socks to put under the shoulder straps of his pack for extra cushion and a piece of venison jerky to nibble on. Henry had a journal book opened on his knees and was busy writing in it. "What are you working on there, Henry?"

"Before we left Saginaw I made a list of things we need to talk about. Just checking some of them off. I don't remember things like I used to."

Will closed his eyes and let his body go limp, trying to rest his sore flesh as much as possible. "I'll tell you, Henry, I got aches in places where I didn't even know I had places. When I was in the army I rode on a limber box just about everywhere we went. I remember on some of those long marches seeing the infantry shedding their equipment and packs until both sides of the road were littered with all manner of things. Then pretty soon we'd see men sprawled out from exhaustion, unable to take another step. I got a better understanding of their misery now."

Henry tilted his head back and took a long pull from his canteen. "You'll harden up, Will. Just give it some time. When we hit the corner of our section this afternoon, we'll lighten our packs and cache most of our supplies. We can make quick sorties and just carry enough to last us a few days at a time."

"Sounds good, Henry. I guess I'm ready anytime you are."

About an hour and a half before dark, they picked up the section line they were looking for and within a few minutes stood at the corner post. Will read the numbers that were carved in the post and used them to verify their location on the map. "Looks like we're there," said Will.

"OK, Will. I say we back track to the little creek we just passed and set up camp. We'll have plenty of fresh water that way. Without prompting, Will set his compass on the post, turned it so the needle was pointing north and sighted along its face in a direction that would take them back to the creek. When they returned the next morning it would be a simple matter to walk the opposite course.

Henry was behind Will a short distance away, watching. When he was sure what Will was doing, he nodded his approval to no one in particular and smiled. "Let's go, son, we're burning daylight. It will take me a little time to teach you how to build a fire and set up a shelter, so we best get after it."

Will laughed and shook his head. "All this walking is bringing on a mighty shit," said Will. "Damn good thing I got you to set me straight about wiping, Henry."

Henry didn't even turn around or break stride but replied, "No need to get all uppity. I ain't the least bit interested in your godless bowel habits. I got enough trouble of my own in that regard."

On a moonless night in the great primal forests of Michigan, the darkness was absolute. The known safe world is reduced to the tiny bubble of illumination that surrounds the campfire. Most nights, the constant sound of wind passing through the distant treetops overhead dies away as the sun sinks below the horizon, taking with it precious heat, and bringing down an unbelievable silence, a silence so complete and unnerving that even the smallest night creatures seem sinister and dangerous. A curious raccoon becomes a hungry wolf; a porcupine digging its nails into a tree as it climbs becomes a bear. On this night, the only real threat to Will was his own memories of the war, of friends who would never grow old, never change from who they were on September 20th, 1863, and of the poor dirt farmer and his son who were just in the wrong place at the wrong time. The memories floated freely, just out of reach of his conscious mind until prodded by some vision, or sound, or smell. Unseen but undiminished, the memories some nights coalesced into horrible, bizarre abominations of the circumstances that created them and burst onto the scene in a wrenching nightmare. Will feared the nightmares more than death. He lay awake long into the night watching the fire burn down and listening to Henry snore. He was tired and sore from hiking with the heavy pack, and he desperately wanted a drink. He was afraid to close his eyes without one. Perhaps it was his overwhelming fatigue that saved him this night, but in the end he finally drifted off to a sleep as dark and silent as the world around him.

Henry and Will fell into a comfortable routine of discussing their objective for the day over morning coffee, hiking with lightened packs to various sections in the township they were working, and making notes on the quality and quantity of white pine they came across. Henry's gruff manner was hard to see through, but secretly he was delighted that Will was such a quick study and an eager student. Unlike some he had worked with who were interested only in learning the rules and committing them to memory, Will always had to see the logic. He said if a thing made sense, it would be there when he needed it. Henry taught Will how to divide a section into forty-acre parcels, the increment used by the lumber companies, by pacing off the distances and then systematically walking the forty and estimating how many board feet it would yield. A forty had to have at least 150,000 board feet of pine in it to be worth the expense of harvesting. The other two factors were the quality of the trees and whether or not there was a river nearby to float them out on in the spring.

One afternoon after returning to their base camp, Will dropped his pack and picked up his rifle, announcing his intention of finding some supper. They had been hearing the drumming of ruffed grouse since the first day, but by now they were tired enough of salt pork or sow belly as they called it, to do something about it. Will disappeared into the underbrush along the creek and was gone about twenty minutes when Henry heard the first two shots followed by four more randomly spaced. He counted them so he could judge Will's marksmanship when he returned. An hour later he heard twigs snapping, and then Will stepped into the little clearing they had made for their camp, carrying six headless grouse by their feet.

"That's a nice piece of shooting, son. I suppose now you're going to tell me you popped 'em on the wing," said Henry. "I hunted 'em for sport in my younger days. Damn things wait till you almost step on 'em before they get up. By the time I was done shitting my pants, they was in the next county."

"No, nothing like that," said Will with a chuckle. "These damn stupid birds just sit in a tree and let you shoot 'em one at a time. Guess that's why some folks call 'em fool hens. Not much meat on them this time of year, but I'll go down to the creek and pull the breasts out of them if you'll be so kind as to heat up the skillet." By the time Will returned carrying the six breasts, still glistening with creek water, Henry had the skillet straddling two logs with a nice little fire going underneath. Will sprinkled the meat with a few pinches of salt, powdered them with flour then dropped them into the sizzling grease. He placed his tin plate upside down over the skillet for a lid and every few minutes he would snatch it off quickly, using a piece of oilcloth to protect his hands, then use his spoon to baste the golden brown pieces of meat with the pork fat.

Darkness had settled on their little camp as the two men sat comfortably with one another and sipped their coffee. "That was a damn fine supper, Will. I'm obliged. Those pats sure have a nice white meat on 'em. Better than chicken, if you ask me."

"I got a question for you, Henry. Something that's been nagging at me for a few days."

"Fire away, son." said Henry.

"It seems to me that there's a passel of beautiful pine that nobody wants because they can't get the logs out. If I was a betting man, I'd say that one day somebody's going to figure out a way to make a go of it."

Henry didn't respond right away, but as he stared in the fire a smile spread across his face. Will had learned to be patient with the older man and trust that a response was coming. Finally he said, "That's a real good question, Will, and one I've pondered on myself at times. The thing is, with me, I'm too old to wait. If I were a young man like you, I'd buy up as much of that cork pine as I could afford, at say a buck and a half an acre, and just sit on it until some smart cookie figures out how to get it to mill. When that happens, those forties are going to be worth some serious money. Besides, all the easy stuff will be gone by then."

This time Will was quiet for a long time, and when Henry glanced sideways at him, he was staring into the fire, smiling.

Chapter 21

The trip back to East Saginaw was uneventful. After only a couple hours' wait, they flagged down a southbound train and settled in on an empty flatcar. It was a cloudless spring day, and as the train rolled along south, Will and Henry lay back, propped on their packs, shoulder to shoulder and brims of their hats pulled low against the sun. Two weeks of running section lines and pacing off forties through swamps and thickets is hard on a man and on his clothes. To anyone watching the train pass, the two men sprawled out on the flatcar would have looked more like hobos on the lam than the wealthy retired land looker and his understudy that they were.

"Ya know, when I was a young man cruising hither and yon for pine back east, I didn't think much about running out of trees, or what the land looked like after they were gone. I guess you seen your share of slash and know what I'm talking about," said Henry.

"Umm," said Will in way of acknowledgment without stirring.

"You mark my words, son, the old pineries will be gone one day and your grandbabies won't even know what you're talking about when you tell them about a grove of white pine with trunks six-foot across and a hundred and fifty feet tall. It'll just sound like a fairytale to 'em."

Will didn't respond this time, but if he had learned anything in the last two weeks, he had learned that Henry had a roundabout way of passing on important things that made it seem like simple jawing. Will let a little time pass while he mulled over what the older man had just said, then pushed the brim of his hat up, turned and looked at Henry. Instead of asking the question he had on the tip of his tongue, he started to laugh.

Henry pushed his hat up and shot an irritated look back at Will. "What the hell you looking at?" he said.

Will tried unsuccessfully to smother his merriment and finally said, "I'm sorry, Henry, I don't mean no offense. It just occurred to me that the dirty, raggedy ass looking old fart sitting next to me don't bear much likeness to the country gentleman I met in Heimbaugh's store a couple a weeks back."

There was a long silence between the two men as Henry squinted down his nose and regarded Will with a look as if he'd just stepped in dog shit. Finally, as if suddenly realizing how bad they both looked, his eyes softened and he laughed too. "Oh, you dumb ass. You ought to show a little more respect for your elders." The two men pulled the brims of their dirty hats back down and fell into a close, comfortable silence in the warmth of the sun and the rhythm of the wheels. Will's thoughts settled back onto the thread of the trees disappearing, and Henry dozed, both enjoying the last hours before returning to civilization.

The two men shouldered their packs, left the depot and headed up Water Street to see if Ben was in his office. Not only was Ben in, but he was standing in front of his office with his arms folded across his chest, watching them come down the street. He had heard the train whistle and figured, knowing Henry's penchant for punctuality, that they would be on this train. He was glad now that he had stepped out to take a little sunshine. It gave him the opportunity to see Henry and Will interact when they didn't know he was watching. The fact that they were even still together was a very good sign. Henry had such a low tolerance for stupidity and laziness that more often than not he came in alone when training was over.

"Well, gentlemen! Good to see you both alive and well after your journey through the vast wilderness of Michigan. And still speaking with one another to boot," said Ben. "You're just a tad scruffier than I like my guests, but come on in anyway."

"Well Lord have mercy on my miserable soul," said Henry. "Bad enough I got to put up with one snot-nosed smartass for two weeks out in the woods, but now I got me another one right here in town," said Henry.

"I don't know how you did it, Will," said Ben with a wink. "You must be a saint."

Will and Henry filed through the door to Ben's office, and Ben shut the door behind them. When all three were seated, Ben put his hands behind his head and leaned back in his chair. "Well, Henry, how did it go?" Even though Will thought he was on pretty safe ground, he still squirmed a little and clinched his butt muscles while Henry collected his thoughts.

"Well, Will here is a pretty sharp boy. He can find and pace out any forty in a section, he's good at picking up section lines, fair hand with figures, and a good woodsman. I'd say he'll do a fine job for you, Ben."

Ben was at a loss for words. Coming from Henry, that amounted to saying Will could walk on water. After a long pause, Ben said "Good... good. OK, come over here, gentlemen, and let me tell you what I want to do." He came around from behind his desk and walked over to a big drafting table on the opposite wall. Will and Henry got up and joined him, looking down at a large scale township map of Michigan that covered the entire top of the table. It was a detailed map and showed rivers, railroads, stage roads, and even the major Indian trails of the Lower Peninsula.

"I want to build a mill in Manistee for the Chicago market. As you know, everything we ship out of here heads east to mostly Ohio and some to New York, but the Chicago market is really taking off. You can see here," said Ben, pointing at the map, "that the Manistee River is impressive and the smaller streams that feed it are numerous. In short, it's an ideal setup. So far this country is mostly untouched, but that won't last forever. Mills are already going up in Manistee. Henry, you've looked over some of that country. What do you think?"

"Well, there's some mighty fine pineries up that way, for sure, and there's a lot of good water for getting the logs out. Seems like three lookers could come up with enough pine to get you a good start. One along the river and one farther out on each side, say here in Antioch and here in Wexford Township."

Ben studied the map in silence for a few minutes before making his decision. "I like it, Henry. That's what we'll do. I was going to send Will out by himself on a short test cruise, but if you think he's ready, I'm going to put him right to work up in Wexford. I got someone in mind for Antioch, but I'm afraid I can't think of a better man than you, Henry, for the close-in river work and especially for picking the best site for a camp. That is, if you'd be willing to come out of retirement one more time."

"Will, I hope you're paying close attention to our boss here. He's been greasing me up since we got here and now he's fixing to go in for the poke. He's a real artist, I tell ya," said Henry. All three men had a good laugh. "I ain't a young man anymore, Ben. On the other hand, city life don't suit me much." After a short silence Henry said, "All right, Ben, I'm in. We'll see how it goes and I may sit out the winter."

Ben slapped Henry on the back and looked over at Will, "What do you think, Will? Sound like a good plan?"

"Well, I'm not sure I would know a good plan from a bad one. I do have an idea that may just show me up as the greenhorn I am."

"Let's hear it, son," said Henry.

"What if we get us a mule and pack in enough supplies to last a couple of months, maybe more if we take some game once in a while. We could set up a base camp around here," he said pointing at the map, "near Sherman, and all of us could stage short quick trips out of there. We could meet at the camp, pool all of our minutes, and take turns running them all back here to the land office."

There was a long silence as Ben and Henry stared at the map and thought through Will's idea. Will figured it must have some merit, since it wasn't rejected out of hand, but he glanced nervously from one to the other.

Finally Henry spoke. "If we had a fourth man, a runner so to speak, we could all three stay in the field and he could bring us fresh maps, prepared by Ben, of course, and then return with our minutes. Damn, I like it. We could cover a lot of ground fast. I told you he had a good head for this work, Ben. I just wish he wasn't so damn ugly. Henry and Ben both laughed at Will's discomfort and Henry said, "Loosen up a little, son.

You keep clinchin' like that you'll end up with a hemorrhoid the size of a summer squash."

Will and Henry parted ways after talking to Ben and agreed to meet at the livery in two days to finalize their plans. Will headed up Water Street looking forward to seeing Jerald and having a night on the town. He was also anxious to get him involved in his plan to invest in passed over stands of pine. As he came abreast of the last mill before coming to the livery, he began to hear the rhythmic pounding of a sledge on hot iron over the receding sound of hissing steam and the screaming of a circular saw. Every smithy had his rhythm, and he would recognize this one anywhere, having listened to it all last winter.

In one of the two work bays of the livery, there was a tote wagon with its back wheels lying on the floor and its rear axle supported by stacked wood blocks. Jerald was bent over his anvil in the back corner and didn't see Will come in. Will watched him for a few minutes and decided that whatever he was working on wasn't going very well. Jerald straightened up, let out a string of curses and tossed the red hot piece he had been hammering on into a bucket of water with a loud hiss.

"Why don't you have a seat and I'll show you how it's done," said Will.

Jerald jumped and spun around, not expecting anyone to be behind him. "You asshole," said Jerald, grinning from ear to ear and shaking Will's hand.

"Damn, Will, is them the best clothes you got? Why, you look like something the cat dragged home and the dog wouldn't eat."

Will looked down as if just now noticing how disheveled he looked and said, "Yes, I need to update my wardrobe a bit. I might even wash up and shave, if you're up for a little pop-skull tonight."

"Throw in a supper and I'm your man," said Jerald, slapping Will on the back.

The two friends sat across from each other in wrought iron ice cream parlor chairs at a square table covered with a red-checkered table cloth and littered with empty dishes that had once contained their supper of spaghetti. One side of the table was pushed up against the wall under a window that looked out on the unpainted side of the next building. The window sash was open about six inches, presumably to let in fresh air, or let pipe smoke out, depending on how you wanted to look at it. What air did come through on the fitful breeze, however, carried the odor of stale urine from patrons peeing in the narrow alleyway, some perhaps even through the window on wilder nights. Jerald tipped his heavy glass beer mug back to wash down his last slice of sourdough bread, and then issued a long, deep belch that got the attention of several of the other patrons, not out of disgust as you would think, but out of admiration.

"Jesus, Jerald, you get any on you?" said Will.

"Never do my friend, never do." With that, he grabbed their empty mugs and headed to the bar. While he was gone, the old lady waiting tables came by and cleared the dirty dishes. On her last trip to wipe the table she remarked to Will how nice it was to have a little fresh air now that the winter was over. When Jerald returned, he set the two mugs of beer on the table, then went back and collected two hardboiled eggs from the bowl on the bar. "How about some dessert?" he said, placing one of the eggs down on the table in front of Will just hard enough to crack the shell. Will nodded his thanks and started picking at the egg. "How would you like to go into the real estate business with me, Jerald?"

Jerald raised his eyebrow without looking away from peeling his egg and said, "Keep going, I'm listening."

Will recounted his conversation with Henry and offered a few ideas of his own on how they would go about it. When he was finished, Jerald said, "Let me get this straight. We start a little land speculation business, split everything fifty-fifty, you find the trees, and I handle the paperwork on this end."

Will nodded and said, "I'll try to be back here about every three weeks to resupply and drop off my minutes. Ben is building a mill in Manistee, so Henry and I will be working up around Sherman for the rest of the summer and then I'll probably go out by myself during winter. Oh, that reminds me…you know anyone that's got a mule for sale?"

"As a matter of fact, I do. I got one in the corral behind the livery. I gotta warn you, though, he's the dumbest, orneriest goddamn animal I ever set eyes on. My partner has been trying to get rid of him since last fall, but nobody can do anything with him," said Jerald.

"OK, I'll take a look at him tomorrow. Let's drink up and head over to the Shanty. I got some serious catching up to do."

From that point on, the evening followed a predictable course. The more Will drank, the more melancholy he became. At one point he and Jerald started retelling each other stories about their best dogs and how they met their fates. They both held up pretty well until Jerald told the story of his beagle, Old Joe. In his younger days, Joe was a crackerjack rabbit dog and could run hard all day long. As he got older, though, he developed a taste for the ladies and would take long junkets into the countryside in search of female favors. Eventually his ardor would burn out and he would come home, thin and exhausted. He would mend and rest up for a week or so and then head back out and do it all again. In his twilight years his legs started to go on him, and Jerald decided one day that he needed to put him down. He dug a hole and loaded his rife. Old Joe walked stiffly over to his master, thinking he was going out for rabbits, and he stumbled and fell in the hole. He sat there looking up at Jerald with his sad beagle look. This is the point where both men were sitting at the bar with tears rolling down their faces. Will had heard the story many times, but it always got to him. Sometime during the night, he got sick and Jerald held him by the back of his suspenders while he hung out a window and puked down the side of the building.

The next morning when he woke, Jerald was already gone. Will splashed some tepid water on his face from the wash bowl and avoided looking at his reflection in the mirror hanging on the wall above the chest of drawers. He needed coffee badly and something to eat that would calm his stomach.

Jerald was back in the corner of the shop pumping the bellows on his forge to get the temperature of the fire up when Will came down the stairs. "Damn, Will, you look like something that was shot at and missed and shit at and hit," said Jerald, shaking his head.

"I been better," said Will a little weakly. "I'm going to walk up the street to the bakery. You want anything?"

"Bring me something really gooey and sweet. I got coffee here that should be hot when you get back."

When Will returned, Jerald poured them both a tin cup of coffee, and they sat in silence on some upturned wood crates and ate their pastries. Finally Will said, "I guess I'll take a look at the mule. You say he's out back?"

"I reckon so. He don't move around much. I'll go back there with you." Jerald pitched the dregs of his coffee out on the floor and set his cup on the shelf over the work bench. "Follow me." The two men walked out through the open bay door and went around to the back of the building. The small corral contained only one animal, and that was the mule in question, standing next to the wall in a sliver of shade. "I told you he ain't nothing special," said Jerald.

"What's his name?"

"Well, I don't rightly know. All I ever hear him called was 'Goddamn mule.'" Will nodded without taking his eyes off the mule.

"You know anything about mules?" said Jerald.

"Well, I know you can't treat 'em like a horse. It's true, he don't look very smart, but I think mules are smarter than horses. You got to treat 'em easy and appeal to their higher intelligence. Once he goes to not liking you, you might as well shoot him, because he ain't going to do nothing for you. They don't never forget either," said Will, looking at his friend out of the corner of his eye to judge his reaction.

Jerald chewed on that information for a moment as he hung on the fence studying the mule. Finally he turned and regarded his friend. "Goddamn it, Will, you're full of shit like a Christmas turkey." Will laughed for the first time that day as Jerald stomped off.

Will retrieved an empty crate from the side of the building, tossed it into the corral, and then climbed over after it. He turned the crate upside down next to the fence boards on the opposite side of the corral from where the mule stood and took a seat. He produced a small jar of apple butter from his coat pocket that he had bought at the bakery, scooped a dollop out with two fingers and walked over to the mule. He slowly reached out, ran the apple butter under the animal's nose, and then smeared it on the top of a fence board. Will walked back over and sat down on the crate and dipped a little of the apple butter out for himself. It was a long wait, but finally the mule turned his head, sniffed at the smear of apple butter, and then gingerly licked at it with his tongue. Will got up and walked over, dipped his finger in the jar and offered it up, keeping his hand just out of reach. His arm was starting to get tired, but eventually the mule took a step forward and put his lips around Will's fingers and then backed away with the reward. Will walked back over and sat down to wait. After about fifteen minutes of watching Will lick apple butter off his fingers, the mule shuffled his feet a little bit and cautiously approached. "Got ya," said Will under his breath. For the next few minutes, Will fed the remaining contents of the jar to the mule, then stood up and scratched behind his ear as he tipped the jar and let him stick his tongue in to clean it out. "I think we're going to shorten your name up a tad to G.D."

Chapter 22

The plan that Ben, Henry, and Will had worked out fell through almost from the first day. Ben could not locate an unemployed man trustworthy enough and with woodsman experience to fill the role of runner. The third land looker he had in mind had decided to freelance, and the last thing Ben wanted was to get in a bidding war over his minutes every time he came in. So it was just Henry, Will, and the mule that headed out in an empty boxcar for Grand Rapids. After a brief side trip to the land office in Ionia for current plat maps of the townships they planned to work, they boarded another train, this one heading north to Newaygo. The rails ended there, but a primitive stage road had been cut through the forest all the way to Traverse City, and they took that to the Manistee River just south of Sherman. They hiked west along the last ridge before the land descended into the river valley and settled on a spot for their base camp on the edge of a grove of mature hemlock trees. An underground spring gurgled to the surface and turned into a small creek just a few feet away. Henry and Will had decided to stick to the original plan and split up after getting squared away, and each would work a different side of the river. Will offered to take the north side and board G.D. with someone in Sherman before he crossed the river.

Since leaving Newaygo they had been set upon by hoards of mosquitoes, and now that they were near the river and the backwaters that were breeding grounds for the pests, there was a constant hum in the air, as if they were near a beehive.

"Let's get a fire going and make a little smoke before we do anything else," said Henry. "These goddamn skeeters are going to suck us dry." Will stopped waving his hand in front of his face long enough to drop his pack and slide a small hand axe from under his belt before disappearing into the hemlocks in search of firewood. When he returned, Henry had a small fire going from some dead grass and small branches that he found close by. This time Henry disappeared while Will built the fire up with the bigger logs. He returned about twenty minutes later with an armload of green balsam branches. He tossed one on the fire and used another to fan the smoke around.

"When we get ready to turn in, I'll show you a little trick," said Henry. The two men spent the rest of the afternoon unloading G.D.'s pack and securing their supplies against varmints as best they could. The nights were still cold, so Will threw a blanket over G.D. and fed him while Henry collected more balsam boughs for the floor of their government surplus A tent.

After supper they sat around the fire taking turns swishing smoke to discourage the mosquitoes. Henry was in a mood to talk, so Will just sat cross-legged, staring into the fire and listening. "There's a lot of high ground hereabouts, especially on this side of the river. If you can find a good climbing tree on a high ridge, you can spot the best pineries for miles around and save yourself a lot of walking. Cork pine sticks up above everything else. Course you got to be mighty careful. You fall and break something you need for walking, you're going die out here. Once the wolves and coyotes get done with you, there won't be nothing left of you but a few bones sticking out of a pile of wolf shit."

Henry glanced over at Will to make sure his point had struck the mark. Will smiled back at him, but in his eyes there was such a deep sadness that Henry couldn't look away. He realized that for a brief moment he was looking at the real Will Castor and that death held no power over him. They sat in silence for a while as Henry turned this new information over in his mind.

"OK, now the first thing you gotta do is make sure you got the back flies of the tent closed up as tight as you can, and make sure the sides are tight to the ground. Crawl inside there and spread your blanket out nice and flat. OK, now back out of there and watch this." Henry flipped the front fly back and with a bough of balsam started pushing smoke into the tent as fast as he could. "Don't just stand there with your mouth hanging open. Lend a hand," he said. Will grabbed a bough of his own and pitched in. "OK, that's enough. Close that fly up tight as you can. We'll give 'em a few minutes."

Will still wasn't exactly sure how this was going to end, so he just did as he was told. "Peel them flies back just a hair." Will lifted the canvas and Henry reached in and carefully slid the blanket out. Almost every square inch of it was covered with mosquitoes. "Damn, Henry, that's the best trick I've seen in a long time. You got anything for black flies and no-see-ums?" said Will.

"Hush up and git on in there quick before they tumble to what we're doing." Will and Henry got in the tent and closed the fly as tight as they could. Henry smacked a mosquito on his cheek and said, "Well it ain't perfect, but at least your eyes won't be swollen shut when you wake up."

The next morning Will and Henry shook hands and went their separate ways after sharing a little breakfast and coffee. They agreed to meet back at the camp in two weeks. Will had no trouble boarding G.D. in Sherman. He gave the lady at the little general store a couple of dollars and agreed to settle up with her on his way back through.

The first week that Will was on his own passed quickly. He wasted time at first pacing off forties that didn't have enough good pine on them to make it worth cutting, but by the second week he could tell just by looking whether or not a forty would yield enough board feet to warrant his effort. When he collected G.D. and met up with Henry at the base camp, he had three adjacent forties that looked good. Henry checked his work and questioned him a bit but seemed satisfied. He gave Will a vulcanized valise to carry their minutes in for the trip back to Saginaw, and with G.D. in tow, they left the next morning. Will switched trains in Grand Rapids and then got off just long enough to enter their minutes at the Ionia land office for Heimbaugh and Sons. By early evening he was once again walking up Water Street in East Saginaw. Will stopped in to let Ben know how things were going up on the Manistee, dropped G.D. at the livery, and had supper and drinks with Jerald. The next morning he headed back north alone, nursing a hangover.

By the end of the summer, Will and Henry had located enough white pine to keep two camps busy cutting all winter. During the first week of September the swampers showed up and began clearing a tote road and putting up log buildings to house the men and animals through the winter. While Henry was busy helping the swampers locate and lay out the camps, Will was making a wide swing north of the main river, looking for good stands of land-locked pine to invest in with Jerald. On the third day of being on his own, he came to a ridge line with a grove of beech trees growing along its spine.

The trees growing high on the south side of the ridge had strong branches close to the ground, just right for climbing. Will's turned-out leg gave him a little trouble, but he was finally able to get up above the tops of the trees sloping away to the south. He was rewarded with a spectacular view of unbroken virgin forest as far as he could see in every direction. Will sat in the tree for a long time studying the treetops, now with the eye of a land looker. From this vantage point it was easy to see patterns in the different types of trees and the ways they grew in relation to one another. As Henry had said, the white pines grew much taller than the other trees, making them easy to spot. What Will hadn't realized before was that the older, taller trees grew close together in solid groves, and the farther out you got from the main group, the pines became interspersed with other trees and less concentrated. To the southwest Will could see where the Manistee River valley curved away from him, and a little further to his right, almost due west, was an enormous stand of white pine that looked like it must cover ten sections at least. When he was back on the ground, he pulled out his map and carefully marked the spot and made up his mind to look it over when he came back out that winter.

Will loved the solitary life of the land looker. There was no one to please but himself, no one giving him "the eye" because of the scar across his face or the permanent limp. He was confident in his woodsmanship and he was making good money. He never once suspected that his fragile link to other human beings was all that had kept him from stepping off the ledge.

Chapter 23

On the face of it, land looking during a northern Michigan winter might have seemed like a great hardship, but in many ways it was easier than land looking in warmer weather. First and foremost, there were no biting insects to contend with. In the spring and summer, swarms of mosquitoes, black flies, and no-see-ums, as the Indians called them, made life miserable no matter how well prepared you were. Long about the end of December, the lakes and swamps froze over and the snow was usually deep enough to cover the underbrush, making it possible, with a good pair of snow shoes, to walk over and not through the obstructions.

As he thought he might, Henry had decided to give up timber cruising in the winter and gave Will his snowshoes. With a little trial and error they were able to modify the binding on the right shoe so that even though Will's foot was turned out at a severe angle, the shoe would track straight. Henry also let Will copy his notes and tracings of old Indian footpaths that he had encountered over the years. There were no regular maps of these trails, so this was invaluable information. Traveling was much easier and faster on one of these trails than striking out cross country.

The fall of 1870 was Will's second as a land looker. Ben Heimbaugh had come to rely heavily on his minutes to keep the mill in Manistee humming along, and the markets in Chicago were gobbling up the lumber as fast as they could get it. This all meant that money was coming in fast and furious for Heimbaugh and Sons and for Will, who was pocketing a third of the take from the pine he found. With the exception of a day or two in town every three weeks when he came in to enter his minutes, he spent his time in the wilderness, living on what he could carry in his pack, or until the snow got too deep, what G.D. could carry. There were enough

Heimbaugh and Sons camps on the Manistee watershed now that it was an easy thing to find a warm place for the mule to spend the harshest part of the winter.

Things were good in the livery business, too, as East Saginaw continued to ride the crest of the lumber boom. Between Will and Jerald converting their profits into land that they hoped would one day be valuable, they had already amassed close to three thousand acres of white pine stumpage. Jerald's contributions had slowed somewhat in recent months because he was planning to build a house in the spring and wed Maribel Kruger, the daughter of a well-to-do salt company owner in town. This new turn of events had also required some serious cleaning up of Jerald's drinking and whoring activities, which left Will somewhat at loose ends.

Will had heeded the advice of his friends and especially the stern warning from Henry and not taken whisky with him into the woods. So far this hadn't been too much of an imposition; he had always been able to go for long periods of time without taking a drink. It was taking that first one that inevitably led to his undoing. On his last trip to East Saginaw he had started feeling low even before he started drinking, mostly because of Jerald's preoccupation with Maribel, and perhaps on some level it reminded him of Jimmy and Amanda. Somehow he woke up the next morning in Henry's carriage house sprawled on the bed of a buckboard wagon under a pile of blankets and a smelly canvas tarp. To think that Henry had collected him out of a tavern or off a sidewalk made him feel worse. He walked back to the livery and gathered his things, even things he normally left behind, like his discharge papers from the army, a few books, and the old cap and ball revolver wrapped in an oily rag that he had brought home from the war. He set up G.D.'s pack and then headed for the land office, hoping to get out of town before he ran into anyone he knew. Jerald was nowhere to be found, and that was just as well. Will bought a plat map and survey notes for a township further east up the Manistee than he had ever gone before and entered his minutes for 320 acres of white pine in the name of the company he and Jerald co-owned. He was still in a foul mood and felt as if he was just throwing good money after bad, but he was in too deep now. On his last stop before boarding the train, Will bought a few staples and three bottles of barrel whisky. He promised himself that he would not touch it until he had his minutes for Ben and was ready to come back in.

It was late fall and the leaves were off the trees, lying deep and light on the forest floor. Several snowfalls had come but vanished quickly on the ground that was still holding some summer warmth. Will and G.D. had been following an old Indian trail since early morning and making good time. He still stuck to the routine of walking forty-five minutes and resting fifteen so he would have a good dead reckoning sense of his distance covered. Will sat on an old windfall log on the edge of a small open boggy area, studying the weather signs. The sky, rather than getting lighter with the day, had started going the other way and was now storm dark. Wind coming out of the northwest was icy cold and carried with it big lake effect snowflakes traveling almost horizontally where there was any fetch to speak of.

"Well, G.D., it don't look all that good. I reckon we better start looking for a place to hole up and ride this one out. Thank you kindly for suggesting I bring those snowshoes along. May get to use them pretty damn quick." When they resumed their trek, the trail took them around the soft, open ground and then plunged back into the hardwood forest. They eventually came to a place where the trail descended into the bottom of a draw and was sheltered from the wind. "I think this is the place, G.D." Will tied the mule's lead to a sapling and dug out his hand axe. Gathering firewood was always the first order of business.

By nightfall Will had a nice fire going at the front of a lean-to he had put together with a heavy sheet of canvas. The pannier packs and pack saddle that G.D. had been carrying anchored the shelter at its base and gave Will easy access to anything he might need. He fed the mule, covered him with a blanket, and made sure the lead was long enough so he could back away from the fire if he got too warm. G.D. chose to stand right at one end of the shelter so he could keep an eye on Will. After supper, Will fished an apple out of one of the packs, took a slice out for G.D., and lay back staring into the fire and listening to the storm rage in the treetops high over their heads. The heat from the fire reflected off the inside of the canvas lean-to and made it so warm that Will took off his coat and used it for a pillow.

This was always the hardest time of the day when he was alone. Tonight the thought of Henry seeing him passed out drunk kept playing over and over in his mind. For the first time since he started drinking in earnest, he saw himself through someone else's eyes, and what he saw wasn't who he thought he was. He felt he had betrayed Henry, and he had betrayed himself, and not just that one time. He thought about the whisky just an arm's length away in one of the packs, and even reached for it once, but he knew if he took a drink, there would be no way to stop.

Will got up just before daylight to put more wood on the fire and set the small pot containing the remnants of last night's coffee on the edge of the coals. He was amazed by the amount of snow that had come down during the night, twenty inches or more, he figured. The wind had died out and the clear star-filled sky ushered in bitter cold. G.D. seemed none the worse for wear. His blanket was still in place, and the snow had collected about six inches deep along his broad back and on the top of his head between his ears. Will couldn't help but chuckle at the sight. "Damn, G.D., you sure are a looker," said Will. "I reckon you're going to get a chance to try out the snow here directly. The next camp is about a day and a half up the trail, and I think you ought to go into winter quarters, as we used to say in the army." Will fried down a piece of salt pork and then stirred a little flour and cornmeal into the grease to make a couple of flapjacks. He washed it all down with a tin cup of very strong leftover coffee. "You ain't much of a talker, G.D., but I appreciate that you're a good listener. I know you like to study on things before you make your move." Back when they didn't know each other very well, Will started talking to G.D. as he strapped the pack saddle on in hopes of avoiding a kick. Now it was just part of the ritual.

They were about four miles further up the trail when G.D. reared his head back and stopped without warning, almost causing Will to fall back over his snow shoes. "Damn it, G.D., what the hell's the matter with you?" G.D. had never done this before, so Will was immediately on his guard. He looked down the trail as far as he could to where it curved to the left and then slowly scanned either side back up into the woods. Nothing seemed amiss. He bent down to sort out his snowshoes after the abrupt stop, and in the act, looked right into the face of a frozen man leaning against a tree. Will was so startled that he yelped and started pumping his legs to back up. In his excitement, he forgot all about the snowshoes and promptly went down on his side in the deep snow. He lay there for a few minutes, trying to calm down and slow his pounding heart. When he finally had his breathing under control, he rolled on his back and slipped his boots out of the snowshoe bindings. He stood up and studied the dead man.

He was sitting on the ground and leaning back against the tree, covered with fresh snow up to his chest. He reminded Will of a white marble bust of George Washington he had once seen in Nashville during the war. Snow had collected on the man's head and shoulders, on the tops of his ears, and even on his eyelashes and upper lip. The skin was devoid of any natural color, but Will recognized the man's features as those of an Indian. He stepped up and pushed on the man's chest. His wool coat had a little give to it, but underneath he was as solid as a block of ice. Will wasn't sure about what he should do, but it seemed like something was called for. Surely someone must be looking for him. He thought maybe he might have a pocketbook with his name in it and started to clear the snow off his lower body. As Will uncovered the arms and legs, the mystery of the Indian's untimely death was solved. His left arm rested on his lap, and the hand still gripped the neck of a whisky bottle that was wedged between his legs. The other hand held the bottle's cork. He had passed out drunk on his way home, wherever that was, and had frozen to death.

Will sat down next to the man, reached over and wiggled the bottle until it broke loose, and then slid it out from under the Indian's hand. "Well, I give up on saying prayers a few years ago, but I'll have a drink with you – even though it don't look like you saved much for company," said Will as he held the bottle up against the sky and peered through it.

Will put the cold bottle to his lips and took a pull. He let out a long sigh. "This shit is even worse than that pop-skull I got. Here's to ya, my friend." Will tipped the bottle back and drained it. "Whew, that stuff will kill ya. But I guess I ain't telling you nothing." Will chuckled at his own humor and then leaned over again and slid the neck of the empty bottle back into the dead man's frozen hand just as he found it. He scooped up a handful of fresh snow and let it melt in his mouth to wash down the whisky. "Come on, G.D., we got places to go," said Will as he stood up. He shook the snow off his snowshoes and then threw them down in front of him and stepped into the bindings. "If we see any of your people, I'll let them know where you are. Otherwise, I s'pose they'll find you next spring." Will picked up G.D.'s lead and started up the trail.

They had only gone about a half mile when Will needed another drink. He retrieved a bottle from one of G.D.'s packs and took a swig. "I think I'll just keep this handy," he said to himself as he dropped the bottle in one of the deep side pockets of his coat. After a few more miles and several drinks, Will decided he'd had enough walking for one day and started looking for a place to camp for the night. They were on a south-facing slope of a ridge that skirted an open meadow, and the warming rays of the sun made it feel right. Will and G.D. left the trail and eased down the ridge about a hundred feet. Will was starting to have trouble walking on the snowshoes, and going downhill was especially tricky, but by mid-afternoon he had a good fire going, and with one of the big shoes, he had scooped the snow out of an area large enough for his lean-to. He had spread his gum blanket over the packed snow under his little shelter to keep things dry, and with nothing more to do, he lay back against one of G.D.'s packs and dozed in the warmth of the sun and the fire.

Will woke with a start and sat up looking around with wide eyes. In his dream Sergeant Hazzard and Big Mike had been frozen like the Indian, exactly as they were just before the old man had shot the horse in the back of the head. Will would never forget the look he had given him that day, and it was the same look that was frozen on his face in the dream. The gun had gone off and Big Mike's head shattered into thousands of slivers of ice turning in slow motion in the sunlight. That's when he woke up. The sun was not down yet, but it was close, just touching the tree line in the west and making a glow on the tops of the bare trees on the east side of the meadow. Will pulled the cork on the whisky bottle, casually noting that it was almost half gone, and took a drink. He washed it around in his mouth to get a little more out of it and then savored the burn all the way down.

As he sat there trying to think through making supper, he noticed a movement out of the corner of his eye on the edge of the meadow below him. Whatever it was had moved slowly and then stopped. When he stared hard at the spot, he could see nothing. Then, as he continued to look on, a deer stepped cautiously into the open.

"He knows something's wrong but just can't figure out what," Will thought to himself. There wasn't much wind, but there was enough blowing through the trees behind him to scatter his scent all over the meadow. Will waited until the deer looked away from him and then reached back over his head and grabbed his Winchester. He rose up on one knee as slowly and smoothly as he could, but he was still wobbly from his afternoon of drinking, and when he focused on the meadow again, the deer was gone. Just then an ear twitched. "There he is," he thought, "an easy shot."

Will put the rifle to his shoulder and squinted down the barrel with one eye closed. He wavered a little, and then when the blade sight on the end of the barrel passed over the chest of the deer, he pulled the trigger. The crack of the rifle going off startled G.D., and he bucked against his lead that was tied to a tree. Will quickly stood up, certain that he would see the deer lying in the snow. But the deer was still standing in the same place, now looking directly at him. He pulled the gun up and squeezed off a quick shot, thinking the deer would bolt at any second. This time the animal's legs buckled and it pitched forward into the snow then flailed its legs as it tried to regain its footing. Will racked the lever of the rifle, preparing to go down and finish him off. The spent shell ejected into the snow, but when he pulled the lever back up, he knew the gun was empty.

Will sat the rifle down and started digging through the packs for a box of ammunition, all the while cursing himself for getting drunk and missing two easy shots. He was on his second pack when he put his hand on the old army revolver. He grabbed the gun, still wrapped in the oily rag, and headed down the ridge toward the clearing. It was slow going in the deep snow without snowshoes, so he stayed inside the tree line where the walking was a little easier, and he skirted the edge of the meadow. As soon as he saw the tracks in the snow, his eyes followed them to the right, and there not ten feet away was the deer.

The deer was lying down with its legs folded under it, as if it had just decided to rest until nightfall. It followed Will with big, dark, bottomless eyes as he approached. There was no fear in its eyes, no understanding. Will stopped and rolled the revolver out of the rag into his right hand. His second shot had struck the deer low, just behind the front leg, and its blood was coagulating in crimson splotches on the cold white snow. It turned away from Will and licked at the wound. When Will pulled the hammer back and brought the gun up, the deer turned its head to the double click and looked up at him.

At that moment, as Will stared down into the eyes of the wounded deer, with his finger taking the slack out of the trigger, the war came rushing up at him with a force like never before. He felt his insides twist into a knot, and the sounds of battle roared in his ears as they had that day when the Confederate shell exploded over the gun. His ability to suppress the unbearable memories of his dead friends and the horrible realities of the battlefield had deserted him. The guilt from not knowing his best friend was mortally wounded, or the guilt from killing a farmer and his son, or shooting his sergeant in the back of the head, or all the other faceless men that had died every time he pulled the lanyard had finally come to claim him, as deep inside he always knew they would. His arm trembled as if it lacked the strength to hold the pistol, and he gasped for air. He couldn't hold on. It was over. His jaw went slack and he crumpled to the ground against a tree. He was ready to die, he wanted to die, here, in the vast, silent forest where his bones and those of the deer would lie together under ever-deepening layers of leaves as the seasons passed, until one day they would dissolve into nothing and return to the soil. He wanted to be with Jimmy and set things right, but he didn't really believe that would happen. When he pulled the trigger and the light faded from his eyes, there would be only an eternity of empty darkness. Will looked at the deer, who was still watching him. He reached out and ran his hand through the coarse hair of its neck and felt the hard muscles tense. "I'm sorry," he whispered. "I'm so sorry." Will stretched out his legs and pulled the deer to him until it rolled onto its side and laid its head on his lap. Eight years afterwards, in the failing light of a winter afternoon, alone in the deep trackless wilderness of northern Michigan, the war for Will was finally over. He would stay with the deer until it died, and then he would use the last round in Sergeant Hazzard's service revolver, loaded so long ago, to end his own life.

With the certainty of the end came peace. Will thought of his mother and father and his happy life before the war. His dad had taught him about honor and dignity, hard lessons learned, but he had squandered them with whisky. His mother had loved him no matter what, and he would leave her only the uncertainty of his fate that would trouble her for the rest of her days. He thought of Jerald, and Henry, and Ben. They would come looking for him, but they would know deep down what had happened. And Mollie, dear Mollie…he had held the one person who could have saved him in his arms, and he had let her slip away. He imagined her this night, reading a bedtime story to her two little nephews by candlelight. The expressions of her beautiful, loving face, framed in soft yellow light, would be changing with the rhythms of the story. It was full dark now, but a three-quarter moon had risen above the trees and cast long dim shadows across the unspoiled snow cover of the meadow. Tremors had begun to course through the deer's body as the chill of death advanced, and Will knew that it wouldn't be long now.

He had saved Amanda until the last. He realized now that it had been only his life that had changed so dramatically when he joined the army back in '61. Amanda's life had gone on as before, save the one part touched by him. It was his need to cling to her that was unfair. This was a need she wasn't even aware of. If ambition was her only fault, then he had sold her short. Those warm, idle summer days when they lay in the tall grass by the creek that ran through her father's wood lot were real and undiminished. Like conspirators, Will and Amanda had held hands and looked deep and long into each other's eyes, secretly professing their love for one another. For both of them it was magic, and the world around them had blossomed into amazing colors and abundance, like wildflowers in a spring meadow. It was real then and always would be.

Will thought of those long-ago Sundays, sitting close to Amanda in church and croaking out hymns just loud enough so that she knew he was singing, but not enough to interfere with her clear, sweet notes delivered in such earnest. At first, for Will, it was the excitement of being seen together in public and the chance to look out at the world as a couple that was so intoxicating, but as time passed, he began to realize that Amanda's motivation had nothing at all to do with him. She was a true believer, and his presence was nice, but incidental. Her unquestioning faith in God had made him look at religion in a light different from the one he had grown up with: the one where decent folks kept the Sabbath, end of story. He knew back then that if he was going to share in Amanda's life, he had some catching up to do. These memories were on Will's mind when he felt the deer shudder, giving up its last warm breath of life and clearing the way for him to make good on his promise.

Will tightened his grip on the gun, opened his eyes to the sky filled with stars and yelled, "God, if you're out there, God, please forgive me. I just can't go on!" As the last echoes of his agony died away in the forest, he raised the old revolver's barrel to the side of his head. He paused to fix in his mind the moment he should have died, with his friends on that flame-swept ridge back in 1863, when the Confederate shell burst over the gun. Before he could pull the trigger, a strange and unexpected sensation coursed through his body. It was a warmth so sudden and so complete that he was stunned. There were no words, no heavenly vision, but the wonderful warmth and peace were unmistakable. He sat there in awe, afraid to move, afraid to think. He just wanted it to go on and on. In those few moments he knew that Jimmy, and Al, and George and Sergeant Hazzard and Corporal VanVleet were all right, that Jack was all right. They were all right. The heaviness he had carried for so many years was gone, and in its place was a certainty that there was more. There was forgiveness, and there was hope. Amanda had known all along, and because he had once loved her, now he knew it, too.

Chapter 24

In the days following Will's experience with the deer, he began to take stock of his life and his future. What he wanted most now was to settle down and start a new life. He still had 160 acres coming from the government for his service in the war, and he had opened a bank account to start putting away money for building a house. There was beautiful unspoiled land just about everywhere he went; the problem was finding good soil. Northern Michigan soil was notoriously sandy, and unless you planned on growing potatoes, it would be used up in a few years. He had two areas left to look at before making his decision: Manistee and Traverse City.

The people who knew Will were amazed by his transformation. Some were skeptical, of course, but for the most part his friends were just relieved that he had taken the cure. Jerald and Maribel were married in late spring at the home of her parents. The brief ceremony was followed by an elegant formal dinner for just a few close family members and friends. Jerald was a little light on available kin, so Ben Heimbaugh, his wife Ellie, Henry, and Will represented his side. As the affair was winding down, the normally reserved Maribel surprised everyone at the door by throwing her arms around Will's neck and hugging him goodbye. She had whispered in his ear that she hoped he would be a regular guest at their house when he was in town. Will and Jerald were both touched.

That same night, after bidding farewell to the Heimbaughs as they settled into their buggy, he walked back to Water Street with Henry. "Well, Henry, I'm starting to think maybe we got in the wrong business," said Will. "Seems like there's some good money to be made pumping salt out of the ground after looking around at Tom Kruger's castle tonight."

"He's done all right for himself, that's a fact" said Henry. "I hear he ain't a walk in the park to work for, though."

"I hope Jerald don't get too uppity for the likes of us," Will chuckled. "You should have seen the look on his face when I told him I was bringing Patty from Cincinnati to his wedding." Henry threw his head back and laughed.

"You're a damned rascal, Will!" They stopped at the corner of Washington and Thompson and watched the horse-drawn streetcar approach, lanterns flickering in the dry wind.

"Are you going out this summer, Henry?"

"I reckon so. I can't take much more than a few months around these city folks. Been thinking of trying my hand up in the U.P. Some fine country up there, I hear."

Will nodded. "Well, I was hoping to share a meal or two with you up on the Manistee if you were thereabouts. This might be my last summer of looking. I've decided to settle in one spot for a while, maybe build a house and do a little farming."

"How much stumpage you and Jerald sitting on now?" said Henry.

"Close to ten thousand acres, give or take. I got a little money put away for a house and a barn, too."

This time Henry looked down and nodded as he thought through what he was going to say next. "I don't know what happened out there in the woods last winter, son; it don't really matter. Being alone in the big timber can have an effect on a man. Whatever you do from here on out, you hang on to what you found out there, you hang on to it real tight, like your life depends on it; because take it from one who knows, it does. You're a good man, Will Castor, and I'm proud to know ya. If I had a son, I'd want him to be just like you." With that, Henry patted Will on the back and turned to head up the street toward his house. After a couple of steps, he stopped and turned around again. "And yes, I will look you up for a partridge supper. Leave a note for me at Sherman to point me in the right direction."

Will had a lump in his throat and couldn't come up with anything to say that seemed right. Finally he called after his friend. "It's kind of a long walk for an older gentleman such as yourself, Henry," said Will, throwing out a little taunt.

"Oh, you don't worry about me, son, I'll dance a jig at your wedding someday… that is if you're able to sneak up on some poor unsuspecting woman that ain't overly bright."

The summer of 1871 was one of the driest on record in the upper Midwest. In Michigan, lumbering had left huge tracts of land covered with tinder-dry slash in the Saginaw valley and along both the Muskegon and Manistee watersheds, extending well into the interior of the state. One of the easiest ways for a settler to clear the land for farming was to simply burn it off, and many, including the Indians, did just that. Once started, these fires were nearly impossible to control by just a few farmers and their families. On any given day that year there were countless local forest fires burning all over the Great Lakes region, making wood smoke part of everyday life. On October 8th, a storm hit the Midwest with hurricane-strength winds, fanning these smaller fires into enormous conflagrations that swept across Minnesota, Wisconsin, and Michigan, consuming everything in their path. Hundreds of people perished, and some fifteen thousand were left homeless in Michigan alone. Whole towns were either swept away completely or in some cases partially destroyed, as was the case with the great Chicago fire. In the town of Peshtigo, Wisconsin, which was totally destroyed, over fifteen hundred people perished. Without question, many Indian villages in these regions vanished without a trace, but there is no record of their loss.

On the night before the big storm, Will and G.D. were camped on a little spring-fed lake a few miles northeast of Manistee. They were on the west side of the lake near an Indian trail that went right to the edge of town. Ben had talked up the place when Will mentioned that he was looking for some land to start a farm on. He also reminded him that his old nemesis, Bellman, was working at the Heimbaugh and Sons mill there.

"Well, G.D., this surely would be a pretty place if it weren't for this damn smoke. If it don't get better by tomorrow, we'll just move on and find us some clear air," said Will. It had been so long since there had been any rain, he had gotten out of the habit of putting up any kind of shelter, and he lay on top of his gum blanket propped up by G.D.'s packs. One good thing about the smoke was that it kept the insects down to a manageable level. As Will watched the mirror surface of the little lake through half-closed eyes, a fish rose to something moving on the water and broke the stillness. G.D. was having trouble with the smoke, too. With increasing frequency he took to fits of snorting and shaking his head in an effort to relieve his stinging eyes and nose.

The next morning the smoke was even thicker and the wind had picked up and swung around to the southwest. By the time he had G.D. saddled up and the packs secure, the sky was an eerie copper color, and he couldn't even see the other side of the small lake. Will heard twigs snapping and the rustling of dead leaves and looked up just in time to see four deer step out of the underbrush, not ten feet away, and look around as if in a daze. They didn't seem to care if Will and G.D. were there or not. Suddenly the woods along the shoreline of the lake were teeming with wildlife. Squirrels, woodchucks, rabbits, skunks, raccoons, and porcupines, all confused and moving slowly, emerged from the smoke-filled forest to the west. Will had never seen anything quite like this before, but it was vaguely reminiscent of defeated soldiers fleeing in front of a determined enemy like those he had witnessed at Chickamauga. Here, the enemy was fire.

Will weighed his options and quickly decided against trying to out-run the fire. He pulled his boots and socks off and stuffed them in one of G.D.'s packs and then picked up the mule's lead and waded out into the lake. He stopped about twenty yards from shore and turned to face the approaching flames. The smoke passing overhead now was solid black, shot through with sparks and long angry streaks of red flame and moving very fast in the high winds. Closer to the ground it was hot and dark as night. Will put his hand on G.D.'s neck, and it was almost too hot to touch. He pulled the mule's blanket from between two of the packs and unrolled it into the water. When it was soaked up, he draped it over G.D.'s back and pulled it forward so that it completely covered his head. Will slowly backed him up into deeper water until just a few inches of his back were above the surface. The edges of the wet blanket hung in the water all around, creating a little pocket of air filtered through the wet cloth for G.D. to breathe. Will was already chest-deep in the lake, so with just a little bend at the knees, he could periodically immerse himself completely to cool off. As a last measure, he tied a wet bandana over his nose and mouth and soaked his hat in the lake before pulling it down low over his eyes.

Above the howling wind they began to hear the deep roar of flames and the crashing of large trees as they toppled over in the approaching firestorm. Will could feel the earth shake through the cool ooze of the lake bottom. G.D. was starting to get nervous, so Will moved in close, put his hand up under the blanket, and rubbed his nose so the animal could take his sent. "Not much longer now, G.D. I reckon we'll know pretty soon how this is going to turn out." By now the heat was so intense that Will ducked under the blanket with GD. There was nothing more to do but wait it out.

Will and G.D. were in the water for about six hours when the worst of the fire finally passed them by heading to the northeast. Fortunately, the wind had shifted again and was coming a little more from the south, causing the hottest winds to miss them. The natural barrier of the lake had caused the fire to split apart as it raced by, leaving a small area of untouched land just to the northeast. Will pulled the blanket back off G.D.'s head and led him into shallow water so they could follow the shoreline around to the only place not scorched black and smoldering. The remaining hours of daylight were spent trying to dry his clothing and digging through the waterlogged packs in an attempt to salvage as much as he could. The front that had spawned the terrible winds was now beginning to move through, bringing with it dropping temperatures. In spite of being nearly consumed by fire earlier in the day, he built a small one to keep the night chill at bay and to aid in drying out his gear.

The next morning they got an early start and headed up the Manistee river valley toward Sherman. A stop at the general store there would give him a chance to replace his food supplies before they headed north on the Traverse City road. The lands along the river that had been logged off were burnt nearly flat, making for fairly easy travel but for the occasional detour around a hotspot. The black ash rose up from their feet with every step and clung to their bodies. G.D.'s legs and belly were black and he had an amusing black ring around each nostril. Will's appearance wasn't much better. The ash from blackened underbrush covered his still-damp canvas pants and coat, and his face was smudged from working itchy insect bites with his dirty fingers. He, too, had black rings under his nose from breathing in the smoke that still drifted in layers along the ground in every direction.

They were just about to take their second fifteen-minute break when they crested a ridge and looked down on what appeared to be a lush green island in a black sea of desolation. By some freak of nature, the fire had swung sharply north after passing over the ridge, perhaps by some concentrated winds funneled up the draw below them from the river. In the center of this patch of green were a small farmhouse and a new-looking barn. In fact, the farm looked newly settled with still a lot of clearing to be done. As Will ticked off the things in his mind that the farmer still needed to do, it dawned on him that there was nothing moving down there. No chickens, no livestock, no people. He and G.D. moved down into the draw and up the other side, keeping an eye out for any sign of life. They stopped by the front corner of the barn where there was a hitching rail for G.D.'s lead, and Will dropped his pack, still feeling uneasy. The white paint on the side of the barn facing the approaching fire had been burned black and still clung to the siding in large curling flakes—a very near thing for this family.

Will started walking toward the house and suddenly stopped, holding his breath and listening. There it was again! Someone was calling for help, but it sounded as if it was coming from far off. He took a few more steps toward the front of the house and the cries faded. He retraced his steps and went around the back of the house and stopped. "Hello!" he yelled and waited for a response. "Help us, please help us!" came the call again. "We're down here!" Instantly Will knew what had happened and started looking for the well. He spotted a rope tied to a tree a few feet from the back door of the house and followed it to where it disappeared into the ground. He eased up to the edge of the well and looked down. The hole was about four feet wide and thirty or so feet deep. At the very bottom looking up at him were five very scared pale faces: a woman and four children standing on what looked to be pieces of furniture. The woman, who was clearly near the end of her endurance, said, "Oh, thank the good Lord you found us, sir. We couldn't go on much longer. My husband put us down here when the fire came, and I haven't seen him since. I fear he has perished, or surely he would have come back for us."

"Well, let's take one thing at a time. I reckon you and the young'uns must be too weak to climb up the rope, but do you think you can hang on if my mule can pull you up?"

"Yes, we will all do our best," said the woman.

"OK, it will take me a few minutes to get ready, but don't fret, I'm going to get you out." Will unhitched all of G.D.'s packs and piled them against the barn. He left the pack saddle on so he would have a place to secure the end of the rope that hung down into the well. The children came up first one by one and stood waiting for their mother, shivering from hours half submerged in the cold well water. It took two tries and a little encouragement, but finally the woman was safely above ground and crouched down hugging her little family close to her.

"Why don't you and your young'uns get on in the house and make a fire to warm up, and I'll poke around a little bit and see if I can figure out where your husband got to," said Will. The woman nodded and looked around as if seeing the house for the first time. "I figured everything was gone," she said, shaking her head. "The last thing he said was that he was going to turn the animals loose."

190

With that to go on, Will figured he would look in the barn first. He walked G.D. over and tied him to the hitching rail and then crouched down and dug in his pack for a little cloth drawstring bag that he kept maple sugar candy in. He thought it might cheer the little ones, and as an afterthought, he held one under G.D.'s nose as a reward for pulling the people out of the well.

Will leaned against the big barn door and rolled it aside, almost to its stops so daylight would fill the large interior space. He stood there for a moment, taking in the tragic scene before him. The stalls were all open, some with a horse or a cow lying half in and half out. Some animals lay on the floor in the center of the barn; all were shot in the head. Sitting on the floor, leaning back against a big chestnut Morgan, was the husband and next to him a black and white long-haired dog, also shot in the head. The man's right foot was bare, the big toe sticking through the trigger guard of an old Sharps hunting rifle, the barrel of which still rested in the man's mouth. Dull red spatter from the back of his head had dried on the horse's side and underbelly and was already attracting large barn flies. Luckily, the colder temperature was keeping the smell down. Will figured that the man had put his family in the well to escape the fire, knowing full well there was no room for himself. When he came to the barn to turn his animals loose and let them fend for themselves, he realized that it was too late. The fire was almost on top of him. Choosing to spare his animals the agony of being burned alive, he had put them down, one by one, then turned the gun on himself; and when all was done, by some fluke, the fire had turned away at the last possible instant. Will took his hat off and slid down the edge of the door to the ground. He bowed his head, letting the sadness of this human tragedy wash over him.

Will walked up to the house and knocked on the door. He stood looking down at the ground and turning over in his mind what he was going to say while he waited. The woman opened the door and motioned him in. Once inside, he took off his hat and nervously began passing the brim through his hands as they stood facing each other. Behind her through the doorway to the kitchen he could see the four children sitting on the floor in front of the open firebox of the cook stove wrapped in a blanket; all four serious little faces were watching him. Will started to speak, but the woman read his face before he could get a word out, and as he looked on he saw the hope drain out of the her small frame. She hunched forward, arms hanging loose in front of her and began to sob. Instinctively Will stepped forward, put his arms around her and hugged her to him, rubbing his right hand gently up and down the center of her back. Her hair still carried the faint sent of moss from the sides of the well. There were no words. There was nothing he could have said more comforting than his embrace, the connection with his soul that felt her loss. Will looked over her shoulder at the children sitting on the kitchen floor in front of the stove. They were still shivering under the blanket, but they had all turned away and were staring into the fire.

Will and the woman stood on the river bank next to a small flat bottom boat. After helping him bury her husband and the family dog behind the house, she had packed a few belongings and loaded them and her children in the little vessel for the short trip downstream to Manistee, or what was left of Manistee. "You got kin downriver?" said Will.

"A sister. Her husband works in a mill there. I reckon they'll take us in until we can get all this sorted out," said the woman as she swatted a stray lock of hair away from her dirty face. Will suddenly remembered the candy in his pocket and stepped up to the side of the boat. The children sat silently but watching intently as he dug in his pocket for the cloth bag. He shook the little squares of maple candy into his hand and held them out for each child to make a selection.

The last little boy took his time and studied the remaining pieces of candy very carefully as if they were precious stones. At last he picked one out and looked up into Will's face. "My daddy is just sleeping, you know. When he gets rested up he will come for us."

Will nodded sadly and squeezed the little boy's shoulder before turning away. He really wanted a drink. "I reckon I'll be on my way," he said. "Good luck to you and your young'uns."

"God bless you for your help, Mr. Castor. We wouldn't have lasted the night in that well." Will tipped his hat and turned away to walk back up to the barn to collect G.D.

Part Three

Chapter 25

The state road that ran from Newago to Traverse City and Northport passed through the tiny village of Sherman about a half mile south of the Manistee River. In fact, it was known first as Manistee Bridge before being renamed in honor of the famous Civil War general. Although the trees and underbrush had been cleared, making the way passable for wagons in the summer and sleighs in the winter, the hilly nature of the terrain made it a difficult journey for settlers going north to stake claim to their homesteads. One old surveyor who helped plan the route reported that any settlers who made the trip to Grand Traverse County would never give up and go back because it would mean battling all those hills again. By the fall of 1871, there was regular stage service all the way to Northport, and farms were springing up along both sides of the road in ever-increasing numbers.

Will and G.D. took their time moving up the road, stopping to chat whenever they encountered another traveler or a farmer out working a field. The latter mostly had nothing but praise for the quality of their soil, which was no surprise. Will still had his doubts, though. The road that ran right past or through this perfect soil was nothing but sand where the sharp wheels of wagons and stage coaches had cut through the fragile loam. It was late afternoon when they crested a hill and looked out over the little community of Monroe Center. One of the first things that Will noticed as they stopped to rest and take the view was the smell of the land. It was different from what they had encountered so far. It had character. Off in the distance, sticking up above the crest of the next hill, he could see a church steeple and the roofs of several buildings clustered close together. "Well, G.D., I got a feeling about this place. I reckon we'll do a little nosing around hereabouts."

They traveled on a little further and stopped next to a partially cleared field where two men and a team of oxen were struggling to pull a large beech stump out of the ground. The pockmarked field where the stumps had already been removed reminded Will of the Confederate line at Stone's River after the rebels had pulled out. It appeared the men had been at this backbreaking work for a good while; they and the animals glistened with sweat in spite of the cool late afternoon autumn air.

As Will approached, the older man looked up and leaned on his shovel, obviously grateful for a little distraction, while the younger man continued to chop away at a big root with an axe. "Evening," said Will with a friendly nod. The older man regarded Will for a moment then said, "What can I do for you, young fella?"

"Name's Will Castor. I'm a land looker for Heimbaugh and Sons out of Manistee and East Saginaw."

"Well, you're a little off the mark for floating logs out on the Manistee, I'd say."

Will smiled and nodded at the man's remark.

"I'm getting a little weary of the solitary life and thinking of putting down some roots. I'm up this way looking for a little patch of good dirt to work and some friendly neighbors." Will knelt down and looked into the hole underneath the stump. "I thought I smelled me some good clay-heavy soil a few miles back, and I see now that my nose didn't deceive."

"It's good and heavy all right, and deep too. Takes some big animals to work it."

"I'd be obliged if you could tell me a little bit about this neck of the woods," said Will.

The old man turned away and yelled at his son. "Edward! That's enough for today. Put them animals away and tell your mother to round up another chicken. We'll be having a guest for supper. I'm Cal Spangler, by the way," said the older man as he offered his hand.

It had been many days since Will had eaten a regular cooked meal with all the fixin's, and he had to force himself to go slowly and remember his manners. Cal's wife Willo was an excellent cook and seemed genuinely pleased to see the pleasure on Will's face as he savored every bite. As soon as they had all eaten their fill, Edward's two younger sisters jumped up and cleared the dirty dishes from the table, returning a few minutes later with apple pie, still hot from the warming oven above the wood fired range.

The lingering smell of the supper, the clatter of dishes being washed in the kitchen, the warm feel of family that filled the room to overflowing was like a tonic to Will. He sat back in his chair with a contented half smile on his face, watching his fingers drum on the side of an enamelware mug of steaming black coffee. "Willo, I'm much obliged for such a fine supper," he said. "I ain't seen the likes of anything half as good in a coon's age, if you'll allow me to say so."

Willo waved off Will's compliment as she squirmed in her chair, but she was clearly pleased with the praise. "Nothing fancy, Mr. Castor. Why don't you young'uns run along now until bedtime and let us old folks talk a bit," she said, dismissing the two girls. "Edward, you're free to do as suits you."

Cal pushed his chair back a little and crossed a leg over his left knee. He took a long sip of coffee and said, "So tell us a little about yourself, Mr. Castor."

"Well, first off, I'd be honored if you folks would just call me Will." Cal smiled and nodded. "I was raised down around Coldwater. Joined the army back in '61 when the war broke out. I was at Stone's River and Chickamauga. That's how I got this bum leg and scar," he said as he brushed the skin of his forehead above his left eye. Spent a year as a teamster for a logging camp north of East Saginaw. Been cruising timber for Ben Heimbaugh since then and doing a little land speculating on the side. I still got a hundred and sixty acres coming from Uncle Sam, and I've saved a little money to put up a house and maybe a barn. Just got to find the right spot, is all."

Cal and Willo exchanged a look as if they had made up their minds about something, but it was lost on Will. "What are your plans for tonight, Will?" asked Cal.

Will glanced out the window behind Cal to see how much daylight was left. "Well, reckon me and my mule will hunt us up a patch of woods and set up camp. Now that you mention it, I better get on it while I still got some light."

"Just so happens I know of a hundred and sixty acre parcel that's for sale not two miles from where we sit. Pretty little spot it is, too. Most of it's good flat land, probably ten acres already cleared. Got a little log shanty on it, stream at the bottom of the ridge on the west side. Might just be what you're looking for."

"If you'll be so kind as to point me in the right direction, I'd like to have a look," said Will as he pushed his chair back and stood up. "I'm truly grateful for the fine meal, Willo. I hope I'll get the chance to do you a proper kindness one day."

Cal and Edward walked Will down to the road where G.D. was tied off to one of the big sugar maple trees that lined both sides of the road for several miles in each direction. "Just go back down the road till you come to the first wagon track heading west. About a mile up you'll see the log house on the left."

"Thank you kindly, Cal. I'll spend tomorrow running the property lines and getting a feel for things. I'll drop back by before I head south."

It took only about thirty minutes for Will and G.D. to reach the little log house, but the sun was already beginning to set behind the trees to the west. The leaves had fallen early this year, probably because of the unusually hot, dry summer, and their dark trunks and branches stood out in high relief against the orange sky where the forest dropped over the ridge. Will walked up to the house and peered through the north-facing window. To his surprise, it looked as though whoever had lived here had just gotten up one morning, locked the door, and walked away. It was too dark inside to see much, but right in front of the window was a crude homemade table with two chairs. In the center of the table was a filmy mason jar full of brown shriveled stems that had once been a bouquet of wild flowers. Against the far wall was a store-bought high chair and a long, narrow, high-leg table holding a wash basin and various cooking utensils.

Will left G.D. by the house and walked the short distance up the track to the crest of the ridge. He was rewarded with a magnificent view of two large sparkling lakes far below, separated by a narrow strip of high ground and nestled in a broad valley of old growth pine forest that stretched away to the smoky blue hills in the distance. The last sliver of the sun winked out below the horizon as he looked on, leaving the whole beautiful expanse bathed in soft light and long shadows. By the time Will had returned to the little house to set up camp, he was already starting to look at this land as his own. There was quite a bit of split wood stacked neatly under a lean-to that was attached to the back wall of the house, and Will availed himself of the convenience. Once G.D. was fed and covered with his blanket, Will wrapped himself in his blanket and sat propped against one of the packs, staring into the fire and thinking about the immediate future. Tomorrow morning he would locate the property lines first, then spend the rest of the day taking the minutes of adjoining land that he could check on at the land office with the idea of using the one hundred sixty acres from the government to increase his spread. He had been looking forward to finding his own place for so long that he had trouble falling asleep and lay awake long into the night looking up at the cold moonless sky, the stars, millions of them, breath-taking and close. A movement in the dead leaves nearby pulled his attention down, and he saw two shiny eyes set in the black mask of a raccoon reflecting the flickering tongues of yellow flame from the fire. He was feeling neighborly, so he let the little visitor nose around as he wished until the howl of a wolf on the ridge finally sent him packing for the nearest tree.

Sunday morning Will was up at first light and preparing to make the trip south to Saginaw. First he had to see Cal Spangler and tell him he wanted to purchase the land with the little log house. He had dipped a bucket of cold water out of the cistern behind the house and washed up as best he could before donning some clean britches and a new white shirt. The shirt was hopelessly crumpled from being packed, but at least it didn't smell too bad, a little smoky maybe, but there were no stains to speak of. G.D. looked on unimpressed, restless now that he recognized the signs of a move. Just after Will turned off the wagon track onto the Newago to Northport road heading to Monroe Center, the bell in the steeple of the little church started to ring. Will stopped and pulled out his gold pocket watch, the one Mollie had given him, and noted that it was a quarter to nine. The peals of the bell were clear and true in the cold morning air, but just a little erratic, and Will remembered with a smile how he and Jimmy used to fight over the bell rope on Sunday mornings, creating the same effect. It seemed like a million years ago.

By the time Will reached the front steps of the church, the first hymn had started and he hesitated, rethinking his spur-of-the-moment idea of attending the service with his future neighbors. Just as he was about to turn away, the right half of the two-sided arched door swung open, and Cal waved him in. Will shifted his hat to his left hand so they could shake, and they exchanged whispered "good mornings" as Cal guided him through the vestibule into the main room of the church.

Will looked to his left and saw a man standing in the corner behind the last pew, holding two unhappy little boys by their collars, one on each side of him. He thought these probably were the bell ringers. The last row to the right of the center aisle was empty, so Will was able to slide in and pick up a hymnal without attracting attention. When the hymn was over, the young preacher made the palm-down motion for everyone to be seated, and Will settled onto the end of his pew. The sermon wasn't especially inspired, even though he liked the story of Zacchaeus, but at least it wasn't fire and brimstone. He was glad now that he had slipped in unnoticed at the last minute and was able to survey the congregation as his mind wandered away from the Word.

It was hard to gather much information by looking at the back of everyone's head, and Will was beginning to tire of the exercise when a bored little girl sitting in front of him decided to spit out a coin she had been holding in her mouth for the offering plate. The noise of it hitting the hardwood floor startled the people close by, and they turned to see who was bad. When the little girl's father leaned forward to retrieve the coin, for just a moment, Will found himself nearly face to face with a beautiful, elegant woman in a black dress who was looking back over her shoulder. The startled look on Will's face must have amused her in some way, and she gave him a little smile before leaning to her side and whispering something to a child who was out of sight behind the high back of the pew. As soon as she turned back and lifted her face to the preacher, the head of a little sandy-haired boy, maybe three or four years old, popped up above the pew and regarded Will unabashed. Will smiled and winked at the boy, and he immediately dropped from sight only to reappear a minute later to see if Will was still watching for him.

The service ended with the benediction and a few liturgical verses that the congregation sang by rote. As the preacher started down the center aisle, turning this way and that, shaking hands and connecting with his flock, Will headed for the door, planning to wait with G.D. by the side of the road until he could have a few words with Cal. The thought had also crossed his mind to watch for the lady in the black dress. G.D. was standing easily, tied to a maple tree next to the road in front of the church. Will remembered that he had stashed a couple of apples a few days back, and he thought a little reward for G.D. might be in order.

As he dug around in one of the side packs he talked absentmindedly, "G.D., I gotta say, as a mule you're doing one hell of a job. Why, any man would be proud to own an animal that was half the mule that you are." Suddenly he felt something grab him tight around the leg and he looked down quickly to see what had him. To his amazement, it was the little boy he had played peek-a-boo with in church. The youngster hugged his leg as hard as he could, not playfully, looking up with a grin to say "got ya," but holding on with a simple desperation that Will recognized but didn't understand. The flood of emotion that was started by the innocent gesture took Will completely unawares. He had never experienced anything remotely like this before, and he was deeply touched. He bent over and gently pried the little boy's arms away from his leg, then eased down onto his knees, still holding the boy's small hands and looking into his face. "Hello there, little one," he said softly.

The boy regarded him with such fascination that Will was transfixed. He raised a hand and slowly traced the scar across Will's face. "Ou ou ou ouch," he said with a little stutter.

"It don't hurt anymore, just looks kind of bad is all. What's your name?"

"Ra Ra Ra Robert," said the child, still looking intently at Will. Anticipating the next question, he held up a hand with four fingers extended.

"Well, I'm pleased to meet you Robert. My name is Mr. Castor, and this here is my mule G.D."

"Da da da does he ta ta ta talk?" said Robert?

Will laughed and shook his head. "I reckon you caught me talking to a mule, Robert. No, he don't talk, but I pretty much know what he's thinking. Right now he's thinking he'd like to have an apple. Maybe you'd like to give him one." Will stood up and fished an apple out of one of the packs and handed it to the little boy.

"I ea ea ea eat 'em ta ta, too," he said. Will laughed again and held Robert up in front of G.D.

"OK, now just rub it on his nose a little and let him take it. Easy does it, G.D." When the mule opened his mouth, Robert lost his nerve and quickly pulled his hand back, letting go of the apple. Will caught it and let G.D. take it out of his hand.

Will had been so distracted by Robert that he had completely lost track of everything going on around him. Robert's mother, the lady in the black dress, was talking with a group of women just to the left of the front steps of the church. She had tried, briefly, to keep Robert by her side when the service had ended, but his pent-up energy from sitting in one spot for an hour was too much for her, and he had made his break, running as fast as his little legs would carry him. Her only recourse was to keep an eye on him from a distance, which she was doing when he ran up to the stranger by the road and grabbed him around the leg. Her sudden intake of breath stopped the ongoing conversation and all the women turned, following her gaze. When the stranger knelt down holding Robert's hands and talking so seriously to him, she was struck by how much he reminded her of David, her late husband who was killed the previous winter when a tree fell on him. When Robert touched the man's face she had to bite her lip to keep from tearing up. All the ladies saw it too and pulled a little closer together, Willo putting her arm around her waist.

Will set Robert down on his feet and once again knelt down to talk to him. "Well, Robert, me and G.D. would sure be pleased to have you as our friend. Next summer we'll take you fishing. Would you like that?" Robert just nodded his head, getting shy as he sensed Will was going to leave. "I think we better go find your mother, but very soon now I'm going to live here, just over that hill," he said, pointing in the direction of the little log house. He was about to stand up when a shadow appeared on the ground next to them.

Robert looked up and bolted for his mother, grabbing her hand and pointing excitedly at G.D. "I ga ga ga gave him a a a apple."

"Yes, I saw that, Robert. Did you thank this nice man for letting you feed his mule?" said the woman.

Will got to his feet and took off his hat. "Good morning, ma'am. That's a very bright little boy you have there. You folks have done a fine job with him." Will saw a fleeting look of surprise pass over her face like a cloud shadow but had no notion of its meaning.

"Are you visiting someone nearby or just passing through?" she said.

"My name is Will Castor. No, actually I'm fixing to settle down here. I work for Heimbaugh and Sons Lumber Company out of East Saginaw and Manistee, locating timber for their mills. Truth is, I'm a farmer by nature. Just took me a while to come around to it."

"Please forgive my manners, Mr. Castor. I'm Emma Reed, the school teacher for this area. I'm pleased to hear that you will be joining our little community. I'm sure you will find that these are all good people and will help you in any way they can."

Will nodded and set his hat back on his head. "Well, Robert, G.D. and I have some miles to cover today, so we best get on our way."

Robert ran up to Will with his arms held high so Will would pick him up. Will blushed and a broad grin spread across his face. He looked at Emma and said, "Looks like I've already made a friend. Truth be told, I never had a young'un fancy me so."

"It seems you are a natural, sir. Come, Robert, we must allow Mr. Castor to get on with his business. Have a safe trip, sir."

Will tipped his hat and started to turn away. "Oh, one more thing. If you and Mr. Reed will permit, I promised Robert I would take him fishing one day soon." Emma gave Will a little smile and nodded as she turned and started up the road, holding Robert's hand.

Will was gratified to see Cal Spangler standing on the front porch of his house as he came over the little hill by the cemetery. He was hoping to state his business quickly and be down the road before much more of the day slipped away.

"Sorry I missed ya after church, Will. I see you was a little preoccupied there and I thought I'd leave you be," said Cal as Will walked up.

"Yes sir, that little Robert is something, all right."

"Damn shame about his Pa. Tree fell on him last winter when he was putting up firewood. Nice enough fella, but pretty green. He never did settle in to this kind of life. The boy saw the whole thing; been having trouble talking ever since." Cal watched as Will looked down at his feet and kicked absentmindedly at the dirt, struggling with this new information. Finally he looked up and said, "I want to buy that place over yonder with the little log house. You know how much they're asking?"

"Being a smart young fella, I'd a thought you would have asked her yourself when you was just talking to her," said Cal.

The older man caught the momentary flash of cold steel in Will's look and realized that he had stepped over some imaginary line. "I'm sure she just wants a fair price and the chance to put the past behind her. She's contracted to teach school here at least through the winter. I 'spect if she gets her money out of that land, she'll move on after that."

Will nodded, stuck his hands in the side pockets of his canvas coat, and turned to look back down the road. "Would you be willing to speak with her on the matter?"

"Yes, I'd be willing to do that. We'll hate to lose her, but I guess it's pretty slim pickin's for a husband around here, and she's got her boy to think of."

"I'll be back here around the end of next month and fix things up with the bank. I'll pay whatever she asks." Cal raised his eyebrows at that but didn't say anything. "I'll be wanting to build a house and barn out there come spring. I'd be obliged if you could recommend someone to do the work."

"There's a couple of brothers out in Leelanau County that do some good foundation work. Let me think on it until you get back. There's plenty of folks looking for work, and we ain't had a proper barn raising in quite a spell. There's a fella in Traverse City got some fine looking draft animals, too. I figure you're going to need the whole shebang."

"I reckon so," said Will. Both men stood side by side on the porch with their hands in their pockets, looking out toward the road and trying to think of anything else that needed saying before Will left.

Cal finally broke the silence. "Now don't get me wrong. I don't mean no offense, but that is by a far piece the scruffiest lookin' mule I ever seen."

Will laughed out loud and turned to face Cal as he stuck out his hand. "He's a good one, but I agree he ain't likely to win any premiums at the fair. I expect to pay you for your trouble, Cal."

"Your money ain't no good with me, son. That ain't the way neighbors are around here."

Will nodded and tipped his hat, then turned away to collect G.D. He was getting a late start, but he felt good, and he had a lot to think over on the long walk south.

Chapter 26

Will didn't know it yet, but his life had already changed more than he could possibly imagine. The terrible forest fires that had swept Wisconsin and Michigan and burned most of Chicago had driven the price of lumber sky high. At almost the same time, a man named Winfield Scott Gerrish proved that a small narrow gauge railroad could be built into previously inaccessible stands of timber and used to transport the logs to banking grounds along rivers or in some cases directly to the mills. When the timber was exhausted in one area, the little railroads could simply be taken up and moved to a new site. This not only gave the lumber companies access to vast tracts of landlocked pineries but also made cutting them a year-round business. Snow and ice for the big logging sleds were no longer needed. The death knell for Michigan's great forests was tolling, but few were listening.

It was nearly dark by the time Will had G.D. put up in his familiar stall at Jerald's livery on Water Street. It had been a good trip south, the Indian summer days dry and warm. He had used the hours of walking to think about the land in Monroe Center and how he would go about turning it into a farm. He found that no matter what problem he was working out in his mind, his thoughts had a way of settling on Emma and Robert. The little boy had awakened something long dormant in his heart in just the few minutes they had been together, and his mother, Emma, was lovely and well spoken with a sophistication and confidence born of a teacher that Will found irresistible. He knew he should nip these daydreams in the bud right now and save himself some trouble later on, but he couldn't help himself, and the hope was too compelling.

The next morning Will was startled awake by the booming voice of his friend Jerald. "Castor, you miserable sack of shit, this is no time to be lying around in bed thumping your melon! We got places to go and people to see! Shake a leg!" Will blinked the sleep out of his eyes to behold what appeared to be a giant standing over him in a red plaid Mackinaw with a wide toothy grin and smiling eyes regarding him from somewhere near the ceiling. "I knew when I see that ugly mule of yours parked downstairs that my long-lost best friend Will was home from the hills." With just the briefest pause to take a breath, Jerald grabbed a straight-back chair, pulled it up to the bed, and straddled it backwards. "OK, I got a good one for you," he said. "Tell me what this is." He leaned in close to Will's face and pooched his lips out past his moustache and beard as far as he could, then lay the index finger of one hand along the top of the upper lip and the index finger of the other hand along the underside of the lower lip and sawed them back and forth. He was so tickled with his own joke that he jumped in before Will could respond. "Why, it's your gal riding a horse!" he said and immediately burst into laughter and slapped his knee. Will looked on in a daze, slack-jawed, until it finally hit him. He groaned and rolled away from his friend, pulling the pillow over his head.

After a cup of coffee from a beat-up enamelware pot, heated on the forge in the usual manner, and some gooey pastries, they headed down to Heimbaugh and Sons. Ben recognized the familiar voices of his two friends harassing his little bald-headed clerk and came charging out of his office to greet them. "Damn, it's good to see you two!" he said as he herded them back to his office. When the hand shaking and greetings were over, the three men settled into chairs around the big desk to get down to business. "You've been out of touch for a while, Will, so I'm not sure how much you've heard about all the changes taking place in our little piece of the world," said Ben.

"I heard about the big fire in Chicago, and barely skinned out of the one that took Manistee. Did the mill survive?"

"The yard burned, and a barge load of boards that was tied in the river alongside. The Old Man's luck held once again, and the machinery was spared. Everyone else was wiped out. The river is still full of wrecks, so we can't get ships in, but no matter, at least not for now. We're running the mill twenty-four hours a day just to keep the folks who are rebuilding in Manistee supplied; a lot of it's charity work. Butler and Tait will be up and running in a few days, and that will take some of the pressure off."

Will and Jerald nodded as they tried to imagine the scenes of devastation and the despair of the people who were burned out of their homes. "I spent the day up to my neck in a lake just a little north of town. That fire was the damndest thing I ever see."

Ben nodded as he fiddled with his pipe. Finally he touched a kitchen match to the bowl and got it to draw. "I heard the damage claims in Chicago have wiped out most of the insurance companies, so even those that had insurance still lost everything. Fortunately for us, it hasn't slowed them down too much. They're already rebuilding and willing to pay just about anything for lumber; which brings me around to a much happier subject. I was in Lima, Ohio last week and bought one of those new little narrow-gauge locomotives, Shays they call them. A fellow named Ephraim Shay from up around Harbor Springs came up with the idea. Ugliest looking contraption you ever saw. Looks like a boiler mounted on a flatcar with little tiny wheels no bigger than that," he said, holding up his hands about two feet apart. "Anyway, I got the engine, ten flatcars, and fifteen miles of track coming up from Toledo by barge next month."

Jerald was already grinning, but Will hadn't fully grasped the significance of this information yet. "If ever there was two people in the right place at the right time it certainly would have to be you two. Lumber has more than tripled in price since the fires, and this little railroad is going to open up all that stumpage you boys are sitting on."

Suddenly the light went on in Will's head and his jaw dropped. Before he could regain his composure, Ben dropped the second bombshell. "What I'd like to propose is this: I'll buy all the land you two own at a fair market price and still give you each a percentage of the profits. Jerald has given me a rough idea of your holdings, and I'd say that you two will be wealthy men when the dust settles on all this."

There was a long silence as Ben and Jerald waited for Will to say something. Finally he spoke. "That's a pretty generous offer, Ben. I don't much like taking advantage of my friends. I always hoped to make a killing someday, but I'd rather do it on someone I don't know." Ben held up his hands palm-out to stop Will, but he continued on anyway. "If it wasn't for you and Henry, I wouldn't even be sitting here. In fact, I'm pretty sure I'd be dead."

Ben was taken a little aback by this last statement but jumped in before Will could go on. "Whoa, whoa! You don't need to worry about me. Think about this for a minute. While everyone is scrambling around sending out lookers to locate passed-over stands of pine, I'd already have enough in my pocket to keep two mills busy for a year at least, and all of it looked at by someone I would trust with my life. My little railroad could go to work right away, and I'd have the jump on everyone else getting lumber down to Chicago. That's good business no matter how you slice it."

Will leaned forward and stared at the floor for a few moments. Finally he looked sideways at Jerald and grinned from ear to ear. "How about it, partner?" Jerald fell back in his chair and let out a long breath of wind like a safety valve going off on a steam engine. "Will, you little asshole, you're going to cause my death someday." Then he sat bolt upright and slapped his hand on the desk in front of him. "Hot damn, gentlemen, we're in business!" All three men laughed and exchanged handshakes to cement the deal.

It took about an hour to work out the details of their arrangement and by then Jerald's stomach was growling so loud that it was interrupting the conversation. "I'm going to leave you two to finish up while I get something to eat. I'll be over at Louie's if you want to catch up later," he said as he stood up and headed for the door.

"Well, I guess we're about done here anyway," said Ben. Will didn't stand up right away, so Ben leaned back in his chair and locked his hands behind his head as he waited for his friend to speak.

"What do you hear from Henry these days?" Will said at last.

"I had a letter just before I went to Ohio. He's up in the U.P. chasing rocks instead of trees now. Seems to think there's going to be a lot of money made mining for iron ore up there—not that he needs the money. The postmark was Marquette, if you want to send him a letter; general delivery should work. I'm sure everyone up there knows him by now," said Ben with a little smile.

Will gave Ben a knowing look and said, "I don't expect he'll ever settle down. It's just not in him." After a moment of silence, Will continued, "I found some land up around Monroe Center that's just what I was looking for, Ben. I'm going to settle in one place for a while and take a turn at farming." He read Ben's face as he spoke but didn't see any surprise. He thought Henry must have tipped him off after their conversation the night of Jerald's wedding.

"Ordinarily I'd be sorry to lose a good man like you, Will, but I'm glad to see you make your move. It's about time you give some thought to starting a family. If there's anything I can do to grease the skids on this end, you just say the word."

Will stood up to leave. "Thank you kindly, Ben. You've already helped me more than I can ever repay. I'm going to build a house in the spring, and I'd be pleased if you and your family paid me a visit sometime."

Ben stood up too and extended his hand. "We'll chat more before you leave town." Will turned to go, but before he could get through the door, Ben called out to him. "Hold it a minute, Will. Where did you say your land was?" Ben had moved over to the far wall and stood looking up at the big township map of Michigan.

"Monroe Center, between Sherman and Traverse City, on the state road." Ben put his right index finger over the dot that represented the little village and looked back and forth between it and some spot to his left. When he dropped his hands and turned around, he had a troubled look on his face. "There's an old acquaintance of yours running a camp for Butler and Tait out of Manistee. I'm sure you remember Tom Bellman, that character with the big nose. You keep your eyes peeled for him. Last time I talked to Ed Butler, he was thinking of building a railroad between Manistee and Traverse City to get at some prime pineries in that area. If he does, that will bring his operation right to your doorstep. You mark my words, Will. He's going to look you up one day to settle that old score."

Will walked into Louie's just as Jerald was pushing back from a big platter that had been heaped with cornmeal mush and thick slices of ham moments before. He pulled up a chair across from his friend and ordered Johnnycake and beef stew off the chalkboard menu hanging behind the counter and a tall mug of sweet cider to wash it down. His friend tipped back in his chair, got a faraway look in his eyes, and tucked his chin into his chest.

Will had seen this look before and steeled himself for what was coming next. At the last second Jerald puffed his cheeks out and swallowed hard, stifling a giant belch. Will laughed and shook his head. "So tell me about married life, Jerald. Looks like Maribel is serious about reforming you."

"I'll tell you, Will, marriage ain't exactly the way I had it pictured. That Maribel is a real peach, don't take me wrong, but damn, she just don't mind very good. The way I was raised, the man was in charge. Not so, my friend. Why the other day she made biscuits and gravy, and I thought, judging by the weight and consistency, a few suggestions about the finer points of biscuit making might be in order. A big mistake! I don't mind telling you, Will, I thought she was going to stick one of those tough little son-of-a-bitches up my ass sideways before it was all over."

When Will had his laughter under control, he briefly considered telling Jerald about Emma and Robert but then quickly rejected the idea. "I'd like to buy a team of Belgians and a sleigh to get me and my gear up north. You know of anyone that got either one for sale?"

"There's a fellow I know runs a little outfit just this side of Bay City that makes a damn good bobsleigh. If you don't need it straightaway, he might be willing to make one that suits you. Probably need one with high sides and maybe no back seat. We could add some bracing to make it a little stronger for the trip. I'll ask around to see who has some horses for sale."

Chapter 27

The November snows began in fits and stops, but by Thanksgiving, winter had settled in to stay, and Will was anxious to be headed north. With the personal attention of Ben's banker, he was able to transfer the majority of his funds, which were considerable by now, to the First National Bank of Traverse City. From there he planned to move a portion to the little local bank in Monroe Center to cover the purchase of Emma's property and the building of a house and barn. He had purchased a 160-acre parcel that adjoined the west side of Emma's land and entered an application for a second 160 acres on the south side under the Homestead Act. The five-year occupancy provision was reduced by one year for every year he spent in the army, so in effect, in just one year the land would be his, free and clear. As he sat on a bench in the outer room of the land office that day waiting for the clerk to draw up his paperwork, he thought of the two sparkling blue lakes separated by a narrow strip of lush green forest that lay in the valley to the west of his land. Henry's words from that long-ago day on the train heading down to East Saginaw came back to him. "One day the great old white pine will be gone and your grandbabies will think it's a fairytale when you tell 'em of trees six feet across and a hundred and fifty feet tall," he had said. Before Will walked out of the land office that day, he had added that strip of virgin trees to his holdings with the idea of protecting them from the lumber companies. From his ridge he could easily keep an eye on any approaching logging operations and head off trespass cutting, a common occurrence in those days.

Will filled a few days updating his wardrobe in the various shops along Water Street. He bought a couple of pairs of summer work boots and a pair of pac-style boots from C. Kull's; britches, shirts, socks, and drawers from Copeland and Barstow's. Along the way he passed a storefront that reminded him of the first time he had laid eyes on Henry. The garments in the window were definitely a cut above what you would expect to see on a regular working man. As he stood outside admiring the handsome green wool hunting coat with leather shoulder and arm patches, it occurred to him that he would need "Sunday go-to-meeting" getup. That was justification enough, but he also had Emma in the back of his mind. When he finally left the shop, he was a little shocked and embarrassed by how much money he had spent, even though it did feel good: a ready-made suit and tie, dress boots, fancy wide-brimmed black hat with a jaunty little red feather in the band, deerskin gloves, and of course the hunting coat that turned out to have roomy game pockets on the inside as well as the outside.

Jerald's inventory at the livery was made up of mostly quarter horses with just a few older draft animals that were still suitable for city work, but he was able to supply Will with several leads on local farmers whom he had bought draft horses from in the past. On his second attempt he found two beautiful palomino Belgians, a three-year-old mare, and a five-year-old gelding that had already been working as a team. Will was sold the moment he laid eyes on the animals, but he feigned uncertainty to stall for time and watch the farmer handle them. He wanted no part of an abused horse and certainly not a team. Once satisfied that all was well, he agreed to return the next day with cash and harnesses. Will planned to have Jerald drop him off early in the morning so he could take his time fitting the harnesses before walking the horses back to town hitched. He could take their measure and still have them put up at the livery before dark.

Will spent the days working his team up and down the streets of East Saginaw as he waited for word that his bobsleigh was ready to be picked up. Annie and Pete were a joy to work with, and the extra time Will had devoted to gaining their trust paid off almost from the beginning. Aside from Pete's tendency to toss his head around a bit and rub his nose on Annie's neck, Will could find no bad habits. Even these minor infractions seemed to take care of themselves once Pete's initial burst of energy was played out. By the time the new sleigh was ready, Will and his team had become something of an item on Water Street. Every day there were a few more faces, Ben Heimbaugh's among them, behind the windows lining the street, watching as he put his team through their paces, deftly turning, backing, and holding with just a soft word or an almost imperceptible touch of rein. He had the best hands Ben had ever seen. Most realized they were watching something special, even if they thought Will was a little daft. Ben, who remembered the war-weary, disillusioned young man who had by chance entered his office five years earlier, was truly amazed at the transformation. Why, he wondered, had so many men returned from the war and just withered, dying a little each day until finally there was nothing left, and some, like Will, had found a way to rise above what they had seen and done? He hoped one day Will would tell him what had happened to him that winter in the forest.

The trip north on the state highway had become much easier in recent years, thanks to the stagecoach stops that had sprung up at convenient intervals between Newago and Northport. They all offered boarding for the animals, and most had rooms and prepared meals as well. At first G.D. seemed a little put off by the new travel arrangement of having his lead tied off to the back of the sleigh, but once he figured out that the big draft horses had the strength to bring him along willingly or not, he settled into the routine.

Ben and Jerald had joined him at Louie's for dinner on his last night in town. The stories and reminiscences ran on into midevening as all three were reluctant to take that first step down their separate paths. When they finally broke up, they were all melancholy and short on words. Lingering handshakes and promises to keep in touch were liberally passed around.

At the Sherman General Store, his last stop before Monroe Center, he was assaulted the moment he stepped through the door by a pack of boisterous little white and brown puppies. The store owner's two little girls tried their best to rescue Will, but every time they were able to pull one of the dogs off his bootlaces or pant legs, another was right there to take its place. The stern look on their mother's face was evidence enough that the girls had been warned about letting the puppies jump on the customers, so to defuse the situation he sat down on the floor and surrendered to the pack. The little girls spun around to their mother and seeing her face soften, squealed with delight and flung themselves on the hardwood floor next to Will. Within a few moments, all three were covered in a squirming mass of little dogs.

"Well, ladies, these are mighty fine looking puppies," he said. "By the looks of those big feet, I'd say you're going to have your hands full when they're full grown."

The girls' father had come out of the back room to see what all the commotion was about and recognized Will from previous visits. "Good afternoon there, Will, nice to see you again," he said. "I see my young'uns and their little pack of devils have wasted no time in working you over. Never seen 'em actually bring down a human before; guess I need to get them started on bears pretty soon.

They shared a laugh, and Will said, "What kind of dogs are these?"

"Well, I'm only sure about the bitch," he said, nodding toward a shallow wooden box by the end of the counter that held a stocky but tired looking white and brown coonhound. "A high roller came through here on the stage a while back, headed for Suttons Bay, as I recall. Had him a real pretty brace of pointers, one black and white, one brown and white, pretty as a picture, they were. I reckon the brown one is the daddy."

On a whim Will said, "I believe I'd like to have one of these pups, Roy...That is, if these two young ladies would be willing to part with one." Will hadn't really thought it through, but it was easy to see that his new life was going to need a dog, and these had a lot of potential, not to mention being nearly irresistible. "You figure a couple of dollars would make the deal?"

"I reckon that would be more than fair, Will. What do you say, girls?"

They looked at each other a little uncertainly until Will opened his hand and showed them two shinny new silver dollars he had gotten a few days earlier at the bank in East Saginaw. "Can we help pick one?" said one of the girls.

Will handed each one a dollar and said, "You sure can. Let me tell you what I'm looking for first." He had been keeping an eye on two pups who were wrestling a few feet away from the others. They seemed to be the biggest of the litter and certainly spirited by the way they were going after each other. The one on top at the moment had one large brown spot in the middle of his back, and the one on the bottom was identical to his brother except he had two large brown spots on his back. "Well...let me see now," said Will as he looked up at the ceiling and played with his chin whiskers as if in deep thought. "I need a big dog. The biggest one you have. He has to have a mostly brown head and a single brown spot on his back. Do you have a dog like that?"

With his new puppy tucked in one of the big inside game pockets of his coat and two pounds of jerked venison wrapped in butcher paper on the seat beside him, Will started out on the last leg of his journey to Monroe Center. The flat bottoms of heavy grey clouds hung close and unbroken above the narrow opening in the stark forest canopy over the road, but the air was calm and mild in the shelter of the trees, making for a comfortable, if unremarkable passage. Will passed the time alternately thinking of possible names for his dog, and possible things he would say to Emma. Sometimes he was confident and came up with clever lines, and sometimes nagging doubts about his chances, marginally educated, scared, and limping as he was, would bring him down. She was certainly pretty enough and sophisticated enough to marry a lawyer or doctor or maybe a successful businessman in town. When he thought of it that way, it seemed very unlikely that she would find a beat-up war veteran with two horses, an ugly mule, and homesick puppy to be her "pot of gold at the end of the rainbow." It seemed so ridiculous, in fact, that he chided himself and put the thoughts of her out of his mind. He had to see her about purchasing her land, and he would let it go at that. It never occurred to him that he was more than just a little successful in his own right. In fact, with a little prudence he could live comfortably for the rest of his life, whether he farmed or not.

A cold northwest wind had begun to blow by the time Will crested the little hill by the cemetery. The dirty clouds were moving fast now with purpose, getting ready to drop the moisture they had picked up on the long fetch across Lake Michigan, in the form of snow. He had already passed several children walking home from school, their colorful wool coats and knitted hats dusted white on the windward side with blowing snow that had begun to drift across the road in sharp ridges. Will thought he had probably already missed Emma and Robert and checked his first impulse to put a little tension on the reins to slow Annie and Pete, but as he pulled abreast of the schoolyard, he changed his mind again and stopped. The puppy was beginning to whimper and squirm inside his coat and he thought this would be a good opportunity to set the dog down and let him relieve himself on the edge of the road. He reached inside his coat with that in mind and immediately felt sharp needlelike puppy teeth close playfully around his index finger.

About the same time, he heard the door on the front of the schoolhouse open and slam back, and when he looked up he saw Robert careening down the narrow path of packed snow as fast as his short legs would carry him. "Gee Gee G.D., Ma Ma Mr. Ca Castor," he yelled at the top of his lungs.

When he reached the sleigh, he pulled up short, not exactly sure what to do next, until Will waved him in. "Robert! I'm glad to see you!" he said as Robert hugged him around the neck, knocking his hat into the back of the sleigh. Robert pushed back and looked into Will's face from about six inches away, not quite able to believe his friend was actually here.

Will was once again struck, as he had been the first time he met the little boy, by his unconditional affection. "I have someone here I'd like you to meet, Robert," he said. Robert looked around quickly as if he had missed something and then gave Will a questioning look. Will unbuttoned two more buttons and held his coat open. Robert bent down to look through the opening just as the puppy's head popped out, and immediately he received several lightning-fast licks on his face.

The little boy squealed with delight and spontaneously clapped his hands. "A pa-puppy, a pa-pa- puppy!" he yelled as he bolted from the sleigh and headed back up the path to the schoolhouse. "Momma! Momma! Ca-ca-come ca-quick. Ma-Ma-Mr. Castor has a pa-pa-puppy!"

Emma had been pulling on her coat in preparation for the short walk up the hill to the Hamlins' house, where she and Robert had been living since her husband's accident, when she saw a rather strange looking sleigh pulled by two large, tan-colored horses stop in the road by the front gate. Before it registered with her who the driver was, Robert had charged out the door and down the path to greet the stranger. When she saw her son put his arms around the man's neck, knocking his hat off, she knew immediately who it was. She took a couple of steps back from the window and watched the exchange between Robert and Will with somewhat more than casual interest. She thought she saw the head of a little dog sticking out of Will's coat, and Robert's reaction confirmed it. Emma finished buttoning up her coat, put the straps of her cloth tote over her shoulder, and waited for her son to burst through the door.

"Well, well, Mr. Castor, this certainly is a pleasant surprise, but I trust you already know that from my son's reception," said Emma. Robert was laughing uncontrollably and rolling on the snow-covered ground beside the sleigh as the puppy worked him over, tugging on his scarf and licking his face.

"It's nice to see you again, Mrs. Reed," said Will as he got up and stepped down from the sleigh. He reached up to tip his hat, only to find at the last second that his hat was not where it should be. Emma quickly brought her hand up to her mouth to cover a little giggle at Will's momentary confusion. He turned back, retrieved his hat from the sleigh and settled it on his head, trying to minimize the damage to his dignity by pretending that nothing unusual had occurred. He gave her a direct look and a little half smile that she found instantly endearing and said, perhaps a little too formally, "I hope you will allow me to give you and young Robert here a ride home, provided we can separate these two," he said turning to the puppy and little boy still wrestling on the ground.

Emma regained her composure and said, "That's very generous of you, sir. We would love a ride, even though we have not far to go, Just to the house yonder on the top of the next hill."

Will handed Emma up into the sleigh and then reached down and snatched the dog off of Robert before he could make a break for it. When they were as settled in as they were likely to get, Emma on one side, Will on the other, with the puppy and Robert still sparring on the seat between them, Will spoke softly to the horses and watched their ears for a reaction. "Annie, Pete…Step up." As the sleigh began to move, Emma stole a quick glance over her shoulder at the general store across the street, but the glare on the big windows hid the eyes she could feel on her.

"Wa-what's his na-name?" said Robert.

"Well, he doesn't have a name yet. I was hoping you could help me out with that, Robert."

"Jack," said the little boy, as clear as a bell.

Both Will and Emma turned to look at Robert, startled by his fast response. "Don't you think you should give something this important a little more consideration?" said Emma. "After all, a name is something you have for a very long time."

"Jack," said Robert. Will threw his head back and laughed. "I like a man who knows what he wants and sticks to it! Jack it is."

Will's and Emma's eyes met as they looked up from Robert. "His favorite bedtime story is Jack and the Beanstalk."

"I had a friend named Jack once. Saved my life back during the war. I reckon he wouldn't mind."

"Where will you be staying, Mr. Castor?" said Emma.

"I believe I'll take a room at the hotel for now. I know they keep stage horses, but hopefully they will have enough room for my animals, too. If not, I reckon Cal will take them in."

"I understand we have business to attend to."

"I reckon so. That is, if you are still willing to sell your land."

"I am," said Emma as she looked down at her hands, remembering her late husband and his enthusiasm when they were starting out. Will sensed her change of mood and fell silent. He talked his team through the turn into the Hamlins' yard and stopped across from the front porch. Robert went running up to the house, yelling his goodbye at Will over his shoulder. He couldn't wait a second longer to tell the Hamlin children about Jack.

"Thank you for delivering us safely home, Mr. Castor, and for being so nice to my son. Losing his father was very hard on him, I'm afraid. It is so heartwarming to see the difference in him when you are around. I hope you will tread lightly, Mr. Castor."

Will didn't respond but stepped down out of the sleigh and then turned and handed Emma down. The silence between them drew out until she was beginning to wonder if he had heard what she said. Will leaned back against the side of the sleigh and reached down, locking hands under the dead weight of the now exhausted puppy inside his coat.

Finally he looked up and into her eyes, and she knew immediately that her words had struck a nerve. She opened her mouth to speak, to explain in softer terms, but Will cut her off. "You need not worry, Mrs. Reed. I'd sooner die than hurt that little boy. The war pretty near sucked the life out of me, I guess. I saw some terrible things, things so bad that they still haunt me most days. Good men…friends, dying for no other reason than they stepped one way and not another. It left me with precious little when all was said and done. Until that Sunday last fall when Robert grabbed me around the leg after church, I had forgotten what pure innocence looked like. Even though he's just a little boy, Mrs. Reed, his spirit renews me."

Emma was momentarily speechless. This was not at all the reaction she had expected. "Mr. Castor, you must forgive my directness. My choice of words and timing are regrettable."

Will smiled at her correctness and looked down at the ground between them. "I prefer directness and honesty, Mrs. Reed; you can always expect both from me."

Emma smiled as the tension between them eased. "You may expect both from me as well, sir. In that regard, I must tell you that my feet are cold and enough time has elapsed that I'm sure the Hamlin family is by now in need of rescue from Robert. Thank you again for the ride, Mr. Castor. We must talk again soon."

Will nodded and smiled and then tipped his hat as she turned to go.

Chapter 28

Will made a point of keeping Emma and thoughts of her at arm's length after their conversation that day. He and Jack were up before dawn each morning, hitching Annie and Pete to the sleigh and setting off before Emma and Robert walked by the hotel on their way to the schoolhouse. There was a lot of new country to explore, and the team needed the exercise. The busy little town of Traverse City on the west arm of Grand Traverse Bay was a frequent destination. It was only about a half-day's ride north on the state road from Monroe Center, but he usually stayed over at one of the hotels on Front Street and returned the next day.

Will and Jack quickly settled into the fabric of daily life in Monroe Center, and the fabric seemed straightforward enough, at least to Will's untrained eye. In time he would come to appreciate the subtle complexities and shadings of society in the tiny community, but for now it was enough to know that Wagner's General Store, across the street from the hotel, was at the center of things. On the days when the weather was bad, Will spent the first part of the mornings playing with Jack in the deep snow alongside the road, trying in vain to burn off some of the puppy's seemingly endless supply of curiosity and energy. With Jack, the world was an all-or-nothing proposition. Back in the hotel, he would play hard for hours, tugging on this or that, throwing things up in the air and then pouncing on them as if they were trying to escape. Then he would just fall over and be asleep in seconds. He hadn't yet mastered the technique of folding his long legs under him to lie down, so he simply crouched as low to the floor as possible and then leaned until he fell over.

"Morning," said Bob as Will pulled the heavy front door of the store closed behind him.

"Morning, Bob," replied Will as he glanced sideways and touched the brim of his hat to the store owner who stood warming his hands over a small potbellied stove and looking out the window.

"How much you say you give for that pooch of yours?" said Bob. Will stopped short and turned around wondering where that question had come from. He followed Bob's gaze out the window and saw Jack lying on his back in the snow with all four feet up in the air. "Seems a might touched, if you ask me."

Will smiled and shook his head. "Sometimes his feet get cold," he replied a little defensively," but I'll admit he don't look overly bright right at the moment."

"What can I do you out of this morning, sir?" said Bob as he turned away from the window.

"Well, I need some ideas about what a four-year-old little boy might like for Christmas, and I need a slab of soapstone for the floorboard of my sleigh."

Bob chuckled and said, "I reckon by 'four-year-old,' you mean Robert Reed, and I suppose it's his mother's feet you plan to keep warm with that soapstone…"

Will's face flushed red, but he fought down the urge to turn away and hide his discomfort. "You don't miss much, do you, Bob?"

"Oh, don't get your drawers in a knot, son. There ain't many secrets in a small town like this. Might as well get used to it; besides, you're something of an item, ya know." Just then there was the sound of canned goods crashing to the floor followed close on by a string of curses. Bob spun around and yelled at the top of his lungs, "Damn it, Cletus, how many times I got to tell you not to cuss and yell when we got customers?" As Bob and Will looked on, a small, stooped old man in dirty bib overalls emerged from behind a long row of shelves that ran down the center of the store. He was pulling a heavy four-wheel cart stacked high with sacks of cornmeal and sputtering under his breath as he headed for the front door. Outside a team and flatbed bobsleigh was pulled up to the wide porch-like loading platform. He had so much trouble coaxing the cart through the front door that Will instinctively started forward to lend a hand, but Bob threw out his arm to stop him. "He's been trying to figure out the swivel wheels on that cart ever since I hired him five years ago, and you can judge for yourself how far he's gotten." When Will looked over at him, he made circles with his index finger next to his temple. "He means well and puts in a good day's work, but the good Lord knows, he tries me some days. I guess I don't know what would become of him if he didn't work here." Will nodded and started to work his way toward the back of the store, sizing up the toboggans that hung high up on the wall over the shelves. "There's some slabs of soapstone on the floor leaning up against the end of the counter there on the left," said Bob. "Oh, and by the way, there's a couple of letters come for you. Remind me to fetch them for you before you leave."

Will was weighing the merits of a large stone over a small one when the front door opened and closed, sending a blast of cold air down the aisle. Cal Spangler stomped the snow off his boots as he surveyed the room. "Morning, Bob," he said.

"Morning, Cal. What can I do you for today?"

"Nothing right at the moment. I'm looking to have a word with Will Castor, and I come across his tracks leading to your front door."

Bob chuckled and said, "You don't have to be no dammed Injun to run him to ground, with that bad leg of his turned out the way it is."

"I reckon not. If I were an Injun, I don't think I'd try to sneak up on him. I have a suspicion you might find yourself looking down the barrel of a gun." Bob considered that information briefly, then looked back over his shoulder to make sure Cletus hadn't run the cart off the front dock before heading back to the little post office room to retrieve Will's mail.

"Me and the missus was thinking you might come to supper tonight and wrap up your business on the Reed place. I 'spect you're wanting to get on with your life, and it would be a good chance to make arrangements with Emma for moving her furnishings."

Will was caught off guard by Cal's invitation, and as much as he wanted to present a plausible reason for declining, nothing came to him in a timely fashion. "Well, that's real neighborly, Cal, and I surely do appreciate the invitation…"

Cal sensed the "but" coming and cut in, "Fine, then, we'll count on you for about 5:30. Bring that new puppy with you if you want. The young'uns will keep him busy." Cal turned to go without waiting for a response but then turned back. Reaching down, he flipped through a couple of the thin slabs of soapstone that stood on end leaning against the counter and pulled one part way out. "This one. Just the right size," he said and quickly turned away.

Will stared at his back as he retreated down the aisle toward the front door. "Seems like everyone knows more about my damned business than I do," he mumbled to himself as he picked up the soapstone that Cal had selected.

Will examined the two envelopes Bob had just handed him as he waited for his change. One was postmarked from Marquette in the U.P. and had to be from Henry. The other was from the Butler and Tait Lumber Company in Manistee. The latter was somewhat surprising, since he had never had any dealings with them before, and very few people even knew he was in Monroe Center. He fought down the urge to tear it open and instead pushed it down into one of the deep side pockets of his coat.

"There you be, sir," said Bob as he dropped some coins into Will's hand. "Soon as you know what you're going to need for next spring, make me a list so I can start working on it. We all like to throw in together and buy in quantity for the best deals, but it takes some doing ahead of time."

Will nodded. "I'll be looking for about thirty apple trees, whips, if you can find a good supplier. Let me know what varieties you can get. Oh, and couple of cases of dynamite and two hundred feet of fuse, too."

Bob raised his eyebrow but didn't look up as he wrote down Will's request. "Gonna do some serious stumping next spring I reckon," said Bob.

"Reckon so," replied Will. "I plan to move fast, once the weather breaks. Good day to you, Bob." Will jumped down off the loading dock on the front of the building and headed across the street toward the hotel with the toboggan and soapstone under his arm. Jack seemed to materialize out of nowhere and fell in at his side, looking up at Will every few steps. He didn't seem to harbor a grudge over his cold feet.

Back in his room, Will sprawled on the bed and picked Henry's letter off his chest. He held it up and examined the envelope with its familiar precise handwriting and thought of his friend. For some reason it made him feel a little lonely, and he dangled his arm over the edge of the bed and scratched behind one of Jack's ears.

Dear Will,

May this note from a fellow woodsman and friend find you in good health and high spirits. Thank you again for sending your notes on that acreage around Walton Junction my way. A very profitable affair all around, that was. With the unexpected proceeds I have purchased part of a new mine just a tad west of Marquette. Thought I might take a turn at mining and leave the pineries to others with younger feet (although it's hard to come by one that can find his ass with both hands these days). Beautiful unspoiled country up here, Will. I hope someday we can share a campfire again and look on it together before I get too old. Well, enough of that crap! I have some business to attend to in Saginaw and will be taking the state road south from Traverse City. I hope to pass through Monroe Center around Christmastime and thought you might show me your new place and catch me up with all the goings on. If the weather allows, I'll be there around the twenty-third.

Henry

Will carefully folded Henry's letter and stuffed it back into the envelope. The missive from Butler and Tait was an announcement of plans to build a railroad from Manistee to Grand Traverse Bay following a roundabout route that would take it past its current logging operation at Nessen City and then on to some of the prime pine forests south and west of Traverse City. Included was a formal offer to purchase the strip of land

226

between the two large lakes west of his farm as part of the right-of-way for the road. Something familiar in the letter nagged at the back of Will's mind, but he couldn't pin it down. He opened the drawer of the night stand and pulled out a pen and ink. On the bottom margin of the Butler and Tait letter he wrote:

To Whom It May Concern,

The land in question between Lake Wahbekanetta and Lake Wahbekaness is not now and will not in the foreseeable future be offered for sale.

Respectfully Yours,

William Castor

Will paced back and forth in his room as the five o'clock hour approached. When he reached the end of his westernmost travel, he stopped and pressed his cheek to the cold window glass and looked up the road in the direction from which Emma and Robert would come. There was still no sign of them. Turning away from the window, he glanced at himself in the mirror over the dresser yet again and considered whether or not the fact that he was wearing a new shirt, vest, and pants was too obvious. He was freshly shaved and the haircut he had gotten the week before in Traverse City was still holding up quite nicely, he thought. Not much to do about the scar across his face, but it didn't seem as noticeable now that he was getting a few wrinkles. When he turned sideways to the mirror and looked over his shoulder at his reflection, he thought it might even lend him a slight aura of mystery and danger. The big clock in the front room downstairs struck the top of the hour, his self-appointed departure time, and broke his train of thought. If he had timed it right, he should be able to intercept Emma and Robert down on the road between the Hamlins' and the Spanglers', and it would appear to be purely coincidental.

"Good evening, Mrs. Reed," said Will as he stepped into the road in front of the woman and her little boy.

"Good evening to you as well, Mr. Castor. How nice to see you again." Will smiled and tipped his hat in his usual way.

Robert, of course, was much less subtle and grabbed Will around the leg. "Wa wa wa where's Jack?" he said. Before Will could answer, the puppy came bounding out into the road, having completed some pressing business in the shoveled path leading up to the front porch of the hotel. "Ja Jack!" Robert cried. Jack, always looking for some action, rose to the occasion and the two were off up the road, leaving Emma and Will standing there shaking their heads.

"Since you seem to have lost your escort, perhaps you will allow me to accompany you to dinner," said Will. Without thinking, he presented his arm and with just the slightest hesitation, Emma placed her hand in the crook of his elbow.

"That's very kind of you, sir."

Chapter 29

Several days after supper at the Spanglers' and the signing of the papers, Will and Jack moved out to the little log cabin on his new farm. Even though Monroe Center was just a small, sparsely populated farming village, it was still easy to bump into a familiar face on the road or find a partner for a game of checkers at Wagner's. The farm, on the other hand, was truly isolated, especially in the winter. Will sat at the small rough-hewn table for the second day in a row, staring out the window at the snow coming down in big fluffy flakes and second-guessing the decision to move out of the hotel. As nice as they were, he suspected that George and Mary Wright, who ran the establishment, were happy to see the last of him and Jack, thanks in part to Jack's indiscriminant pooping and part because of Will's nightmare a few weeks earlier that woke everyone up at three in the morning—including Jack, who added his mournful howl to his master's disquieting sounds.

The evening at Cal and Willo's had given Will and Emma a chance to sit across from each other and engage in conversation for the first time since they had known each other. Will's inclination was to attempt an on-the-fly clean-up of his grammar to match Emma's correct English, but the first cumbersome sentence that came out of his mouth convinced him to abandon the effort and let the chips fall where they may. He was struck by Emma's understated beauty and sophistication as they all lingered over coffee and pie at the end of the meal. She was at once unimposing yet self-assured and confident in her knowledge, a natural teacher. She knew the effect her looks had on men, and she knew her command of the language would give her the upper hand in any test of wills, but she chose to use her advantage to draw Will out and bolster his confidence. Will was smart enough to see what she was doing, but try as he might, he could find no malice in her method. The one thing he could not accept was that someone like her would ever be the least bit inclined toward someone like him. Over the years since the war, he had given up the idea that any woman of Emma's ilk would be able to see past his bad leg and disfigured face. He also knew if he revealed himself as a suitor and failed, it would mean his fears were justified.

Jack, who had been sleeping on the floor with his belly turned to the little cast iron cook stove, suddenly rolled up and gathered his feet under him, intent on the shelf next to the back window. Will had heard the rustling sound, too, and he turned his head toward the source of the sound. Nothing happened for a moment, and then suddenly a little brown field mouse with a chest full of white fur emerged from behind a two-pound coffee can and stopped on the edge of the shelf to regard them. Jack growled and lunged at the shelf but fell hopelessly short each time. The little mouse just held his ground and continued to look on. "I don't think he's all that impressed, Jack. I'd say our little neighbor has some grit." When Will stood up, the mouse spun around and disappeared behind some boxes on the back of the shelf. Will walked over and moved some things around to make sure nothing important had been gnawed. When he was satisfied, he said, "Well my little friend, I think we'll call you Ned. Ned, I'll tell you straight out, I don't want you messing with my coffee. Anything else here Jack and I will share. Just don't mess with my coffee." Will reached to the back of the shelf and retrieved a tin of crackers to place on top of the open coffee can. When he pulled the crackers out he noticed a piece of chinking missing from between two of the big logs that were part of the back wall of the cabin. Wedged in the empty space was a worn black journal book. He reached in, pulled the book out, and ran his hand over the cover to dislodge the layer of dust. The scent of moss that was used to chink the logs rose up to him. The cover revealed nothing, but on the first page were neatly printed the words "The Reed Farm—Monroe Center, Michigan." It was the farm diary of Emma's late husband. Will flipped through it quickly and noted that it had an entry for almost every day until it ended abruptly a little over a year ago. The volume spanned four years. He slowly sat back down and started reading.

Tuesday August 4th. Spent the day stump'n. The Nickerson boys worked with me and brought a team. Hot. Emma found a blueberry patch at the bottom of the ridge near the river. She smelled a bear but didn't see one. Returned directly.

Wednesday August 5th. Rained off and on today. Set some fence posts out by the road and split some cedar rails. Went to Wagner's in the afternoon and found out that Ken Batzloff has decided to move to Missouri. Spent afternoon fixing Dannie's harness.

Thursday August 6th. Sunny but cooler today. This forenoon pulling stumps again. Hard work, but they make a good fence. Progress slow. Worked corn on the west side between the stumps for a spell after dinner. Will need to fix the roof of the lean-to for the team.

Most of the entries were similar, with good information about the area's weather and timing for crops and such, but what held Will's interest was the occasional comment about the couple's home life, and he soon found himself skimming ahead for any mention of Emma. Near the end of their first year, Emma was pregnant with Robert.

Monday May 5th. Plowed the garden and picked up stones. I'll borrow a drag from Cal tomorrow. Emma feeling poorly again this morning. She thinks we are going to have a young'un!

Will read on, feeling a little guilty now, but he couldn't resist. The short winter day was beginning to close down, so he lit his only oil lamp and trimmed the wick to burn bright and clean. Jack was a little restless, so Will gave him a hambone he had picked up at Wagner's and put a couple of pieces of wood in the stove.

Sunday January 13th. Sun came out today. Very mild for January. Emma very sick last night and this morning. Went to fetch Willo and she started Johnny after the doctor. Mary and Dr. Kilpatrick came shortly after noon. Little Robert born at 3:30. I have a son! He is healthy but Emma is taking it very badly. Doctor and Mary left before dark. Willo and Clara will attend the night.

Monday January 14th. Bad night for Emma. She is very weak still. Held Robert and said prayers. Doctor Kilpatrick called at 11:00 and is very concerned. Took Willo home after dinner. Clara stayed on. Robert doing very well.

Tuesday January 15th. Praise God! Emma is better this morning! Fever broke during the night and she can sit up. She held Robert for the first time. Willo, Mary and Cal called this forenoon. Dr. Kilpatrick called and was pleased with Emma's progress. We are warned that she may not survive another birthing. Held Robert and gave thanks to our Lord. Split wood till dark.

Will closed the cover of the journal and stared at the thick lazy flame wavering in the glass chimney of the oil lamp.

Chapter 30

The church in Monroe Center was filled nearly to capacity with the faithful for the late afternoon Christmas Eve service. To be sure, the church was plenty big enough to accommodate the faithful every other day of the year. It was the not-so-faithful that worshiped only on this, one of most sacred of days, that filled the pews. Henry and Will stood shoulder-to-shoulder against the back wall with the overflow people, sharing a hymnal as the congregation sang "Oh Come All Ye Faithful." Will glanced sideways at his friend and was surprised to see him delivering the words with such intensity. It occurred to him that in spite of all the long talks they had shared over many a campfire, they had never discussed religion.

The music ended and the congregation was seated amid a soft rustling of skirts and shuffling of shoes on the hardwood floor. The young preacher, Reverend Pauling, stepped up to the pulpit, and instead of addressing the congregation, simply held out his right arm in a gesture to focus attention on a pleated fabric partition in the dark front corner of the room. As everyone looked on, the partition wobbled a bit, and then a solemn procession of children emerged, all dressed as characters of the nativity, and they all took their places around a makeshift manger overflowing with straw. Will spotted Robert standing slightly apart with two other little boys, wrapped in sheets and all holding what appeared to be ordinary walking canes, but in their small hands they were transformed into shepherds' crooks.

Will bumped Henry's arm with his elbow. "Robert's the one on the left." Henry cast a knowing sideways glance at Will and nodded, then continued looking on. He was just in time to see the tallest of the three boys shove Robert closer to the manger in an attempt to realign him with their designated spot on the floor. Robert's reaction was swift, if not exactly appropriate for the occasion. He changed his grip on the cane and raised it over his head as if to slay his tormentor. Time stood still for a moment as every woman in the little church inhaled sharply, waiting for the blow to land. Emma stepped out from behind the partition and spoke a single word, hushed in form but loud enough to be easily heard by all in the tense silence. "Robert!" she hissed. Robert checked his swing abruptly and looked around, finally remembering where he was. He slowly turned back to face the congregation and once again took up his shepherd's stance as if nothing at all had happened. Emma clutched at her neck and quickly ducked back behind the partition, clearly rattled. Will glanced to his left, and Henry was grinning from ear to ear.

The rest of the service proceeded without mishap. Reverend Pauling retold the story of the first Christmas, timing the important parts to match the series of skits performed by the children of the nativity. Following the benediction, the organist played a soft preamble to "Silent Night," and on cue, several men of the congregation started down the center aisle, lighting the candles of people on the ends of the pews. They in turn stood up and passed the flame to their neighbor, and so on until every face was cast in soft candlelight framed by darkness. When the last verse began, the oil lamps that lined the walls of the church were trimmed down, and everyone held their candles over their heads. Taken apart, each was a simple enough gesture. As a whole, it was mystical. From the back of the room, Will and Henry looked out over the little sea of flickering lights as they sang, softer now, "Holy night, all is calm, all is bright." It was easy to feel the spirit move amongst them, to feel the presence of Jimmy and Al, and George, of Sergeant Hazzard and Jack. It was not the same as in the forest with the dying deer, but it was there.

Cal and Willo had invited Emma, Robert, Henry, and Will for Christmas Eve supper, so following the service, they all made the short walk down the road to the Spanglers', Emma hanging onto Henry as they negotiated the deep ruts in the road and Robert sitting on Will's shoulders. The melancholy that had gripped Will earlier in church lingered on through the meal, but only Willo and Henry seemed to notice his mood. Willo thought that something must have gone awry between him and Emma in spite of her best efforts. She was partly right, but Henry's guess that it had something to do with the war was closer to the mark. Neither had time to draw him out; Willo had the dinner to think of, and Henry had Robert. The fact that Henry seemed to suddenly appear in Monroe Center on Christmas Eve with his white hair and beard, even though both were well trimmed, convinced the little boy beyond any doubt that Henry was indeed Santa Claus. He would not be dissuaded of this notion and sat on the old man's lap studying his face and hanging on every word. Near the end of the evening, Henry pulled a beautiful brass lensatic compass from his vest pocket and quietly handed it to Robert. It was worn smooth from years of riding in the pocket of the old land looker's coat, and it shone deep gold in the light of the parlor oil lamps. Will had seen it many times and knew the value of the gift, and perhaps more importantly, its meaning. Robert's eyes were big as Henry turned it in his hand and explained about the needle always pointing to the North Pole. To Robert it was pure magic and even more proof, if any were needed, that he had been right all along about Henry's true identity.

Willo wanted Cal to hitch Pea to the cutter and give Emma and Robert a ride up the road to the Hamlins', but Emma reasoned correctly that it would take longer to harness Pea than it would to walk the short distance, and besides, she would have Will and Henry as escorts. A quarter moon reflecting off the snow-covered landscape made it easier to keep their footing, but Emma still clung tightly to Henry's arm. A little ahead of them, walking in the same rut, Robert once again rode on Will's shoulders. This time, however, he was exhausted from the evening's excitement, and with his arms wrapped tightly around Will's hat just above the brim, his head rested sideways on the flattened crown. Will was aware that Henry and Emma were engaged in a conversation that seemed something more than casual, but he could not distinguish any of the words over the sound of their footfalls in the crusty snow.

At the Hamlins' front door, Will gently handed Robert off to his mother so as not to wake him. Henry bade her farewell and then stepped off the porch and waited for Will a few feet away. Emma spoke first, thanking him for carrying Robert home and then wished him a merry Christmas. Will sensed she wanted to say more, but as soon as she finished her sentence he gave her a little smile, tipped his hat, and turned away. He had only taken a couple of steps when she called out to him.

"Mr. Castor, if the weather permits, would you consider taking me out to the cabin to fetch my things?"

Will stopped and turned. "It would be my pleasure, Mrs. Reed. Day after tomorrow…around nine?"

"Yes, that would be perfect. I shall be ready, sir." With that, she turned and disappeared into the house.

"A fine woman, that one," said Henry. "Shame about her husband."

"Reckon so," said Will.

"You got something on your mind, son?"

There was a long pause while Will framed a response. "I don't know, Henry, I guess Christmas just makes me a little sad, is all."

"I'm sure you know you got a lot of blessings to be thankful for… or maybe you need an old coot like me to point them out to you." Will stopped in the road and looked hard at his friend. Even in the dark, Henry could feel Will's eyes boring into him, but he held his ground. "If you want my nickel's worth, and I'm obliged to give it to you whether you want it or not, I'd say the only thing you lack is a good woman and some young'uns, and the answer to that problem is right under your nose."

Will was speechless as he fought down his temper. Finally he said, "Well, not that it's any business of yours, but women like Mrs. Reed are looking for lawyers and doctors and such, not some uneducated crippled-up farmer like me. Besides, she's planning to move on when school lets out next spring."

There was another long pause as Henry gathered himself. "Goddamn it, son, sometimes you ain't got the sense God gave a goose! Women don't think the same as we do. You don't need to understand it, just know that they don't. Now you just get her alone so you can talk and ask her straight out. I'm telling you, if you let her slip away, you're going to end up with four bags worth of sorry shit and only three bags to put it in."

By now Will's fury had subsided and he realized that Henry was probably right. There was really nothing to lose. He just nodded and they walked on to the hotel in silence.

The next morning Will and Henry shared a big breakfast before the early stage arrived. Their conversation was much lighter than the night before, and Will was feeling better about life in general. They said their goodbyes as the driver and George the innkeeper finished hitching the traces of a fresh six-horse team to the coach. "Sorry if I ruffled your feathers a little last night, son. I only want the best for you. You ought to know that by now. You marry her and teach young Robert how to use that compass. She's the one you want." With that, he locked eyes with Will and took his outstretched hand. "If I still live, I'll be back through here next October for some pat hunting. You teach that mutt of yours to find some birds so I don't have to walk all over hell's half acre looking for 'em myself." He gave Will a nod and swung up into the coach. Will shouted at him to give his regards to Jerald and Ben as the stage pulled away, rocking and creaking on its springs.

Will snow shoed out to the cabin after seeing Henry off. Jack followed close behind to avail himself of the easier walking on the packed snow and occasionally stepped on the back of a shoe, throwing his master off balance. Normally Will would have found this amusing, but today he was deep in thought about what he would say to Emma, and it was just an annoyance. "Dammit Jack! You're going to send me ass-over-apple-cart if you don't stop that!" As was usually the case, Jack showed little remorse. They spent the rest of the day tidying up and splitting wood for the little stove. Will wanted everything to be just right when Emma stepped through the door, as if a clean, orderly house would tip the scale in his favor.

At the appointed time the next morning, Will turned his bobsleigh into the Hamlins' farmyard and gave Annie and Pete a touch of rein, bringing them to a stop across from the front porch of the house. Robert had been watching for him and darted away from the window, leaving the drapes swinging, and yelling something unintelligible when Will waved. Emma stepped out onto the porch so promptly that she must have been waiting also. "A good morning to you, Mr. Castor," she said pleasantly. "I must say you are very punctual, sir."

"I learned the hard way some years ago it's best not to keep the teacher waiting." Emma half smiled at yet another well-worn reference to her profession as he handed her up into the sleigh. When they were both settled, Will unfolded a heavy black bearskin robe across their laps and draped it down over their legs and feet. "The last time you rode in my sleigh you suffered a case of cold feet, Mrs. Reed," said Will, floating the double meaning. "If you will allow me?" he said as he threw caution to the wind and reached under the robe to slide her feet over onto the hot soapstone that lay wrapped in canvas on the floorboard between them. Emma was starting to warm to the verbal sparring and said, "Oh my, Mr. Castor you are fresh, but I must admit, that does feel heavenly! It is a wise man who knows the way to a woman's heart is through her feet." Will threw his head back and laughed as he snapped the reins lightly to start them forward.

It was cold but still a beautiful winter morning for a sleigh ride, and Will let Annie and Pete pace themselves. He was in no hurry to end the intimacy of sharing the warmth of the robe with Emma. Snow clung to every limb and branch of the big dark trees lining the way, and the low sun sparkled like scattered diamonds between the long shadows on the smooth, white windswept fields where the trees had already been cut. There was no wind to speak of this morning. It was quiet, save only the restless power of the horses moving in their harness, the rhythmic jangle of the sleigh bells that hung around Annie's neck, and the continuous slice of the runners on the frozen road. Puffs of hot breath from the horses hung back on the frigid air in little clouds as they passed. Will shot a sideways glance at Emma. Her brown fur hat was fashionably tilted forward, and her hands rested easily together on her lap inside a matching fur muff.

The turned-up rabbit collar of her red wool coat framed her smiling face, cheeks blushed from the cold as she looked off across the pristine winter landscape. Will was pleased to see the beauty of the picturesque moment was not lost on her.

It took only a few minutes of stoking the fire and adding several pieces of split wood to the cook stove to bring the interior of the small cabin up to a comfortable temperature. If seeing things from her former life stacked against the wall in the once-familiar space had given her pause, she hid it well. While Will fiddled with the draft of the stove, Emma walked slowly around the room, picking up this, looking behind that. The liberal sprinkling of mouse turds on nearly every shelf was not missed by her, but she could tell that Will had made an effort to make things respectable. "I'm afraid I can't offer much in the way of a libation besides coffee, Mrs. Reed."

"That would be fine, Mr. Castor, thank you," she replied, with an amused half smile. Will had a brief moment of discomfort when he was ready to serve the coffee, and he realized that he owned only one beat-up tin cup. Emma dug around in one of her crates for a few minutes and produced a china cup to save the situation. In the process she came across the farm journal that Will had tucked in the side of one of the crates. When she was packing up her things after her husband's death, she had wondered about it, but it was nowhere to be found.

Henry had been right about one thing. Being alone together put them on an entirely different footing. They sat at the little table sipping their coffee in silence for a few minutes while Emma thumbed through the pages of the journal. Finally she laid the little black book on the table between them and met Will's look. "Please forgive me for being so forward, Mr. Castor. I'm sure you know by now that there are few secrets in a small town like Monroe Center. I must assume you know the story of what happened to my late husband, even what our daily lives were like," she said nodding at the journal. "I feel at somewhat of a disadvantage because I know almost nothing about you." Will showed no remorse over reading the journal; his look was steady and unrepentant. After all, any farmer worth his salt would jump at the chance to gain some advance knowledge of local weather or the best times to plant. The fact that there were things of a more personal nature mixed in was none of his doing.

Will didn't respond right away and finally looked down at his hands wrapped around his tin cup and considered his next move. In the end he decided to lay all his cards on the table, face up. He told her about his experience in the war, about his friends who were killed, and how he broke his leg. He told her about Jack and Mollie and killing the bushwhacker who had left him with the scar across his face. He told her about the lumber camp and his drinking problem and about how his experience in the woods had turned his life around. At some places in his story he had to stop and collect himself before going on. This was the first time he had ever told someone the whole story, or most of it anyway, and when he was through, he was dismayed that it painted such a bleak portrait of his life. He hadn't even mentioned the worst things: putting Sergeant Hazzard out of his misery and killing the unarmed farmer and his son. He would go to his grave with these.

As Will spoke, he seldom looked up from the tabletop, and Emma studied him closely as the difficult emotions played across his face. She was surprised at his candor and the deeply personal nature of his disclosures. To her, his story was anything but bleak. The man she saw had overcome his demons; he was a survivor who had every right to be hardened off by the war but yet was determined to open himself to love and a family. He was a man who had killed other men in mortal combat, yet was powerless to resist the affection of a four-year-old little boy. Emma was captivated by what she saw.

There was a long silence between them, and Emma was just getting ready to speak when Will looked up from the table and locked his eyes on hers. "Well, Mrs. Reed, there it is in a nutshell, the sorry truth of the matter. I reckon as long as I've gone this far, I got nothing to lose. I might as well say the rest of my piece. Come spring, I plan to build a proper house and barn on this spot. Maybe even burn down this cabin when I'm through. I did pretty well in the lumber business, so I have some means. I guess more than anything, little Robert…" Will had to stop for a moment because of the lump in his throat. "Your little Robert is…well, he touches something in me." Once again Emma started to speak, but Will held up his hand. "I know I ain't much to look at, and I got this bad leg, but I know farming and I know the woods. If you'd be inclined to marry me, I'd help you raise Robert like he was my own, and I'd see to it you both lived a pretty good life." With that, he fell silent and watched closely for Emma's reaction.

She wasn't completely surprised by Will's proposal, but it still jolted her to hear the words, and she was slightly off balance when she spoke. "You should never shush the teacher, Mr. Castor." She said it in a kind of nervous, light-hearted way, but she regretted the utterance the moment she gave it wing. Will looked at her as if she had just slapped him. She immediately leaned across the table, wrapped her hands around his as they lay there, and looked up into his face. "Oh Will…dear Will, please forgive me! That is not at all what I meant to say. You are a rare one indeed, sir, and I can scarcely believe my good fortune that you have stepped into my life, seemingly out of thin air, at an especially dark time. You have been in my thoughts a great deal since Robert grabbed you outside of church last fall, but I dared not chance a hope. I would be honored to be your wife, Will, but are you sure, knowing what you know about Robert's birth from my late husband's notes?"

The strain in Will's face gave way to something like astonishment at Emma's words. He hung his head and let out a long sigh, silently saying "thank you" before looking up into her eyes again. He shifted his hands until each of his held one of hers. "I want you and Robert as my family; that's all I will ever require."

Chapter 31

Over the next few weeks, Emma and Will met several times to make plans and work out the details of merging their lives and that of Robert into a family. On most occasions Will and Jack would meet Robert and his mother at the schoolyard gate by the road at the end of the day, and they would go next door to the hotel for an early supper. Once word of the pending wedding had circulated around town, Mary, the innkeeper's wife, was much more tolerant of Jack, and of course Jack was on his best behavior as long as Robert had food on the table in front of him and was willing to slip him a bite here and there.

One of the things that Will worried over the most was what the boy would call him. To be referred to as "father" or "Pa" didn't seem fair to his departed birth father, and "Will" or "Mr. Castor" was certainly out of the question. When he mentioned it to Emma, she had shrugged it off as something that would likely resolve itself, not fully grasping the weight it had with him. As a matter of fact, it was the first thing that came out of Robert's mouth when he was told the news. He had tried to say "Papa," but in his excited stutter it had come out as "PeePaw." That name held for a short time but was shortened to the much handier "Peep" when they discovered that Robert could say that without stuttering. Emma seized on it immediately, and that's all it took. The name was struck.

It was decided to delay the wedding until the new house and barn were completed in the spring. That way Emma could finish out the school year and her teaching commitment as a single woman, which the custom of the times required. The notorious Northern Michigan winter lashed the Grand Traverse Bay area unmercifully during the months of January and February. Twice the men of Monroe Center were called out to rescue the stage and its occupants from the deep snowdrifts. Wherever the road ran through open fields, snow would accumulate and drift smooth in the wind, completely obscuring any recognizable features that the drivers relied on to keep the road. Once when the men arrived on the scene, they found the coach lying at a forty-five degree angle and buried up to its roof on the low side. As the driver pushed the six-up team relentlessly to pull the coach out of the gully, they had gradually sidled to the right and off the road. Eventually all six horses were buried up past their bellies and too exhausted to fight on. Will was always included on these missions for his experience with artillery and logging teams but mostly for the almost magical way he had with the big animals.

Regardless of the harsh weather, Will was warmed from within by his prospects. As he and Emma spent more time together, what had started out as a sensible engagement began to blossom into a proper romance. Part of the allure for both of them was just the excitement of leaving the old familiar but incomplete life behind and starting a new one full of possibilities. But that was only the beginning. To their mutual delight, as time passed, they became friends, and then lovers. On one of their long sleigh rides to Traverse City to shop for furnishings for the yet-to- be-built house, they kissed for the first time. With their cold noses touching, they looked into each other's eyes, taking each other's inner light. Will had felt this magic once before, and he recognized it for what it was. He vowed he would never in life be without her.

One Sunday early in March, Will, Emma, and Robert were sitting in church as the Reverend Pauling's sermon began closing in on the eternal message of "turn the other cheek." To the left of Will, Robert was lying on his side in the pew, trying to amuse himself by arranging and rearranging several small but special stones he had carried into church with him that morning. To his right, Emma was rapt as if she were hearing the story for the first time and didn't know how it would come out. The church was nearly full, but oddly, the pew in front of them was empty except for one person, Cletus, from the general store. He sat all alone on the end of the pew nearest the wall, fidgeting nervously with the hymnal and scratching himself behind the bib of his Sunday overalls.

Will's thoughts were drifting in and out of the sermon, and he began to consider the reason no one wanted to sit next to Cletus, when out of the corner of his eye he saw Emma shoot an annoyed glance over at the old man. At the same moment, coincidence or not, Cletus looked back at her, gave her a broad toothless smile, leaned sideways rolling up on his right bun as if to point at her and let a resounding fart. It was so loud that Reverend Pauling pulled up short mid-sentence, and several soft groans from nearby ladies filled the void. Emma inhaled sharply as she brought her hand up to cover her mouth. She bent forward, and her shoulders began to quake. Will's first impulse was to burst out laughing, but when he saw the effect the incident had on Emma, he became alarmed, thinking, as did the lady sitting on the other side of her, that the assault on her proper sensibilities had sent her into some kind of terrible fit. To test Will's composure even further, Robert sat up and started tugging on his sleeve while pinching his nose with his other hand.

By now the service had ground to a halt and everyone was looking on with concern. Still covering her mouth and bowing her head, Emma continued to shake uncontrollably. It dawned on Will that she might actually vomit, so he gently helped her to her feet, and they headed quickly for the vestibule. He grabbed their coats from one of the pegs next to the door, draped hers over her shoulders, and donned his own while still supporting her with one hand. Once outside, Emma stopped on the shoveled path leading to the front steps of the church and bent over at the waist, still shaking and gasping for breath. Will looked around helplessly, trying to form a plan, but he just wasn't sure what to do next. He was even beginning to wonder about the wisdom of marrying a woman who was this unstable. After all it was just a fart, no matter how grievously delivered. At last he decided to carry her across the road to the hotel and see if he could calm her down.

Without warning her of his intentions, he bent over and put one arm around her back as he swept her legs out from under her, cradling her against him. It was at once apparent that this was not a good move. Not only was she heavier than he had expected, causing him to fight for balance, but her fit became worse. She started to shriek and kick her legs, beating on his chest with her outboard fist. Losing his patience now, Will looked down at Emma's face, tears streaming down her cheeks, and realized for the first time that she was laughing. In fact, the whole episode had been a laughing fit! Will, still cradling her in his arms, threw back his head and started to laugh as well, so hard that he lost his footing and tumbled backward into the deep snow bringing Emma down on top of him. As they lay there catching their breath, Will studied her face against the pale blue sky, cheeks pink from the bite of the cold air and big snowflakes catching in her eyelashes. Reaching up, he cradled her face in his warm hands, and proper or not, they shared a lingering kiss, lying right there in the snow in front of the church. The muffled sound of the organ and the congregation singing "Seek Ye First" floated away on the air above them. That's when they knew.

The frost was finally out of the ground by the third week of March, and a small army of men descended on Will's land, tools of their trades and building materials piled high in buckboard spring wagons. Farmers from all over, most of whom Will had never even met before, brought wagonloads of field rocks that had surfaced in their fields as they did their spring plowing. The stonemasons, two brothers all the way from Leelanau County, laid up the foundations for the house and barn while loads of rough-sawn lumber from a mill on the Boardman River south of Traverse City accumulated in large, strategically placed stacks.

The house was built along the same lines as the others in the area, four rooms downstairs, parlor and living room in the front, kitchen and dining room in the back, and four bedrooms upstairs with a staircase open on one side going up through the center of the house. The most noticeable feature that set this house apart from its neighbors was a broad covered porch that wrapped around all four sides. The house was set back a short distance from the edge of the ridge that overlooked the valley containing Lake Wahbekaness and Lake Wahbekanetta. Will planned to hire a crew of unemployed jacks later that summer to cut a pie-shaped swath through the woods to the southwest, and another to the northwest, from the house, to halfway down the ridge. From her kitchen window in the back, Emma would have a grand unobstructed view of the beautiful valley below stretching for nearly twenty miles, and in the evenings they could sit on their front porch and watch the sun set over the lakes. As a surprise for Emma, Will had installed an indoor hand pump water well. It was located in the pantry off the kitchen and drastically cut down the labor and time spent each day fetching water for cooking, laundry, and bathing.

Emma and Will were married in the front parlor of their new house during the second week of June. Reverend Pauling performed the ceremony, and Emma was attended by Clara and Sally, the two Spangler girls. For them, this was a dream come true. They had spent every day after school the previous week making decorations for the parlor, creating little knickknacks to adorn the dining room table and working on their dresses. Some of the Monroe Center ladies, Willo, Mary, and Phyllis Wagner, had taken over the cooking and put out an amazing spread of smoked ham, fresh baked breads, pies, and fresh strawberries. Even Jack did well, quickly identifying the easy marks, working them for scraps and perfecting his "needy" dog routine. Despite their apprehension over how Robert would react to once again living on the land where he had seen his father crushed by a falling tree, the boy seemed to take it in stride. Will had cut the trees back and dynamited the stumps from the area where the accident had occurred to make sure it bore no resemblance to the way it had looked on that fateful day.

By mid-summer the barn was up and sided. It lacked only hardware to hang the two big main gallery doors and some finishing touches to the stalls on the lower level to be complete. During the dinner break on the first day of the barn raising, a neighbor who had a small place over on Hilltop Road and worked as a lumberjack during the winter months approached Will about the property between the lakes in the valley. When he was satisfied that Will was indeed the owner, he pressed even further about his intentions for land. Will quickly became annoyed with questions regarding his personal business but stayed with the conversation a while longer, partly because the man was his neighbor and partly because he was helping put up Will's barn. It was good that he did. Eventually he learned that some of the men in the camps around Nessen City and Thompsonville were becoming restless. They thought their jobs would be in jeopardy if Butler and Tait were forced to abandon their plans to build a railroad north, on the high ground between the lakes, to some of the best pinerics between Manistee and Traverse City. Camp Number Five a little south of Nessen City was especially bad, being stirred up by the foreman there, Tom Bellman.

Chapter 32

Building a house and barn and dealing with the myriad of tasks involved in setting up a new farm had ruled out any thought of putting in a crop that first year. With the help of the Weber boys from the next farm over, they were at least able to put in a respectable garden for potatoes, beans, pickles, and onions, things they could put up and keep in the fruit cellar. Will also put in a small apple orchard, thirty trees, off the south end of the barn. Emma's tasks setting up housekeeping in the new place were no less daunting, and they had to be accomplished in addition to her regular daily chores that kept the family going. Just to cook a decent meal, she had to quickly learn the idiosyncrasies of the new wood-fired range. Even so, with one notable exception, it went smoothly. About a week after Emma and Robert moved in, Emma asked Will to bring her crated things from the little log cabin up to the house so she could sort through them and put them away. The crates contained soft goods such as bedding, tablecloths, and towels, most of which had not been unpacked since they were shipped up from downstate several years before. As Will was walking out to the barn from delivering the last crate, he was stopped in his tracks by the terrified screams of a woman, his woman. He turned and raced back to the house as fast as his bad leg would allow, expecting the worst. When he opened the back door to the kitchen and surveyed the confused scene before him, he had to close his eyes and then look again. Emma's screams had devolved into desperate whimpers as she swatted wildly at the floor and along the base of the wall with a corn broom, long wisps of her normally carefully fixed hair flying every which way. Robert's butt and short legs were sticking out of a lower cupboard as he lay on his stomach, and Jack was frozen in an impressive birddog point at something in the walk-in pantry. In fact, Will was so momentarily thrilled with Jack's performance, he forgot all about Emma's problem and just stood there with a big grin on his face.

He was abruptly brought back from the moment by a well-placed whack from Emma's broom and the delighted shout from Robert "I got one, I got one!" as he backed out of the cupboard holding a small brown and white field mouse by the tail, its tiny legs clawing at the air.

"Robert!" Emma screamed, brandishing her broom as if she would strike down all comers. "Outside with that thing!"

Evidently at some point Ned and his "people" from the log cabin had taken up nesting between two warm and comfy quilts in one of Emma's storage crates. When she pulled the top quilt off, Ned and his startled family made a break for it in all directions at once, setting off to parts of the house unknown. With a few reassuring words and a quick hug, Will disarmed Emma and took up the hunt. He couldn't resist working with Jack a little bit as he held his first point on whatever was still in the pantry. "Easy, Jack, easy now, easy now, hold it," he said as he inched past the dog and held the broom out in front of him. "Good boy, Jack." Two mice pups were disoriented and huddled together in the far corner, and with a quick one-two move, he trapped them with the wide broom head and scooped them up with a dustpan for immediate relocation. Before getting back to work, Will pawed through the remaining crates to make sure Emma would encounter no more surprises, and then the two of them sat facing each other and holding hands across the dining room table as they caught their breath. They were both becoming a little frazzled.

The exact opposite was true for Robert, Jack, and G.D. Will wasn't sure of G.D.'s numerical age, but he knew the mule was getting on. His earlier years had not been easy ones, and when Will had rescued him in Saginaw, he counted every human as an enemy. He was still leery of strangers, but around Will, and now Robert, he behaved like a devoted pet. Will had fenced in a half acre next to the wagon trail that crossed the front of his property, and G.D. whiled away the warm sunny days of retirement dozing and munching pasture grass as the spirit moved him. His only job now was to be Robert's charge so the boy could learn about responsibility, and as it turned out, he was a pretty fair watchdog, too, giving off a mighty wee-snaw whenever someone passed the farm, which wasn't very often.

Robert and Jack had become inseparable. At first Emma wasn't too keen on the idea of having a dog in the house, but Will took up Robert's case and convinced her to give it a try. Jack still took his meals and water outside on the back porch, but every night he slept on the floor next to Robert's bed. You never knew how most pups were going to turn out until they were about a year old, Will said, but Jack was different. He seemed to have a wisdom that was unusual in a dog his age. When Emma and Robert had first moved in, Jack was more of a partner in crime with the boy. What one didn't think of the other would. Now, after a summer of running wild and scouting the edges of the dark, mysterious forest that surrounded the farm, just far enough in so he could still see the bright sunlit farm field between the trees, Jack was becoming more of a guardian.

Chapter 33

"**M**orning, gentlemen," said Bob Wagner as Will and Robert pushed through the well-worn screen door of his store.

"Morning, Bob." Robert was too distracted for pleasantries and made a dash for the long row of fishbowls filled with penny candy that lined the lower shelf below the cash register. Will shook his head and chuckled.

"Gets 'em every time," said Bob with a big grin.

"Guess I can't blame him. I fancy a caramel myself from time to time," said Will. "Any word from Purvis about those barn hinges?"

"Naw, nothing yet. I think he's a little backed up this time of year. He's a good man, though. I'll have Cletus run them out to you as soon as I get 'em. That reminds me…There was a man in here last week looking for you. Cletus talked to him. Cletus! What the hell you doing back there, anyway? Come on out here for a minute," said Bob, a little impatiently. The old man came shuffling up from the back room and stood, shifting his eyes between Will and his boss and covering his toothless mouth with his hand every time he gave up a nervous giggle. "Tell Mr. Castor here about that man that was looking for him last week. You know the one I mean, God-awful big nose and the manners of a wild boar with the butt itch." Before Cletus could respond, Will looked up at him sharply, getting another nervous chuckle in response. The hairs on the back of Will's neck were tingling.

Several weeks passed and Will's busy days had almost wiped the thought of Bellman from his mind. Robert had started getting up a little before dawn and taking breakfast with Will and Emma before tending to G.D. and setting him out to pasture. Will was still keeping a close eye on him to make sure he didn't get distracted and get himself in a position to be kicked or stepped on. His routine was to sit on the top rail of one of the stalls and watch Will harness the morning team. Each day Will would show him a different component of the harness and explain its purpose, then the next day he would quiz the boy. Will looked forward to the day when Robert was big enough to throw a harness on his own. "OK, Robert, you ready for a little learning?"

"Yes sir, I reckon I am," replied Robert with gravity beyond his years. Will reached down and grabbed a heavy horizontal strap that attached to one of the hames by the collar and led back along the length of the horse and then trailed off onto the floor with a piece of chain on the end. "We used to call these traces in the army, but folks around here usually call them tugs. Either way is OK. Now if I'm plowing, the chains hook to the doubletree. Pete's got the same setup on his side. When both horses are hooked into the doubletree, it hooks to the plow, and I'm set to go. You got all that?"

Robert studied the harness for a minute and then shook his head "yes" a little uncertainly.

"OK, what's this?" said Will as he put his hand on the thick strap that wrapped around Annie's hindquarters.

Robert's back and head snapped up straight so suddenly that Will started to reach for him, sure that he would tumble backwards off the side of the stall. Even Jack, who was curled up on a little pile of hay, sleeping off his morning meal, was startled awake and gave an uninspired bark. "That's a britchin!" Robert shouted.

Will laughed at his enthusiasm. "Good! Now what's it do?"

"Well, it lets Annie and Pete slow down your wagon or what-have-you," he said, quoting Will's exact words from the day before.

"That's right, son. You're doing real good, Robert. I guess that's enough to think on for one day. Let's get G.D. out to pasture, and then you and Jack do as you please until dinnertime." Will got G.D. out of his stall and started on the path to the front pasture before he handed the lead to Robert. "There you go, son. You mind your business now and don't get behind him. Most animals don't want to hurt nobody, but sometimes they get spooked. You want me to go along and open the gate for you?"

"No! I want to do it, Peep!"

"OK, you tie him off like I showed you before you start monkeying with the gate, and be careful!"

About thirty minutes had gone by since Robert, Jack, and G.D. had walked up the path by the side of the barn when two quick shots rang out followed by a third a few seconds later. Will was making a minor adjustment to Pete's harness when he heard the "pop pop… pop." He knew what it was immediately. He had heard the same thing during the war when tired, scared men on picket duty would fire at shadows in the half light of early morn. Will spun around, bolted up the steps, and threw open the trap door to the main floor of the barn. His old .44-40 Winchester was leaning against the front wall next to the open door, and he picked it up and automatically racked a shell into the chamber as he took in the scene before him. G.D. was lying on the ground on his side, and Robert was screaming and running as fast as he could toward the house. A hundred yards away on the edge of the road, were three men, two sitting on horses and the third kneeling over G.D. with a rifle. Will snapped the Winchester to his shoulder and drew a bead on the man with the rifle. If he even so much as twitched before Robert got safely to the house, he was going to kill the man where he knelt. It seemed like an eternity as Will studied him over the barrel of his gun, but finally he heard the kitchen screen door slam, and he knew the boy was safe. Even from a hundred yards away the man's enormous nose was clearly visible as he stood up, trotted over to his horse, and with his companions, headed up the road toward the edge of the ridge.

Will's mind was racing as he considered his next move. Once the wagon road crested the ridge, it became more of a trail and turned south to traverse the steep ground at a shallower angle. Here the horsemen would be traveling single file. Behind the barn there was an old Indian path that led straight down over the ridge to the river and blackberry patch, and it also crossed the trail the men were on. Will carefully eased the hammer of his rifle down and headed out the back of the barn on the run. If he hurried he could cut them off.

Will waited until Bellman, the lead horseman, was about fifty feet away up the trail before he stepped out of the underbrush and blocked the way. The horse was startled by his sudden appearance in the middle of the trail and bucked, nearly throwing Bellman off. Amid a flurry of curses and flailing arms, he started to reach for the rifle that was tucked in a scabbard under his leg but thought better of it when he saw that the man blocking his way had beat him to it and already had his rifle up to his shoulder. The other two men pulled up even with the first horse so that they sat three abreast across the trail, looking very intimidating. Most men probably would have been intimidated, but Will was way past that now. He was so mad that he was struggling with everything he had to keep control. This day had been a long time coming, and he had given some thought to what he would do, but none of those plans mattered much now.

Bellman had given this day some serious thought as well, but now that they were face to face, the reality of their last meeting was hard to ignore. He knew that Will would have killed him then if not interfered with, and he knew that Will would certainly shoot to kill now. If he had any doubt of that before, there was no question about it now as he looked back into the eyes fixed on him over the gun barrel. Will Castor's cold eyes knew what it was to kill a man. Few other times in his life had Tom Bellman been frozen in fear, but he was now. He knew he was about to die.

The two other men saw Bellman's uncharacteristic resignation and began to look around for an escape route, but the path was too narrow and the woods too thick. Will tightened his grip on the stock of his rifle and dipped his head to the rear sight. Bellman closed his eyes and let his hands fall to the top of the saddle horn, waiting for his final seconds to tick down. Will hesitated, and out of the corner of his eye he saw Robert a few feet away, standing on the Indian path, watching everything with a look of sheer terror frozen on his young face. At the last second, Will nudged the gun sight a bit to the left and pulled the trigger. The impact of the bullet at

254

such close range cart-wheeled Bellman off the back of his horse, and the sound of the shot caused the other two horses to rear, nearly dismounting their riders. Will quickly racked another shell into the gun and swept the barrel over the two companions to let them know they could be next. "You boys get on down and keep your hands out in front of you where I can see them; there's plenty of lead here to go around," said Will.

"You just killed a man over a broken-down old mule, for God's sake!" said the one on the left.

"That mule was part of my family. Now step back, go on, step back, I said." Will prodded the men back up the trail with his gun barrel. "OK, take off your coats and shirts, and throw them on the ground in front of you. Turn out the pockets of your britches."

The two men looked at him for a moment as if he were crazy. Will pulled the rifle up to his shoulder and aimed it at the head of the man who had spoken. "Goddamn it, do it now!" he shouted. "I ain't in the mood to repeat myself." That's all the convincing they needed, and both men were quickly reduced to boots, britches, and braces. Meanwhile, Bellman had come around and let out a groan as he sat up holding the side of his head where his right ear used to be. Bright red rivulets of blood were oozing out from between his fingers and running down his forearm into his sleeve, turning the elbow of his coat dark. He glanced up at Will, but there was no fight left in him. He was just glad to be alive.

Will stepped up to him, shoved his upper body back flat on the ground with his foot and rested the barrel of the rifle on his forehead. "I got about half a mind to shave a tad off that damned big nose of yours while I'm at it. This is the last time you and I are ever going to speak, so I hope you can hear me good, you miserable sack of shit. God knows you're plum out of ears. If I ever see you passing anywhere near my farm or my family again, I'll kill you straightaway, no questions asked. You won't even hear the shot."

Will turned to Bellman's companions. "Get him up and wrap one of those shirts around his head. You boys got a long walk ahead of you, so you better get after it. If the mosquitoes don't suck you dry and leave you for dead, tell Butler and Tait they better come in person and talk to me if they want these horses back."

While Will waited for them to fashion a makeshift bandage for Bellman, he glanced up the ridge and saw Emma's form silhouetted against the tiny patch of blue sky where the trail parted the trees before disappearing over the crest. She held his double barrel shotgun across her body. The sight of her reminded him of Robert, and as soon as the three men had walked a ways down the trail, he hurried over to where the boy sat crying into his hands. Will knelt down and wrapped his arms around him. "It's OK, son, I didn't hurt him too bad. Just had to teach him a lesson so he won't bother us again." Robert looked up at Will with tears still rolling down his face, leaving tracks in the dirt smudges on his cheeks. "Jack," is all he said and started crying harder.

Emma stood by, pressing Robert into her skirts so he wouldn't see the ugly wound in Jack's side. When Bellman had shot G.D., Jack stayed back to cover Robert's retreat, and the third shot had struck him a glancing blow along his rib cage leaving a ragged tear in his skin and exposing bone. Will knelt down and gently stroked his head as he checked him over. He was still alive, but just barely. His eyes were fixed and vacant and his breathing was shallow. Emma had stopped and draped her apron over the gaping wound on her way to the ridge, and that at least had prevented flies from getting in.

"Robert, I need your help, son." Robert turned and looked at Will, still sniffling. "Jack is hurt bad, but he ain't dead. I need you to be brave. You go to the barn and bring the cleanest blanket you can find up to the house. Emmy, we'll need a bowl of hot water, some button thread, and the biggest sewing needle you have." Will carefully picked Jack up and started for the house with Emma. Robert took a long swipe at his runny nose, starting at the inside of his elbow and ending at his knuckles while he thought it over and then ran as fast as he could for the barn.

Emma started awake early the next morning, and she lay there in the darkness, trying to sort out what was amiss when the clock in the parlor downstairs struck three chimes into the silence. When it came to her, she quickly patted the bed to her left and found that Will was not there. She sat up and lit the small oil lamp on the dresser and tip-toed out into the hallway so as not to wake Robert. She need not have bothered. When she stuck the lamp through the door to check on him she found that he was gone too. Emma was starting to get concerned now. She made her way downstairs and through the still house to the kitchen. When she stepped through the wide doorway from the dining room, there sitting on the floor and leaning back against the wall, asleep across from the cook stove was her husband. Sitting on the floor next to him, sound asleep also and nestled into Will's side under his arm, was her son. Jack lay on Will's lap, wrapped in the old blanket with just his head sticking out. Emma watched him for a minute to see if he was still breathing. His eyes were closed but as she looked on, his ample lips puffed out and then lay flat again. The vents along the bottom of the stove's firebox glowed deep red, casting her slumbering little family in a soft warm glow. Emma retrieved a straight-back chair from the dining room table and sat in the doorway keeping watch and enjoying the warmth of the room. If she had imagined a perfect life for her and Robert a year ago, it would have looked very different. Nevertheless, somehow, by some grace, here it was.

Chapter 34

It took about a week for news of what had happened to Bellman and his friends to travel back down the line to the main office of Butler and Tait Lumber Company in Manistee. Will had just started toward the house for the midday meal when Robert came tearing across the field from the Indian path, yelling, "Peep! Peep! Sa Sa Somebody's ca ca coming!"

Will stopped and waited for the boy to catch up. "You go on up to the house and tell your mother that I'll be up directly, as soon as I have a word with our visitor. Robert hesitated, clearly disappointed at being left out, but he knew the look on Will's face offered him no wiggle room.

The man who came over the ridge was well dressed, but not excessively so for the errand he was on. He sat astride a beautiful tall black quarter horse, rolling easily with its gait like a man who had spent many a long day in the saddle. As he drew near, Will could see that he was a man of some means by the tooling work on his saddle bags, his tailored coat with dark velvet trim on the collar and cuffs, and the elegant gold-braided watch chain that draped across the front of his vest. He was a portly man, the likely result of easy living in recent years, but he had the face of a man who had seen much and bent but little. The only thing slightly out of place about him was the well-worn black slouch hat pulled low over his eyes. Years of hard service had given it a personality all its own. It reminded Will of the war.

Will leaned against the top rail of the fence, waiting for the stranger to speak first. The man reined in his horse and immediately dismounted as soon as its legs were still—a good start, Will thought. "Name's Ed Butler," said the man without offering his hand. "I'm looking to have a word with Mr. Castor."

"You found him," replied Will. Butler nodded and then studied the ground between them for a moment while he organized his thoughts. Finally he looked up at Will and said, "I'm here to apologize and make amends for the wrongs done to you by three of my employees. I hope you will believe me when I say that they acted on their own with no encouragement from me or anyone else who works for me. I'm an honest man, Mr. Castor, and I don't abide the kind of ugly business that I understand took place here a week or so ago. Tom Bellman is a bad one all right, and I had a feeling when I hired him I would regret it someday. If I'd known how much I was going to regret it, I would have shot him myself and saved us both some trouble. Anyway, I hope you will let me make this right, sir."

As much as Will was prepared to give this man a dressing down, no matter how rich and powerful he was, he found instead a kindred spirit. Will regarded Butler in silence a few moments longer and finally said, "That's a fine looking animal, Mr. Butler. Reckon he could use a little rest and a drink." Will swung the gate to G.D.'s corral open and waved them in. "I was just going up to the house for dinner when you rode up. It's simple fare, but you're welcome to join me."

"That's mighty generous of you, Mr. Castor. I'd be obliged."

"Name's Will," he said, holding out his hand.

Emma was a little put off by having an unexpected guest for dinner, but Will was the only one who caught "the look" that promised more discussion at some time in the near future. Robert was still leery of Mr. Butler, and even after he was excused, he lingered in the kitchen and peeked around the door from time to time.

"Ben Heimbaugh is a good man. It speaks well of you that he's your friend," said Butler. "He's done a lot of good work in Manistee, rebuilding after the fire."

"I saw a bit of that fire myself," said Will. He went on to describe taking refuge in the lake with G.D. and pulling the woman and her children out of the well.

"A man can get attached to an animal when you roam the forest alone like you did. I can see now how Tom Bellman got under your skin."

"He and I had some unfinished business from a winter we spent at a camp down near East Saginaw."

"Have something to do with that other ear?" said Butler with the trace of a smile. Will smiled too and nodded as he looked down at the table. "Yeah, that's my work, too."

Emma hadn't said much so far, aside from the initial pleasantries, being content to listen and learn more about Will's past. Ed Butler was clearly taken with her grace and elegance and more than once arched an eyebrow at her proper spoken English. Once she did begin to interject herself into the conversation, he was surprised by her quick mind and a little envious at how well she and Will complemented each other. The three of them lingered over coffee and a slice of cake from the covered glass pedestal stand that graced the center of the table. "Well, Mrs. Castor, I must apologize once again for dropping in on you out of the clear blue. That was a fine meal. If I could trouble you for the recipe for that marvelous cake, it would please my wife greatly."

"It would be my pleasure, Mr. Butler," she said as she got up from the table and cleared their dishes away.

"Now don't take me wrong, Will, I don't mean nothing by it except to satisfy my own curiosity, but what is so special about that property down in the valley that's behind all these goings on?"

"You ever hear of a fella named Henry Bolton?"

A smile spread across Butler's face as he nodded in the affirmative. "Quite a character, as I recall. Forgot more about lumbering than most of us will ever know."

"That's him. He told me once that the day will come when all the big trees will be gone, and that folks that come after us will never know how it used to be. It seemed a little far-fetched to me then, but after seeing all the slash and clear cuttings around Saginaw, I come to believe he is right. I plan to save that little piece of forest."

Butler sat quietly playing with his fork as he thought over what Will had said. "Would you be willing to ride down there with me and show me around?" Will unconsciously shot a glance toward the kitchen before answering, and as if on cue, Emma called out that she would pack a few things for them to eat. Butler smiled and rolled his eyes as Will smiled and said, "Yes I would."

Dusk did not linger this time of year as it did in early summer, but there was still enough light from the sun, now well below the horizon, to define the distant hills surrounding the lake. Under the canopy of the great trees on the edge of the forest where it descended down a steep bank to the water, it was almost full dark. Sluggish evening lake waves lapping the shore and the pop and crackle of pine logs in the fire were the only sounds in the vast silence.

Will and Ed Butler sat next to each other on the ground, studying a plat map that was spread out between them and tilted toward the fire for light. "This river that joins the north ends of these lakes is the key to this whole area," said Ed. "Once it leaves here, it runs all the way to Lake Michigan." Will nodded his agreement but didn't offer anything. Ed folded the map up and slid it down into one of his saddlebags. "I planned this whole swing north from Thompsonville from my office in Manistee, with that map on my desk and a pile of survey notes. It never occurred to me to come out here and see this land for myself."

The two men lapsed into silence as they stared into the fire, each lost in his own thoughts, but revisiting very similar memories. Finally Will spoke without looking away from the flames. "You strike me as someone who saw service during the war, Ed."

"24th Wisconsin. Signed up in '61, mustered out in '65. Don't seem like that long ago, sitting around this fire. How about you?"

"Battery D, First Michigan. Got this leg at Chickamauga. Lost a lot of good friends on that last day. Even after these many years, I can still see some of their tired, dirty faces looking back at me over the fire." The two men shared a knowing look and savored the connection before being drawn back to the flames.

"I was there, Lytle's brigade. They don't come any better than him. It was hot work that day, my friend—mighty hot work…" said Ed. They fell silent again with their memories. But now, and forever more, they were linked by a bond of trust and respect, linked by what they had seen and what they had endured – linked because they had stood up, with all they had, and all they ever would have, and faced down death.

The next morning Will and Ed watched the sunrise over Lake Wahbekaness as they stood knee deep in the warm water, pant legs rolled up, fishing for their breakfast with a couple of poplar saplings. Will was amused by Ed's childlike excitement when he caught a nice Bluegill. "Well, Lord have mercy!" he exclaimed when the fish fought back, turning its flat iridescent blue flank perpendicular, catching the light and bending the pole down to the water. "By God, this one's a fighter, Will!"

"Good thing I saved that butcher paper from last night. If we can't eat all of him, you can wrap up what's left and take it home," said Will with a chuckle.

After breakfast they cleaned up their campsite and saddled their horses for the ride back. "I haven't had this much fun in a long while, Will. I want to thank you for your hospitality and for showing me this place. I agree with you, it needs to be protected. What would you say to this…I throw my land on Lake Wahbekanetta in with yours, and we go down to Lansing and make a gift of the whole shootin' match to the state, with the provision that they make a park out of it? That way everyone could enjoy this spot, and nobody would ever be able to log it off. Of course, you'd need some way to get people here…"

Will threw his head back and laughed and said, "Why, I reckon we'd need us a railroad running right up the center of the park!"

"Damn, Will, you're smarter than you let on. Just so happens I got a railroad with nowhere to go just south of here." Will nudged his horse forward until he was next to Ed and stuck out his hand. "You got yourself a deal, Mr. Butler. I like you, Ed, even though I had a mind not to. I say we meet back here next summer with our families and make a camp. Teach our young'uns a thing or two about the woods."

"That's a grand idea, Will. My boys would love it. You keep those horses as payment for your mule. I figure that little paint ought to be just right for your boy. You tell him I said so."

Chapter 35

The Butlers and the Castors did meet the following year, and every year thereafter, until the children were grown and off pursuing their own dreams. After that, Will and Ed kept the tradition alive for a time, spending a few pleasant days each year in the forest they had saved from the loggers' crosscut saw, fishing and sharing stories by the campfire. As they grew old and their lives lay mostly unfolded behind them, they came to see what the war had truly cost their young friends who had died so many years before. The second gifting of life had left both men with a burning need to give something back, something that added meaning to the gift. The armor of youth had melted away, leaving their old memories vivid and near the surface, cloaked only in a thin fabric of melancholy.

The unique location of the forest, situated as it was on a narrow strip of land between two large lakes, saved it from the huge forest fires that swept the area in the early 1880s, leaving thousands of square miles of Michigan a vast wasteland of black smoldering stumps. Butler's railroad, the Manistee and Northeastern, was completed through to Traverse City, and it carried passengers as well as logs to the sawmills. Where it interlocked with the Pere Marquette Railroad near the site of Michigan's first state park, a small community called Interlochen sprang up.

When Michigan's forests were gone, Ben Heimbaugh followed the timber west, eventually settling in St. Paul. He had amassed great wealth over the years, and being a charitable man, used it to right many social wrongs he encountered along the way. He was an especially soft touch for down-and-out veterans and their families. Unfortunately, his own children and grandchildren did not benefit much from their father's example, and after his death in 1922, it took only a few short years of greed and a Great Depression for the money to evaporate.

Jerald and Maribel ended up with eight children, five boys and three girls. It was a common sight to see the whole clan come walking down the street in Saginaw, one child riding on her father's shoulders, two being pushed by their mother in a strange looking double stroller that Jerald had devised, and a pack of out-of-control boys punching each other, trying every door latch and swinging on every lamp post they encountered. Maribel's father was a shrewd businessman, and between him and his daughter, they were able to keep Jerald out of trouble financially. Jerald was in his element hammering something into shape or figuring out how to make something work better, but he had little use for money other than what it would buy. Will, Emma, and Robert came for visits a few times, but with the responsibilities of family and the absence of alcohol to ease them back into their old ways with each other, the meetings left them both uneasy.

The last time they were in Saginaw, Will left Emma and Robert at the depot to sit out the long wait for the northbound train while he walked down Water Street to the livery. On the way, he stopped and bought two sticky sweet rolls. As he approached the big front doors, he once again heard the familiar cadence of hammer blows on hot iron that he remembered so well. Jerald looked around, sensing someone behind him, and without the slightest hesitation, reached up to the shelf over the bench, pulled down two battered tin cups and filled them with steaming coffee from the pot on the edge of the forge. That was how they left things. When they said goodbye, they held their handshake a long time.

Henry made it back to Monroe Center for two fall bird hunts before he passed away at his iron-red brick townhouse in Marquette. Even though he disparaged Jack by calling him every unflattering thing he could think of for a dog, other than his name, the two were made to hunt together. If Jack would point up a grouse and Henry would miss the shot when the bird flushed, he would lie down and give the old man a disgusted stare until it elicited the predictable "What the hell you looking at?" Will and

Robert would always remember those late fall Indian summers with Henry, tramping the margins of the golden poplar groves along each side of the little stream at the bottom of the ridge, hunting with their shirtsleeves rolled up and following Jack's easy pace as he worked birds.

On those mild evenings when they sat on the front porch to take the sunset and watch the waves of Canada geese break formation and pass low overhead before settling onto Lake Wahbekaness for the night, Will liked to recall for him their conversation on that long-ago afternoon while riding the flatcar south to East Saginaw. "Those are your trees, Henry," he would say. Henry would cast a knowing glance at Will, but he always kept his silence as he looked away to the stately old white pine forest on the strip of land between the lakes.

Henry didn't have any close family, so he left the majority of his wealth to what he considered worthy organizations in and around East Saginaw and Bay City. The one exception was his bequeath to Robert, of his majority shares of the iron mine near Marquette. Henry wisely stipulated that Robert work in the mine himself for two years before the shares would be turned over to him.

Robert eventually grew out of his stutter, but he never quite overcame his streak of wildness, and it would surface from time to time throughout his life. One cold day in January when he was eight years old, he and several other boys from neighboring farms decided it would be fun to climb up on the roof of the schoolhouse and stuff the chimney of the wood stove with pine boughs. The theory, which proved correct, was that the classroom would quickly fill with backed-up smoke, and school would have to be canceled. The one flaw in the plan, and the one that led to their undoing, had been the noise their boots made on the flimsy tin roof. Emma cried for a bit and then became furious, demanding that Will march Robert out to the barn and administer a sound whipping. It was the first time that Robert had been on the receiving end of Will's murderous, scar-faced looks, and by the time they reached the barn, he had died a thousand deaths. Will tortured him a bit longer by making him stand at attention while he mulled over the situation. Finally, he had simply said, "I don't like it when your mother cries. Don't make her do that again." As Robert was leaving to go back up to the house, Will continued. "The next time you decide to smoke out old man Neiddlemyer" (the old schoolmaster who replaced his mother), "you wet down an old horse blanket, and stick it up there with a long pole. Use your brain, son." Robert never forgot that day.

Until he turned seventeen and began to spread his wings a little, Robert spent his days working the farm with Will and becoming more and more helpful each year. Early on Will recognized in him a natural curiosity about everything he encountered, and he nurtured that every chance he got. One late spring afternoon Emma looked out the back door of the kitchen and saw her husband and son lying in the tall grass on the edge of the apple orchard, looking up at the sky and pointing here and there as they talked. A short time later she looked out again, and they were further away, doing the same thing. Over supper, she learned that Will was showing Robert how to locate a beehive, so they could steal the honey, by watching their little bodies silhouetted dark against the pale sky when they made a bee-line from the apple blossoms to their combs.

Robert eventually took a wife from Marquette, Michigan, and they settled there on the west side of town, a short distance from the mine. They were blessed with four boys, all of whom had the same zest for life their father had at that young age, so there was seldom a quiet moment. That was fine with Robert. He doted on the boys and loved teaching them how to hunt and fish and enjoy the beautiful but rugged wilderness of the Upper Peninsula. Most importantly, he passed on the things that Will had taught him about respect, honor, and discipline. For several years when the boys were old enough to travel on their own, they took the train to Traverse City and spent their summers on the farm with Grandma Emmy and Peep. Eventually they stopped coming, and the letters from Robert, always spotty at best, dwindled to yearly Christmas cards. Robert's second boy would later be killed at Belleau Wood during World War I.

Jack was getting on in years by the time Robert left home, but he never quite gave up the notion that his lifelong friend would one day come walking back up the road. He and Will hunted pats alone for several seasons, but they both came to enjoy the solitary afternoon naps on the edge of the forest more than shooting birds. They would find a sunny place near the bottom of the ridge by the river, where the carpet of fallen leaves was deep and Will could lean back against the trunk of an old beech or maple tree. Jack would lie close, rest his gray muzzle on his master's lap, and they would doze to the peaceful murmur of timeless water, gurgling over rocks and under fallen trees, its constant silver thread coursing through the forest floor and through their sleepy minds. Eventually Jack's back legs would only carry him a short distance from the house, and he spent his last days sleeping on the back porch or a warm corner of the kitchen in the winter. Will never stopped grieving for Jack after he finally passed on one January, and every spring thereafter as his plow turned up field stones behind the house, he would drop a few of them on Jack's grave in the far corner of the orchard.

Emma and Will considered themselves equal partners in the business of living, and gaining the upper hand in any issue held no sway with either of them. Will always made sure that there were hired hands around to help with the daily chores so he and Emma would be free to enjoy some fun things in life and do a little traveling during the winter months. When the first real warmth of spring arrived, Will would be out in the forty-acre field behind the house at sunup with a team, following a walking plow and turning the earth. Sometimes Emma would step out onto the back porch to ring the dinner bell, but before she pulled the rope, she would stop and watch her husband, moving slowly away down the rich, moist field with his team of Belgians, while a swarm of white ring-billed gulls, luminous in the slanting light, turned, circled low, and dipped into the freshly opened furrow for earthworms. She was reminded of pictures she had seen of a Gloucester fisherman returning to port. Row after row after row, Will walked all morning and then hitched a fresh team after dinner and walked all afternoon. The land was in his bones, and it called him home again and again. He would walk the furrows of these fields until his legs would no longer carry him.

In their later years, Will and Emma would spend winter days in the cozy warmth of the kitchen, sitting at a table just big enough for the two of them. They read stories to each other from Emma's books and baked angel food cakes. At first, Will's only job was to control the temperature of the oven, opening a vent here, closing one there, throwing in a stick of elm or birch or oak, as the need arose. As time passed, he picked up the tricks of the delicate process and could bake a pretty fair angel food cake himself, but he didn't let on. In the afternoon he would hitch up one of the horses to the cutter and together, snuggled under a bearskin robe, sleigh bells jangling with every footfall, he and Emma would deliver the cake. All their neighbors and their neighbors' children for miles around would receive one of these wonderful creations to mark their birthday. Even Robert and the grandkids would get one in the mail.

Emma came down with jaundice and died suddenly in the summer of 1914. Since his experience in the forest years earlier, when he was about to end his life, he had carried a certainty with him that there was something more to life than just living and dying, and whatever came next would be OK. Still, he was heartbroken and missed her so badly he didn't want to go on. He wanted only to be with her again. It was all that mattered now, but he had to wait for his time, like an apple that hangs on through an autumn blow and two days later drops quietly to the ground in the still of early morning darkness. After her passing, Will stepped back from life as if he were stepping back from a Monet, and what at first seemed like random brush strokes, came together, bringing the beginning, the middle, and the end into soft focus. He read again the stories that he and Emma had read together in the kitchen, and he talked to her as if she still sat across from him while he stirred the ingredients for another angel food cake.

Will lived on alone for five more years. In the spring he plowed in the back forty every day until he tired, usually after only a few rows. He never got enough ground opened up in time to plant, but that was OK. He only wanted to feel the plow handles alive in his hands, smell the freshly turned earth, and hear the sweet music of the horses moving in the harness. In the fall he put up wood for the winter, just enough to heat the rooms he lived in downstairs. One February day during a short warm spell, he hitched his team to the farm wagon and spent the afternoon out in the woodlot, filling it with small logs that were already cut to length by a couple of neighbor boys. He hadn't been feeling well for a few days, and he thought a little fresh air might do him some good. As he was pulling up to the side of the house, the dark angry clouds of a front were amassing on the western horizon, and he decided to wait until the next day, after the storm had passed and he was rested, to unload the wagon. Will stepped in between the horses and bent over to unhook the traces from the wagon, when he felt a sudden jolt of pain in his chest that rippled quickly up through his shoulders and neck, and set off a ringing in his ears so loud that all other sounds were lost. His legs buckled, dropping him hard to his knees on the frozen ground, where he held for a moment before toppling over onto his side under the horses. He folded his arms tight across his chest and braced for another stab of pain, but it never came. Instead, he felt the muscles in his body relax in succession, starting in his chest and moving out, like the waves from a stone dropped in a pond. Peace coursed through him, followed by warmth, warmth like he had felt only once before. The roaring in his ears subsided, and he could hear raindrops hitting the frozen ground next to his head, but he was warm, as if he were deep in his feather bed under one of Emma's quilts. He could hear voices – far away, but coming closer, calling for him. Will smiled. Jimmy was coming for him, just as he had all those years ago. And his beloved Emma, her voice was there, too, but it held the edge of youth that he hadn't heard in many years. The voices were close now, and they were calling his name, calling him to get up.

The next morning just before ten o'clock, Lloyd the mail carrier stopped his buggy next to Will's mailbox and started thumbing through a bundle of letters for the one he knew was in there for Will Castor. When he had the one he wanted, he pulled down the heavy counter-weighted door and looked over the mailbox at the team standing in the drive as he dropped the letter in. Something wasn't right, but it took a moment for him to settle on what it was. Finally it hit him. The two horses were covered with a thin coating of ice from the sleet storm the night before. There were deep ruts in the drive where they had nervously shuffled their feet, waiting all night and most of the next morning for their master to softly give them the words "Step up."

Beneath the horses lay the undisturbed body of Will. Lloyd squatted down and looked under the horses at the old man's face. There was a translucent layer of ice covering the upper side of his body and partially obscuring his frozen smile. "Always meant to ask him about that scar," he thought. Lloyd reached for Will's hat that lay upside down next to his head with the thought of covering his face, but like its owner, it too was frozen to the ground; instead, he patted his neighbor's shoulder and whispered, "Goodbye, old friend."

Epilogue

Paul woke from his nap as something flitted close by his face with a little buzz. When he opened his eyes, two black-capped chickadees were watching him from a lilac bush a few feet away. He stood up, brushed off his pants, and took one last look at Emma's and Will's headstones before heading back to the car. According to his research, William and Emma's property should be just a couple of miles away to the south and west. He had it circled on the plat map. A mile down the road he came to an intersection and was surprised to see the road to the west was called Castor Road. "This is almost too easy," he thought. He turned and followed the road for about a mile, slowing when he saw the sign warning trucks of a steep downgrade ahead. On the left was the property he was looking for. He was a little disappointed that there was no old farm house or dilapidated barn still standing, but at least there was a trace of a drive with two big rambling rosebushes, one on each side, sending off tendrils studded with pink blossoms along the ground in all directions. A rusty real estate sign faced the road to the left of the drive. Heavy snow from the blades of county trucks had bent it backwards, and unlucky hunters, determined to fire their guns at something before heading home, had left it with rusty pockmarks from birdshot. Paul pulled his car into the driveway and shut off the engine.

Where the house had once stood was a fieldstone foundation surrounded by overgrown lilac and forsythia bushes. There was a single pipe sticking straight up out of the ground by the back wall, perhaps a well at one time. He stepped out of the car and walked up the drive a short distance. To his right on a little knoll was a similar foundation, only much larger, where the barn used to be. Ancient pieces of rusty horse-drawn farm implements poked up through the tall weeds here and there like the bones of a man's life.

Paul walked up to the high ground by the back of the barn, and suddenly the rolling forty-acre field to the south opened up before him. He stood there for a long time gazing out over the golden meadow surrounded by deep green hardwood forest. As he looked on, puffs of wind sent waves rippling down the big field through the tall grass. He was mesmerized. It was beautiful and it touched something deep inside him, something familiar. He turned away, shaking his head, wondering how he could be so foolish. When he rounded the corner of the barn foundation and looked northwest, he was brought up short once again. Stretching away for twenty miles or more was a wide verdant valley with two beautiful sparkling blue lakes, side by side. Towering white cumulus clouds with low flat bottoms marched up the valley from the south, casting shadows on the green carpet of second-growth treetops, adding a lovely texture to the vista. It was a breathtaking sight, and he could no longer deny the pull he felt. Paul looked at his watch and started for the car. If he hurried, he could make it back to Traverse City before the real estate office closed.

Author Note

With three notable exceptions, the characters in this novel are fictional, and as they say, any resemblance to persons living or dead is purely coincidental. Paul Castor, who appears in the prologue and epilogue, is my "real life" cousin whose passion for genealogy sparked my interest in family history and started me down the path to write this book. The characters Mollie and Jack Dean are based on two of my ancestors from the Civil War time period. Jack Dean was, in fact, shot by Yankee bushwhackers and left on a neighbor's porch near Raus, Tennessee as an example for the local population of Bedford County. The letter from Mollie to Ailcey Dean, Jack's wife, relating the circumstances of his death, is nearly verbatim from the actual letter.

I have taken the liberty of using the names of men from the original Battery D First Michigan Light Artillery, but that is as far as any similarity goes. Serious scholars of the Battle of Chickamauga will no doubt find discrepancies in my retelling of events, but it was my first priority to give the reader a feel for what the common soldier experienced during those horrific two days in the autumn of 1863. That afternoon, Battery D was overrun in fierce combat with Confederate forces under the command of General Longstreet. When the artillery horses were killed, the battery was able to save only one gun. The conversation that took place between one of the Battery D gunners and Confederate General Preston during a chance meeting on the battlefield was taken from a news story written shortly after the battle.

The man who deserves the credit for saving the area now occupied by the Interlochen State Park and Interlochen Center for the Arts from being logged off is Willis Pennington. Pennington built a tourist hotel on shores of Green Lake (Lake Wahbekanetta) and was later instrumental in luring Dr. Joseph Maddy to the area, who at the time was looking for a scenic and secluded location to start a music camp for high-school age youngsters. Over the many years since 1928, Dr. Maddy's vision has not only taken root but has flourished to become what we now know as Interlochen Center for the Arts, a world-renown institution devoted to developing and encouraging the arts and education in young people. Its beautiful campus, covered with stately old-growth trees, is a perfect backdrop for the wonderful work that goes on there. So, too, has Interlochen State Park evolved since Willis Pennington convinced Michigan lawmakers to purchase this unspoiled land and turn it into a park for the enjoyment of everyone. Interlochen State Park, Michigan's first, has become one of the most beautiful and popular parks in the state, giving countless children and adults a chance to glimpse the past and see first-hand what Michigan must have been like when the great trees covered the land.

Acknowledgment

Occasionally in life a chance encounter or an offhand comment will brush past us, almost unnoticed at the time, but in retrospect will prove to be a great turning point, as a seed dropped in just the right place will find contact with the life-giving soil, germinate and flourish. Such was the case when I visited a close friend's mother in Florida back in the 1970's. Over a cup of morning coffee, she asked me to name the one thing I most wanted to do before I died. When I answered, without much hesitation, that I wanted to write a book someday, she nearly spit up a mouthful of coffee all over the both of us. Her words, and I can still hear them as if they were just spoken, have stayed with me: "Son, you don't have the vocabulary to write a book." I remember being a little put off at the time, but nevertheless, her comment piqued a young man's innate indignation over being told there was something he could not do. What began that day as a quest has since turned into a labor of love and fulfillment. For that, I thank you, Pat.

I also want to thank the good people of Monroe Center, Michigan (Bob, Phyllis, Peggy and Brent Wagner, Jim and Maxine Steinmiller, and Cal and Willo Spangler to name a few), for sharing so many stories and pictures of the "old days." The wonderful folks of the Northwest Michigan Draft Horse and Mule Association not only answered my endless questions but allowed me to drive a beautiful team of horses around a plowed field to get a feel for the power of these gentle giants. Thanks to Dave Pennington for sharing his wonderful collection of old photos and for coming up with truly obscure information at the Traverse Area Historical Society archives.

Along the way, while researching material for this book, my path crossed that of Dr. Rob Taylor and his wife Joanne from Arab, Alabama.

Rob and I are descended from the Dean family in my story, and we spent an enjoyable afternoon sharing stories and identifying the people in his handed-down collection of daguerreotypes.

To all the men and women of the reenactment group, Battery D First Michigan Light Artillery, I tip my hat. Their passion for bringing Civil War history alive for thousands of youngsters every summer honors the veterans of that conflict, both North and South, in a very special way. I will never tire of seeing the look of pure astonishment on the young faces as they stand with their hands over their ears watching a cannon erupt with a thunderous roar and a cloud of smoke.

Last but certainly not least, I want to thank my wife Maurine, not only the love of my life, but also my "live-in" English teacher and editor who keeps not only me, but my punctuation, on the straight and narrow.